SURRENDER

the

NIGHT

MaryLu Tyndall

BARBOUR
PUBLISHING

Other books by MaryLu Tyndall

SURRENDER TO DESTINY SERIES
Surrender the Heart

CHARLES TOWNE BELLES
The Red Siren
The Blue Enchantress
The Raven Saint

THE LEGACY OF THE KING'S PIRATES
The Redemption
The Reliance
The Restitution

The Falcon and the Sparrow

Cover image: Faceout Studio, www.faceoutstudio.com
Cover photography: Steve Gardner, Pixelworks Studios

Published by Barbour Publishing, Inc., P.O. Box 719, Uhrichsville, Ohio 44683, www.barbourbooks.com

Our mission is to publish and distribute inspirational products offering exceptional value and biblical encouragement to the masses.

 Member of the
Evangelical Christian
Publishers Association

Printed in the United States of America.

ABOUT THE AUTHOR

MaryLu Tyndall

MaryLu Tyndall dreamed of pirates and seafaring adventures during her childhood days on Florida's coast. She holds a degree in math and worked as a software engineer for fifteen years before testing the waters as a writer. Her love of history and passion for storytelling drew her to create the Legacy of the King's Pirates series. MaryLu now writes full-time and makes her home with her husband, six children, and four cats on California's coast, where her imagination still surges with the sea. Her passion is to write page-turning, romantic adventures that not only entertain but expose Christians to their full potential in Christ. For more information on MaryLu and her upcoming releases, please visit her Web site at www.mltyndall.com or her blog at crossandcutlass.blogspot.com.

❖ DEDICATION ❖

To those who have been wounded by life

❖ CHAPTER 1 ❖

Baltimore, Maryland, August 3, 1814

*G*ong. *Gong. Gong.* The evening air reverberated with warning bells from St. Peter's church. Rose McGuire halted in her trek to the pigsty and gazed across the shadowy farm. Musket fire echoed in the distance. The British were on the move again. Punctuating the unrest crackling through the air, shards of maroon and saffron shot across the western sky, bringing into focus the line of cedar and pine trees that marked the end of civilization and the beginning of the dense forest of Maryland.

Gong. Gong. Gong. The eerie chime scraped a chill down Rose's spine. She glanced back at the brick house in the distance. Though she had yet to spy a redcoat anywhere near her farm, she should go back inside. Swallowing her fear, she emptied the bucket of slops into the pig trough. Grunts and snorts amassed in the putrid air above the enclosure, drawing her attention to her favorite pig, who waddled toward her to receive his evening scratch. Kneeling, she reached her hand in between the fence posts. "Hi, Prinney." His moist, stiff hair bristled against her hand as he lifted his head beneath her caress and nudged against the wooden railings, while the rest of the pigs devoured their kitchen scraps.

"You'll miss your dinner, Prinney. Better get some before it's gone." Rose stood and dabbed her sleeve over the perspiration on her forehead. A light breeze, laden with the smells of hay and honeysuckle, brushed her golden curls across her face. Flicking them aside, she drew in a deep breath, hoping the familiar scents would calm her nerves.

Men and their wars. She hated the war, hated the alarms, hated the violence. But most of all she hated the fear. Two years was far too long to live in constant terror of being overrun by a ruthless enemy.

Picking up her bucket, she hastened to the barn, gazing at her tiny garden as she went. Even in the dim light, she could make out the patches of red and yellow of the nearly ripe tomatoes and the spindly silk atop ripe ears of corn. She smiled. Despite the war, life went on.

Musket shot peppered the air. *Pop. Pop. Pop.* Somewhere close by, soldiers were being shot at or a settler was defending his land—somewhere close by, people were dying. Fear prickled her skin. Just a few more chores and she would go inside. Rose began humming a song her father taught her when she was young. She could still hear his baritone voice as he sang the words—words that always seemed to calm her.

Oh fare thee well, my little turtledove,
And fare thee well for awhile;
But though I go I'll surely come again,
If I go ten thousand mile, my dear,
If I go ten thousand mile.

Setting the bucket down on the dirt floor of the barn, Rose eased beside Liverpool, her milk cow. Why the song allayed her fears she could not say, for it was nothing but a lie. Her father had not even gone ten thousand miles away. Yet he had never returned. Rose shooed a fly from the animal's face and planted a kiss on her nose, eliciting a moo from the friendly cow and a jealous neigh from Valor, Rose's filly in the adjoining stall.

"Don't vex yourself, Valor. I'll take care of you next."

"Rose!" Aunt Muira's voice rang from their home across the small yard.

Rose needed no further encouragement. She would attend to the animals later. "Coming!" she shouted as she made her way through the barn, nearly stumbling over Georgiana, one of her chickens. Squawking, the bird darted across the hay-strewn floor.

Gong. Gong. Gong.

Alarm gripped Rose's stomach. Did the signal mean what she thought? Surely the British would not come this close to Baltimore. Hurrying her steps, she approached the two-story brick house. Light cascaded from the windows like the golden water of Jones Falls in the summer sun, luring her inside to the warmth of the fire and comforts of home. Home. At least she had called it her home for the past five years.

Rose stepped into the kitchen, closing the door behind her. The smells of venison stew and fresh bread wafted around her as she removed her straw hat and hung it on a hook by the door. Cora, the cook, knelt over the massive fireplace, stirring something that bubbled inside the iron pot hanging over the fire.

"There you are, Rose." Aunt Muira, attired in a blue cotton gown with a white sash about her high waist, strutted into the room as if she wore the latest Parisian fashion. "Didn't you hear the alarm? For goodness' sakes, you know you are to come inside when the alarm rings. Oh, look at you dear, covered in dirt again." Her jewel-laden silver earrings—so at odds with her plain attire—twinkled in the lantern light as her sharp green eyes assessed Rose.

Rose glanced down at her gray linen gown and saw not a speck of dirt. But then again, her aunt had a propensity for spotting stains.

"Wash up and take off those muddy shoes, dear. Mr. Drummond awaits his supper." With that, Aunt Muira swung about and swept from the room like a fast-moving storm.

Cora stepped from the fireplace, hand on her back and gave Rose a look of reprimand. "Best do as she says, child." The dark-skinned cook scowled and nodded toward the sink. Black spongy curls peeked from beneath the red scarf wrapped about her head. "You know how the missus can get when her orders aren't carried out."

Slipping off her shoes, Rose skirted the food preparation table and poured water from a pitcher over her hands at the sink. "Do not think poorly of her, Cora. She only wants me to comport myself like a lady."

"Humph." Cora grabbed a cloth, opened the Franklin stove and pulled out a loaf of bread. Setting it beside one that was already cooling on the table, she mumbled, "I don't know nothin' 'bout that, miss. But have you seen Amelia? I could use some help carryin' this food into the dining room."

Rose dried her hands on a towel and smiled. "I have no doubt she will make an appearance when all the work is done."

Cora chuckled and handed her a platter. Together they entered the dining room and placed bowls of steaming stew, fresh corn, and platters of cornmeal cakes on the table.

"Good evening, lass." Rose's uncle, Forbes, smiled from his seat at the table. Short-cropped gray hair sprang from his head in a dozen different directions and framed a ruddy face lined with the trials of a long life. The skin around his eyes crinkled as he squinted at the food-laden table. "Now, what have we here?"

Rose bent and kissed his cheek, then took a seat beside him. "Lose your spectacles again, Uncle?"

He chuckled. "Ah, they'll turn up somewhere, I'm sure."

"Wherever he last placed them, no doubt," Aunt Muira added from her seat next to her husband. "Where is Amelia?"

Cora returned to the kitchen, mumbling under her breath.

Rose shrugged beneath her aunt's questioning gaze. "I saw her this morning. She mentioned heading into town."

"You should discipline that woman, Forbes." Aunt Muira huffed. "She's out of control."

"Come now, dearest," Uncle Forbes said. "She's a grown woman and not our prisoner."

"But we took her into our home to be a lady's maid and companion to Rose. It would certainly be propitious if she would attend to her duties."

"You worry overmuch." Forbes smiled at his wife and took her hand in his.

"And you, dear Forbes, do not worry enough."

Rose shifted her gaze between them as they shared a chuckle. "Amelia has been a great companion to me, for which I thank you both very much. But as a lady's maid"—Rose shrugged—"well, let's just say I have no need of a silly maid anyway."

Uncle Forbes took Rose's hand and gave her a wink. "It pleases me that you two have become such good friends. Now, shall we pray over this grand feast?" Bowing his head, he asked God's blessing on the food, then ladled stew into his and Muira's bowl before passing the pot to Rose.

"You must come inside when you hear the alarm, dear." The candle-light shimmered over Aunt Muira's copper-colored hair streaked with gray. At eight and fifty, Muira retained a beauty and a bearing that gave evidence of her privileged upbringing.

An upbringing similar to that which Rose had experienced, save in her case, all signs of fine breeding had long since dissipated. "But nothing ever comes of them." Rose glanced out the window where darkness had stolen the remaining light, then back at her aunt whose expression had scrunched into a knot.

With a sigh, Aunt Muira rose, circled the table, and wiped Rose's face with her napkin.

Rose gave her a timid smile. "My apologies. I thought I had washed sufficiently."

"I suppose I wouldn't recognize you if you were clean, dear." Her aunt returned to her seat.

Uncle Forbes swallowed the bite in his mouth. "They sound the alarms for a reason, lass. You should heed them as your aunt says."

"But I've yet to see a British soldier anywhere near here." Rose bit into a chunk of meat in her stew, savoring the aromatic flavors. "They wouldn't dare come close to Baltimore. Not after General Smith has gathered such a strong militia."

"I wouldn't put anything past those redcoats." Uncle Forbes spooned corn into his mouth. "Why, they have turned the Chesapeake Bay into nothing but a British pond. A pond from which they emerge like crocodiles to raid upon our poor citizens."

"Leaving hundreds of widows in their wake," Aunt Muira added glumly. "Ruined women and orphans."

A breeze fluttered the calico curtains at the open window and sent the candle flames sputtering.

Ruined women. Rose's stomach soured. She set down her spoon, her appetite gone. "Thank goodness for your charities, Aunt. You and Mrs. Pickersgill are doing much good for those women."

"And you could too, dear. If you accompanied me more often." Aunt Muira gave Rose a look of censure. "They need someone who understands what they have endured."

Uncle Forbes chomped on a piece of venison. "You know, my love, Rose does what she can. We must be patient with her as God has been patient with us."

Aunt Muira smiled at her husband. "I understand." But when his knowing gaze refused to leave her, she huffed. "Well perhaps I'm not patient. It has been five years, after all."

Familiar guilt pinched Rose. "You know I care for the women devastated by this war," she said. "But I'm not as strong as you are, Aunt Muira. I don't have your courage." Though Rose longed to be brave, once had even considered herself brave. But after. . . Well, afterward, her courage had abandoned her like everything else—like every*one* else, including God. "When I look at those women, when I look into their eyes, I see myself." Rose stared down at the cream-colored table cloth. "If only the nightmares would end."

Reaching across the table, Aunt Muira took Rose's hand in hers. "Forgive me, my dear. I simply wish you would learn to trust God."

Trust? Rose grimaced. She had trusted God after her father had been murdered—had kept trusting Him after her mother died. But how could she trust a God who had allowed such a horrific thing to happen to her? "I am trying, Aunt." She winced at her lie.

Aunt Muira drew in a deep breath and shook her shoulders as if to shake off the gloom that had descended on their conversation. She grabbed a johnnycake and placed it on her plate then glanced over the fare. "Oh I do miss having rice. And coffee." She moaned. "And chocolate. It seems years since we've had such luxuries."

Uncle Forbes snorted. "We are fortunate to have food at all with the British blockade."

"More than missing food"—Rose leaned back in her chair and sighed—"I miss peace. I long to feel secure again."

Uncle Forbes grabbed her hand and squeezed it. His brown eyes sparkled with understanding. "You have been through so much in your short life, lass. Peace will come again soon. God will take care of us."

Shrugging off the platitude that had been proven false in her own life, Rose chomped on her corn cake, but the grainy, buttery flavor soured on her tongue.

Uncle Forbes took a swig of cider, dribbling some on his brown waistcoat, and set down his mug. He scratched his thick hair. "Let us pray this war will be over soon, and our lives can return to normal."

"My word, Uncle. Normal only if we win." Rose shook her head. If not. If America once more became a British colony, things would never be normal again.

"Of course we'll win." Aunt Muira nibbled on her corn cake, reminding Rose that true ladies took smaller bites. "It is too much to think otherwise."

"Ever the optimist, dearest." Uncle Forbes gazed lovingly at his wife.

She returned his gaze, then moved her eyes to Rose. "And then perhaps you can finally marry. Goodness, you are all of two and twenty and fast becoming a spinster."

Rose opened her mouth to protest but her aunt continued, "I was eighteen when I married Forbes." The couple exchanged another adoring glance, sending a twinge of jealousy through Rose.

Rose glanced at her food, hoping for a resurgence of her appetite, but it did not come. "I have yet to meet a man who interests me." Or one who didn't sicken her. Truth be told, after rumors of her plight spread through Baltimore, very few suitors had come to call. And even if an honorable man took an interest in her, and she in him, Rose could only hope to have a marriage as good as her aunt and uncle's. If not, she wanted no marriage at all.

"What of Mr. Snyder, the councilman?" Aunt Muira drew a spoonful of stew to her lips. "He's been coming around quite often."

"He is a fat wit."

"Rose, lass." Uncle Forbes squinted toward her. "It isn't kind to say such things."

"I know he doesn't come from an honorable family." Aunt Muira dabbed her mouth with a napkin. "But he has become successful on his own merit."

Rose let out a sigh. "If I do ever marry, it won't be to a man with a dubious character." No, she needed a man she could trust implicitly—someone who would never take advantage of her.

"But dear—" her aunt started to protest when the sound of carriage wheels grated over the gravel in front of their house.

Pound. Pound. Pound. The front door resounded.

The heavy knock at this hour could only mean trouble. Rose's body tightened. Her glance took in the Brown Bess musket perched atop the fireplace.

Pound. Pound. Pound.

"Ah, yes." Uncle Forbes rose from his chair, as he no doubt

remembered that Samuel, their footman, was no longer in their employ. "I keep meaning to hire a new man," he mumbled as he disappeared through the dining room door as if he hadn't a care in the world—as if there weren't British soldiers raiding the coast. Rose heard the front door open and anxious words exchanged. The intruding voice sounded like Mr. Markham, Uncle Forbes's assistant from church. Sharing a look of apprehension with her aunt, Rose headed toward the foyer.

A warm summer breeze trailed in through the open door and swirled about the room. Upon seeing Rose and her aunt, Mr. Markham dragged off his hat. "Sorry to disturb you, Mrs. Drummond, Miss McGuire, but there's trouble down at the church."

"Calm down, man. What sort of trouble?" Uncle Forbes squinted at Mr. Markham and laid a hand on his shoulder.

"Some men in town caught a redcoat, sir. And they're threatening to string 'im up." He fumbled with his hat and cast an anxious gaze out the open door. "He's hurt pretty bad too." He glanced at Rose's aunt.

"Oh my." Lifting her skirts, Aunt Muira headed upstairs only to descend within seconds, medical satchel in one hand and a pair of spectacles in the other. "We should alert Dr. Wilson just in case the man's injuries are beyond my abilities."

Grabbing his overcoat from the hook by the door, Rose's uncle swept it over his shoulders.

"A lynching?" Cora entered the room, fear pinching the features of her face.

"Never you mind, Cora. Keep an eye on Rose and we'll be back soon," Aunt Muira ordered.

"Can't I come with you?" Rose said as the familiar fear clenched her gut once again. "I don't feel safe here without Samuel." She glanced at Cora.

"Don't be blamin' me for him runnin' off." Cora wagged her finger. "He was nothin' but trouble, that one."

"You're safer here than in town," her uncle said. "Mr. Markham will stay with you, won't you, sir?"

The gentleman nodded, seemingly relieved he did not have to return to the mayhem in town. "Indeed, I will."

Uncle Forbes patted his pockets and scanned the room. "My spectacles. Where are my spectacles?"

"I have them, dearest." Aunt Muira handed them to him, then faced Rose. "Promise me you won't leave the house."

Rose swallowed. With the British afoot and the crazed mob in town, her aunt and uncle were venturing straight into danger. "I promise, but please be safe."

Without so much as a glance back, they sped out the door and slammed it behind them. The thud echoed through the lonely house. *Oh God, I cannot lose my family. Not again.*

Alexander Reed trudged through the thick mud. A leafy branch struck his face. Shoving it aside, he continued onward. All around him the chirp of crickets and croak of frogs joined other night sounds in an eerie cacophony. An insect stung his neck, and he slapped the offending pest. Behind him eight men slogged through the woods as silently as the squish of mud would allow, and before him, at their lead, marched Mr. Garrick, first lieutenant of the HMS *Undefeatable*.

The troops of men from various British warships blockading the Chesapeake had barely hauled their cockboats up on the land when darkness had descended. Alex huffed under his breath. This was a job for marines and soldiers, not sailors. Why Admiral Cockburn insisted that naval officers go ashore on these raids eluded Alex. He'd rather be back in the wardroom aboard the HMS *Undefeatable* sipping a glass of port than stomping through the backwoods of this primitive country.

Alex tried to shake the visions of senseless destruction, rape, and murder of civilians ordered by Admiral Cockburn and carried out by his small group that night, but they haunted him with each step. His stomach turned in revulsion. At least he'd been able to slip into the shadows during the worst of it and avoid forever scarring his conscience. Yet he didn't know how much more he could endure. As horrendous as war was, true gentlemen fought with honor and integrity, not by assaulting innocent farmers and their families. When he joined His Majesty's Navy, he had not signed up for this madness. He wanted to make an honorable name in battle and perhaps gain some prize money that would go a long way to erase the stain he'd made upon his family's name. Then maybe his father would welcome him home again.

Home. Alex had been without one for so long, he'd forgotten what it felt like to have a place to call his own. And a family who loved him. Yet these raids brought him anything but honor. To defy orders, however, would bring court-martial upon him and most likely a sentence of death or worse—cashiering, a dishonorable discharge from the navy.

Garrick slowed and slipped beside Alex. Doffing his bicorn, he wiped the sweat from his brow with his bloodstained sleeve. "Easy prey, these ruffians, eh, Reed?"

"They are but farmers. I would not allow your pride to swell overmuch."

"Egad man." Garrick snorted. "You always were a sour pot."

A marine chuckled from behind Alex. "Did you see the look on that woman's face when we burst into her home?"

The purl of rushing water caressed Alex's ears, and he longed for it to drown out the men's malicious commentary.

"This silver tea platter will please my wife back home," another man whispered.

Alex's anger rose. "The silver is not yours, Grayson."

"Aye it is, Mr. Reed. A prize of war."

"Don't mind him lads," Garrick shot over his shoulder. "Reed's always been a stuffed shirt. His father's a viscount. *Lord Cranleigh.*" He mimicked the haughty tone of the London aristocrats then snapped venomous eyes Reed's way. "Perhaps you believe this type of work beneath you, Reed? Don't like to get your hands dirty, eh?"

Ignoring him, Alex trudged forward. Sweat streamed down his back beneath his waistcoat.

Thankfully, a light ahead drew Garrick's attention away from him. "A farmhouse, gentlemen." Excitement heightened his voice.

Reed peered through the darkness. A small house with light streaming from its windows and smoke curling from three chimneys perched in the middle of a patch of cleared land. A barn nearly as big as the house stood off to the right, and a smaller one sat in the shadows to the left.

"Upon my honor, Garrick. It's just one farm. Leave them be," Reed said. "Captain Milford instructed us to strike towns, not single farms."

Garrick gazed up at the black sky, then turned to face Alex. His expression was lost in the darkness but his tone indicated nothing but sinister glee. "It grows late. You take the men and circle around back toward the ship. I'll meet you on board."

Alex released a heavy sigh and watched as Garrick turned, gripped his pistol, leaped over the short fence, and crept toward the unsuspecting farmhouse. If Alex were a praying man, he'd say a prayer for the poor souls within.

But he wasn't a praying man.

Rose hooked the lantern on a nail by Valor's stall. The bells and musket shots had ceased, giving her the courage to venture forth from the protection of the house and finish her chores. Although Amelia had returned, she and Cora had long since retired to their beds. How they could sleep at a time like this baffled Rose. Neither Mr. Markham's snores from the sofa in the parlor nor his meek demeanor when he was awake provided Rose with enough security to risk slumber.

Leaning her cheek against the warm horse's face, Rose drew a breath of the musky scent of horseflesh. "I'm sorry to have forgotten you, precious one." She pulled away and ran her fingers through Valor's mane.

Something moved in the reflection of the horse's eye. Something or someone.

Rose froze.

"Well, I daresay, what do we have here?" The male voice struck her like a sword in the back. Heart in her throat, she jumped and swung about. A man in a British naval uniform, dark blue coat and stained white breeches, glared at her with the eyes of a predator. A slow smile crept over his lips. His dark eyes scoured the barn and then returned to her. He took a step forward. Valor neighed.

Rose's legs wobbled. "I insist you leave at once, sir. This is a civilian home, and my uncle is within shouting distance," she lied, wishing her uncle hadn't left for town.

Wishing she'd kept her promise to stay in the house.

"Indeed?" He cocked a malicious brow and took another step. Blood stains marred his white shirt.

"You are a pretty thing, aren't you?"

"Please sir, I am not at war with you. As is no one in my family." Rose's pulse raced. Her vision blurred.

"Ah, but that is where you are wrong, miss. All Yankee rebels are at war with Britain, the mother country." He grinned and rubbed the whiskers lining his jaw. "And what does a parent do with a rebellious child? Why, he gives the brat a spanking."

Rose's breath crushed against her chest. She darted a quick glance toward the open barn door behind her.

"You will give me what I want," the man continued. "Or"—he sighed and flattened his lips—"I'd hate to see this barn and all your animals go up in flames."

Liverpool mooed in protest.

Rose's head grew light. The barn began to spin around her. She could not endure this. *Not again.* "Please sir, I beg you." Her voice squeaked. "If you have any decency, leave me and my family be."

"Ah, there's the rub, miss. In truth, I have no decency."

Clutching her skirts, Rose made a dash for the door. Meaty hands gripped her shoulders and tossed her to the ground. Pain shot up her arms and onto her back. She screamed. Hay flew into her face. Valor neighed and stomped his foot. The frenzied squawk of chickens filled her ears.

The man shrugged out of his coat and tossed it aside. Never removing his eyes from her, he slowly drew his sword and pistol and laid them on the ground.

Terror seized her. She scrambled on her knees to get away. He grabbed her legs, flipped her over, and fell on top of her. His heavy weight nearly crushed her.

Rose closed her eyes and prayed for a rapid death.

❖ CHAPTER 2 ❖

A woman's scream pierced the air. Alex dashed across the open field. *Blasted Garrick,* he swore under his breath. He halted midway and listened. Barn or house? Another scream, followed by the distraught whinny of a horse. The barn. Alex darted in that direction, glad he'd stayed behind to see what mischief Garrick was about, instead of heading back to the ship with the other men.

Chest heaving, he barreled through the barn's open doors. Squinting in the glare of lantern light, his eyes latched on Lieutenant Garrick lying atop a struggling woman. Fury consumed Alex. He charged toward his superior, laid a muddy boot on his side and kicked him off the lady. Garrick moaned and tumbled over the dirt and hay. He snapped to his knees, raking the barn with his gaze. A pair of searing brown eyes met Alex's. The look of shock on Garrick's face faded beneath an eruption of rage.

"What is the meaning of this, Reed?" He leaped to his feet and brushed the hay from his shirt.

Alex dared a quick glance at the woman. Disheveled golden hair, a muddied gown, and crystal blue eyes that screamed in terror stared back at him.

"The meaning of this, sir"—he swung his gaze back to Garrick—"is that I tire of your cruel treatment of innocent ladies."

"I care not a whit what you tire of." Garrick scowled. "She is rebel trash and therefore no lady."

Alex forced down his anger. He wanted nothing more than to pummel this nincompoop into the ground. "You disguise your licentious appetites behind the shield of war. It is beneath you, sir, as an officer in His Majesty's Navy." Yet even as he said the words, he wondered if anything was beneath a man like Garrick.

"Captain Milford will have you court-martialed for assaulting me." Garrick spit hay from his mouth. "Return to the ship at once." His tone held no possibility of defiance on Alex's part. "Now!" he added with a spiteful gleam in his eye.

Alex remained in place.

A flicker of uncertainty crossed Garrick's expression. "Go now, and I'll forget this moment of insanity." His tone softened.

"Please help me, sir," the woman managed to squeak out, shifting pleading eyes toward Alex.

He drew a deep breath of the muggy, manure-scented air. Seconds passed, affording him a moment of clarity. He could return to the ship and continue with his plan to gain honor and fortune in the navy, or he could defy his superior officer, defend this woman, and lose everything. Why did he care if one more American woman was ravished on a night when dozens had already suffered the same fate?

"Be gone! What is one rebel woman to you?" Garrick chuckled as if reading Alex's thoughts. He wiped the spit from his lips, then leaned over the lady with such lustful disdain it sickened Alex.

Whimpering, she clambered backward.

Alex clenched his fists, silently cursing his infernal conscience. "Upon my honor, I fear I cannot do that."

Garrick flinched and cast an incredulous gaze at Alex. "What did you say?" He lengthened his stance. His narrowed eyes shot to his sword and pistol lying atop his coat on the ground, but then he shook his head and grinned. "Ah, you want the woman, too. By all means, Mr. Reed, you may have her when I'm done." He waved a hand through the air.

"You misunderstand me, sir." Alex forced the anger from his tone. "I'm ordering you to leave the woman alone and return to the ship with me."

"You are ordering?" Garrick's incredulous tone was ripe with spite. Anger flared in his otherwise lifeless eyes. He inched closer to his weapons.

"I would not attempt that if I were you, Garrick."

"No, *you* wouldn't." In one fluid motion, Garrick leaped for his sword, grabbed it, and swept it out before him. "But I would." He grinned. "In fact, there are many things I would do that you would not, which is the great difference between us."

Anguish brewed within Alex as he watched his glorious naval career scuttled. Gripping the hilt of his sword, he slowly drew it from its sheath. "To be different from you, sir, has been my greatest aspiration." Alex gave a mock bow. Why couldn't the libertine relinquish this one lady? Why had he forced Alex's hand? Visions of his own body swinging from a hanging post at Portsmouth flashed before his eyes. But he couldn't think of that now.

"I've been looking forward to gutting you with my blade for a long time, Reed." Garrick sneered.

Alex raised a brow. "Then let us delay your attempt no longer."

Heart cinched in her chest, Rose eyed the two men. When her rescuer knocked the hideous man off of her, terror had given way to hope. But now as the two sailors lunged toward each other, swords in hand, her fears returned in full force.

Clang! Steel struck steel as their blades crossed. The man called Garrick forced her rescuer back beneath the blow. Or was he her rescuer? She could not be sure that this Reed, as Garrick had addressed him, didn't harbor the same plans for her as her assailant. He was British, after all.

Reed shoved Garrick back then narrowed his eyes upon him. He leveled the tip of his sword at Garrick's chest. A confident grin played upon his lips.

Garrick's face reddened and a sweat broke out on his brow. "You'll hang for this, Reed."

"We shall see."

Fear clogged Rose's throat. Her gaze landed on Garrick's pistol lying atop his coat. Pressing her palms against the dirt, she struggled to push herself up, but her legs turned to jelly. She plopped down again and began to hum her father's song in an attempt to calm her nerves and give strength to her limbs.

Sword raised, Reed charged Garrick, and the two parried back and forth. The chime of steel on steel echoed through the barn. Liverpool mooed.

Tears stung Rose's eyes. She gasped for breath as she tried once again to rise.

Garrick dipped to the left and thrust his sword at Reed's side, but the taller man leaped out of reach, then swung about and brandished his blade across Garrick's chest. A line of red blossomed on the man's shirt. Garrick stared at it as if he hadn't realized up to that point that he could bleed.

Valor snorted and stomped her hoof against the wooden rail. Rose struggled to her knees and began to inch toward the pistol.

Garrick's face grew puffy and red. Fear clouded his brow. "Enough of this!" He spat and lunged toward his opponent. Reed jerked backward then veered to the right and brought the hilt of his sword down on Garrick's hand. Garrick's blade flew from his grip and landed in the dirt.

A chicken squawked.

His chest heaving, Garrick gaped at his sword lying in the mud. He raised seething eyes to his opponent.

Reed kicked Garrick's sword aside then lowered his blade. He ran a sleeve across his forehead. His features twisted in a mixture of anger and regret. "Let us put this behind us, Garrick. We are in the midst of war. Tempers are high. Forget the girl, forget this incident, and let's return to the ship."

Yes, indeed, forget about me. Rose shuddered. Almost within her reach, the pistol gleamed in the lantern light, taunting her, daring her to pick it up. To shoot it as she had those many years ago. She could still feel the unyielding wood of the pistol's handle in her grip, could still smell the sting of gunpowder. She had no idea if she could even touch it, but she had to try. Inching forward, her legs became hopelessly tangled in the folds of her gown.

Garrick's vile chuckle bounced off the walls of the barn. "Are those your terms, Reed?" She heard his boots thudding toward her.

She reached for the pistol.

"Fair terms, to be sure, considering I won our little contest." Reed's voice carried a hint of distrust, of hopelessness, which did not bode well for Rose's future.

"Well, stab me, Reed. I didn't take you for such a ninny." Garrick's black boot stepped in her view. He grabbed her wrist and tossed her arm aside. The pistol disappeared.

The cock of a gun sounded. Rose felt the hard press of a barrel against her forehead. She slowly lifted her chin to gaze into Garrick's face, twisted in fury and bloodlust. His eyes sparked like a madman's. Rose's blood grew cold.

"Leave, Reed, or I'll kill your precious rebel," Garrick said.

Reed huffed. "What the deuces, Garrick? Why must you be so difficult?"

For an instant, anger chased Rose's fear away—anger that once again a man had used his superior strength to subdue her. Struggling to her feet, she glared at Garrick as he kept the barrel of his pistol pressed against her forehead. Perhaps she deserved to die at the end of a gun, after all. "Let him kill me, sir. For I prefer that to the alternative."

Garrick blinked then snorted. "Very well, as you wish."

Lord, take me home. Rose's mind went numb as she closed her eyes.

The twang of a sword spinning through the air. The squish of steel into flesh, and the cold barrel left her forehead. Rose pried her eyes open to see Garrick's stunned expression. He glanced from her to Reed, and then down at the blade planted in his gut.

Staggering backward, he gripped the embedded sword with one hand, his pistol still in his other. "To the devil with you," he muttered and leveled his gun at Reed.

The pistol exploded with a loud crack. The shot reverberated in Rose's ears. Smoke filled the air as the smell of gunpowder drifted over her. Dropping the weapon, Garrick crumpled to the ground.

Rose snapped her gaze toward Reed. His eyes met hers. Red burst upon his white breeches. He bent over, clutched his thigh, then stumbled backward. His head struck the wooden post of Liverpool's stall, and he too toppled to the ground.

"Amelia!" Rose nudged the woman, wondering how anyone in the house had slept through the gunshot. "Get up, Amelia."

Amelia batted Rose away with a moan as Rose set the lantern atop a table in her maid's bedchamber. Grabbing a petticoat and gown from a hook on the wall, Rose tossed them at the girl—no, woman. In fact, at two and twenty, Amelia was the same age as Rose. "Get up, Amelia. I need your help. There's a man in the barn."

"A man?" Amelia opened her eyes and struggled to sit.

Rose would laugh at the silly woman's infatuation with the male gender if the situation weren't so harrowing and Rose wasn't still trembling. "Yes, and I need your help."

Rubbing her eyes, Amelia peered in her direction. "A man, miss?"

"As I said. Now get dressed, gather some bandages from my aunt's chamber, and meet me in the barn." Rose's stomach lurched within her. Oh my, what was she to do? Though Garrick was dead, Mr. Reed was very much alive. At least for the moment. But not for long with all the blood pouring from his leg. A wave of dizziness struck her, and she halted and pressed a hand to her chest. Oh why did her aunt and uncle have to be gone on this particular night?

"Whatever is the matter, miss?" Amelia, fully alert now, sprang from the bed. She flung her gown over her head and settled it over her nightdress. She touched Rose's arm. "Miss? Are you ill?"

Rose drew a deep breath. "We need to hurry." She had no time to think about Mr. Garrick's assault. No time to calm herself. "Gather the bandages as I said and Aunt Muira's needle and thread." Grabbing the lantern, Rose headed for the door. She must also get a knife from the kitchen and the aged scotch her uncle kept hidden under the cabinet.

"But, miss—"

"Please do as I say, Amelia. A man's life depends on us."

Rose rushed out the door. A British man's life. The enemy.

Bottle of scotch and knife in hand, Rose stormed into the barn. Mr. Reed's pain-filled groan pierced the air as he struggled to rise. Swallowing her fear, Rose knelt beside him. A circle of maroon mushroomed across his white breeches. The metallic smell of blood filled the air.

"Be careful, sir. You've been shot."

"I am fully aware of that, miss," he said in an unmistakable British lilt that carried a bit of hauteur. He gave up on his attempt to stand and leaned his weight back on his arms. A pair of deep hazel eyes shot a look of curiosity her way. Brown hair the color of rich earth drifted in waves about a strong masculine face, then gathered behind him in a queue.

Rose set down the knife and bottle. A wave of unease crashed over her. Could she trust this man—this *enemy*? Regardless, she should not be alone with him. Despite his injury, he could possibly still do her harm if he so desired. She glanced toward the open door. Oh where was Amelia?

"Would you assist me in rising?" Wincing, he bent his injured leg until the heel of his boot lodged in the dirt.

"I will do no such thing, sir. I'll not have another dead man in my barn."

His glance took in Garrick lying in a heap at the edge of Valor's stall.

"Yes, he's dead." She thought she saw pain cross Mr. Reed's gaze before he closed his eyes.

Amelia burst through the open barn door, her gown sitting lopsided on her shoulders and her long braid of dark hair swaying behind her. "Oh my."

"I need to get back to my ship." Reed moaned.

"You'll bleed to death first, Mr. Reed." Rose examined the wound. Blood seeped from the opening. She knew a little about doctoring from her aunt, and if she didn't extract the slug and stop the bleeding, he may not survive. "We need to get the bullet out and patch you up."

"Bullet out." Beads of sweat broke out on the man's face. His glance took in the barn, Liverpool and Valor, the rafters above, Squeaks, one of Rose's chickens crossing the ground—anywhere but the wound on his leg. He frowned. "But surely you are not a surgeon."

"Lie back, Mr. Reed." Rose gathered some hay to form a pillow. Fortunately, he had fallen near the doorway where fresh hay had been piled to feed Valor, for she doubted she and Amelia could move his large, muscular frame very far. At least the hay would make a soft bed and absorb some of the blood.

"Amelia, the bandages." Rose nudged Mr. Reed's shoulder. Nothing but hard muscle met her touch. He did not budge.

"I insist you lie down, Mr. Reed."

His quizzical gaze took her in as if she were some newly discovered species. "If you'll assist me to my feet, I'll be on my way."

"You will do no such thing." Rose nudged him again.

Reed shook his head as if he were dizzy. "What the deuces, madam. If you please."

Ignoring him, Rose grabbed the knife. "My word, Amelia, the bandages please!" Rose glanced up. Her lady's maid stared at Garrick's body, her face a mask of white.

"Amelia, look at me. I need the needle, thread, and bandages you brought."

The woman shifted wide, frightened eyes to Rose. "What happened, miss?"

"It doesn't matter now." Rose shook her head, trying to scatter the memories.

Reed stared down at his wound as if he had just seen it. He moaned.

"Shouldn't we wake Mr. Markham? Shouldn't we call a physician?" Amelia knelt and handed Rose the bandages and the needle and thread as her gaze took in Mr. Reed's uniform. "He's British, miss."

"I am aware of that." Rose laid them on the cloth she'd spread over the dirt. "Which is why we cannot alert Mr. Markham nor call for the physician. The fewer people who see him, the better." She held up the half-empty bottle of scotch. "Now, Mr. Reed, I suggest you have a sip or two of this." With her other hand, she held up the knife to the lantern. "This may hurt a bit."

Mr. Reed swallowed, and his eyes shifted from the knife down to his wound and back to Rose. "Ladies, if you will but help me to my feet, I will trouble you no further," he said as if he were simply leaving an evening soiree. But then he glanced back at the blood bubbling from his wound. His face grew as white as fresh snow on a crisp winter's morn. His eyes rolled back into his head, and he plopped back onto the hay.

❖ CHAPTER 3 ❖

The sound of squawking rummaged through Alex's ears. *Cluck. Cluck. Cluck.* An infernal noise that defied description. It seemed to peck upon his brain, sending pain shooting down his back. No, down his leg. His left leg. Was it on fire? Was *he* on fire? His throat burned. Sweat tickled his skin as it streamed down his cheeks.

The gurgle of water sounded. A cloth touched his face—its coolness jarred him.

"Oh fare thee well, my little turtledove. And fare thee well for a while." A sweet melody drifted in an angelic song around him. Was he in heaven?

Quite impossible.

"But though I go I'll surely come again. If I go ten thousand mile," the sweet feminine voice continued.

The cloth moved across his forehead as humming replaced lyrics.

"How is he, miss?" another feminine voice asked.

Several moments of silence. "He is feverish. We must pray, Amelia. Pray very hard."

Then the sounds drifted into silence.

Rose dipped the cloth into the bucket of water and wrung it out.

Laying it gently atop Mr. Reed's forehead, she sat back with a sigh. On the other side of the naval officer, Amelia gazed at him from her spot perched on a stool. A morning breeze drifted in through the open doors of the barn and rustled the maid's silky black curls.

"Do you suppose we should call for the apothecary?" Concern tightened Amelia's face.

"As I said, we cannot risk it."

"But surely they wouldn't toss an injured man in prison?"

"He's British," Rose snapped, hearing the venom in her own voice. "You heard what they did to that redcoat they caught in town two nights ago." She shook her head. Had it already been two days since that vile man, Garrick, had entered Rose's barn and attacked her? Every moment since then, Rose had been so consumed with keeping Mr. Reed alive, that she'd had no time to sleep let alone recover her nerves from the incident. She gazed at the blisters on her palms—red, puffy, and sore to the touch.

Evidence of the crime committed in her barn—and her duplicity in covering up the murder.

It had taken Rose and Amelia—well, mainly Rose—hours of hard work to gouge out a hole in the soft earth large enough for Mr. Garrick's body. After saying a few words over the man—out of Christian duty— Rose had left his grave unmarked, leaving Garrick in God's hands to face whatever judgment he deserved.

What else could she have done? Should any more British soldiers happen upon their farm and see their fallen comrade, only God knew what they might do to her and her family. She grabbed a piece of hay from the ground and twirled it between her fingers, allowing a bit of strain to seep from her knotted muscles. Yet even so, her head still spun with all that had happened. If not for these blisters and the injured officer lying before her, the entire incident would seem more like one of the many nightmares that so often haunted her slumber.

Amelia pressed down the folds of her violet gown, a puzzled look on her face. "How can you be so kind to this man after what the British did to your family?"

Rose lowered her chin. She gazed at Mr. Reed's pistol and sword lying atop his blue coat by the barn door—reminders that he belonged to the same nation who had murdered her father. And caused her mother's death. "British or not, this man saved my life. If he hadn't, rest assured, I'd have already turned him over to General Smith."

If he hadn't, she'd probably be dead.

Or worse.

"He's quite handsome," Amelia said, a devilish twinkle in her eye.

Rose shook her head. "You are incorrigible, Amelia. You have just as much reason as I to hate the British."

"He is first a man, isn't he?" Amelia quirked a smile that formed a dimple on her cheek. "Besides, it's so romantic the way he dashed to your rescue."

"There was nothing romantic about it." Rose huffed. A chicken approached, cocked her head quizzically at Mr. Reed, then hopped into Rose's lap. Rose stroked Georgiana's feathers as it settled onto her gown.

"You and your chickens, miss." Amelia said as a grunt sounded from the doorway, drawing both ladies' gazes to the pig. Prinney waddled into the barn and made his way toward Rose. "And your pigs." Amelia scrunched her nose. "How do you expect anyone to court you when you smell like a barn?"

Liverpool pressed her nose against the wooden posts of the stall beside them and mooed. The pungent scent of pig droppings drifted on a stiff breeze as if confirming Amelia's words even as Prinney nuzzled up against Rose. Reaching out to pet him, she smiled. "I prefer my barn and my animals to most of the men I've met."

"I simply will never understand you, miss." Amelia flattened her lips. "With your inheritance, you could wear the finest gowns and attend monthly balls at the Fountain Inn"—she leaned toward Rose, a gleam in her eye—"and no doubt catch the eye of a wealthy man."

Memories flooded Rose. Memories of men wealthy in coin but devoid of conscience. Men who thought nothing of stealing a young woman's fortune—and future. "I shall leave the fine gowns and frivolous soirees to you, Amelia." Rose gazed beyond the barn's open doors where the morning sun cast rays over the distant oak trees and lit the wildflowers dotting the field in bright purple and red. The distant rush of the Jones Falls River settled her nerves like a soothing balm. "Besides, I doubt I'll ever find a man I can trust."

Mr. Reed groaned, drawing Amelia's concerned look his way.

"Poor man. What are we to do with him? You can't keep him out here forever."

Nudging the chicken from her lap, Rose took the cloth from his forehead and dipped it into the water. Georgiana squawked in protest as she strutted across the hay-strewn ground. "Just until he recovers. Then I'll send him on his way."

Amelia pinched her cheeks, bringing color to the surface, though no man—at least not a conscious one—was in sight. "I do not see how you can keep him from Cora and your aunt and uncle for that long."

Rose wrung out the cloth and placed it back on Mr. Reed's forehead. "I will fetch the eggs and milk Cora needs from the barn. Aunt Muira is in Washington DC assisting at the orphanage for the next few days, and Uncle Forbes spends most of his time at his church. Besides, he keeps his carriage and horse in the stable, so he has no need to come out to the barn." Rose wiped a strand of hair from her face. "I am sure Mr. Reed will be long gone before anyone finds him."

She laid the back of her hand against the man's flushed cheek. Still hot. Two nights ago, after he'd drifted into unconsciousness, Rose had poured scotch over Mr. Reed's wound and dug out the bullet. Then she sewed up the opening with needle and thread. Just like she'd seen her aunt do a dozen times. Rose supposed she should be thankful that Mr. Reed had swooned at the sight of his own blood—as humorous as that was—for at least he had not been awake to see how violently her hands shook. But now she wondered if she had done something wrong, for his fever indicated an infection. And that did not bode well for Mr. Reed.

Rose eased the blanket up to his chin and watched as his eyelids twitched and his breath grew labored.

"Do you suppose he's wealthy?" Amelia asked.

"My word, Amelia. Appearance and wealth. Is that all that matters to you? Why, this man could be part of the very crew who were responsible for your husband's disappearance."

Amelia cocked her head and puckered her lips in that delicate way that seemed to turn most men to mush. "We can't know for sure what happened to Richard."

Rose studied her companion. Each of them had suffered great losses. Two years ago, Amelia's husband had gone missing at sea. A simple seaman aboard a merchant ship that had never been heard from since. Reports filtering back to Baltimore from a fishing boat told a tale of a British frigate's seizure of the merchant sloop. Soon after, Aunt Muira had found Amelia, destitute and starving, scrabbling for scraps of food on the city streets. Of course Rose's benevolent aunt had brought the lady home and given her a position as Rose's companion and maid.

"I cannot bear to think of it." Amelia batted the air aside as easily as she seemed to bat away her husband's memory. But Rose knew better. She'd often heard Amelia's quiet sobs during the long hours of the night.

Mr. Reed moaned and tossed his head. Sweat streamed down his forehead onto the dark hair at his temples. A few days' growth of whiskers shadowed his jaw and chin.

Amelia's forehead suddenly wrinkled. "What would the magistrate, or worse, General Smith think if they found him here?"

"No doubt they'd accuse me of being a traitor. Not just me but my aunt and uncle too."

"And me." Amelia's brown eyes grew wide.

Prinney grunted as if he included himself in the conspiracy.

Rose bit her lip. Amelia had a propensity to gossip with the other ladies in town. "You must tell no one, Amelia. Can you promise me that?"

"Of course, miss." She laid a hand on Rose's arm.

Rose swallowed. She could not put her aunt and uncle at risk. Not after all they'd done for her. Not when they were her only family left—the only ones who cared about her. "We must pray he recovers soon, Amelia. Pray hard."

"If I prayed, miss, I would join you." Amelia shrugged. "But I shall wish really hard."

Rose was about to comment on the woman's lack of faith when a "Hi ho, Miss McGuire!" shot into the barn from outside.

Rose's and Amelia's wide eyes latched upon each other. "My word, it's Councilman Snyder," Rose said. Why hadn't Rose heard his carriage drive up? "Hurry, Amelia, cover Mr. Reed up with hay. I'll delay him."

Amelia gazed at Rose as if she'd lost her mind.

"Just do it, please." Rose scrambled to her feet, stepped over Prinney, and dashed out the door, hearing the crackle of hay behind her.

The summer sun struck her like a hot poker. She squinted against its brightness and nearly bumped into Mr. Snyder, who was strolling toward the barn with tricorn and cane in hand.

His bergamot scent assaulted her. "So nice to see you, Mr. Snyder," she lied. Truth be told, the man made her nerves tighten into hopeless knots, though she could not say why. He had been nothing but kind to her, and he had certainly not hidden his interest in furthering their relationship.

A slick smile that reminded her of a hungry cat curved upon his lips. "Whatever are you always doing in the barn, Miss McGuire?"

"Brushing my horse, milking the cow, feeding the chickens," she waved a hand through the air. *Tending to wounded British sailors.* "The usual chores."

Prinney ambled up behind her as the other pigs grunted from the pigpen.

Plucking a handkerchief from his waistcoat pocket, Mr. Snyder held it to his nose. "You should leave this type of work to a stableboy or farmhand. A lady as lovely as yourself shouldn't be getting her hands dirty." He took her right hand in his and lifted it to his lips, but then halted at the sight of dirt smudged across her knuckles. He lowered her hand with a sigh.

She snatched it from him, restraining a smile. "We don't have a stableboy, Mr. Snyder. Our last groomsman ran off and joined the British army.

"Indeed." He sidestepped her. "What do you expect from a freed slave?" The sunlight shone over his perfectly styled auburn hair cut short to his collar and gleamed over his silk-embroidered waistcoat and spotless cravat. Strong features that could have been considered handsome tightened as he peered toward the barn. "Show me what interests you so much in the barn, miss. I'd like for us to get better acquainted."

Alarm squeezed the breath from Rose's lungs. Though she hated to touch the man—any man—she clutched his arm and swung him around. "You would find it dull, I assure you, Mr. Snyder. I know how you loathe getting dirty."

Halting, he faced her, his blue eyes drifting to her cheek. "Unlike you, I see?" He grinned.

Rose lifted her hand to rub the dirt from her face, but Mr. Snyder grabbed it before she could.

"Is this blood? Are you hurt, Miss McGuire?" His urgent tone filled with concern as he pointed toward dark red stains on her palms. "And these blisters." He pinched his lips. "What have you been doing?"

Pulling from his grip, Rose swallowed a burst of guilt at Mr. Snyder's genuine regard. He had always been kind to her and her family, and she hated the lie that rolled off her tongue. "I. . .I. . .killed a chicken for dinner."

"You?"

Prinney ambled about the hem of Rose's gown and bumped into Mr. Snyder's leg. Releasing her hand, he leaped backward and swatted the pig away with his handkerchief. "Filthy beast!"

Suppressing a giggle, Rose knelt and scratched Prinney between the ears then leaned down to whisper, "Good pig, Prinney. Now run along."

A moan sounded from the barn. "That sounded like a man." Swinging about, Mr. Snyder headed that way.

"A man?" Rose emitted a nervous chuckle. "What sort of lady do you think I am, sir?" She yanked on his arm, halting him. "Why, that was Liverpool, my cow. Can you not tell a moo from a man's voice?" She offered him a sweet smile as she once again dragged him away from the barn. "Come into the house for some tea, Mr. Snyder. I'm sure you didn't come here to discuss my farm chores."

"Indeed I did not, miss." He dabbed at the perspiration on his brow with his handkerchief. "By the by, you should not be out here alone without at least one male servant to watch over you. Why, there are British soldiers afoot, as well as Indians and various unsavory sorts."

Longing to remove her hand from his arm, Rose grimaced. In truth, she had felt safer before Mr. Snyder imposed his presence upon her. "I agree, sir. My uncle is searching for a new man of work as we speak."

He gazed across the lush field toward the Jones Falls River. The rush of water accompanied the twitter of orioles flittering about the tree tops. "But I do so enjoy a glimpse of such natural beauty."

Rose studied him as he perused the thirty acres of Drummond land that extended to the river on one side and was bordered by a line of trees on the other. The twinkle in his eye bespoke an admiration and longing she had never seen when he looked at her. "Why, Mr. Snyder, if I didn't know better, I'd think you came out here to see my land instead of me." She feigned a grievous tone that ended up sounding giddy. Perhaps because the idea caused her no distress.

"Preposterous!" He snorted then smiled at her and patted her hand that still clutched his elbow. "No land could hold a candle to you, Miss McGuire."

Rose eyed him with suspicion. Despite his charming facade, an insincerity lurked about him—in his mannerisms, his expressions, and even his compliments.

"You know my feelings, Miss McGuire. I would like to ask your uncle's permission to court you." He led her around the corner of the house to the front porch.

"As you have already informed me, Mr. Snyder. And though I am flattered, I must tell you I am not ready to court anyone."

He stopped her at the door, set his tricorn and cane down on a rocking chair and took her hands in his. "It has been seven years since your parents' deaths. Surely you are ready to start your own family." The yearning in his eyes made her stomach fold in on itself. Retrieving her hands, she lowered her gaze. She didn't want to cause him pain— had tried to dissuade his advances, yet still he pursued her. Perhaps she should agree to his courtship. The only other suitors who had come to call had been quickly turned aside by her hoydenish ways and her timidity around men. And with most of the men in town gone off to war—some never to return—Rose's choices were limited. Mr. Snyder was handsome, successful, and kind, and her aunt spoke well of him. *An honorable councilman, my dear. You could do much worse.*

Then why did everything within Rose rebel at the thought of marrying him? "It's the war, Mr. Snyder. I loathe the death and violence and cannot possibly think of courting during a time like this."

He lifted her hand to kiss it then, no doubt remembering the dirt and blood, he released it again. "The war should remind us all of the brevity of life, Miss McGuire. And the need to take advantage of every opportunity." The way he said the word *opportunity*, like a greedy merchant haggling over a purchase, gave her pause. She wished to be more than an opportunity to her would-be husband. In truth, she had a feeling the favorable chance he spoke of had nothing to do with her at all.

And everything to do with her land.

Though her inheritance money had purchased this farm and provided a reasonable living for Rose and her aunt and uncle, when her uncle died—and he was already sixty—Rose would lose the farm unless she married.

And with no other prospects, Rose could not put Mr. Snyder off forever.

Sooner rather than later, she'd have to marry him or risk losing everything and throwing her aunt, Amelia, and Cora out onto the streets.

❖ CHAPTER 4 ❖

Splash. Splash. A familiar yet strangely unfamiliar sound of moving water drifted through Alex's mind, jarring him awake. The guttural and drawn-out moan of some kind of beast ground over his nerves. A cow, perhaps? Alex shook his head. Searing pain stabbed him and sped down his back. The malodorous smell of manure stung his nose and filled his lungs. A dream. A nightmare. *Cluck. Cluck.* Something pecked his arm. His neck. His cheek.

"What the deuces?" Alex raised his hand with difficulty to bat the offending varmint away. Squawking ensued as he rubbed his eyes in an attempt to pry them open.

The splash halted and footsteps approached. Despite the pounding in his head, he opened his eyes to the sight of an angel—albeit a rather disheveled, dirty angel—leaning over him. Golden curls that caught the sunlight in a glittering halo hung about her face. Blue eyes peered down at him with concern.

"Am I in heaven?" His voice came out cracked and dry.

"No, Mr. Reed. Far from it, I'm afraid." Spreading the folds of her gown, she sat beside him. On the ground. Not on a stool, nor a chair. And he was in no bed. He grabbed a handful of hay with his other hand and felt dirt shove beneath his fingernails.

"Where am I?" Momentary terror struck him. He struggled to rise on his elbows, but he felt weak, as though he were pushing through molasses. And his head. Had it been replaced with a twenty-pound cannonball—a pain-filled cannonball?

"You should rest, Mr. Reed." The angel poured water from a pitcher into a glass. "You've been quite ill."

"Ill." Alex glanced at the bloodstained bandage on his thigh and memories flooded him. Garrick. The sword fight. The firing of a pistol. He raised his eyes to the angel. *The rebel farm girl.*

"Yes, a fever." She lifted the glass to his lips. "Drink this."

Alex's mouth felt like it had been stuffed with cotton. He gulped the water hungrily until it dribbled down his chin. The liquid saturated his tongue and poured down his throat, cooling the parched places and giving him back his voice.

"Easy now." She withdrew the cup and set it down on a small stool beside him.

"Thank you," he managed before his arms began to wobble and he toppled back down onto a bed of hay that he found remarkably soft.

The pain in his head dulled only to be replaced by the one in his leg. "My thigh."

"I removed the bullet," the angel said, as if she performed the task on a daily basis. "It is healing nicely."

"You. . .a *woman?*"

"Yes, I assure you, sir, women are quite capable of such complicated procedures." Her tone was caustic.

Caustic and biting—like an enemy. She *was* his enemy. And he was at her mercy. She leaned over him and ran the cloth over his forehead and cheeks. Loose curls sprang from her bun and fell across her delicate shoulders. She smelled of hay and fresh milk. Feminine curves filled out the folds of a plain blue cotton gown. Despite his muddled state, his body warmed at her gentle ministrations. "I meant no offense, miss. . .miss. . ."

"Miss Rose McGuire." She sat back and eyed him quizzically. Her gaze drifted to his chest then quickly snapped away.

Alex glanced down at his open shirt sprinkled with blood. Memories of the sword fight flooded him: Garrick leveling his pistol at this ministering angel before him; her cowering on her knees;

Alex's blade protruding from Garrick's gut. Had Alex truly killed him? Or was it all a nightmare conjured up by his feverish mind? "Garrick?"

Pain skittered across her crisp blue eyes. "Your friend is dead."

Remorse fell heavy on Alex. "He was no friend of mine." He tried to rise again but his strength failed him. Should any British soldiers find Garrick's body, there would be an inquiry and a court-martial, followed by a hanging—Alex's hanging. He glanced over the barn. Bales of hay were stacked in a corner, farm tools hung on hooks against the far wall, a ladder led to a loft above, chickens strutted across the floor. No sight of Garrick's body. "What did you do with him?"

"Amelia and I buried him four days ago." Miss McGuire stood and brushed the hay and dirt from her skirt.

"Buried? Four days?" He struggled to lift himself once again. This time he managed to sit. "I must get back to my ship."

Miss McGuire's eyes widened, and she took a step back as if frightened of him. "I assure you, sir, I would love nothing more, but you are in no condition for a long march. Now, I insist you lie down and rest. You need to recover your strength." She gazed at the open doors before facing him again, anger pushing the fear from her face. "The sooner you are out of here the better." With that, she turned around and disappeared into the glaring light as if she had, indeed, come from heaven.

Alex's head spun. Caged in on both sides by wooden railings, he appeared to be lying in some sort of animal stall. The snort of pigs sounded from outside. The stench of manure, aged wood, and horseflesh assailed him; and he fell back onto the hay. Movement caught his eye, and he turned his head to see a pair of giant brown eyes staring down at him from the stall beside his. The cow munched on green twigs and gazed at him with pity. If not for the angel who had just left, Alex would have thought he had died and gone to hell.

Or worse, America.

Rose cradled the bowl in her hands and made her way to the barn, trying not to spill the savory broth. Steam rose from the meaty stew. Her stomach growled. She'd been so anxious to feed Mr. Reed, she'd neglected her own dinner. High in the sky, the hot August sun poured its own steamy rays on her.

"Hello, Prinney." She smiled at the pig as she passed by his sty. He gave her a forlorn snort, but she couldn't stop to let him out now. The redcoat—or bluecoat, she supposed because Mr. Reed was in the navy—had developed quite a voracious appetite since he'd awoken from his fever the day before. Other than bringing him food and checking on his wound, Rose had avoided him as much as possible. She would do only what was necessary to save his life and send him on his way. Anything more would be an insult to the memory of her mother and father. Thankfully, the man seemed even less interested in conversing with her than she did him. Though he spent much of his time in slumber, his eyes were regaining their clarity and his body its strength. A strength that caused Rose to feel increasingly uneasy in his presence—which was why she had elicited Amelia's help today to change his bandage and move him to the icehouse. So far she'd managed to keep his presence from Cora and her aunt and uncle, but it was only a matter of time before one of them ventured to the barn.

Skirting the barn doors, Rose approached him, surprised to see him alert and lying on his back with one arm behind his head. He snapped his hazel eyes her way, giving her a start. A gentle smile curled his lips. "I did not mean to frighten you, Miss McGuire."

"You didn't frighten me." Rose knelt beside him and lifted her chin. "I have brought you some stew."

Gripping the wooden post of Liverpool's empty stall, Mr. Reed lifted himself to a sitting position with minimal effort. Dark wavy hair grazed the collar of his white shirt—a shirt devoid of the waistcoat and cravat that would offer him a modicum of modesty. Instead, the garment hung open over a well-muscled chest. Rose cleared her throat as a heated blush rose up her neck.

"Your color has returned, Mr. Reed." She kept her eyes on the ground as she handed him the steaming bowl.

"Indeed. I feel stronger every day." The sound of his accent grated down her spine. Lifting the dish to his lips, he took a sip, then another and another as he hungrily devoured the stew. "Thank you. I realize that aiding the enemy does not bode well for you or your family."

"No sir, it does not. And the sooner you are gone the better."

"I assure you, I am of the same mind." Dark eyes as deep and mysterious as the swirling water in Jones Falls River remained upon her. "Regardless that our countries are at war, I do not wish you or your family harm."

Rose found no insincerity in his gaze. But that didn't mean she could trust him. She lifted her chin. "Yet when you are well and return to your ship, you will continue to terrorize my friends and neighbors."

Regret clouded his eyes. "I am a part of a war that I did not start nor chose to engage in, miss." He stretched his shoulders, flexing the muscles in his chest.

Averting her gaze, she plucked fresh bandages, a knife, and a satchel from the pocket of her gown. "My aunt returns from Washington tomorrow. If you think you can walk, we should move you to the icehouse where you'll be hidden."

"Sounds rather cold." He gave a mock tremble, followed by a grin.

Ignoring his playful demeanor, Rose pursed her lips. "We have not used it in years, Mr. Reed, but it's down by the river and out of the way. Nobody goes there."

He glanced over the barn, his nose wrinkling in disgust. "And with whom am I to share these chilled quarters? Pigs, chickens, rodents? Or perhaps a sheep or two?" A slight grin toyed upon his lips, but his tone held a hint of hauteur. "Will I at least have a bed?" He grabbed a handful of hay and flung it to the side. "Or do all Americans sleep in the straw?"

Rose grimaced. *Pompous bore.* "No sir. We reserve our barns strictly for odious beasts."

He quirked a brow. Instead of the outrage she expected, amusement settled on his face. "Well, at least I know my place."

"I doubt that, Mr. Reed, since you find yourself in my country instead of your own."

He chuckled. "Indeed." Yet the supercilious grin remained on his lips and something else—a flicker of admiration—crossed his eyes that made Rose's stomach squirm.

She tore her gaze from him. He taunted her. Enjoyed taunting her. Rose glanced over her shoulder out the door. Oh where was Amelia? Rose shouldn't be here alone with this man—this enemy who was twice her size and getting stronger by the minute.

Picking up the knife, she studied the bloodstained bandage wrapped around his leg. The hole she'd been forced to tear in his white breeches offered her a view of a thigh as thick and hard as a tree trunk. She'd never seen a man's bare leg before—barely noticed the muscular tone of it during the harrowing moments when as she'd plucked the bullet out. But now the vision sent an odd sensation through her. Ignoring the feeling, she began to slice through the bandage. Her hand shook.

He touched her arm. She froze and met his gaze, her heart racing.

Releasing her, he shook his head, his eyes searching hers. "Do not fear me. I have no intention of doing you harm, Miss McGuire."

"Yes you do, Mr. Reed. You intend to rob me of my freedom." Rose continued her work, reminding herself that despite his attempt at kindness, Mr. Reed was her enemy. In fact, *because* of his kindness, Rose must never trust him. No doubt finding himself at her mercy, he merely attempted to worm into her graces for his own preservation. When he regained his full strength, she would use her uncle's musket to encourage him to leave. She shuddered at the thought of holding the vile weapon. But she may have no choice.

"I did not mean to sound ungrateful." He rubbed the thick stubble on his chin and eyed her. "Why do you not turn me in to your military?"

"You saved my life, Mr. Reed. How can I do any less for you?"

"War changes the rules of civility, Miss McGuire."

She sliced through the bandage and began to peel it away. "Not for me, it doesn't. Now stay still."

Wishing Mr. Reed would stop talking to her, and in particular stop looking at her, Rose focused her attention on the task of removing the final bandage. She poked at the skin around his wound. No puffiness, no swelling or discoloring to indicate infection. Just firm muscle met her touch.

"Thank you for tending my injury." Despite the British lilt, his deep voice soothed over her, untying her nerves.

"As I said, I was obligated to help you." She forced spite in her tone.

"As I was to prevent Mr. Garrick from ravishing you."

A shiver coursed through her at the memory, and she lifted her eyes to his. "Then we are even, Mr. Reed. And when you are well and are gone from here, we shall owe each other nothing more."

But he didn't seem to be listening to her. Instead his gaze focused on her neck, and a smile played at the corners of his mouth. "You have dirt on your. . ." He pointed toward her upper chest.

Looking down, Rose wiped a muddy smudge from the skin above her neckline then she scoured him with a sharp gaze. "And you are covered in dirt as well, Mr. Reed."

He glanced down the length of his filthy uniform and chuckled. "Indeed."

Amelia floated into the barn on a stiff breeze that fluttered the lacy trim of her lavender gown. She held a sack in one hand. "I've brought the clothes you requested, miss." Her eyes trained on Mr. Reed while a coquettish grin danced over her lips.

Despite the woman's flirtations, Rose released a sigh of relief at her presence. "Mr. Reed, may I present Mrs. Amelia Wilkins, my companion and lady's maid."

"My pleasure, Mrs. Wilkins." Reed nodded toward her. "Forgive me if I do not get up."

Amelia giggled. "No need, Mr. Reed. We are most happy that you did not die."

"I share your enthusiasm." Mr. Reed grinned revealing an unusually straight row of white teeth.

Reaching into her pocket, Rose opened a small pouch and spread saturated leaves over Mr. Reed's wound.

"Poison?" He chuckled.

"Comfrey. To speed the healing process." Giving him a lopsided smile, she wrapped a fresh bandage around his thigh. "So you can leave as soon as possible." She tied it tight, eliciting a wince from him and bringing her a measure of satisfaction, albeit only momentary.

Stretching his leg, he gripped the wooden rail of Liverpool's stall. "Then I will be happy to accommodate you, miss. Do you have a horse I may borrow?"

"Not one I'm willing to forfeit."

"Why not lend him Valor?" Amelia glanced toward the filly's stall where the horse stood watching the proceedings.

Rose gave her a measured look. "Who is to bring her back to me after Mr. Reed boards his ship?"

Amelia took a step toward Mr. Reed. "I will go with him and bring her back."

"Don't be a goose, Amelia. All alone? With British soldiers raiding the countryside?"

Mr. Reed's brow gleamed with sweat as he strained to pull himself up. Leaning upon his good leg, he blinked as if trying to clear his head. "Miss McGuire is right. It isn't safe for a woman alone." He faced Rose. "A carriage perhaps? You could bring your footman for protection."

Rose packed her bandages and salve and slowly stood. "You presume too much, Mr. Reed. Besides, both our carriages are in use."

Mr. Reed's breath came in spurts as he fell against the wooden railing. "I will walk then."

"When you cannot even stand?" Rose took a timid step toward the man who if he were standing to his full height would surely tower over her by at least a foot. The last thing she needed was for him to fall and injure himself further. "It must be miles back to your ship."

"And you're in enemy territory, sir," Amelia offered as she slipped beside Rose. "You'll either open your wound and bleed to death or be caught and hanged."

Mr. Reed peered at them both through half-open lids. Hot wind swirled about the barn, swaying a strand of his hair across his stubbled jaw. "Either way, ladies, I shall not impose on you any further." He glanced down at the hay. "Now where, pray tell, have you placed my coat and weapons?"

Rose grimaced. She wondered when he would ask about them. Thank goodness she'd had Amelia store the heinous things in a trunk in the loft. "They are hidden, Mr. Reed. Out of your reach where you can do no harm with them."

"Do you think me so base as to assault the woman who saved my life?" Incredulous pride saturated his tone. "Or to assault any woman for that matter. I am second lieutenant aboard the HMS *Undefeatable*, miss, an officer in His Majesty's Navy and not without honor."

"I believe your Mr. Garrick gave me a taste of your navy's idea of honor," Rose retorted, tossing her nose in the air.

Amelia fluttered her lashes. "You were so brave to come to Rose's defense."

"I could do no less." His admiring gaze swept to Rose.

Confusion jumbled her thoughts and tore through her contempt. She took a step back.

He frowned. "Very well, I shall leave without my things." Releasing the railing, he took a step forward on his good foot, but started to wobble.

Dashing toward him, Rose shoved her shoulder beneath his arm, gesturing Amelia to do the same on the other side. He smelled of hay and man, and she nearly toppled beneath his weight. Amelia gripped his other side and they managed to assist him out of the barn and across the field.

"Oh my, he's quite heavy, miss." Amelia exclaimed in wonder.

"My apologies, ladies." His murmur came out weak as they led him step by painstaking step to the icehouse and propped him against the front wall.

Rose opened the door and a waft of cool, moist air tainted with mold blasted over her, refreshing her hot skin. She and Amelia assisted Mr. Reed inside and helped him down onto the bed of hay Rose had prepared earlier.

"I am not without compassion." She sighed. "You may stay a few more days until you are well enough to walk."

Mr. Reed propped himself up on his hands and studied the gloomy room.

Amelia handed her the bundle that had been slung across her free arm. "I've brought some of Samuel's old clothes."

Grabbing the sack, Rose tossed it at Mr. Reed's feet. "You may want to change. If someone does find you, it would be better if you weren't dressed like a British naval officer."

"Thank you." Mr. Reed nodded.

Rose glanced at the dreary walls, the empty space, anywhere but into his kind dark eyes. "I shall bring you some food and water later. There's a bucket in the corner where you can relieve yourself."

He wrinkled his nose, and a brief glimmer of repulsion crossed his face before he dipped his head in her direction. "I am completely at your mercy, Miss McGuire."

"So it would seem." Rose started to leave, confusion tumbling within her at his accommodating attitude.

"Why do you hold me with such scorn?" His indignant tone turned her around.

Rose threw back her shoulders. "As I said before, because you are attempting to rob me of my freedom, sir." Sorrow weighed on her heart. "And because your countrymen murdered my family."

His throat moved beneath a swallow, and he opened his mouth as if to say something but then quickly slammed it shut.

"And because of that"—retribution surged through Rose, tightening her voice—"you will keep hidden and behave yourself, Mr. Reed. Or mark my words, I will gladly turn you in to the American military where you will rot in prison until the end of the war."

❖ CHAPTER 5 ❖

Rose adjusted her sprigged muslin gown and fingered the lace trim on her collar. She gazed out the window of the landau as they traveled down Calvert Street. Beside her Amelia pinched her cheeks and chattered incessantly about who she was going to see at church, which couples she had heard were courting, and which privateers might be in town.

Amelia glanced out the coach's small window with a sigh. "Privateering is so romantic."

Aunt Muira exchanged a smile with Rose at the woman's fanciful views of life. Dressed in a plain cotton gown of emerald green, Rose's aunt looked much younger than her fifty-eight years. Perhaps it was the love she shared with Uncle Forbes that kept her so young and vibrant. Rose wondered if she would ever find such happiness with a man.

She turned her gaze back to Amelia and saw her wistful expression. "Privateering is anything but romantic, Amelia." Rose clasped her gloved hands together in her lap, noticing the tremble that went through them. "It is difficult and dangerous work."

"Oh why must you be such a crosspatch, Rose." Amelia closed her eyes as the breeze blowing in through the window sent her dark curls twirling over her neck. "I daresay I hope I am never as frightened as you are of everything."

Rose lowered her chin beneath the affront, yet before her anger had a chance to swell, she remembered her trembling hands. As curt as Amelia was, her maid spoke the truth.

Aunt Muira leaned forward and touched Rose's hands. "How are you faring, dear?" Her dress brought out the deep green in her eyes— eyes full of concern.

"It grows easier each time I travel into town." Rose smiled and her aunt squeezed her hands and leaned back on the leather seat. Though Rose knew her aunt referred to the tragedy that had befallen Rose years ago, it was the recent assault by Garrick that had Rose's nerves twisted in a knot. In fact, despite her trembling hands, she was proud of herself that the incident had not kept her from her Sunday trip into town. A trip she'd only found the courage to take during the past few years. Before that, constant dangers that lurked on the city streets had kept her home frozen in fear. Yet now she was beginning to wonder whether her farm offered her any refuge at all.

Bright morning sun angled across the carriage windows and glittered over Aunt Muira's pearl earrings—a remnant of the lady's former wealth. Her jewelry being the only luxury she had kept from her past.

As they turned down Baltimore Street, Rose adjusted her bonnet and gazed at the brightly colored homes passing by in a rainbow of colors. Mulberry and hackberry trees lined the avenue while pink and red hollyhocks dotted the landscape. Turning, they ascended a small bridge that crossed over Jones Falls River into the east side of the city. The wooden planks creaked and groaned beneath the weight of the carriage. The *clip-clop* of the horses' hooves echoed over the sparkling water that frolicked over boulders and fallen branches toward the sea. On days like this, it was hard to imagine that their country was at war. It was hard to imagine being frightened of anything.

Aunt Muira smiled at Rose—a calm, loving smile that reminded Rose of her mother's. A pang of longing pinched her heart. Oh how she longed to talk with her own mother—to share her fears, her hopes, her disappointments. Though Aunt Muira didn't hide her love for Rose, neither did she harbor much patience for Rose's timid temperament.

The smell of salt from the nearby port mixed with the sweet nectar of flowers blew in through the window, and Rose drew a deep breath. She looked forward to Sundays—a day of rest and worship. Safely surrounded by family, it was a day she could get away from the farm. Away from her problems.

From the British officer hiding in the icehouse.

A twinge of guilt stiffened her. While it was the Christian thing to do, Rose felt like a traitor to her country for helping Mr. Reed. She should hate him. She should want him dead for what his countrymen had stolen from her. But after he returned her insults with courtesy and her threats with graciousness, she could conjure no feelings of contempt toward him. Regardless, she must put him from her mind. His strength was returning and he'd soon be gone. Back to his ship. Back to his nightly raids.

Back to being her enemy.

"You seem lost in your thoughts today, my dear," Aunt Muira said.

"Yes, forgive me." Rose gripped the window frame as the coach jostled over a bump in the road. "How was your trip to Washington?"

Her aunt's lips pursed. "Worthwhile." She shook her head as a breeze sent her red curls dancing. "My heart saddens for those poor little ones. This war has stripped many children of their parents. And of course, Reverend Hargrave takes them all in. Why, the orphanage is bursting at the seams with lost, desperate children." The lines on her face seemed to deepen as she spoke. "And with only dear Edna there to assist him. No one in Washington seems to care. They are far too busy with their politics and their fancy balls."

Amelia tore her gaze from the window. "I see no harm in an occasional ball. It is most agreeable to have a pleasant diversion from the war."

Rose cringed at the impropriety of her maid chastising the lady of the house.

Yet Aunt Muira only smiled. "I quite agree, Amelia." She tugged upon her white gloves. "I myself enjoy a good soiree now and then, yet never at the expense of the comfort of those in need."

Amelia nodded as the landau pulled up in front of Uncle Forbes's small stone church. Mr. Markham leaped down from the driver's perch and assisted them one by one to the cobblestone walkway leading to the front door. A sign by its side read FIRST PRESBYTERIAN CHURCH.

REVEREND FORBES DRUMMOND. Pride swelled within Rose for her uncle's accomplishments.

An odd assortment of people ambled through the open front doors, ladies in gowns of calico and pastel muslin, trimmed with ribbons and long colorful scarves. Wide-brimmed bonnets decorated with brightly colored plumes graced their heads. The more fashionable men wore silk breeches and white stockings, cocked hats, lacy cravats, and high-collared coats. Fishermen and seamen dressed in stained cotton shirts and breeches that smelled of fish and brine entered the church right alongside the ladies and gentlemen in their finest and took seats in the back or along the upper balcony.

Rose smiled at the diverse crowd her uncle drew to church as she slipped into their assigned pew near the front. Amelia and Aunt Muira eased in beside her. Cool air swirled around her, enveloping her in the musky aged smell of the church—a smell that always seemed to settle Rose's nerves. As Mr. Smithers, the organist, began to play, a white blur brought Rose's attention to Marianne, her good friend, waving her gloved hand. Her one-year-old son, Jacob, crawled up in her lap as her husband, Noah, eased in beside her and nodded his greeting to Rose.

Rose waved in return. Her heart lifted to see her friend so happy. And also to see that Noah was back in town. Although their relationship had not begun on the best of terms, Marianne and Noah were truly blessed with a great marriage. Rose had no idea how Marianne endured his long absences or the danger he was constantly under as a privateer during wartime. But the sweet woman had a peace about her that Rose envied. Her uncle stepped out from a side door and took his place by the retable. After leading the congregation in several hymns, he began his message. Though his sermons were usually quite thought-provoking, Rose found her mind unable to focus today. Instead, she gazed at her uncle, admiring the man who had once been nothing but an indentured servant.

After the sermon, they stood to sing another hymn before the crowd slowly filtered out of the now stifling church into the stifling summer sun. Rose led Amelia and her aunt to stand in the shade of an elm tree while she peered through the crowd for Marianne. Several young gentlemen and not a few seamen cast admiring glances toward

Rose and Amelia. Giggling, Amelia drew her fan out and waved it enticingly about her face.

"Be careful, or you'll signal one of them to come this way." Rose stiffened her jaw. The last thing she needed was to endure some man's amorous dalliance.

"Perhaps that is what I wish." Amelia gave her a playful glance. "At least the rich ones."

"Oh my." Aunt Muira gave a hefty sigh. "What are we to do with you?"

Smiling, Marianne emerged from the crowd, young Jacob in her arms and her sister, Lizzie, by her side. "There you are. I was hoping you hadn't left. We have so much to catch up on." The shorter woman gazed up at Rose just as Jacob grabbed the edge of her bonnet and pulled it down over her eyes. "Oh drat. He's become quite a handful." Marianne nudged her bonnet back up and kissed Jacob on the cheek.

Lizzie cocked her head, sending brown curls bobbing. "Good morning, Miss Rose."

"I can't believe how big you are getting, Lizzie," Rose said.

"I am nine now. Almost ten." The girl announced with a bit of pride.

"Indeed." Rose leaned over. "You have become quite a lovely young lady. Before we know it, you'll be all grown and married like your sister."

Lizzie smiled up at her sister as a blush blossomed on her cheeks.

Aunt Muira brushed her fingers over Jacob's soft skin, a look of longing in her moistening eyes. "He is absolutely precious, Mrs. Brenin."

Rose grabbed her aunt's hand and gave it a squeeze. Why the good Lord had not given children to such wonderful people, Rose would never understand.

Her aunt leaned toward Lizzie. "And my niece is correct. What a young lady you have become, Miss Lizzie. Is that a new dress?"

The little girl beamed and twirled around, sending the flowered calico fluttering in the wind. "Yes, it is."

"It is lovely."

"And I have good news." Marianne's brown eyes glowed. "I am with child again."

"Truly? I am so glad!" Rose's eyes drifted down to Marianne's belly just barely rounding beneath her gown.

Noah appeared by her side and took Jacob from her arms.

"You are looking well, Noah." Rose gazed at his sun-streaked hair and bronzed face. "Privateering agrees with you."

He shared a knowing glance with his wife. "It is my calling, to be sure. My duty to my country. And I won't complain that it is also quite lucrative." He tossed Jacob into the air, eliciting a giggle from the boy. The babe's white lacy gown billowed in the breeze, revealing his chubby legs. "I do, however, long for the day when I can spend more time home with my family."

Marianne's eyes brimmed with love. "You'd be bored silly at home. As it is, I'm happy with the time we have together."

She faced Rose. "Would you care to spend the afternoon with us, Rose? And Amelia and your aunt and uncle, of course. We plan to have our meal at an inn by the docks then take a stroll down Market Street."

Rose hesitated. The docks meant ships and ships meant sailors. Yet surely with Noah and her uncle along, she would be safe. Ignoring the fear gurgling in her belly, she lifted a questioning brow toward her aunt. Amelia crowded beside her, nearly bursting with excitement.

Aunt Muira tightened her lips and glanced toward the port. "I don't know, dear. I hoped you would accompany me to Mrs. Pickersgill's. She's most anxious to inform us of her new charity for women and children orphaned by the war. You did say you wanted to help, didn't you?"

Rose bit her lip, guilt and longing waging war in her thoughts. Yes, she did. But after what happened with Garrick, the thought of facing women who had suffered as she had caused a lump to form in her throat. "Please forgive me, Aunt, but I. . .I. . .do not think I am up to the task today. Can we go later in the week?" She avoided looking at the frown that must certainly be upon her aunt's lips and focused instead on Noah tickling his son beneath the chin.

"I shall be with them every moment, Mrs. Drummond." Noah came to her rescue. "And I will drive Rose and Amelia home in my carriage before sundown."

"Oh do say they can join us, Mrs. Drummond." Marianne held her bonnet down against a burst of salt-laden wind. "Amelia would be such a help with Lizzie while Rose and I catch up on news."

Aunt Muira glanced at her husband who was still greeting people as they left the church.

"Very well, I suppose so." Aunt Muira withdrew a handkerchief and dabbed at the perspiration on her neck. "But be home in time for supper, my dear. You know how cantankerous Cora gets when we are late."

Rose kissed her aunt on the cheek and watched her join her husband, then she turned toward her friends. "Shall we?" She threaded her arm through Marianne's as they sauntered down the pathway toward Pratt Street and the docks.

"You have come a long way, Rose," Marianne whispered as they neared the water.

Rose glanced over the harbor that was bustling with activity. "Not as far as you think. My nerves are a bundle of knots even as we speak."

Marianne patted her hand. "Well, all the more reason I'm glad you joined us. You are safe with us." She glanced at her husband walking ahead with Jacob in his arms. "My husband can handle the fiercest rogues, I assure you."

Rose admired Noah's strength and confidence as he strolled down the street. She longed for her own protector. But how could she trust any man after what had happened?

As they approached the water, the bare masts of dozens of ships rose like a thicket of bare winter trees. Bells clanged, workers shouted, street vendors hawked their wares, children laughed, and somewhere in the distance music played. The malodorous smells of the harbor mixed with pleasant scents of food as the group hurried to get out of the hot sun and gathered into Chamberlain's tavern. There, they claimed a table on the open patio and enjoyed a refreshing pitcher of lemonade, spiced cake, and fresh crab.

A breeze wafted in from the port, cooling the perspiration on Rose's arms. Lizzie sat beside Amelia, who seemed most pleased to have finally found someone who would listen to her opinionated narrative on the fashion, status, wealth, and courting rituals of those citizens who had the misfortune of passing by the tavern. Noah entertained his son while Marianne and Rose drew their heads together catching up on all that had passed since they'd last visited.

When the sun began its trek toward the western horizon, the group strolled down Market Street. With Jacob in his arms, Noah led the way past an endless succession of one-story brightly colored houses of white, blue, and yellow lining the cobblestone road on both sides, broken up by the occasional quaint entrance of a rich merchant's brick mansion. Locust trees and the rich blooms of honeysuckle, butternut, and Virginia creeper decorated the pathways between the buildings.

Rose leaned toward her friend. "I do believe Noah gets more and more handsome every time I see him."

"I agree." She gave a sultry smile.

"Incredible since, if I recall, you once loathed the very sight of him." Rose chuckled and tugged the brim of her bonnet further down against the setting sun.

"God does work in mysterious ways." Marianne eased her fingers over her belly. "If Noah were in town just a bit more often, my life would be perfect."

"Apparently he's in town quite often enough." Rose giggled and Marianne joined her.

Thinking of a new baby reminded Rose of Marianne's ailing mother. "How does your mother fare?"

"Ah, she is well. Thank you. We have enough money now to hire the best physician in Maryland. Though she requires a great deal of rest, she has flourished under her new medicines."

"I am so pleased to hear it," Rose said as a great throng of gentlemen and ladies dressed in a rich display of brocades and taffetas passed by, flirting, jesting, and enjoying the warm summer air. Ahead, Amelia was thankfully too preoccupied with Lizzie to notice the attention flung her way by some of the passing young men. Rose flattened her lips. With Amelia's comely appearance and coquettish ways, she was bound to draw the wrong kind of attention sooner or later.

The thought had barely drifted through her mind when two handsome gentlemen, attired like London dandies, tipped their hats first toward Amelia and then toward Rose as they passed.

A sudden queasiness gripped Rose, followed by anger.

"You garner quite a bit of attention, Rose." Marianne gave her a sly look.

"I wish I didn't." Rose huffed. She hated the way some men ogled her as if she were a sweetmeat, but at Marianne's frown, she decided to make light of it. "Of course they find me appealing when I am dressed like this. But when they see me petting a pig and my face covered with mud, they simply"—she attempted to mimic the tone of haughty society—*"cannot tolerate such unsophisticated, unladylike behavior."*

Marianne giggled. "A man will come along who finds those things adorable, you'll see."

But Rose was not so sure. Nor was she sure she even wanted a husband anymore. The clip-clop of a horse and carriage bounced over her ears as it passed, laughter spilling from within. "You would hardly know we are at war," Rose said.

"Indeed. But I believe it is important to carry on with our lives as normally as we can even in the midst of war," Marianne said. "Otherwise we will go mad."

Rose played with a curl that dangled over her cheek. "It sickens me to think the British fleet is just miles off our coast."

"Did you hear the pistol shots a week ago?" Marianne placed her hand on Rose's arm. "I heard that British troops were spotted nearby."

Amelia coughed.

"In fact, a poor woman, Mrs. Davison—perhaps you know her?" Marianne asked.

Rose shook her head, afraid to hear any more.

"Why, she was attacked in her own home, and then the brigands burned it down while she watched from her field."

Noah shot a stern glance over his shoulder. "Which is precisely why you and your mother are staying at my father's house while I am away." His commanding voice reminded Rose why he was a captain at sea.

"And I have hired additional footmen for your protection," he added. "Blasted British."

"Were you not impressed upon one of their ships?" Amelia's admiring gaze fixed upon Noah.

He nodded toward his wife. "Both Marianne and I were, yes."

Amelia slipped back beside Marianne, dragging Lizzie by her side. "You were, as well, Mrs. Brenin?"

"Yes." She exchanged an adoring look with her husband. "But we survived."

"Their cruelty is inexcusable," Noah remarked, switching Jacob to his other arm.

Amelia lowered her chin, and Rose knew she thought of her husband.

"Oh look, isn't that Mr. Snyder?" Marianne pointed. "Over there talking to General Smith."

Rose followed her friend's gaze to see the councilman, dressed in his usual lace cravat and double-breasted tailcoat, cane in hand. Her stomach dropped. Could she not escape him? "Let us turn around, shall we?"

She spun Marianne about and headed the other way, but Mr. Snyder's shout slithered down her spine, halting her. "By the by, Miss McGuire."

Rose released a shaky sigh, gave Marianne a look of defeat, and swung back around.

General Smith, with Mr. Snyder on his heels like an obedient puppy, wove between two passing horses and marched toward her as if on a mission. The gold epaulets and brass buttons on his dark military coat glimmered in the sunlight. What could he possibly want with her? Surely he couldn't have discovered her secret. Yet the pointed look on his face made Rose's throat close.

The general halted before her. At least sixty years of age, he carried himself with the authority of a man accustomed to command. Now in charge of the Maryland militia and ordered to fortify Fort McHenry, he had quickly become the most important man in Baltimore. He nodded toward them all. "Miss McGuire, Mrs. Brenin, Mr. Brenin. Good day to you."

Noah and Marianne extended their greetings.

"Good day, General." Rose's smile felt stiff. "Are you enjoying your Sunday?"

"As much as one can during wartime."

Mr. Snyder eased up beside the general, rubbing against his arm as if he hoped the man's authority and wisdom would somehow transfer to himself.

"Miss McGuire." The general directed his gaze toward Rose. "There were several reports of musket and pistol fire near your uncle's land eight days ago."

"Indeed?" Rose forced her breathing to calm.

"Did you hear anything?"

"Me? No." She batted the air. "I sleep quite soundly, sir."

Amelia leaned on a nearby tree, clutching Lizzie to her side.

"Are you all right, Miss Amelia?" Lizzie asked.

Ignoring them, Mr. Snyder shot Rose a look of concern. "Your neighbor, Mr. Franklin, insists he saw British forces on your property." He tapped his cane on the ground.

"Confound it all." Noah's jaw bunched. "I cannot believe the audacity of those redcoats."

Rose lifted a hand to her neck. "My word! On my property?"

Mr. Snyder narrowed his eyes and leaned toward her. "Are you well? You've gone suddenly pale."

Rose drew out her fan and waved it over her face. "It's the thought of British soldiers on my property, sir. Far too distressing to imagine. But certainly I would have seen them."

"I am not implying otherwise." The general cocked his head and stared at her quizzically. "However, for your protection and the protection of Baltimore, I would like to come and ensure all is well."

Noah nodded his approval.

General Smith leaned toward Rose as if he had a grand secret to tell her. "Though this may shock you, miss, there are British sympathizers among us."

Rose's chest felt as though an anvil had landed on it. "Here in Baltimore? I cannot believe it." She feigned a gasp. Wondering if the man was playing with her, if he knew exactly what he would find on her land.

The general huffed in disdain. The lines of his face tightened. "And if I should discover any of them aiding the enemy, I'll have them hanged for treason."

"As well you should, General," Noah added.

The air around Rose grew stagnant and stifling. She gasped for a breath. "Indeed" was all she managed to mutter.

"General, you've upset the ladies." Mr. Snyder furrowed his brows in concern.

"Of course, forgive me." General Smith flipped open his pocket watch. "Nevertheless, I plan to send a few of my men to your farm. Councilman Snyder will accompany them, if that would make you feel more at ease."

"Well, I cannot say." Rose's voice came out shaky, and Marianne took her arm in hers and gave her a curious look. "You should seek my uncle's permission first."

"In wartime, I need no permission, Miss McGuire." General Smith snapped his watch shut and plopped it back into his pocket. "I can have a small band of militia formed within the hour. I assure you, it won't take long. We shall be in and out before your evening repast."

❖ CHAPTER 6 ❖

Alex leaned back against the open doorframe of the icehouse and gazed over the lush green farm. Farm indeed. For it appeared the fields had not been plowed nor planted for quite some time. No doubt the cow and the horse, both of whom now grazed among the grass and weeds, were the only things that kept the forest from reclaiming the land. From the icehouse, which was situated at the edge of the property near the tree line and not far from a river—the mad rush of which had soothed him to sleep the past few nights—Alex possessed a grand view of the property. Smoke curled from the small brick house at the center of the land, evidence that at least one person remained at home. Most likely a servant since Alex had seen Miss McGuire, Amelia, and an older lady leave in a landau hours ago. An elderly gentleman had left on a lone horse at dawn.

The barn where Alex had fought with Garrick and where he'd been tended to by the lovely Miss McGuire stood to the right of the house, while a smaller barn or stable perched on the other side. A quaint manor, to be sure, a rich and fertile land that was well placed beside the river. Yet quite rustic compared to the Reed estate from which Alex hailed. In fact, one might even call this American farm barbaric.

Yet there was something soothing, something peaceful about the scene that eased through Alex like a warm elixir, loosening his coiled nerves and calming his mind. Or perhaps that elixir came in the form of the angel who had tended him so faithfully these past eight days.

An avenging angel, to be sure. Though Miss McGuire appeared angelic on the outside, the fire burning in those blue eyes and her occasional caustic retort spoke otherwise.

She hated Alex. Simply because he was British. He'd never experienced that level of prejudice before. But how could he blame her? Her parents had been murdered by the British. And now his countrymen were attempting to reclaim her country for the Crown.

Alex gripped the knife and continued whittling away at the thick branch he'd found among the trees. Miss McGuire had stolen his pistol and service sword, but she'd not found the knife he kept hidden within one of his boots. He studied his handiwork. Soon he'll have fashioned a crutch that would aid him in his trek back to the Gunpowder River, where he'd first landed. With God's help and a bit of luck, he'd come across a cockboat from one of the ships. God's help. Alex wondered if God had anything to do with any of this. Or if the Almighty took note of Alex's life at all. Lately, it seemed, God had forgotten all about him.

Leaves rustled and a twig snapped. Alex jerked toward the sound, knife before him. A gray squirrel eyed him with bored curiosity before it darted away, pinecone in its mouth. By now, Alex expected Captain Milford to have sent a band of men to search for him and Lieutenant Garrick. It wasn't every day a British frigate lost both its first and second lieutenants. But it had been eight days, and he'd not seen a single British soldier. Either they were otherwise engaged in important battles or Alex suffered from an overinflated view of his own importance. He hoped it was the former. He had spent too many hard years serving His Majesty's Navy to accept such callous dismissal.

He scratched his arm and then his chest—yet again. What pesky varmint inhabited this loathsome clothing the lady had given him to wear? The fabric was course and stiff and the shirt and breeches were far too small. Not to mention the foul smell that permeated his new attire. No doubt the garments had not been properly washed since they were last worn. But he'd had no choice. Miss McGuire had been correct on one point: It would be best if he were not discovered in his uniform.

Alex stretched his leg out over the dirt and winced. It had healed nicely and only pained him when he attempted to stand. Despite being a woman, Miss McGuire had done a good job of extracting the bullet and dressing the wound. In a day or two, Alex should be able to walk the distance he needed back to his ship, back to his people. Oddly, he found no joy in the prospect. He drew in a deep breath of warm air and allowed the scent of honeysuckle and pine to fill his lungs. Though he knew he'd have to go back to his ship eventually, this brief respite from the horrors of war did his soul good. As long as he kept hidden away and did not endanger this rebel family, why should he rush back and risk reopening his wound?

Leaning his head back against the wooden doorframe, he thought of the lovely Miss McGuire. Rebellious curls that refused to be restrained framed her face in a silken web of glittering gold. Her eyes, the turquoise color of the sea he'd once seen in the West Indies—clear and sharp. With a wit to match. So outspoken. So unlike the women he'd known back home. One woman in particular came to mind. Miss Elizabeth Burgess, demure and sweet at least in etiquette and mannerisms. But beneath the outward facade of feminine perfection, a devious vixen raged.

On the contrary, despite Miss McGuire's harsh words and her obvious hatred toward his nationality and uniform her inner kindness overwhelmed him. She had every reason to turn him over to the military authorities. Yet she saved his life, healed his wound, protected him. He'd never been on the receiving end of such true Christian charity.

Slipping his knife inside his boot, he propped the end of the crutch into the dirt and hoisted himself up. The muscles in his back and arms ached and his thigh throbbed, but he felt strength surge through him. Shoving the handle of his crutch beneath his left arm, he tested it with his weight, careful not to place any strain on his injured leg. Perfect. This would do nicely. A gentle breeze wafted over him, cooling his sweat and bringing the smells of the earth, the forest, and life. Sunlight set the field aglow in various shades of green that waved before him like a mossy sea. America was indeed a beautiful land.

But it was Britain's land. And these people were British subjects. The sooner they faced that, the better. Arrogance and greed had made them forget their homeland—the parent country of their birth. Like rebellious children, they needed to be reminded who was in authority. Hopefully, that reminder would not take the lives of too many people. Or of one lovely lady in particular.

Alex released a sigh of resignation. Regardless of the lady's allure and the peace of this land, he should leave tomorrow night. The longer he stayed, the more danger he placed on her and her family. Alex would rejoin his ship and secure his future as an honored British naval officer. No one need know what had happened with Garrick. Alex had taken the only action available to him in the defense of an innocent woman. It mattered not that she was an American. He had done the honorable thing. And if he continued doing the honorable thing on board the HMS *Undefeatable*, this war would not only bring him the prize money he needed, but the accolades he required to earn the forgiveness of his brother and respect of his father. And maybe even a welcome home.

The clomp of horses' hooves and the grating of carriage wheels filled the air. He glanced toward the road leading to the house. The family returned. But it wasn't the same landau that left that morning. Alex froze. Behind the carriage, a band of horses trotted. He squinted at the sight. Men, armed with muskets and swords, some in blue-and-white uniforms, spread like a stormy wake behind the landau.

So, Miss McGuire had alerted the authorities after all. Alex's heart raced as his mind sped, searching a course of action. There was no way he could outrun them in his condition.

Ignoring Mr. Snyder's outstretched hand, Rose leaped from the carriage, trying to contain her fear behind a polite mask of composure.

"By the by, Miss McGuire," Mr. Snyder said as he assisted Amelia behind her. "You seem flustered." His eyes gleamed as if he knew something.

As if he knew she was about to be accused of treason.

"Not flustered, sir." She offered him a tight smile. "Simply tired after my long day in town and anxious to rest."

"Of course." He nodded, then searched the area—no doubt for a groomsman to take his horse—before he tied the reins to a post with a huff. "Someday I shall be able to afford a coachman." He grumbled under his breath. "And you a footman, perhaps?"

Rose frowned. A ridiculous comment in the midst of wartime.

Amelia brushed past Rose and entered the house, terror screaming from her eyes. The thunder of horse hooves pounded the air and shook the ground as a dozen men, both regular army and militia stormed toward them.

Rose struggled to breathe. In the western sky, the setting sun barely grazed the tops of the trees, sending spindly bright fingers across the farm, poking and prying into every dark corner. Her gaze shot unbidden to the icehouse in the distance. The door was shut. Was Mr. Reed inside or outside? If inside, he'd never be able to leave unnoticed.

Cora came running through the front door, wiping her hands on her apron. "What is happenin', child? Why are these men here?"

"Never fear, Cora." Rose took her arm in hers and led her back inside. The spicy smell of roast rabbit and wood smoke filled her nose. Normally Rose found them to be comforting aromas, but under the circumstances, they only enhanced her fear of losing everything that was dear to her—family, home, and freedom. She faced the cook. "They are here to protect us."

Or arrest us as traitors.

The cook's chubby cheeks quivered as her dark eyes skittered toward the door. "Then why are you shakin', miss?"

Rose snatched her arm back. "I'm just tired." She glanced up the stairs, wondering where Amelia had gone. "Now please run along and finish preparing the meal. Aunt Muira and Uncle Forbes will be here shortly."

With a frown, Cora turned and waddled toward the kitchen, muttering something about soldiers having no business searching the farm.

Taking a deep breath, Rose faced General Smith and Mr. Snyder as they marched through the front door. The general's thick boots thumped over the wood, grinding Rose's nerves to dust. He removed his bicorn and held it by his side. "Miss McGuire, we shall be no bother to you, I am sure."

"No trouble at all." Rose tugged off her gloves if only to keep her hands from shaking. She tossed them onto a table lining the wall of the foyer as she took a mental inventory of any incriminating evidence lying about the farm. Mr. Reed's coat and weapons were in a wooden chest on the top rafters of the barn. Other than that and the freshly dug dirt of Garrick's grave, there should be no sign of any traitorous activities.

Unless the soldiers looked in the icehouse.

If they did, at least her aunt and uncle wouldn't be here to witness Rose's arrest.

Five soldiers entered behind the general, two of whom Rose recognized as men from town who had joined the militia. They wore the same white trousers as the regular army but their dark blue jackets were devoid of the golden stripes and red trim that marked them as military. They both tipped their straw hats in her direction. "Miss McGuire."

"Mr. Cohosh. Mr. Blake." She gave a tremulous smile.

"My men will search your home." General Smith's commanding tone left no room for argument.

Mr. Snyder stood by the door, hat and cane in hand, and a worrisome look on his face.

Rose clenched her jaw. "General, this is pushing matters rather far. Do you think I wouldn't know if British soldiers were in my own house?"

"They are sneaky little devils, Miss McGuire," the general said. "It is for your own protection."

With a huff, Rose gestured toward the stairway. "You are wasting your time, gentlemen. Please be advised that my lady's maid may be in her chamber."

The men scrambled up the stairs, muskets in hand and swords flapping against their breeches.

Rose took a deep breath to steel herself. Then after a moment she turned. "May I offer you some tea, General, Mr. Snyder?" She sauntered toward the parlor, hoping to act nonchalant, but stumbled over the rug.

"No, thank you, miss. I need to direct my men." Swinging about, General Smith plopped his hat atop his head and marched outside as quickly as he had come.

Mr. Snyder hung his hat and cane on a coatrack by the door, then approached her. "I am here, Miss McGuire." He dabbed his fingers on his tongue then raked them through his perfectly styled copper-colored hair. "Nothing will happen to you. I can see these military affairs cause you great distress."

Rose merely stared at the man, hoping he, too, would find an excuse to leave.

"I will accept your offer of tea if you will join me," he said. "Perhaps I can help allay your fears." He gestured toward the parlor and a floral-printed settee that sat in the center of the small room.

Rose's palms grew sweaty. Her stomach bubbled. "Very well." Using the tea as an excuse to leave the man, Rose entered the kitchen, and leaned back on the wall beside the door. Her head grew light, and she raised a hand to rub her forehead.

Cora turned from stirring a pot over the fire. "Are you all right, child?"

"Yes. Would you prepare a tea tray for me and Mr. Snyder?"

The cook frowned and shook her head. "O' course," she sassed. "Along with makin' dinner and cleanin' the house and everythin' else I do around here. Yes, I'll serve tea to you and your gentleman caller." Pulling a tray from a shelf, she set it on the preparation table and eyed a kettle already steaming on the Franklin stove.

Ignoring her, Rose darted to the window above the sink and peered out through the mottled green glass. Blurred figures spread across her field like a swarm of locusts. Several men entered the barn. She could hear Prinney and the other pigs snorting accompanied by the squawk of chickens.

"Search the icehouse!" General Smith's command shot like an arrow through Rose's heart. She swung about and leaned on the sink, nearly collapsing.

Cora's brow wrinkled and unusual concern flitted across her face. "Child?"

Oh Lord, save us. The prayer rose up, unbidden. But when had God ever come through for her? When had He ever answered her pleas? Rose dragged in a breath that stuck in her throat and ignored the numbness that had taken over her body. "I believe Mr. Snyder and I will take that tea now."

Slapping a hand onto her rounded hip, Cora faced the fireplace, muttering under her breath. Her legs trembling, Rose left the kitchen.

If she were to be arrested for treason, she would abide it with dignity. She would pay the consequences of her actions. Memories of another equally terrifying event from her past threatened to leech the last of her strength and send her tumbling to the floor. Not all involved in that fateful night had lived to see the dawn. At the time, she had wished to be among those who had not survived. But now, she longed to live. To remain on this farm with her aunt and uncle, and when she was able, to help other women who had suffered the same fate as she had.

She gulped as she made her way to the parlor, trying to dislodge the vision. The soldiers clomped down the narrow stairs, casting smiles her way—*knowing* smiles. The wood creaked in laughter beneath their boots as they stormed toward the kitchen.

Cora burst through the kitchen door, tray in hand, and screeched at the sight of the men. They marched past her, nearly knocking her aside. Tossing a string of choice words over her shoulder, she entered the parlor, slammed the tray down on the rosewood serving table perched before the settee, and left.

"Difficult to procure decent servants these days." Mr. Snyder shook his head.

Taking a cloth, Rose lifted the teapot and attempted to pour a cup of tea for the councilman, but her hands shook, spilling the steaming liquid onto the tray. She set the pot down with a clank and sank onto the settee.

"They are simply soldiers ensuring your safety, miss. I've never seen you so distraught." Mr. Snyder took the opportunity to sit beside her. Her trembling increased. "Why, whatever is the matter, Miss McGuire?" He took her hands in his.

"My apologies, Mr. Snyder." She snatched them back and stood. "I fear I am unwell."

General Smith barged through the front door, two armed soldiers behind him. A fierce look rode on his face.

"Miss McGuire, we have found something most distressing."

❖ CHAPTER 7 ❖

Rose's legs wobbled, and she slumped onto the settee. She lifted her gaze to General Smith and then to the two armed soldiers behind him. The general's face was a cold mask, devoid of emotion. A breeze drifted in from the door and stirred the golden fringe of the epaulets crowning his shoulders. The pinpricks of a thousand needles traveled up her legs, through her stomach and chest, and onto her arms. "You found something, General?" Her voice rasped.

A British naval officer, perhaps?

Dread enveloped her. They had come to arrest her—had probably already bound Mr. Reed and placed him on a horse to escort him to the fort.

Mr. Snyder stood.

The general took a step toward her. His boots pounded like a judge's gavel over the wooden floor.

Rose's heart stopped beating.

"Yes, miss. We discovered this bloody cloth in your icehouse." He flapped the offending scrap through the air before her.

Rose's vision blurred. "In the icehouse?" Her voice cracked. Was he toying with her?

The general studied her. "Are you all right, Miss McGuire?"

"General, if I may." Mr. Snyder waved a palm toward Rose. "Surely you can see the sight of blood frightens the lady."

"Ah, of course. My apologies, miss." General Smith flicked the cloth over his shoulder to one of the men behind him.

Rose laid a hand on her heaving chest and struggled for a breath. "What do you make of it, General?"

Behind him, the kitchen door opened a crack, no doubt so Cora could listen to the proceedings.

"It's obvious," the general said, causing Rose's stomach to clamp again. "A wounded enemy soldier must have taken refuge there. Have you seen or heard anything during the past few weeks?"

Rose searched his hard eyes for any sign of trickery. "No sir." She wrapped her arms around her aching stomach. "We haven't used the icehouse in years. What need would I have to go out there? I can't believe a British soldier was so close. My word." She clutched her throat to stop her nervous babbling.

Mr. Snyder sat down beside her and took her hand. "It's all right, Miss McGuire." True concern burned in his eyes. He faced the general. "You've upset her. Obviously she knows nothing about this."

Rose slid her hand from his.

The general studied the room with censure. "What of your aunt and uncle?"

"I assure you, General," Rose said. "If they spotted an enemy soldier on our land, they would have alerted you immediately."

The general nodded, seemingly satisfied with her answer. "Well, it seems that whoever it was has long since gone. I am sorry to have upset you, miss, but we are at war. And one cannot be too careful."

"Of course. I thank you for your diligence, General." But all Rose heard was "has long since gone." Had Mr. Reed indeed left? Without so much as a by your leave or a thank you for all she'd done for him—all she had risked? She nearly chuckled at her own foolishness. What was she thinking? Mr. Reed had saved her life. He owed her no thanks. She should be happy that he was gone.

"I shall relieve you of my company." The general gave her a short bow, turned, and marched from the room, his men following after him.

Only then did Rose fully release the breath that had jammed in her throat. Only to have her lungs constrict again as Mr. Snyder caressed her bare fingers. Why did the man always have to touch her?

Rose leaped from the settee. "I thank you for coming to my defense, Mr. Snyder."

He shrugged. "It was my pleasure to shield you from the general's harsh demeanor. You know how these military sorts are." He waved a lacy cuff through the air as the last rays of the setting sun glinted off the jewel on his finger.

Shadows blossomed like hovering specters throughout the parlor, adding to her unease. Rose lit a lantern from the embers in the fireplace. When she turned back around, Mr. Snyder stared at her with the most peculiar look. The realization struck her that she was inappropriately alone with him. She could not hear Cora rumbling about in the kitchen. Perhaps the cook had gone out to the privy. And where was Amelia when Rose needed her?

Rising to his feet, Mr. Snyder sauntered toward her, a gentle smile on his lips. "Never fear, you are safe now, Miss McGuire. I shan't allow any harm to come to you."

Then why did Rose feel so uneasy? "We should not be alone without benefit of an escort, sir." She snapped her gaze to the door. "I must ask you to leave."

"You have nothing to fear from me." His forehead wrinkled. "I simply wish to discuss our future."

"I am unaware that we have one." She tried to sidestep him, but he blocked her path. Clenching her fists at her side, she stood her ground. Though the man was annoying, Rose doubted he would do her any real harm. Not with his reputation as city councilman at risk.

"But that is what I wish to discuss, my dear." He loosened his cravat. One golden brow rose above a pair of pleading eyes.

"Mr. Snyder, you overstep your bounds. I am most certainly not your dear." Rose started for the door, but he stepped in front of her yet again. The bergamot cologne he doused himself with stung her nose.

"Rose, I beg you." He took her hand and placed a wet kiss upon it. "Do not deny the affection I see in your eyes. Accept my courtship. I'm sure your uncle would find the match agreeable." He offered her a timid smile. "I cannot bear to live without you."

Tugging her hand from his—yet again—Rose took a step back, a battle of mind and heart waging a war within her. She should accept his offer. He had everything to recommend him and she had nothing, save this piece of land. But something in her heart forbade her—she did not love him. Could barely tolerate his presence. But perhaps she could learn. Couldn't she? To ensure herself a future? "I need more time."

He frowned and lowered his chin.

Rose pursed her lips. "I fear my feelings for you do not go beyond friendship."

He seemed to shrink in stature. "I see. Yet, surely after we are married, your love for me will grow?"

"Perhaps."

"Consider the prestige you will acquire from being a councilman's wife."

"And what will you acquire from the match?"

"A beautiful wife." His mouth remained open as if he intended to say something else.

"And my land." Rose snapped, leveling an incriminating gaze upon him.

His eyes widened, then he shrugged. "I daresay it is not so uncommon to covet such a sweet dowry. Any suitor would feel the same."

Rose knew he was right. Most marriage contracts revolved around money and land. And this man seemed to admire and love her as well. Could she hope for any more? "Mr. Snyder, though I am flattered by your offer, I ask you to wait a little while longer."

Disappointment rolled over his angular face.

"Now, if you please." Rose softened her tone. "For propriety's sake, I must ask you to leave."

He did not move. Fury chased the kindness from his face. "I will not wait forever for you. And I doubt you'll get a better offer."

The truth of his words sliced through her like a hot blade. "Perhaps not. Still, I insist you leave at once."

A cool breeze blew over them. The ominous thud of a boot step.

"I believe the lady asked you to leave." A deep voice that rang with a British lilt floated in on the wind.

Leaning on a crutch, Mr. Reed's body consumed the open space of the doorway. His dark eyes shifted from her to Mr. Snyder.

The councilman spun around at the intrusion. "Of all the. . .who the devil are you?"

"Forgive me, Miss McGuire." Mr. Reed nodded in her direction. "The door was slightly ajar, and I thought it best to ensure you were safe."

Rose tried to form the words "thank you," but nothing came out of her mouth. The kitchen door opened, and Amelia entered, a look of shock pinching her features.

Rose swept her gaze back to Mr. Reed, her mind trying to process what the daft man was doing.

Mr. Snyder stepped toward Mr. Reed. "I asked you to identify yourself, sir."

Mr. Reed's brows lifted as his glance shifted to Rose.

"He's our new man of work, Mr. Snyder." She blurted out the first thing that came to mind.

Mr. Snyder swerved about. "Your man of work? I wasn't aware you'd hired a man." His face grew red and puffy. "He sounds like a British aristocrat!"

Rose's mind reeled. "Yes. . .well. . .his accent. . ."

Amelia halted just inside the foyer.

Mr. Reed hobbled toward the parlor, his boots scraping over the wooden floor. He faced them with the confidence of a man who had nothing to hide. "What Miss McGuire is trying to say is that I spent my formative years in England living with my mother. I suppose I've never quite lost my accent."

"Indeed!" Mr. Snyder's eyes turned to steel. "What happened to your leg, sir?"

"Shot by the enemy."

Amelia slipped beside Rose and squeezed her hand. When Mr. Reed had first announced himself, Rose thought all was lost. But now as she watched him counter Mr. Snyder's insolent questions with grace and bravado, her heartbeat slowed from frantic to flurried.

"Are in you in the army?" Mr. Snyder continued his interrogation.

"Vermont State militia. Wounded at Odelltown, Quebec," Mr. Reed replied with calm assurance.

Rose bit her lip and wondered how he knew such things. But no doubt the British navy kept abreast of recent land battles.

Mr. Snyder's cold eyes swept to Rose. "Your uncle hired a crippled servant? I just saw him today in town, and he failed to mention it."

"What business is it of yours?" Rose shrugged, sharing a glance with Mr. Reed. Even leaning on his staff, he stood tall and bold. Not a hint of fear shadowed his face. He adjusted his makeshift crutch and shifted his broad shoulders as a breeze wafting in the door played with loose strands of his dark hair.

"Yet when I arrived"—Mr. Snyder faced Mr. Reed and fisted a hand on his hip—"you did not come out to take my horse."

"Forgive my negligence, sir. I was mending a fence at the perimeter."

"Ah, such unforgivable behavior." Mr. Snyder's eyes flashed indignant fury. "A good servant hears his master's guests arriving and anticipates their every need." He turned to Rose. "Your uncle needs a lesson in hiring qualified staff." His disdainful glance drifted over Amelia.

"Which is also none of your concern, Mr. Snyder." Rose gestured toward the open door. "Now, if you please."

His gaze shifted from Rose to Mr. Reed, who eyed him with an authority unbefitting a servant. Grabbing his hat and cane from the rack, Mr. Snyder barreled toward the door just as the sound of a carriage crunched over the gravel outside.

"By the by, here are your aunt and uncle now." Mr. Snyder hesitated in the doorway.

Amelia gasped and drew a hand to her mouth.

Rose's heart took up a rapid pace once again. Mr. Snyder was no fool. As soon as her aunt and uncle denied knowing Mr. Reed, he would figure out where he had come from and all would be lost. Releasing Amelia's hand, Rose dashed forward just as her aunt and uncle came through the door. "Uncle Forbes, Aunt Muira, Mr. Snyder was just leaving."

"I can see that. Good evening to you, Mr. Snyder." Uncle Forbes entered the room, his wife on his arm. His glance took in Mr. Reed standing staunchly to the side. "And who, pray tell, are you?"

"As I suspected!" Mr. Snyder swung about and slammed his cane on the floor.

"Uncle." Rose grabbed Uncle Forbes's arm and gestured toward Mr. Reed. "Remember you mentioned to Mr. O'Brien that you were looking to hire a man of work, and he recommended Mr. Reed." Rose lifted her brows and gave him a pleading *please-play-along* look.

Her uncle shifted his gaze between her and Mr. Reed as Aunt Muira released his arm and circled the tall British man.

"And you hired him sight unseen based on his recommendation?" Rose forced sincerity into her tone.

"Pure rubbish." Mr. Snyder took a step inside.

Ignoring him, her uncle scratched his gray beard. "Indeed, the incident grows clearer in my mind."

"Well, this is Mr. Reed." Rose turned her back to Mr. Snyder and mouthed *Please, Uncle.* Out of the corner of her eye, she saw Amelia gripping the stairway post for support.

A curious look claimed Uncle Forbes's face, but deep within his aged brown eyes, Rose spotted a glimmer of understanding. "Mr. Reed, you say?" He glanced over his shoulder.

"At your service." Mr. Reed bowed regally, ever the statue of serenity.

Rose heard the swish of Aunt Muira's skirts as she approached. "Ah, good, Forbes, you finally found someone." She beamed at her husband causing his cheeks to redden.

Uncle Forbes grabbed the lapels of his coat and swung about. "Yes, Mr. Reed, of course. Welcome."

Mr. Snyder huffed his displeasure from the doorway.

"Mr. Reed," Uncle Forbes said. "Can you see to the councilman's equipage?"

Mr. Reed tucked an errant strand of dark hair behind his ear. "I have already prepared Mr. Snyder's horse and carriage for his departure, sir."

Uncle Forbes smiled. "Very good. Very good. See, the man is already fast at work." He faced Mr. Snyder. "Good evening to you then."

Mr. Snyder's face grew as red as his hair. Rose would have laughed if her heart were not still in her throat. Amelia, however, seemed to have no such impediment and let out a merry giggle. The councilman stormed out the door, and Mr. Reed closed it behind him.

Sweeping off her shawl, Aunt Muira handed it to Mr. Reed. "Well, aren't you a fine figure of a man," she exclaimed, looking him over. "I do believe he'll do quite nicely, Forbes. I shall feel very safe with Mr. Reed here protecting the girls."

"I do my best to make you happy, dear." Uncle Forbes handed Mr. Reed his coat, and the poor man gave Rose a quizzical look. She gestured toward the coatrack by the door, and he obligingly hung up the garments.

"Well." Uncle Forbes rubbed his hands together. "I, for one, am famished. What is that delicious smell?"

Only then did Rose once again detect the aroma of roast rabbit and apple dumplings. Withdrawing a handkerchief from her sleeve, she dabbed at her neck and dared a glance at Mr. Reed. Wayward strands of hair the color of cocoa drifted over his collar. Dark stubble lined his jaw and chin, and his deep eyes locked on hers.

He had risked everything to protect her—again. The thought slammed against every opinion she'd ever held of the British. That any man, save her uncle, would risk his life for her caused a storm of confusion to rage within her. It frightened her. It elated her.

It frightened her *because* it elated her.

She shook off the traitorous feelings. He must have something to gain from keeping her safe. But what?

"Mr. Reed, have you been shown to your quarters yet?" her uncle asked.

"No, sir, I have not."

Rose cringed at his British accent.

"I shall show him," Amelia offered excitedly.

Aunt Muira patted her hair and headed toward the stairs. "Do you have any luggage?"

"No, madam."

She turned to Forbes. "Oh dearest, always taking in those in need. So like you." They shared a loving gaze.

During which Rose tried to move her feet to flee to her chamber but found them still frozen to the floor from the shock of all that had transpired.

Uncle Forbes laid his folded hands across his portly belly. "Though normally, Mr. Reed, you'll take your meals in the kitchen with Cora, do join us tonight. We would love to get to know you better."

His eyes widened in shock before a smirk played on the edges of his lips. "I shall be delighted." He leaned on his crutch and the muscles in his forearm bulged beneath the snug cotton shirt.

Rose wondered if Aunt Muira would recognize Samuel's clothing on Mr. Reed's much larger frame. Tearing her gaze from him, she searched her heart for a morsel of anger against his heritage, against him, but found none.

"I'll show you to the groomsman's quarters." Tugging on his arm, Amelia led him toward the front door.

"First, please tend to our landau and horses, Mr. Reed," her uncle ordered.

Mr. Reed's haughty brow rose, but at Rose's insistent nod, he flattened his lips and hobbled outside.

After Aunt Muira excused herself to freshen up for dinner, Uncle Forbes approached Rose, a look of reprimand on his face.

"I'm sorry, uncle. I should not have hired him without your approval." She bit her lip. "But I see he displeases you. I shall relieve him of his duties at once." She hoped he would agree, so there would be no need to explain when Mr. Reed suddenly disappeared. She started toward the door, but her uncle grabbed her arm.

"No, my dear. Your aunt finds favor in him. And he seems well-suited to the task. I trust your judgment." He cocked a brow and for a second, she thought she saw skepticism cross his brown eyes. "Does he come highly recommended?"

Rose smiled at the opportunity to impugn the British man and hence procure his immediate dismissal. "No, not at all. In truth I hardly know him." She leaned toward her uncle and whispered. "He could be a criminal."

"Nonsense, dear." Aunt Muira chuckled as she floated downstairs. "I find him charming. There's a nobility about him that adds elegance to our home."

"I agree." Uncle Forbes straightened his waistcoat. "Let us at least give him a fair chance."

"But—" Rose began, but her uncle lifted a finger, silencing her.

"No arguments," he said.

No arguments. Rose sighed. If only they knew they had just hired a British naval officer to be their man of work, there would be plenty of arguments.

If they knew they had just invited the enemy into their home, they would never forgive Rose.

❖ CHAPTER 8 ❖

Shifting his weight onto his good leg, Alex gripped the back of his chair and waited until Mrs. Drummond, Miss McGuire, and Amelia took their seats. Across the spotless white linen that covered the table, pewter plates, silverware, and glass goblets shone beneath the glimmering light of several candles set in brass holders. A modest display, to be sure, but far more than he expected from these backwoods farmers. Amelia burst into the room, then slowed her pace as she pinched her cheeks and approached the table, offering him a coy glance. She'd exchanged the lavender gown she'd worn earlier that day for one of cream-colored muslin with a pink velvet bow tied about her waist. Alex shifted uncomfortably beneath his drab, stained garb. Never in his life had he attended the evening meal so shabbily dressed. Even aboard the HMS *Undefeatable*, he'd always worn his cleanest uniform.

He glanced at Miss McGuire who slid into her seat across from him. She had not changed for dinner from the simple muslin gown she'd worn all day—a definite breach of proper etiquette. Yet the flowing lines and delicate pattern of the fabric flattered her feminine figure and brought out the glow in her face. He longed for a glimpse of her sea-blue eyes, but she kept them hidden from him and glanced instead at her uncle sitting at the head of the table—the man seemingly oblivious to his lapse of decorum. Both in the fact that he had taken his seat before the ladies and that he had invited Alex, a mere servant, to sup with them. Unheard of!

As soon as the ladies lowered into their seats, Alex moved out his chair and sank onto the hard wood, stretching out his injured leg beneath the table. A plump colored woman whom he assumed was the family slave slapped a steaming bowl and two trays of food in the center. His stomach growled as the spicy smell of gamy meat and butter filled his nose.

"Shall we bless the food?" Mr. Drummond bowed his head, the ladies following suit. As the man prayed, Alex cast a curious glance across the group. It had been years since his own father had prayed before a meal. When had he stopped? He couldn't recall. Yet as Mr. Drummond's voice shook with emotion and his words rang with sincerity, Alex couldn't help the lump that formed in his throat. These people actually believed God had provided this food and would bless it to strengthen their bodies. Yet the fare that sat before him, though it smelled delicious enough, paled in comparison to the nightly feasts Alex had partaken of at the Reed estate back home.

Where thanks had so rarely been given.

Their harmonious "amens" rang over the table, and Miss McGuire handed him a bowl of buttered potatoes. She continued to avoid his gaze as he took the dish from her and spooned a portion onto his plate. No doubt, she was not altogether pleased at his presence at her family's table. But how could he have avoided it? He'd watched the soldiers leave the farm from his spot behind a bush along the tree line. But as he waited, it occurred to him that the foppish gentleman he'd seen enter the house had not left along with them. It was beyond objectionable that the man should be alone with Miss McGuire. Alex intended only to ensure her safety before returning to the icehouse, but when he approached the front door and heard Miss McGuire order the man to leave and saw that he did not oblige, Alex had no choice but to step in.

He handed the bowl to Amelia beside him. The young woman had no trouble keeping her gaze locked on Alex. Creamy skin surrounded by waves of raven hair and sharp brown eyes assessed him with brazen impunity as she flitted her lashes and took the potatoes. Like so many of the ladies he'd known at home, Miss McGuire's companion was a coquettish tease. With the proper attire—and pedigree—she would be the belle of the London season...if she weren't such an unsophisticated American.

Ruffians, he huffed to himself. Again, he found it beyond the pale that they would invite a servant to dine at the same table with the masters of the house, but Alex would not complain. The few minutes he'd spent with their cook in the kitchen convinced him he would no doubt suffer from indigestion should he be forced to dine while listening to her incessant grumbling. Besides, being the son of Lord Cranleigh, he had every right and more to sit at any table he chose. *If they only knew.*

Alex stabbed a chunk of some type of meat from a platter that barely held enough for all of them and placed it on his plate.

"Please forgive our meager fare," Mrs. Drummond said as if reading his mind. "I'm afraid that the British blockade of the Chesapeake has restricted our diet and tightened our purse strings. And with no one to hunt game for us, we are forced to purchase what we can from the local trappers."

Alex glanced into her green eyes and was startled at the intelligence he found there. Intelligence and a speck of hauteur that together with her stately bearing could match any of the accomplished, society matrons back home. A sparkle drew his gaze to elegant jewels dangling from her ears—an odd accessory to her plain gown. What a dichotomy. Yet despite the wrinkles lining the corners of her eyes and mouth and the touch of gray that ran through her auburn hair, Mrs. Drummond possessed a refined comeliness Alex had not expected to see among these crude Americans.

"However, we must thank Rose for the potatoes." She gazed lovingly at her niece. "She grows them in her garden, you know."

"And Cora for her delicious apple butter." Mr. Drummond nodded as he snagged a biscuit from the tray. "Best in all of Baltimore." He dipped his spoon into a serving bowl filled with the brown, gooey substance and slathered it over the bread.

"Indeed." Alex smiled at Miss McGuire, but still she would not look his way. "Has the blockade caused you much discomfort?"

Something struck his foot, and he peeked beneath the table, thinking perhaps a dog wandered about seeking scraps of food.

"As you know, Mr. Reed." Mrs. Drummond's tone was edged with pride. "We are a hardy people and have become quite accustomed to living off the fruits of our labors." She sighed. "It is the luxuries we miss. The exotic fruits, sugar, coffee, and rice from the West Indies. The satin, taffetas, and velvets from England and France. Why, I haven't had a new gown in over a year. And the millinery was nearly empty the last time we visited."

"I couldn't agree more." Amelia shook her head, sending her dark curls dancing. "It has been insufferable."

"Come now, my dear ones," Mr. Drummond gently admonished them as he bit into a biscuit, scattering crumbs over his waistcoat. "These are trifling problems compared to the suffering some citizens have endured due to these infernal British raids." His gaze traced to Miss McGuire.

A twinge of guilt struck Alex. Miss McGuire dropped her spoon onto her plate with a clank.

Mrs. Drummond smiled at her husband. "You are right, dearest. Forgive me."

"So, Mr. Reed." Mr. Drummond faced Alex. "I'll warrant my niece has a good explanation for hiring you without my consent, but before I agree to it, tell us a bit about yourself. Where did you meet my niece, and how did you come to be in Baltimore?"

Out of the corner of his eye, Alex saw Miss McGuire stiffen like a mast. "In truth, Mr. Drummond, I was passing by your farm, saw a gentleman enter your house and heard a scream shortly after. Not wishing to pry, but worried for the safety of any ladies within, I crept up to the open door to investigate."

"Such kindness, Mr. Reed." Mrs. Drummond took a sip of her drink.

Amelia sliced her meat and smiled his way. "It's so romantic."

Feeling his throat go dry, Alex poured a glass of the amber-colored liquid from a pitcher and drew it to his lips. Sweet mint filled his mouth. A tea of some kind. Cold but pleasant tasting.

Mr. Drummond drew his brows together and cast a harried glance at Miss McGuire then back at Alex. "Who was the scoundrel, sir?"

"Nobody, uncle." Miss McGuire found her voice, although it sounded as strangled as if she'd swallowed a piece of rope. "The whole event was of no consequence."

Ignoring her, Alex chuckled. "Why, it was none other than your Mr. Snyder. At first glance, I feared his intentions were less than honorable, so I ordered him to leave."

"How gallant you were, Mr. Reed." Amelia took a bite of potatoes.

Mr. Drummond snorted. "I wish I could have seen his face." Crumbs flew from his mouth onto the table. Alex cringed at the man's lack of manners.

"Now, Forbes. That isn't kind." Mrs. Drummond laid a hand on her husband's arm. "Mr. Snyder is a respectable councilman." She directed her gaze toward Miss McGuire. "And quite taken with you, Rose."

Miss McGuire toyed with the food on her plate but offered no reply nor did she lift her gaze.

"But I'm confused, how did you come to be my new man of work?" Mr. Drummond pointed his fork at Alex—once again showing a lack of good breeding.

Miss McGuire lifted her chin. Wayward strands of honey-drenched hair dangled like glimmering threads about her neck. "Uncle, truth be told—and I'm sorry if this impugns your opinion of Mr. Snyder, Aunt Muira—but the man would not leave at my request. He was being quite obstinate. If not for Mr. Reed's intrusion, I cannot imagine what would have happened."

Mrs. Drummond's features wrinkled. "Surely you do not think he would do you harm, Rose. Preposterous." She chortled as she glanced around the table.

"I didn't think so either, Aunt, but then the infernal man wouldn't leave."

"Our sweet Rose creates a dither out of every little thing." Mr. Drummond tossed the last bite of his biscuit into his mouth.

Miss McGuire's shoulders slumped, and Alex pitied her for her uncle's nonchalant attitude toward her safety. What was the man thinking? Leaving two young ladies at home alone without a man in attendance to protect them?

"You should try this apple butter, Mr. Reed." Mr. Drummond handed the bowl to Amelia, who passed it to Alex. "It is quite delicious."

Amelia slid her fingers over Alex's as he grabbed the dish and set it down on the table. "I think Mr. Snyder left because he was frightened of Mr. Reed."

Ignoring her flirtations, Alex placed a piece of meat into his mouth and was instantly rewarded with a spicy, succulent flavor. Certainly not the hard tack and dried beef he normally received when out to sea. Rabbit, if he remembered the taste, though it had rarely been served at the Reed table.

A breeze swirled in from the open window, sending the candles sputtering, and bringing with it the scent of hay and evening primrose. Mrs. Drummond patted her coiffure back in place. "I imagine that Mr. Snyder was indeed frightened. You make quite an imposing figure, Mr. Reed. But do tell us what happened to your leg?"

"Pistol shot," he replied casually. He spooned potatoes into his mouth, finding himself suddenly quite hungry.

Someone kicked his leg beneath the table again. He winced and leveled a gaze at Miss McGuire. She frowned and jerked her head toward the door, no doubt prodding him to excuse himself and leave.

But his stomach resisted the notion.

Mrs. Drummond's green eyes flashed. "Shot! Indeed, from whom, where?"

"In the battle for Odelltown, Quebec, madam. Vermont militia." Alex cringed at the lie once again, but it could not be helped.

"Good heavens." Mr. Drummond set down his spoon, his ruddy face reddening even further. "So you are a soldier?"

Amelia leaned her chin on her hand and gazed at him adoringly.

"He is simply a wanderer, Uncle." Miss McGuire speared Alex with another icy gaze. "With a wounded leg and no particular skills. I only told Mr. Snyder that Mr. Reed was our man of work to get rid of the councilman." She straightened her shoulders and gave him a caustic smile. "So after you've partaken of our hospitality, sir, I assume you'll be on your way."

"Ah, not so quick, my dear." Mrs. Drummond set down her fork. "Your uncle has had a difficult time finding an appropriate replacement for Samuel. I, for one, find Mr. Reed an interesting candidate and wish to hear more about him."

"I quite agree, dearest." Mr. Drummond heaped a second helping of potatoes onto his plate. "Most of the men of Baltimore have either joined the militia defending the fort or have become privateers." He lifted kind brown eyes to Alex. "Or are fighting in Canada as you were, Mr. Reed."

"Yes." Alex spread a dab of apple butter onto his biscuit and took a bite. The creamy flavor of sweet apple exploded on his tongue, but instantly soured beneath his deception.

A smudge of apple butter guarded the corner of Mr. Drummond's lips as they formed a frown. "Were you shot by the British?"

A mixture of fear and anger leaped from Miss McGuire's crisp blue eyes.

"A British naval officer, to be exact," he answered never taking his eyes off Miss McGuire. She kicked him beneath the table. On his bad leg. Pain shot through his thigh. He coughed into his hand to cover up a groan.

Amelia exchanged a harried glance with Miss McGuire.

"Oh my." Mrs. Drummond played with the tiny jewels dangling from her ears. "Thank goodness you survived."

"The wound is healing nicely. I had the best of care." Alex hoped his compliment would assuage the fury pouring from Miss McGuire's face, but it only seemed to agitate her further. Did she think him such a fool that he would divulge his true identity? Upon his honor, he would be gone soon enough.

Amelia took the liberty of refilling his goblet from the pitcher.

"May I ask where your family is from?" Mr. Drummond paused in cutting a piece of meat. "Your accent rings with nobility, sir."

Alex tore his gaze from Miss McGuire's piercing eyes. "Indeed. I am told that quite often. A curse of my upbringing, I fear. But my family is all gone now."

"Oh my." Mrs. Drummond gasped. "Please forgive my husband's impertinence. We did not mean to intrude."

Mr. Drummond plopped his last piece of rabbit into his mouth then directed his gaze at Miss McGuire. "But Rose, lass, I must chastise you. You rid yourself of Mr. Snyder, yet place yourself at the mercy of a complete stranger."

Seconds passed as Miss McGuire pushed a pile of potatoes about her plate. Finally she looked up. "We have met before, Uncle."

"Have you, dear? Pray tell, where?" Mrs. Drummond dabbed her napkin over her lips.

"On the farm a few weeks past."

"I came by looking for work, but your niece turned me away," Alex said.

"I did not think you would approve." Miss McGuire sipped her tea and sat up straight. "In fact, now that you know more about him, I'm sure you'll agree he is not suited for the position."

A smile twitched on Alex's lips at her attempt to be rid of him. The fire sparking in her blue eyes tempted him to goad her further—if only to draw her gaze his way once again.

Mrs. Drummond shook her head. "Oh dear, you shouldn't say such things in front of Mr. Reed. Why, he's a soldier wounded while fighting for our country." She gave him an admiring look. "I for one am in favor of giving you a chance to prove yourself as our new man of work."

Amelia flinched beside him. A loud clank drew Alex's gaze to Miss McGuire. Her goblet lay on its side, the remainder of her tea spilling onto the white tablecloth. "Forgive me." Miss McGuire tossed her napkin over the puddle as her aunt frowned in her direction. "I am sure that Mr. Reed wishes to return to the war." She squeezed the words out through clenched teeth and a tight smile. "Do you not, Mr. Reed?"

"Whatever is amiss with you tonight?" Mrs. Drummond said.

Mr. Drummond brushed the crumbs from his shirt and held up a hand. "Before you accept, Mr. Reed, I should inform you that the position requires you to handle a multitude of duties. As you can see, we are unable to afford many servants. We have Cora, our cook and housekeeper—"

"Then she is not your slave?" Alex had not intended to interrupt, but the way Mr. Drummond had spoken the cook's name inferred that she was more of a family friend than slave.

"Oh goodness no, sir." Disgust shadowed Mr. Drummond's face. "I purchased her ten years ago from a slave trader and offered her freedom and a position in our home should she desire to stay. She's been with us ever since."

An unavoidable admiration for the man blossomed within Alex.

Though England's Slave Trade Act forbade British ships from transporting slaves, both Britain and America had not yet removed the scourge of slavery from their colonies. "Commendable, sir. Especially since so many of your fellow countrymen think nothing of keeping slaves."

"My countrymen?" Mr. Drummond's gray brows rose. "Are they not your countrymen as well?"

Amelia coughed. Miss McGuire froze and Alex stiffened at his foolish blunder. "Indeed, I misspoke. It has been a long day."

But Mr. Drummond's smile indicated he took no suspicion of it. "Nevertheless, as I was saying, when Rose came to live with us, we also hired Amelia as her lady's maid and companion. So we are in need of a general man of work to perform the duties of footman, groomsman, and farmhand."

Alex swallowed the meat in his mouth and took a sip of tea to stifle the chortle that longed to emerge from his throat. The son of a viscount hired as a common servant? And by a man with half Alex's intelligence, breeding, and education. It was most comical. "You do indeed have a pleasant piece of land, Mr. Drummond."

"Can I get you another biscuit, Mr. Reed?" Amelia smiled his way, and Miss McGuire glared at her maid.

"No, thank you, miss." Alex withheld a chuckle at the woman's continued flirtation.

"The land." Mr. Drummond waved a hand in the air, "Oh, that's Rose's doing."

"Indeed?" Alex raised brows at Miss McGuire, but she had plucked out her fan and was waving it about her face.

"It does not deserve a mention," she mumbled.

"Of course it does, lass," Mr. Drummond said. "We bought the land with Rose's inheritance."

"And her money provides us with a comfortable living," Mrs. Drummond added. "This home, our carriages and horses, and Cora and Amelia's salaries."

"I am all astonishment." Alex said. And indeed he was. Miss McGuire's eyes chilled. "Is it so unbelievable?"

He grinned.

"You see, Mr. Reed," Mrs. Drummond continued, "Mr. Drummond brings home but a meager salary from his church."

"Your church?"

"Yes. I am the reverend at the First Presbyterian Church in Fells Point."

Alex shook his head. A reverend? Certainly the last profession he would have guessed for this unrefined, bumbling man. "A rewarding position, no doubt."

"It is. And much more than I deserve." The sparkle left Mr. Drummond's eyes. "I came here as an indentured servant—a captured thief from Scotland, and now look what God has done."

Alex cringed. A criminal. His father Lord Cranleigh would choke on his food were he to learn of the depravity of Alex's dinner companions.

Amelia placed an overbold hand on Alex's arm. "Ouch!" She jerked back her hand and speared Miss McGuire with a gaze. Alex smiled. No doubt the poor woman had also fallen victim to the point of Miss McGuire's shoe.

Composing herself, Amelia continued, "Forgive me. I. . ." She took a breath, then went on without explaining her outburst. "Theirs is such a romantic story. Mr. Drummond was an indentured servant in Mrs. Drummond's house."

"I was known then as Miss Muira McGuire, you see." Mrs. Drummond gazed adoringly at her husband. "We fell in love."

"Aye, after I repented of my sins and came to know the Lord." Mr. Drummond cocked his head toward his wife. "Due to your brother's godly influence, I might add."

"Rose's father, Robert. God rest his soul." Sorrow tugged upon Mrs. Drummond's features. "He was a good man."

Alex set down his fork, his stomach suddenly churning.

Mrs. Drummond shrugged. "Of course my father disapproved the match."

"Her family disowned her," Amelia added. "But she ran away with him anyway." She released a wistful sigh.

Left everything? For love? Yet hadn't Alex nearly done the same years ago?

"Is it warm in here?" Miss McGuire huffed as she fluttered her fan over her face and neck.

Mrs. Drummond scooped potatoes onto her plate. "You see, Mr.

Reed, my family grew quite wealthy building ships in Norfolk."

"Indeed?" Alex watched as Miss McGuire pushed her uneaten plate of food aside and pleaded with her eyes for him to leave.

"We were poor for many years." Mrs. Drummond took her husband's hand in hers. "Yet so much richer than most."

Alex turned away from the intensity of affection he saw in their eyes—an affection stronger than any he'd witnessed between a man and wife. A strange longing welled up within him to be loved with such passion.

Miss McGuire hurried her fan, sending wisps of golden hair dancing about her neck. "I would never have had such courage to do what you did, Aunt Muira."

Mr. Drummond kissed his wife's hand then faced his niece. "If you would only put your trust in God you could."

"How can I after what He allowed me to endure?" She swallowed, and her gaze flitted over Alex. Could she be speaking of her parents' deaths? Yet the depth of sorrow in her eyes bespoke of something more.

"So you see." Mr. Drummond wiped his mouth with his napkin and tossed it onto the table, though crumbs still speckled his gray beard. "If God redeemed this poor old sinner, how can I not give as much as I'm able into His service?"

Mrs. Drummond leaned back in her chair and folded her hands in her lap. "Our work takes us away from the farm often, Mr. Reed, so we are in desperate need of someone to watch over things."

"You leave the ladies alone? Without protection? In wartime?" Alex found the idea inconceivable. Visions of Lieutenant Garrick's body atop Miss McGuire resurged his anger.

"Only recently. And out of necessity. Samuel our last man of work ran off two weeks ago. Joined the British army. You have no intentions of doing that, do you?" He chuckled.

Amelia clutched her throat, then grabbed her glass and sipped her tea.

Another blow to his leg. Pain speared up his thigh. Alex winced and tightened the muscles in his jaw. "The British army? No sir. That would be my last choice." And indeed it was. He was a navy man through and through.

Alex tapped his napkin over his lips, then sat back in his chair and patted his full stomach. He'd not felt so satisfied and rested in months. If he were back on the ship, he'd have to assume his duties and carry out the commands of his volatile and berating captain. In addition, he'd no doubt be sent out on further raids where he'd witness unspeakable atrocities in the name of war. Or worse, where he might have to perform acts that violated the strictures of decent humanity. No, he was in no rush to return.

He gazed over his dinner companions. Though uncultured at best, the kindness of these simple people eased over his soul like a warm tropical breeze. Besides, he hated the thought of leaving the women alone without protection—of leaving Miss McGuire at the mercy of the next British raid. He shuddered. What harm would it do to stay on and protect them while his leg healed?

Mr. Drummond's eyes twinkled in the candlelight. "Do say you'll stay on as our man of work, Mr. Reed."

Rose thrust her foot once again at the pompous man's leg, no longer caring if she hurt him. Surely he would not agree. But just in case, she wanted him to know her wishes on the matter. Her foot met air, and his smile confirmed that he had retreated his leg to a safer position.

Aunt Muira frowned. "Dear, you've hardly eaten a bite. Are you ill?" She placed the back of her hand against Rose's cheek.

"Now that you mention it, I do believe I'm not feeling well." Turning her face away from her aunt, Rose gave Mr. Reed a venomous look and glanced toward the door.

He grinned.

She'd love to slap that haughty smirk off his lips. He'd done nothing but toy with her through the entire meal! And toy with her aunt and uncle as well. In addition, he had refused to take heed of her numerous hints for him to leave. My word, didn't he understand she had the power to turn him in to the authorities? But of course, he was no fool. Since he had been introduced to Mr. Snyder as the Drummond servant, she could no longer do that without implicating her entire family as traitors.

Mr. Reed nodded toward her uncle but kept his playful eyes upon her. "I'd be happy to accept your offer, Mr. Drummond, but only until you can find a replacement for me. When my wound is fully healed, I must return to my shi—regiment."

What? He couldn't stay! Rose bolted from her chair, tipping it backward. It landed on the floor with a thump. Her uncle gave her a curious look. "Whatever is the matter with you, lass?"

Aunt Muira took her arm. "Perhaps you should retire. You look a bit pale."

Mr. Reed struggled to his feet. "Indeed, Miss McGuire. I fear the events of the day have taken their toll on you."

Rose's jaw hardened until she felt it would snap.

"I commend your loyalty to our cause, Mr. Reed." Uncle Forbes scraped his chair over the wooden planks and stood. He tugged upon his waistcoat. "Such courage and dedication is difficult to find. I accept your offer. In the meantime, I shall make every attempt to procure a replacement for you as soon as possible."

Nausea gripped Rose's stomach. She wrapped her arms around her waist and glared at Mr. Reed. By bringing the enemy into their home, she had endangered all their lives. Why didn't the blasted man return to his ship? He certainly was well enough. What could he possibly want with them?

And then it hit her.

Mr. Reed hobbled to the side and pushed in his chair. Leaping to her feet, Amelia gathered his crutch and handed it to him. He thanked her with a smile as Rose's uncle and aunt crowded around him, welcoming him to the family.

Yes, Rose knew exactly what the man was up to. No doubt, he intended to use his time here to spy for his country—make trips into town, under the guise of running errands, to get a good view of the city's defenses. But he would not succeed, for Rose would do everything in her power to stop him.

❖ CHAPTER 9 ❖

Bucket in one hand, lantern in the other, Rose yawned and plodded through the weeds that surrounded the back of the barn where her uncle kept his horses and carriage. Katydids chirped their nighttime chorus as she peered through the predawn shadows and halted before the door of the servants' quarters attached to the building.

Where Mr. Reed had spent the night.

A chilled breeze coming in from the forest swirled around her with the sweet fragrance of cedar and Virginia creeper. Despite the pleasant aromas, a shudder ran through her as she set down the pail and lantern—a shudder that had nothing to do with the wind. She fingered the handle of the knife she'd stuffed into her leather sash and hoped she'd have no need of the vile weapon. But one could never be careful enough when it came to a man she did not know. Rose had learned that lesson the hard way. She banged on the door.

After a few moments, a loud groan that sounded like an angry bear filtered through the wood. Plucking out the knife, she knocked again.

"What the deuces?" The words, followed by a string of expletives, grated over her ears before the door squeaked open.

Mr. Reed, bare-chested and with loose breeches hanging about his hips, gaped at her through puffy eyes. Hard muscle rounded his chest and arms, and Rose gripped the knife in both hands and held it out before her.

"Miss McGuire." His gaze lowered to the blade trembling in her hands. "Have you disturbed my sleep just to kill me?" More humor than fear filled his voice.

"Only if I have to, Mr. Reed."

"I assure you, I will give you no cause."

"And I assure you, sir, that I will give you no opportunity to give me cause." The words that had made sense in her mind twisted nonsensically in the air between them.

Mr. Reed's brows furrowed. He shook his head. "You are befuddling my mind, miss." He shifted his stance. "What need do you have of a weapon?"

"I do not know you, Mr. Reed. Yet, by circumstance I find myself forced to be alone with you."

"Miss McGuire." He sighed and rubbed his eyes. "If I had wanted to hurt you, I have had ample opportunity." Anguish rolled across his face. "Why are you so frightened of me?"

"I am frightened of many things, Mr. Reed."

He studied her. "As your uncle declared at dinner." He stretched his back, his muscles rippling across his chest.

An odd warmth sped through her. Rose dragged her gaze from him to the dark form of her house in the distance. When she faced him again, she found him staring at her inquisitively. "Why are you looking at me like that?"

"It's just that you don't seem the skittish type, Miss McGuire. You endured the assault of an enemy, went ably toward his gun, removed a bullet from a man's leg, and then nursed him back to health at the risk of your own and your family's safety. Egad, if I recall, you even begged Garrick to shoot you!" He shook his head. "Those are not the actions of a fearful woman."

Rose nearly snickered at his compliment. What Mr. Reed didn't realize was that she had been out of her wits with terror every second of those encounters. "I did what I had to."

"Precisely." One eyebrow lifted and a look of admiration flickered in his hazel eyes.

Against her will, his ardor nestled into a soft spot of her heart. Lowering the blade, Rose stuffed it back into the sash of her gown. "You should know, Mr. Reed, I intend to have this knife on me at all times."

He chuckled. "I consider myself duly warned."

Yet when her eyes drifted once more to his muscled torso, she realized how foolish her statement was. This man would have no trouble overpowering her.

"Please cover yourself, sir," she said, clearing her throat and touching the knife handle again.

Hobbling, he disappeared into the dark room and returned wearing one of Samuel's cotton shirts. "Forgive my state of undress. I did not know it was you at my door."

"Who else would it be, Mr. Reed?" Rose flicked a curl from her face, trying to ignore the heat flushing through her body.

He rubbed his eyes again and gazed over the farm still shrouded in darkness. "Certainly not you at this ungodly hour."

"Enough of this." Rose huffed. "You cannot stay here."

The green flecks in his eyes glinted playfully in the lantern light. "I believe your aunt and uncle have given me their blessing."

Rose clenched her jaw. "You may find your little charade amusing, but I assure you it is anything but."

He leaned on the doorframe and crossed his arms over his chest. "I find you sneaking out here in the middle of the night to see me quite amusing, miss."

Rose's stomach knotted in fury. "I insist you leave at once and go back to your ship."

"Though I would love to oblige you, I fear I am not yet capable." He sighed and glanced down at his leg. "When I saw the soldiers descend upon your farm, I tried to make my escape in the woods. Before too long, I found my strength spent and my pain unbearable."

"Perhaps I should give you some of my aunt's laudanum to assist in your journey."

"Or a horse."

"You know I cannot do that." A light wind played with the hem of her dress and tossed Mr. Reed's loose, dark hair over the top of his shirt. "How long must you keep up this pretense? My aunt and uncle are not imbeciles."

He cocked his head and studied her as if he disagreed with her assessment.

Of all the impertinent... A muscle tightened in her neck. Grabbing the lantern, Rose held it up to get a better look at his face. "Can you not see that every minute you spend here puts me and my family at great risk? Any honorable man would leave us be."

"I assure you, I would never harm you or your family, nor do I wish to put any of you in danger."

"Then leave us, I beg you."

His jaw tightened. "In truth, my honor forbids me to leave you and Amelia without protection. Not after what happened with Garrick."

Blood surged to her face. "Oh do not pretend, sir, that you have a care for what happens to us. You are an enemy to everything I hold dear."

The katydids ceased their buzzing. Sorrow passed over Mr. Reed's features before his eyebrows shot up. "Perhaps you forget that it was I who saved you from being ravished a week ago?"

Rose lowered her chin. "I have not forgotten your kindness. Yet I do wonder at your reasons." She gazed up at the man towering over her and gathered both her fury and her resolve. "You have placed yourself in a grand position to spy upon my country, Mr. Reed, and I'm here to inform you I will not allow it." She stomped her foot for effect but the man merely smiled.

"Spy?" Mr. Reed's hearty chuckle tumbled over her, dissolving the power of her accusation. "What could I possibly learn from simple farmers that would aid the British cause?"

The katydids resumed their incessant droning.

Rose's face heated. "Why you pretentious, pompous, overbearing. . ." —the rest of the names popping into her mind should not be uttered by a lady—"We may be farmers but we are not as beef-witted as you assume."

Instead of being insulted at her tirade, he grinned even wider.

Rose sighed. "Besides, you could learn something of import when my uncle sends you into town on errands."

"Miss, unless I were given access to your city's plans of defense, I cannot see how the cost of a pound of flour or whether you wish to purchase beeswax or tallow candles would be of any use to me."

"Is that what you believe to be the extent of our knowledge? How to buy flour and candles?"

He flattened his lips and ran a hand through his loose hair. "I meant no insult, miss. But upon my honor, I am no spy."

"Good. Because I shall see that you have no opportunity to discover any military secrets."

Mr. Reed stretched his shoulders and gazed into the darkness.

His features tightened beneath a pensive look. "I realize you hold my countrymen responsible for the death of your parents. I understand your hatred of me."

Rose backed away. "I doubt you understand much about me or my country."

"I assure you that I have no intention of staying but a few days."

"Is that a promise?"

"Unless unforeseen circumstances arise, yes."

"Do you even know how to be a servant?"

He shrugged. A breeze tugged at a loose tendril of his dark hair. "I passed the lieutenant's exam with honors; how hard could it be?"

A giggle rose in her throat. This highbrow had no concept of hard work, at least not the kind required by the only male servant in the house. Perhaps that was how she could get rid of him. She would give him the most vile tasks—tasks that a man of his breeding would consider far beneath him. Tasks so repulsive that his pride—which was obviously enormous—could not suffer the humiliation. Then perhaps he'd leave when he promised. Or better yet, even sooner.

Picking up the pail, Rose held it out to him. "Milk Liverpool."

"Milk who?" Mr. Reed stared at her as if she were an apparition floating outside his door.

"Milk the cow." She gave him a supercilious smile. "Did you think this was merely a social call?"

Mr. Reed gazed past her, confusion wrinkling his face. "What hour is it? Where is the sun?"

"It is five thirty, Mr. Reed, and the sun shall make its appearance soon, I assure you."

"Five thirty." He yawned. "Only thieves and murderers lurk about at this hour, Miss McGuire. Go back to bed and call upon me in a few hours." He started to close the door.

She shoved her foot against the wood and the pail against his chest. "We milk the cow before dawn."

"Need I remind you, I am an officer, not a farmer?"

"Need I remind you that you are under my employ and will do what I say? Or"—she shrugged—"my uncle will discharge you, and you'll have no choice but to return to your ship, Mr. Reed, injured leg or not."

One side of his lips lifted in a smile. "So you plan on driving me away with work?"

She released the bucket. It fell onto his good foot with a thud.

"Ouch." Mr. Reed winced.

"I'll meet you in the barn."

An hour later, Alex found himself sitting on a stool staring at the underbelly of a huge, portly beast. A stench he dared not describe but one that had haunted his dreams while he'd been feverish assailed his senses. Beside him, Miss McGuire lowered herself to another stool and rubbed her hands together.

"Make sure your fingers are warm," she began instructing him, but her words rummaged past his ears unintelligibly. Instead—as a rhythmic *splat, splat* echoed in the bucket—Alex found himself mesmerized by the slight tilt of Miss McGuire's head, the way the lantern light glimmered over her curls, and the moist sheen covering her lips.

"There," she sat back. "Now it is your turn."

Alex shook his head. A rooster crowed in the distance. "My turn?"

"Yes." She faced him with a satisfied smirk. "This will be your job every morning."

Alex stared at the four pink teats with disgust. Yet how hard could it be? "Very well, allow me." He slid onto the stool Miss McGuire vacated. Flexing his fingers, he leaned beneath the beast and grabbed hold of one of the teats. It was warm and slick to his touch.

The cow let out an ear-piercing bellow and swung her enormous face toward him. Alex grabbed his crutch and leaped off the stool in horror.

Miss McGuire giggled. "Afraid of a cow, Mr. Reed?"

"Only when she bares her teeth at me." He regained his composure.

"She won't bite." Miss McGuire placed her hands on her hips. "Try warming your fingers first. I doubt you'd enjoy an icy touch to your. . ." She halted, dropped her arms to her side, and glanced away.

Alex withheld a laugh, enjoying the red blossoming over her fair cheeks. "No, I daresay, I wouldn't."

He took his seat again. Then, after rubbing his fingers together, he placed them on the teat and began to squeeze. The cow let out a long and arduous moo.

Miss McGuire sat on the stool beside him, maintaining some distance between them. "Like this, Mr. Reed." She pressed his fingers onto the top of the teat near the udder then ran them down to the tip. A squirt of milk shot into the pail. "See?" Her eyes met his. Too close. Her fresh feminine scent pushed the malodorous smells of the barn from his nose, and he resisted the temptation to bury his face in her hair. Her lips parted and he stared at them, moving closer.

She jerked her hands back and stood, retreating to the wall of the barn. He grinned, hoping their closeness had a similar effect on her.

But why? When he'd be gone in a few days?

Pushing the unwanted thoughts aside, he returned to his task and attempted to duplicate her action, but the cow stubbornly withheld her milk.

Miss McGuire giggled again.

Alex continued to coax the beast into compliance. "You are enjoying this, aren't you?"

"Immensely." She smiled.

"I am no stranger to hard work, miss, if that is what you are trying to prove. I have served on His Majesty's ships for the past nine years." Finally a squirt of milk shot from the teat.

Onto the dirt.

"Try hitting the pail, Mr. Reed."

He growled his frustration. "Perhaps people were not meant to milk cows. Have you ever considered that? It seems highly unnatural to me."

"Unnatural or not, someone with your education and skills should have no trouble with a simple task that any milkmaid can perform."

Alex shook his head and switched to a different teat. Liverpool let out a guttural groan as dawn painted a luminous glow outside the barn door. Miss McGuire swept past him, her cotton gown rustling.

"Have no fear. I am sure I will master the technique before too long." He glanced up at her. The morning sun formed a golden halo around her head.

"I should hope so, Mr. Reed." The halo faded beneath her biting tone. "You have many more tasks to complete before the day is done."

Alex massaged the teat. Another squirt. This time into the pail.

"Now I have it." He shot Miss McGuire a confident glare then squeezed the same teat again. A stream of warm milk shot him in the face. He slammed his eyes shut as the liquid dripped off his chin onto his shirt. Releasing the cow, he swiped the creamy fluid from his cheeks and neck.

"Yes, I'd say you have it now, Mr. Reed." Miss McGuire's feminine laughter bubbled over him. But instead of stirring his indignation, it had the opposite effect.

He smiled up at her. "Quite amusing, I'm sure." They laughed together, and for a moment joy sparkled in her eyes. But then a cold shield lifted over them once again. She pursed her lips. "When you're finished, bring the milk to Cora. Then ask her for the kitchen scraps and return to me in my garden. I'll show you how to feed the pigs."

"You named your pig Prinney?" Shock jarred Alex, followed by a disgust that halted him in midstride.

"I did." Rose knelt to pet the massive beast.

"After the Prince Regent of England?" He still could not believe it.

"He does resemble him, don't you think?" Miss McGuire scratched the pig behind the ears then moved her fingers to do the same beneath his chin. "There you go, Prinney. That's a good boy."

Indignation churned in Alex's belly. How insolent, ungracious, and ill-mannered! He shifted his gaze to the cow in the barn, and he grew more outraged. "Liverpool. You named the cow after our Prime Minister, Lord Liverpool!"

Miss McGuire stood, a grin twisting her luscious lips. A smudge of dirt angled down her neck and despite her blatant disrespect, he longed to wipe it off.

She handed him a shovel. "Time to clean out the pigsty."

Alex gazed up at the sun. Only halfway in its ascent, its hot rays already seared him. Sweat beaded on his neck. "Clean it of what?" He glanced at the clumps of mud and hay and other less desirous nuggets that covered the floor of the enclosure.

"Of the pigs' messes, of course." A sarcastic twinkle shone in her eyes. "You should be good at it by now. Being in *His Majesty's Navy*, don't you often have to shovel Prinney's waste?"

Alex opened his mouth to respond but outrage strangled his voice.

"Afterward, you may clean out the barn as well. And chop the firewood." She pointed toward a pile of thick branches stacked along the side of the barn. Then flashing him a curt smile, she sashayed away.

Rose poured a cup of tea and sat down at the preparation table in the center of the kitchen. Amelia and Cora jostled each other for a position at the window that pointed toward the barn.

"You sure got him working hard, child." Cora returned to her spot at the table and began kneading a lump of dough.

"He's a servant. He's supposed to work hard." Rose took a sip of the tea, bitter like the guilt that soured the back of her throat. She plopped another lump of sugar into the hot liquid and gave it a stir.

"But you never made Samuel do yer chores. I thought you loved carin' for the animals yourself." Cora's tone was tinged with disapproval.

Amelia continued to gaze out the window. "Oh my."

"Amelia, for goodness' sakes, quit drooling."

"He's taken off his shirt," Amelia responded breathlessly.

Rose and Cora both darted to the window, nudging against each other for a better view. Mr. Reed's form came into shape beyond the blurry glass. His shirt hung limp over a fence post as he raised the ax over his head, bringing it crashing down onto a log. Muscles that were anything but limp swelled firm and round on his biceps and chest. Dark hair the color of cocoa loosened from his queue and feathered his broad shoulders gleaming in the sunlight. The sweat indicated he was working hard. But the muscles indicated that he, indeed, was no stranger to work. She should have realized that when she'd seen his bare chest that morning. Perhaps her plan would not succeed after all.

"My, my, my." Cora clicked her tongue. "Ain't seen nothin' like that in quite some time."

A flush of heat waved over Rose. She tried to pull her gaze away but found it riveted on the man. Forcing her eyes closed, she backed away, tugging Amelia with her. "We shouldn't stare at him. It's improper."

But Amelia wouldn't budge.

"Amelia!" Rose dragged the enamored lady from the window and forced her to sit down. "And where have you been all day? It's nearly noon." Rose had long since given up expecting Amelia to assist Rose with her morning toilette.

"I did not feel well, miss. I'm sorry." Amelia poured herself some tea and gave a little pout. "Too much excitement yesterday, I fear."

Cora tugged at the red scarf she always wore tied around her head and picked up the lump of dough. She slapped it back down on the floured table. "What excitement you talkin' 'bout, Amelia? I thought you'd be glad to see a bunch o' handsome soldiers pokin' about here."

Rose and Amelia shared a fearful glance.

"I suppose it's just the idea that we could be invaded by the British at any moment." Amelia tossed her raven curls over her shoulder. "And lose everything—this home, this farm, and the family I've come to love."

"Humph." Cora's thick arms flapped as she pressed down on the dough. "You both don't know nothin' about losin' everything. About bein' torn from those you love when you was but five and sold as a slave to strangers."

"I know you have suffered, Cora." Rose laid a hand on the woman's arm, stopping her kneading. "What happened to you was evil of the worst kind."

Dark eyes lifted to hers and a rare glimpse of understanding crossed over them before they hardened again. "I know the both o' you lost your parents too." She looked at Amelia. "But at least you know they're no longer on this earth. I have no idea where mine are. Probably still slaves somewhere, or died in their chains."

"You have us now, Cora. We are your family." Rose dropped two more lumps of sugar into her tea.

"Goodness' sakes, child. You'll use up all our sugar." Cora shook her head and sprinkled flour atop the dough. "Family, humph. I am your cook. I knows my place."

"My word, Cora, you are so much more than that, and you know it." Rose reassured the cook for what felt like the thousandth time.

Amelia smiled. "I certainly don't feel like your servant." Reaching across the table, she squeezed Rose's hand. "You have treated me so kindly, I feel as though we are sisters."

Rose forced back the moisture in her eyes. "I'm so thankful God brought you both into my life."

"Your aunt and uncle have been kind t' me." Cora slapped the dough into a bread pan. "But how can I ever be free while my people are still slaves?" She scratched her curly black hair beneath her scarf and fisted her hands at her waist. "And what has God got to do wit' any of this?"

Rose gazed into the fireplace that took up nearly an entire wall of the kitchen. Iron pots bubbling with the noon meal hung on a crane over the flames. Yet, a chill coursed through her. She understood Cora's attitude more than she cared to admit, for Rose had great difficulty finding God's loving-kindness in any of the events of her life.

Amelia sipped her tea. "God brought you Samuel, Cora. He'd still be here if you hadn't chased him off."

Cora tossed the pan aside, her face deepening to a dark maroon. "That no-good, lazy, sluggard. I'm glad he's gone."

"He loved you, Cora." Amelia shook her head and shifted her shoe over the floor.

Spinning around, Cora grabbed a ladle from a hook on the wall, but not before Rose saw a mist cover her eyes.

"That man don't know how to love no one." Bitterness sharpened her tone as she stirred the pot hanging over the fire.

But Rose wondered. She had always found Samuel to be a hard-working man of honor. A man who had not hid his interest in Cora. But in the end, he took off without a word to Cora or any of them. Rose had heard through gossip in town that he had joined the army— the British army.

Amelia stood and headed toward the window. "I miss my family too."

Rose clutched the woman's hand in passing. "The plague took many of the townspeople. You're fortunate to have survived and to have been married to Richard at the time."

She gave Rose a look of derision. "What did it matter? He is gone now."

Rose released her hand along with a sigh of resignation. Her aunt and uncle had admonished Rose to always trust God, to not complain, and to share her hope with others. But how could she encourage her friends when she held to her own hope with nothing but a thin thread? "We should trust God," was all she could think to say.

Cora gave a cynical chuckle. "If this is God's doin', I want no part o' Him."

Amelia leaned on the window ledge and gazed out. "It seems He has taken everything from me as well."

Rose stared into the amber-colored tea swirling in her cup. No amount of sugar could dissolve the bitterness in her throat. Was it by the hand of God they had all lost so much? She could make no sense of it. If God loved them, then why had He taken their families from them? She knew God existed. She understood that Jesus had come to earth and died and rose again so those who believed and followed Him would go to heaven. Maybe that was enough. Certainly it was more than any of them deserved. Despite what her uncle declared, perhaps their lives here on earth were meant to be lived without God's help. Certainly that made more sense than thinking He purposely allowed His children to suffer so much pain.

Alex thanked Cora for the meal as he opened the door to the kitchen and stepped outside. All he received in return was a grunt from the peevish cook. Her dinner of wild goose and corn bread soaked in buttermilk was far better than her disposition. Closing the door, he gazed at the scorching sun that made one last effort to sear his skin as it dipped below the tree line in the western sky. He'd never experienced such sweltering heat. At least not since he'd sailed to Jamaica three years ago. How did these colonists bear it?

Adjusting the crutch beneath his arm, Alex hobbled over to examine his work. A dozen rows of cut logs sat neatly stacked beside the house. How he had managed to do all that work with one good leg, he could not fathom. Especially in the afternoon's blazing heat. He pressed a hand against his back where an ache had formed hours ago. His wound throbbed, causing him to lean on his good leg, but even that appendage burned with exhaustion.

Turning, he gazed across the farm. He had not seen Miss McGuire since she had turned her pert little nose up at him that morning and sauntered away. Egad, she'd armed herself with a knife. Did she really believe he would hurt her? The thought saddened him.

His glance landed on the pigsty where the stinking beasts grunted and wallowed in the mud. The one named Prinney poked his snout through the wooden posts and looked forlornly toward the barn as if he were waiting for Miss McGuire's appearance.

Infernal woman. Naming a pig after the Prince Regent! Yet Alex couldn't help the smile that played on his lips even as his insides churned with indignation. Truly these colonists were every bit the unrefined, uncultured ruffians he'd been led to believe. And Miss McGuire. He'd never encountered such a woman in all his days. Hair consistently out of place, gowns stained with dirt, consorting with pigs and cows. Yet a healthy, fresh glow brightened her face much more than any powder and rouge he'd seen on the ladies back home, and her eyes—those lustrous eyes as clear and sparkling as the turquoise sea in the West Indies.

He really couldn't blame her for wanting him gone. Despite the pain spiking up his back, he felt his strength returning. Soon enough he would relieve her of his company and head back to the crazy ramblings of Captain Milford and the tight confines of the HMS *Undefeatable*. So unlike the open spaces of this beautiful land. The western sky lit up with splashes of maroon, orange, and gold. He drew a deep breath of air and instantly regretted it. Lowering his chin, he took a whiff of his shirt. He smelled of sour milk, pig droppings, and sweat. If only his father, Lord Cranleigh, could see him now.

Squawks shot from the barn, and Alex hobbled in that direction. Prinney grunted at him as he passed, and Alex made a face at the filthy beast before he swept his gaze to Miss McGuire's garden divided into neat rows of tomatoes, some type of squash, lettuce, potatoes, and corn. Guarding either side of the open barn doors stood two flourishing rosebushes, boasting pink and red blossoms. Yet their sweet scent did nothing to assuage the stench emanating from within. As Alex shuffled inside, he flinched at the sight that met his eyes. Miss McGuire sat in the dirt at the center of the barn, gown spread out around her, with a chicken in her lap. Unaware of his presence, she spoke softly to the bird while she stroked the chicken's feathers. The bird clucked and snuggled against her gown like a cat, and Mr. Reed stood frozen in astonishment. His crutch shifted and struck the wooden doorframe.

She jerked her face up. "Mr. Reed." Her eyes widened. "I thought you were partaking of your supper." Shooing the bird from her lap, she jumped to her feet.

Alex repositioned the crutch and shuffled inside. "I was. Forgive the intrusion, Miss McGuire, but I heard squawking and thought something might be amiss."

"No, I was just. . .just. . ." She lowered her gaze.

"Petting a chicken?" He grinned.

Her eyes narrowed. "Yes, if you must know. They are my pets."

"Indeed? I thought you ate them." He wrinkled his nose at the smell of horse and cow dung that permeated the barn.

"Shhh." She cast a harried gaze around her. "You shouldn't say such things."

If Alex didn't realize she was serious, he would have laughed out loud. As it was, he simply gazed at her, amazed that she always managed to astonish him and bring a chuckle to his lips.

"You have dirt"—he brushed a finger over his own cheek—"there on your face."

She swiped at it, a look of annoyance crinkling her features.

Alex stretched his tight shoulders and took another step toward her. "Did you miss your dinner?"

"Supper. And no, Aunt Muira, Amelia, and I ate earlier in the dining room."

"Ah, I've been reduced to a servant again."

"Not reduced, sir."

"Ah, you are correct, madam." He gave a mock bow to which she pursed her lips and glanced out the door as if planning her escape.

"Where is your uncle?" he asked, longing to extend his conversation with this bewildering, charming lady.

"In town, I assume." She moved toward Liverpool and began to stroke the cow's head. "He does much work ministering at the taverns by the docks."

The cow groaned her approval, then swept her huge brown eyes toward Alex as if to prod him into jealousy at the attention she was receiving. *Fiendish beast.*

"I see you finished the work I gave you." Miss McGuire continued petting the cow.

"As I informed you, miss, I am accustomed to hard labor." He rubbed his sore palms where blisters stung in defiance of his statement.

"I thought perhaps your wound would slow you down." She lifted her gaze to his.

He took a step toward her.

She stepped back, fingering the handle of the knife still wedged in her leather sash. "But I see you are getting stronger."

Alex halted. He hated that she feared him. A breeze blew in, sending the wisps of her hair fluttering about her shoulders even as the last traces of sunlight set them aglow. He shifted his stance uncomfortably and tried to do the same with his gaze. But his eyes refused to let go of their hold upon her as if losing her visage would leave them cold and empty.

Miss McGuire blinked. "Why are you staring at me like that?"

Alex hesitated but the truth spilled unbidden from his lips. "Because you are quite lovely, Miss McGuire."

Shock flashed in her eyes before she swept them down to her soiled gown, then over to Liverpool. She huffed. "You tease me, sir."

"I never tease."

Darkness stole the last shreds of light from the barn, leaving only the light from a single lantern hanging from the post.

"I should be going inside." Miss McGuire headed toward the door. "Please douse the lantern when you leave."

Alex stepped aside to allow her to pass when a *gong, gong, gong* rang through the night air.

She froze and stared wide-eyed at him.

"It's only a bell, miss."

"It's the bell from St. Peters." She glanced out the door, her lip quivering as her chest rose and fell rapidly.

"What does it mean?"

Gong. Gong. Gong.

"It's to warn us." She swallowed. "British raiders have been spotted near town."

A mixture of shame and anger battled within Alex. With his only thought to comfort her, he drew her into his arms. She tightened in his embrace stiffer than a sail at full wind. He nudged her back. "Go into the house. I'll keep you safe."

"No!" She jerked from him, anger darkening her features. "You are one of them."

Alex felt her statement slam into his gut. "I told your uncle I would protect you, and I will."

"You owe me nothing." Grabbing her skirts, she started to leave when Alex clutched her arm.

"I will never allow anyone to hurt you."

"Go join your friends, Mr. Reed." She hissed, then tore from his grasp and dashed out the door just as the crack of a musket shot split the evening sky.

❖ CHAPTER 10 ❖

Gripping the banister in one hand and the folds of her nightdress in the other, Rose crept down the narrow stairway. The aged wood creaked beneath her bare feet and she halted, holding her breath. No sounds met her ears save the slight hiss of wind swirling about the outside of the house. She inched down a few more steps. From the parlor on her right, a single candle sent flickering ribbons of light out the door onto the dark foyer floor. She eased to a spot halfway down the stairs.

Then she saw him. Mr. Reed.

A traitorous wave of relief sped through her, for she had assumed she would not find him at his post. Sinking onto one of the stairs, Rose positioned herself for a better view and drew her knees to her chest. With only a single candle to light the parlor, Mr. Reed stood by the fireplace, one boot atop the base of the hearth, her uncle's Brown Bess stiff in his arms.

Wide awake and guarding them like a protective father. . .or *husband*.

Despite her angry demands that he join the British raiders, he had ushered her inside the house and once they had gathered Amelia and Aunt Muira, he had assured them that in Uncle Forbes's absence, he would guard them with his life. Amelia nearly swooned in his arms, while Aunt Muira remained the epitome of feminine courage. Rose wondered how brave her aunt would be if she knew it was a British naval officer who offered them his protection.

But when her aunt had handed Mr. Reed the Brown Bess that hung over the fireplace in the dining room, Rose's fear had risen another notch. It was bad enough to have an enemy in their home, but an armed one was beyond the pale. Now he could do with them as he pleased or worse, hail his compatriots wandering about in the forest to come join in the siege.

But no. Rose no longer believed that.

Mr. Reed let out a long sigh, rubbed his eyes, then took up a hobbled pace across the room. Raindrops pattered on the roof as he paused at the corner of a window and lifted a flap of the wooden shutters to peer into the night. Releasing the tab, he resuming his shuffle. Fatigue tugged at his stern features. At well past midnight, the man must have been beyond exhaustion. Especially after all the hard work he'd done that day—work Rose had forced upon him. Guilt pinched her heart. She had expected him to either be gone or fast asleep. Certainly not standing his post as if he were on watch aboard his ship.

With musket propped in one arm, he took a turn about the room. Lines of concern edged his face. Concern for them? Concern for his countrymen? Confusion threatened to crush Rose's disdain for this British man. He moved out of her sight for a moment. His boots thudded over the floorcloth of coarsely woven wool. But then he emerged once again on the other side of the parlor. He stretched his neck and eased back his broad shoulders. Despite his limp, with his head up and stubbled chin jutted forward, he walked with the authority of a man in command. A man who was well equipped to deal with any situation that came his way. She envisioned him in his dark blue navy coat with brass buttons and service sword at his side, and a burst of warmth flooded her—no doubt due to the hot humid night.

Surely as a second lieutenant aboard a British warship, he carried a great deal of authority. The weight of that responsibility seemed to sit heavy on his shoulders tonight. Or perhaps it was the dichotomy of protecting Rose and her family against his own countrymen. She had not considered, until now, the conflict the poor man must be suffering.

Because she had not considered that he would protect them at all.

Reaching the fireplace again, he leaned one arm upon the mantel and released a sigh. He rubbed his tight jaw and gazed across the room. Resolve and deliberation reflected in his hazel eyes. And something else—an anguish that set Rose aback.

Her thoughts drifted to the way he had looked at her in the barn. A look that had sent her belly aquiver. A look as if she was something precious to cherish and protect.

Rose squeezed her eyes shut and shook her head. No. What was wrong with her? He was a British enemy. A spy, most likely. And he would soon be gone.

A sob caught in her throat at the thought. He froze at the sound and glanced her way. Rose's pulse quickened. He approached the door, peering into the darkness. Leaping from her seat, she darted up the stairs into her chamber and quietly pressed the door shut behind her. Her heart crashed against her chest as she leaned back against it. But no creak of stairs sounded. When her breath settled, she grabbed the lit candle on her desk and dropped to the floor beside a trunk at the foot of her bed. Lifting the lid, she rummaged through the contents: a stack of books, an old jewelry box, a deck of cards. A cool musty smell saturated the air. She grabbed the blanket her mother had knitted for her when she was a child and drew it to her nose, but her mother's lilac scent had long since faded. Beneath it, the McGuire family Bible stared up at her. Setting down the candle, she began sifting through crackling pages—pages she hadn't read in years. There, stuffed somewhere in Psalms, was the letter.

The letter she needed to rekindle her hatred of the man downstairs.

With tender care, she fingered the broken wax and gazed at her mother's name on the front. Tears filled her eyes as she opened it and read.

My beloved Rossalyn,

The days pass with mindless toil and an empty heart since I left you, and I begin to wonder whether it was a wise choice to join this country's navy and be so often gone from your side. Though the Chesapeake *is a grand ship and I a fair boatswain,*

the glory of the majestic sea cannot compare to your beauty, my
lovely wife. I find Commodore Barron to be a good captain with
much battle experience, yet his pride expresses itself in harsh
methods one minute followed by neglect the next.

Tomorrow we hoist our sails for the Mediterranean, and I
shall not see you for months. Please know, my darling that you are
and always will be my love and my life. My thoughts will ever be
consumed with you and Rose, and I shall write you daily, though
I know not when the posts will arrive in your hands. Do not be
anxious, my love. I am in God's care now.

Please kiss our sweet Rose for me and tell her I shall return to
beat her at whist as soon as I can.

Yours forever,
Robert McGuire

Even through her tears, a slight giggle choked in Rose's throat at
her father's last sentence. Like warm summer days, countless joyful
memories passed across her mind of the hours she'd spent playing
cards with her father in the sitting room of their home.

But those days were gone forever.

She folded the letter and pressed it to her breast. Tears streamed
down her cheeks as she placed the faded letter within the Bible—the
Bible she hadn't read since her mother died. Then clinging to the holy
book, she lay down on the floor and placed her head on her mother's
blanket.

Sometime later, in the midst of nightmares filled with cannon
shots and British warships, she was awakened by the sound of her
uncle's voice—its comforting cadence nestled around her like a warm
blanket and she drifted into peaceful sleep.

Forcing his leaden eyelids to remain open, Alex circled the quaint
but rustic parlor one more time, if only to keep himself awake by
invoking the pain in his thigh. He knew if he dared to sit on the
sofa or one of the cushioned wooden chairs, he'd be done for and the
slumber that beckoned him would win. With each turn of the room,
however, his anger grew at Mr. Drummond's complete indifference

toward his family's safety. During such harrowing times, and especially after warning bells had been sounded, the man of the house should be home standing firmly in defense of those he loved. His behavior was reprehensible! But what did Alex expect from a former thief and indentured servant? Alex would never tolerate such a lackadaisical attitude on board his ship. However, it angered him more that he could not order the man to step up to the task. In fact, as a servant, Alex possessed no power at all.

A first in his life.

A floorboard creaked beneath his boot. His spine stiffened. What was wrong with him? Egad, fatigue must be tying his nerves into knots. As his thoughts had done to his gut. All night long, he'd pondered what he should do if British raiders attacked the house. And he had come up with only one possible course of action—a course that frightened him to the core, for that course was spurred on by a pair of luminous turquoise eyes.

No, he could never allow harm to come to Miss McGuire.

He halted at the fireplace yet again and ran a hand through his hair, tearing strands from his queue. What kind of British officer was he? What sort of man could be swayed from loyalty to his own country by a lady who had nothing to recommend her but a plot of land and a bevy of farm animals?

He chuckled as he pictured Miss McGuire petting the chicken in her lap.

The clomp of horse's hooves jolted Alex to attention. He cocked the musket and lifted the flap of the shutter to see Mr. Drummond's horse enter the stable. Finally.

Minutes later the elderly man burst through the front door, a draft of wind spiced with rain swirling on his heels. Shrugging out of his coat, he ambled into the parlor. "Mr. Reed." His gray eyebrows leaped. "What are you doing in the house at this hour?" He motioned toward the musket in Alex's hand. "And with my Brown Bess."

Alex cleared his throat to stifle his annoyance. "I am protecting *your* family, sir, as you ordered."

Mr. Drummond approached Alex and handed him his coat. "Ah, yes, the warning bells. Very good, Mr. Reed. Very good indeed."

Hot blood surged through Alex's veins as he took the garment.

Mr. Drummond should be the one hanging up Alex's coat, not the other way around. If the man knew he entertained the son of a wealthy viscount, he'd no doubt be buzzing around Alex, seeing to his every need.

Or would he?

Something in Mr. Drummond's light brown eyes bespoke of a humility not easily impressed by rank and wealth.

"Have you seen my spectacles, Mr. Reed?" The old man patted his pockets. "It seems I have misplaced them again." He stumbled over the edge of the rug then shook his head with a chortle.

"No sir." Alex's impatience rose at the man's lubberly behavior.

Blowing out a ragged sigh, Mr. Drummond sank into one of the cushioned chairs beside the fireplace and spread his hands over his portly belly.

Tossing the coat onto the back of the settee, Alex circled the sofa, intending to chastise Mr. Drummond for his negligence of duty and family. But he halted when he saw red splotches marring the old man's wrinkled hands. "Is that blood?" he asked.

Mr. Drummond gazed up at him, his tired eyes distant with sorrow. "Yes. But not mine. There was a bit o' trouble down at Gorsuch's Tavern tonight."

Alex flinched. "The British?"

"I wish it had been. That enemy I know how to fight." Mr. Drummond huffed then gestured toward the sofa. "If you intend to stay, have a seat, son. Your leg surely could use the rest."

Son? Alex cringed at the man's familiarity, yet the tender way in which he spoke the word filled Alex with an odd longing. Alex obliged him and lowered himself onto the soft cushions. Immediate relief swept through his tired legs.

"No, my enemy, Mr. Reed, is far more formidable than the British military." Mr. Drummond took a brass-tipped poker and began stirring the lifeless coals in the fireplace.

Alex restrained an insolent chuckle. "Upon my honor, sir, what or who could be more formidable than the British?"

"The powers of darkness." Mr. Drummond's quick and solemn reply startled Alex. "The powers that lure a man to drink too much, to steal, to curse his fellow man, and even to kill." He poked at the dark chunks of coal like a swordsman against an evil foe.

Alex snorted. *Simple-minded Americans.* "You speak of the devil, sir? But I doubt he exists."

Intense brown eyes snapped his way, the candlelight reflecting an intelligence that surprised Alex. "He would love for you to believe that, Mr. Reed. But he exists, I assure you." He turned back to the fireplace. "I have seen his work too often to deny it."

Alex studied the man. Short and bulky of stature with a full head of rebellious gray hair, and a beard to match, he normally exuded a kind, benign demeanor. But tonight as he stared deep in thought at the dark fireplace, he seemed burdened by an enormous weight. Lines folded across a ruddy face that possessed a wide forehead and a stout nose. Perhaps there was more to this man than Alex had first assumed. "What happened tonight?" Alex leaned forward.

Mr. Drummond expelled a long sigh. "Too much drink, too much anxiety about the war, too many opposing sides." His shoulders slumped. "Add to that mix those who have lost friends and family in recent battles. And before I could settle things, someone ended up with a knife in his gut."

Alex's chest constricted. "A friend of yours?"

"Aye, died in my arms." Mr. Drummond stabbed a dark coal in the corner of the fireplace and flung it across the pit. "It fell to me to inform his widow." His voice broke.

Alex shifted uncomfortably, uneasy at the man's display of emotion. "Why you, Mr. Drummond? Why not allow family or friends to tell her? Surely your vocation doesn't require you to perform such agonizing tasks?" At least Alex had not seen the vicars back home do much of anything save attend parties and put people to sleep with their Sunday sermons.

"Oh no, Mr. Reed, a man of God does everything he can to assist and bring comfort to those in need. We who follow in Christ's footsteps are to be an extension of God's love to everyone we come across."

Alex stared into eyes misted with tears yet hard with purpose, and it struck him—the man truly believed what he said. Despite his ineloquent speech and reprehensible manners, wisdom and determination poured from him. Alex searched memories of his childhood for any moments of intimate conversation he and his father had shared, but all he found were visions of a stiff chin bordered in satin and lace and the cold sheen of pomposity that had covered his father's dark eyes.

Then he remembered Mr. Drummond's sordid past, and the man's intentions became clear. "No doubt one must perform many acts of charity to atone for past sins." Something Alex could well understand—exchanging charity and honor for the shameful acts of a rebellious youth. But instead of trying to live up to the impossible rules of a distant God, Alex sought to make restitution by becoming an honorable naval officer.

"Atone?" Mr. Drummond scratched his stiff gray beard and smiled. "All the good deeds in the world wouldn't make up for what I've done. No, I do these things out of love for my Father in heaven."

Father. Emotion clogged in Alex's throat. God as Father? Absurd.

Uncomfortable with the direction of the discussion, Alex struggled to rise, leaning most of his weight on his good leg. "I cannot stay in your employ much longer, Mr. Drummond. I hope you will be able to procure a replacement soon."

Mr. Drummond nodded, but Alex thought he saw a slight smile on the man's lips. "I already have someone in mind, Mr. Reed."

"Very good." Alex said. "I'll leave you to your rest." Turning, he shuffled toward the door.

"Sleep well, son." Mr. Drummond's kind tone threatened to undo the tight bands Alex had formed over his heart.

For never had he heard those words from his own father's lips.

❖ CHAPTER 11 ❖

Standing in front of the house beside her aunt and Amelia, Rose pressed a hand over her churning stomach. The last thing she wanted to do today was take another trip into town. Especially with Mr. Reed escorting them. But she had promised her aunt on Sunday that she would visit Mrs. Pickersgill, and Rose could not go back on her word. Oh why had she made such a vow? What if someone recognized Mr. Reed? What if he came across some valuable military information to take back to his captain?

Rose squeezed her forehead as her thoughts spun a knot of fear and guilt—a knot she saw no way to untangle at the moment.

"For heaven's sake. Where is Mr. Reed?" Aunt Muira clutched her medical satchel and shot a harried gaze toward the stable.

Rose glanced at Amelia. "I imagine he's attempting to harness Douglas to the carriage."

"But he's been in there for over thirty minutes." Aunt Muira bit her lip impatiently. "What sort of servant is he?"

Amelia giggled. "One who isn't skilled with horse and equipage, I imagine."

Aunt Muira cast the maid a curious gaze as Rose headed toward the stable to see if she could assist the poor man. She'd only taken two steps when Mr. Reed appeared, wearing Samuel's used livery and plodding forward on his crutch as he led Douglas and the carriage out from the barn. His black coat and breeches—far too small for his large frame—strained across his chest and thighs, outlining his firm muscles beneath.

Rose averted her gaze and elbowed Amelia to do the same, but the insolent woman gaped at him unabashed.

"Ah, there you are, Mr. Reed." Aunt Muira took Mr. Reed's outstretched hand and climbed into the coach. "We thought you'd become lost."

"Just familiarizing myself with your equipage, madam." He turned a half-cocked smile to Rose and offered her his hand. But when she placed her still-trembling fingers into his firm ones, his look of playfulness faded into one of concern.

Snatching her hand away, she entered the carriage and sat beside her aunt as Amelia's delicate hand lingered far too long on Mr. Reed's before she joined them. Then leaping into the driver's seat, Mr. Reed snapped the reins.

Per Mrs. Drummond's directions, Alex pulled the coach to a stop before a small stone house on the corner of Pratt and Albemarle Streets. He was more than impressed by what he'd seen of the quaint little town on his way here. He'd expected to see nothing but dirt streets lined by dilapidated shops and open-air taverns inhabited by swine, both animal and human. Instead, he'd counted at least five churches, two theaters—albeit rustic theaters—several watchhouses, five inns, two libraries, three markets, two banks, and three newspaper printing offices.

Despite the war, the citizens of Baltimore scurried about their business on foot or in carriages or on horseback. Ladies and gentlemen strolled down the cobblestone streets in finery and frippery that could equal any to be seen among the *haut ton* sauntering down Bond Street—well, almost.

Alex leaped down from the driving seat, set down the step, opened the door, and held his hand out for the ladies. Though the demeaning status grated against his pride, he found being a servant an easy and innocuous occupation—a great respite from the responsibility and hard work of an officer in His Majesty's Navy. He briefly wondered if Captain Milford was searching for him and Garrick or had he assumed them dead or worse—deserters. But what did it matter? The issue would be resolved as soon as Alex returned with his wound as evidence of his tale of being shot in a skirmish and then cared for by a rebel farmer until Alex could make his way back to the ship.

"Wait here," Miss McGuire said. Leaping down, she waved a gloved hand toward him and lifted her pert nose in the air. In fact, since they had begun the journey, her attitude had transformed from a humble farm girl to a pretentious chit that reminded him of certain noble ladies he'd been acquainted with back home. Yet the act was so at odds with her true nature that it appeared more adorable than annoying.

"No, no." The ostrich feathers atop Mrs. Drummond's gold bonnet fluttered in the breeze. "Do come in, Mr. Reed. I would like you to meet Mrs. Pickersgill."

Alex raised a victorious brow in Miss McGuire's direction.

A maid answered the door and ushered them inside to a sitting room, where a short, elderly lady dressed in a plain gown rose from her seat. Gray hair sprang from beneath a white mob cap fringed in lace. She gave them a wide smile as she greeted them warmly. Finally her gaze landed on Alex.

"My, my, who do we have here?" Approaching him, she took his hands. Cold, boney, yet strong fingers gripped his.

Shocked by her familiarity, Alex stiffened.

"This is Mr. Reed, our new man of work," Mrs. Drummond said, pride lifting her tone. "Mr. Reed, Mrs. Mary Pickersgill."

"A pleasure, madam." Alex nodded and kissed her hand.

Mrs. Pickersgill squealed with delight. "My goodness. I haven't heard an accent so regal since I was a little girl in Philadelphia."

Over the elderly lady's shoulder, Alex saw Amelia exchange a fearful glance with Miss McGuire.

"It has been my family's curse." Mr. Reed gave a lopsided grin, to which the elderly lady released his hands and gestured toward a maid standing by the doorway. "Dorothy, please bring everyone some cocoa."

Mrs. Drummond tugged off her gloves and took a seat on a

cushioned oval-backed chair. "Mrs. Pickersgill is a flag maker, Mr. Reed."

"Indeed?" But Alex could not take his eyes off Miss McGuire. Her simple walking dress of periwinkle blue brought out the sharp color of her eyes and made her skin glow. She untied the pink satin ribbon of her bonnet and drew it from her head, dislodging a few golden strands.

"She made the enormous flag that flies over Fort McHenry. Have you seen it?" Mrs. Drummond drew his gaze back to her.

Flag, indeed. Alex grumbled silently. These colonies had no need of their own flag for soon the Union Jack would proudly wave once again above their city squares. "I have not had the pleasure."

Mrs. Pickersgill gestured for them to sit, but Alex remained standing.

"I must say I was quite surprised when Major Armistead, General Smith, and Commodore Barney came to call on me that day to commission the ensign." She chuckled. "In their own words, they wanted 'a flag so large that the British would have no difficulty seeing it from a distance'!"

Alex felt the muscles in his neck tighten as the maid brought in a service tray with china cups and a steaming pot of the sweet-smelling drink.

Miss McGuire speared him with a sharp gaze and nodded for him to leave. She tossed her reticule onto a floral-printed sofa, then took her seat beside Amelia. Mrs. Pickersgill slid onto a chair to their left.

The maid poured dark liquid into each cup then scurried from the room.

"I hope you don't mind hot cocoa, ladies. I never did favor tea." Mrs. Pickersgill handed each of them a cup and saucer.

"Not at all." Amelia lifted the cup to her lips. "It is my favorite too."

Mrs. Pickersgill frowned. "Hard to come by with the blockade. I fear my supply is nearly depleted."

Again Alex felt a thread of guilt wind through him.

"Mr. Reed, the flag Mrs. Pickersgill sewed measures thirty feet by forty-two feet." Mrs. Drummond boasted.

"Astonishing," Alex remarked, trying to envision the enormous flag filling the room. "How did you accomplish it?"

"I had help, sir." Mrs. Pickersgill opened a palm toward an empty seat in the corner, but Alex remained rooted in place. Why did these Americans insist on treating their servants as equals?

"My daughter, two nieces, and two servants assisted me, but we had to move the massive cloth to a warehouse nearby just to finish it." She smiled. "I was happy to do it," she waved a hand through the air. "It does present a fine ensign above the fort."

Mrs. Drummond took a sip of hot cocoa. "Perhaps we will take you to see it later, Mr. Reed?"

"Surely a servant has no interest in flags or forts." Miss McGuire shot into the conversation with the force of a cannon. Her cup clattered on the saucer she held, and she set both on the table. Opening the fan hanging on her wrist, she fluttered it about her face. "Perhaps you should check on the horse, Mr. Reed. We will be discussing things which could not possibly interest you."

Mrs. Drummond's eyebrows bent together, and she gave her niece a look of reprimand.

But Mrs. Pickersgill did not seem to notice. "Ah yes, the reason for your visit," she added. "I am most anxious to discuss my idea for a new charity devoted to widowed ladies who have lost their husbands and cannot support themselves."

Alex flinched. To find such generous kindness among these poor colonists. Astonishing. His family and most of his associates back in England possessed far more wealth than these people could ever imagine, yet Alex had not once witnessed such benevolence among them. "Most commendable, Mrs. Pickersgill," he couldn't help but say as he stretched his back against a shirt that seemed to shrink with each passing moment.

"God has blessed me with a skill to make flags, Mr. Reed. Passed down through my mother." Mrs. Pickersgill's expression grew somber as she glanced over the ladies. "But many women do not have the same opportunity to run their own businesses and provide for themselves."

Mrs. Drummond nodded. "And Rose is most interested in helping you, my dear Mary."

At this, Miss McGuire's face brightened. "Yes, indeed I am, Mrs. Pickersgill."

Alex felt his brow wrinkle. Though he sensed Miss McGuire possessed a kind heart, he had not supposed this frightened woman's charity to extend beyond her family and those of her closest acquaintances—people with whom she felt safe. The revelation caused his thoughts to tangle in confusion. And he didn't like being confused. Confusion caused bad decisions. Any emotion caused bad decisions. And one bad decision by a naval officer could cost lives. Distinct lines must be drawn between good and evil, enemy and friend, rebel and patriot. Excusing himself, Alex stepped outside and tested his leg. He must leave tonight. If he didn't, he feared those distinct lines would forever be blurred in his mind, and then all would be lost.

Rose peered at Alex from beneath the brim of her bonnet as they made their way to the brick building behind her uncle's church. He hobbled beside her with difficulty, the hot sun forming beads of sweat on his forehead. Forcing down her traitorous concern for him, she continued walking. She must make his day as a servant such an unbearable prick to his pride that he'd be desperate to return to his ship at nightfall. She must also keep him as far away from Fort McHenry as possible. Oh wouldn't he just love to go see Mrs. Pickersgill's flag. Along with the armament at the fort!

Halting, Rose shrugged out of her spencer and handed it to him. "Aunt Muira, Amelia, do give Mr. Reed your wraps. It is growing far too hot and will only be more oppressive in Uncle's sickroom." She smiled at Mr. Reed as the two ladies complied.

Once they had gone, Mr. Reed's brows arched. "And what am I to do with these, miss?"

"Why, put them in the coach, Mr. Reed." She forced an air of pretension that did not settle well in her stomach. "Or you may carry them until we have need of them again. It matters not to me."

He narrowed his gaze and headed back toward the carriage, wrestling out of his own thick black coat.

"No, no, no, Mr. Reed." Rose called after him. "A footman must always be dressed with the utmost of propriety."

He groaned, and Rose followed her aunt and Amelia into the makeshift hospital before she could make out his curt reply.

Once they stepped inside the dark room, however, all thoughts of annoying Mr. Reed into leaving vanished as the smell of sickness and despair slapped Rose in the face. Shabby cots lined either side of the long narrow room. Lanterns, bloody cloths, mugs, and Bibles covered small side tables wedged between the beds. Two tiny windows perched above allowed barely a breeze and a modicum of sunlight to pass into the dank room. In the distance, Uncle Forbes hovered over one of the beds.

Aunt Muira had already pulled up a chair before the first cot on the left and began to dab a cloth over the man's forehead. Amelia leaned against the side wall, covering her nose. It had been months since Rose had joined her aunt on her weekly visits to this place. Why had she stayed away so long? A wave of guilt swept over her, but she shrugged it off and took a step forward. She was here now. Clutching Amelia's arm, she dragged her down the aisle, promising herself that she would do her best to never again allow fear to keep her from helping others.

Alex stared as Mr. Drummond, two Negro men, and the three women flitted about from cot to cot, caring for the sick. Though sweat streamed down his back and the stench stung his nose, he allowed no complaints to form in his mind in light of the scene of tragedy and despair before him. No doubt Miss McGuire was as hot and uncomfortable as he was, yet she offered caring smiles and gentle ministrations to each patient she visited. Alex tried to picture any of the ladies of his acquaintance back home doing the same, but the vision would not form in his mind. In fact, most of them would not come within a mile of such sickness and misery.

Mr. Drummond greeted his wife with a kiss and then made his way down the aisle. His gaze met Alex's and he slipped beside him.

"Who are these people?" Alex asked.

"These are the outcasts of society, you might say," Mr. Drummond replied with a sigh. "When the main hospital is full, they send those who cannot pay and those who suffer from prolonged drunkenness or who have been injured in tavern brawls to me. Some simply need to sleep off last night's drink and have nowhere else to go. Others need a bit o' loving care and that my wife kindly supplies. While others need the kind of care only God can give."

Alex bristled at the mention of God's care for he had never

experienced it in his life, and he wasn't all together sure God was around enough to care for anyone. "What of those who need a doctor's care?"

"A charitable physician from the hospital visits once a week, but in the meantime, my lovely wife does what she can."

Alex watched as Miss McGuire unfolded a letter and began reading it to one of the men. "Does Miss McGuire assist here often?"

"Not as much as she'd like, I'm sure." Mr. Drummond folded his arms across his portly belly and lowered his voice. "She has suffered greatly in her young life. I've never seen a heart so pure and kind, but fear has kept her home. It's the only place she feels safe anymore."

Alex tried to rub the tightness from his jaw. Mr. Garrick's attack certainly hadn't helped her in that regard. "She still suffers from her father's death?"

"Aye, but it is more than that." Mr. Drummond's brow wrinkled for a moment before the gleam returned to his eye. "But she has shown improvement lately, and we hope she'll be able to join my wife on her visits here more often and also when Mrs. Drummond travels to Washington."

"Washington?"

"Aye, my wife assists at an orphanage there, but Rose refuses to travel that far from home."

Alex's gaze followed Miss McGuire around the room, wondering what further tragedies had struck the lady. A hollow ache formed in his gut at the thought of anyone doing her harm.

"Your presence seems to have done her good, Mr. Reed." Mr. Drummond used the end of his stained cravat to wipe the perspiration from his face.

"Me?" Alex stifled a laugh. "I fear you are mistaken, Mr. Drummond."

"Am I?" He scratched his beard, and once again Alex saw a deep, lingering intelligence behind his brown eyes. "I knew it would take someone very special to bring joy again to the lass. Someone we would least expect." He winked at Alex as if they shared a grand secret—as if he knew Alex was British. But how could he?

Besides, joy was the last thing Alex brought Miss McGuire. No point in bringing the error to Mr. Drummond's attention since Alex would be gone soon. "I trust you have been searching for someone to replace me as your man of work, sir?"

Mr. Drummond frowned and patted his waistcoat as if searching for something. "As best I can, Mr. Reed. Meager pickings here in town."

"Regardless, I fear I'll have to be go—"

"Well, I best be getting back to my work." Mr. Drummond slapped his hands together, interrupting Alex. With a nod, he sped off to join his wife.

Alex shook his head and watched as the two of them along with Miss McGuire continued to wander among the cots, holding hands, praying, and conversing with the patients. They received no pay for their trouble, no reward, no public honor—all the things Alex fought so hard to acquire. Things that suddenly seemed as useless as the dust beneath his boots.

Those distinct lines he fought so hard to keep firmly in his mind began to blur even more.

Two hours later, Alex walked behind Amelia and Miss McGuire down Baltimore Street on their way to purchase some fabric for a new dress. He wondered what his father the viscount would say if he could see his son dressed in an ill-fitting footman's livery strolling through a rebel town, ducking into shops filled with ladies' garments and feminine fripperies.

No doubt he'd say what he'd always said.

You'll never amount to anything, boy. Why can't you be more like your brother?

Alex sighed. Perhaps the man was right all along, for if Alex truly admitted it to himself, he was enjoying his time with these humble rebels and dreaded returning to his ship.

Doffing his hat, he dabbed the sweat from his forehead and allowed the breeze blowing in from the bay to thread cool fingers through his hair. The clip-clop of horses' hooves, the grate of carriage wheels, and the chatter of citizens filled the air. Bells rang from the harbor, and somewhere in the distance, a peddler hawked his wares. Pressing forward, Mr. Reed offered his arm to Miss McGuire.

"A footman walks behind his mistress, Mr. Reed, not with her." She snapped at him keeping her eyes straight ahead.

He gave her a crooked smile and drifted back a few steps. "As you wish, miss." He knew he should be angry at her for her condescending treatment, but her ill-fitting cloak of pomposity only endeared her to him more.

They crossed over a wooden bridge, making way for a horse and rider to their left. Beneath them the Jones Falls River slapped its banks and tumbled over rocks as it dashed toward the bay.

As they proceeded, Alex studied the homes that lined the cobblestone street. Square, two-story structures stood back from road with beautiful gardens stretching before them to the street. The sweet fragrance of roses, pinks, sweet williams, larkspurs, and hollyhocks filled the air. Most of the homes boasted a smokehouse off to the side or peeking out from the rear, where no doubt the family cured its bacon and baked biscuits and other varieties of bread and cake. Though nothing like the stately homes in Cranleigh, Alex found the dwellings quite charming—in a rustic sort of way.

He scanned the faces of those they passed. Aside from the occasional grimy slave, tattered beggar, or common worker, most of Baltimore's citizens appeared well groomed and fashionable. Not a few men turned to smile or tip their hats at the ladies.

Miss McGuire ignored them entirely, but Amelia seemed to thrive upon the attention as she pinched her cheeks and returned each greeting with a coquettish smile or a wave of her fan. More than one gentleman seemed intent on answering her call—that was until they saw Alex following close behind.

Farther down the street, Alex became enamored with the signs hanging in front of the shops. Instead of words describing what wares could be found within, pictures and symbols told the passersby what type of shop it was. Alex had never seen anything like it. Were all Americans so unlettered? He passed beneath a sign etched with the picture of a golden fan and umbrella. He peeked in the window to see an assortment of fancy haberdashery. An engraved sundial hung above the watchmaker. The importer of Irish linens depicted his goods with a painting of a spinning wheel, though the store appeared empty when Alex peered within.

A ship's bell drew his gaze toward the east where, in between warehouses and shops, a crowd of bare masts jutted into the afternoon sky, swaying with the gentle movement of the bay. He wondered if any of them belonged to the notorious Baltimore Clipper he'd heard so much about—those swift ships that continually harassed British merchants. He thought to ask Miss McGuire, but knew she'd only accuse him of spying. Instead, Alex drew in a deep breath of the salty air but, oddly, found no longing within him to return to the sea.

After a brief stop at the drapers where, much to Amelia's dismay, she did not find her desired fabric, they turned down Calvert Street to visit, as Miss McGuire informed him, the best millinery in town.

Aside from the aching wound in his thigh and the heat of the day, Alex enjoyed this brief foray into civilization. Having spent months out to sea, any city, even one as primitive as this one, reminded him that life was more than wind and weather, grapeshot and broadsides.

Amelia dashed inside Brekham's Millinery before Alex reached the front of the shop and stopped beneath a sign painted with a large purple hat.

"Stay here, Mr. Reed, if you please." Miss McGuire thrust out her chin and turned to follow her companion.

Alex grabbed her arm, turning her to face him. "I know what you're doing, miss."

Holding her bonnet against a hefty breeze, she tugged from his grasp. "And what is that, Mr. Reed?"

"Trying to humiliate me into leaving." He brushed dust from his coat. "I promised I would return to my ship, and I am a man of my word." He offered her a look of appeasement. "So why don't we spend our brief time together being polite instead of impertinent?"

She seemed to be pondering his suggestion when Amelia burst from the shop.

"There are no hats," the woman grumbled as the bell hanging from the shop's door clanged her disapproval before shutting. Tipping the edge of her bonnet against the sun's bright rays, she gazed down the street. "There is no silk, no satin, no velvet, nothing with which to make an appropriate gown." Her lips drew into a pout. "I tire of this war."

"Amelia." Miss McGuire looped her arm through her friend's. "There also is a shortage of food and medicines, things which are far more important than such fripperies."

Alex grimaced beneath another wave of empathy. What the deuces was happening to him? These Americans deserved discomfort and much worse for their rebellion against England.

"I know." Amelia shrugged. "I know I am spoiled, and I shouldn't say such things. It's just that I heard there will be a ball at the Fountain Inn next week, and I was so hoping to go. I know it won't be like the balls we had before the blockade, but at least we can forget the horrors of war for one night and enjoy the company of the good citizens of Baltimore." Her eyes lit up. "Besides, I think Mr. Braxton intends to ask your uncle if he can escort me."

Miss McGuire smiled, but her eyes were riveted to something in the distance. "Look, there are Marianne and Cassandra."

Alex followed her gaze to a crowd of people across the cobblestone street. A tall muscular man in gray trousers with a double-breasted black waistcoat stood beside a woman in a stylish pink gown. Alex's heart froze.

Noah Brenin.

He'd know that bronzed face and light hair anywhere. He squinted against the sun at the two men who stood by his side. Neither could he mistake the coal-black hair of the one and the brawny frame of the other, nor the smiling face of the lad standing beside his father. Luke Heaton and Blackthorn along with his son, Daniel. All of them had been impressed aboard the HMS *Undefeatable* two years ago—dragged aboard as slaves to the British Crown.

Surely they would recognize Alex as easily as he had recognized them.

"Marianne!" Miss McGuire shouted as she made her way across the street, Amelia on her heels.

Alex turned his face away and scanned the street. People strolled down the avenue, weaving among carriages and horses. He could escape into the crowd, make his way back to the farm to get his uniform, and head to his ship directly.

But that would leave Miss McGuire and Amelia unescorted.

Clenching his fists, he glanced behind him at the millinery shop just as a feminine voice shouted "Rose!" from across the street.

❖ CHAPTER 12 ❖

Grabbing Amelia, Rose darted in between a stream of carriages and made her way to her friends. But instead of the expected smiles and greetings tossed her way; all of them, with the exception of Daniel, stared curiously at the spot she had just vacated.

Glancing over her shoulder, she saw nothing unusual to draw their attention, although she did wonder where Mr. Reed had run off to. Scanning the street, she was about to ask Amelia when Noah spoke up. "I could have sworn I saw Lieutenant Reed."

Mr. Heaton flipped the hair from his face, his dark brows furrowed. "Indeed."

"Impossible, gentlemen." Marianne's skeptical tone belied her words as she turned to Rose with a smile. "What a pleasure to see you in town."

"Mr. Reed?" Rose shook her head. Surely she heard the name incorrectly.

"Aye, Mr. Alexander Reed of the HMS *Undefeatable*," Daniel, whose voice had deepened considerably since Rose had last seen him, announced with a hint of pride.

Rose's knees turned to mush.

"Are you ill, Rose?" Cassandra, her dear friend, gripped her arm and steadied her.

Amelia eased between Rose and Marianne and took her other arm, but from the sound of her maid's ragged breathing and the tremble in her grip, Rose guessed she suffered from the same confusion and terror that consumed Rose.

"I'm quite all right, thank you. Just a bit warm." Rose plucked out her fan and waved it frantically about her face. Anything to keep her wits about her. "My word, what would a British naval officer be doing sauntering about on the streets of Baltimore?" She attempted a laugh that only brought curious gazes her way. "Why, he'd be arrested on the spot."

Amelia's grip on her arm tightened.

Mr. Heaton's jaw knotted. "Or worse, if I ever see him again."

Cassandra placed her hands on her delicate hips. "Come now Mr. Heaton, why are you always so eager to use your fists before your reason?" Ignoring her playful smile, Mr. Heaton huffed and looked away.

Her heart tight in her chest, Rose swept her gaze to the last place she'd seen Mr. Reed. No trace of him remained. But where had he gone? And how did her friends know him? Rose searched her mind, but only one possibility surfaced. Two years ago, Marianne and Noah had returned from the sea with an adventurous tale of capture aboard a British navy ship, of a mad captain, of sabotage, escape, and victory. Rose drew a hand to her head to quell a sudden dizziness. Of all the ships in the royal navy and all the second lieutenants. . .

Mr. Blackthorn, whom Rose had been introduced to three weeks prior as Noah's first mate, continued to stare at the millinery store as if expecting Mr. Reed to reappear. "That man and his cap'n kept me an' my boy prisoner on board his ship for three years."

"Papa, it wasn't his fault," Daniel said. "He was only following orders."

"Mr. Reed was an honorable man." Noah gripped the pommel of his sword, sending Rose's stomach churning. She had no doubt that regardless of his sentiments, he would not hesitate to arrest Mr. Reed and toss him into prison.

"Don't forget, he allowed my precious wife to escape from his ship," Noah continued.

Rose squeezed her eyes shut, trying to wrap her mind around

these shocking revelations. A flurry of wind tugged on her bonnet and cooled the perspiration on her neck. The clip-clop of horses' hooves, the prattle of passing citizens, and the occasional bell from the port swirled past her ears. Nothing out of the ordinary.

Mr. Heaton's gruff chortle snapped her eyes open. A breeze stirred his coal-black hair. He narrowed his eyes. "We owe him nothing. He allowed Marianne to escape only to save himself and his career."

"I don't understand. How could letting an enemy go save his career?" Rose asked.

Mr. Heaton crossed his arms over his chest. "He allowed her to keep a weapon on board. That's treason."

A weapon? Rose sped up the fluttering of her fan.

"For my protection," Marianne added. "Against that vile Lieutenant Garrick."

"Oh my word." Rose's knees wobbled and Cassandra steadied her. So Marianne had experienced Mr. Garrick's licentious appetites as well. And once again, Mr. Reed had played the chivalrous hero.

Marianne smiled. "And I threatened to tell his captain if he didn't allow me to escape."

Though the sun had begun its descent in the western sky, its searing rays seemed hotter than ever. Rose ceased her useless fanning.

"God had a plan for Mr. Reed." Daniel nodded with a grin. "To help us escape."

Blackthorn shook his head. "Only you could see God's hand in such a disaster, son."

"God's hand is everywhere." Daniel's gaze shifted to Rose and remained there so long she thought there might be dirt on her face again. "God has a plan for you too, Miss McGuire," the boy said it stoically as if he were speaking directly from another's prompting. "Something important for you to do."

Blackthorn's lips slanted. "Are you sure, Daniel?"

"Yes, father, I'm sure."

Something important to do? Confusion once again jumbled Rose's thoughts. For God? She hadn't exactly been on speaking terms with the Almighty these past years.

Marianne squeezed her arm and smiled. "I would listen to him if I were you."

"My son is a prophet, Miss McGuire." Blackthorn scratched his linen shirt.

A prophet? The explanation did nothing to ease her confusion. Prophets existed only in biblical times. God did not speak to people through prophets anymore. Any fool knew that.

As if to confirm her thoughts, Mr. Heaton let out a skeptical snort.

Blackthorn shrugged and ruffled Daniel's thick brown hair. "He's not often wrong. An' my other son, who's only five, appears t' have the same gift. Got it from me wife, God love her. An' we are now expectin' our third. Mebbe we'll have a whole family of prophets."

Noah slapped his first mate on the back. "Indeed. We could use more prophets in this city."

Pursing her lips, Rose directed her gaze at Daniel. "Well in this case, I fear you are entirely incorrect, Daniel, for I am not destined to perform any great feat." Nor did she want to be. Truth be told, she just wanted to be let alone—to live out her life in peace.

Instead of frowning at Rose's rebuke, Daniel smiled—a knowing smile that sent an odd shudder through her. She glanced toward the millinery. The shadow of a tall man shot back from the window. *So that's where Mr. Reed went.*

Best to be on her way and rescue him from his hiding place.

"We should be going. My aunt will be worried." Rose snatched the fan back from Amelia.

Noah cast a harried glance over the street. "But surely you and Amelia aren't without escort?"

"No. My footman is with us." At his questioning look, she continued, "I sent him to the chandlers to purchase some candles."

"Well, allow us to escort you there," Noah said.

"No need. It is just another block." Rose waved her fan in the air and dragged Amelia away. "Do continue to enjoy your day."

"Very well." Noah touched the tip of his cocked hat. "Good day to you then, ladies."

Cassandra waved. "I hope to see you soon, Rose."

"Yes, soon. Let's get together for tea, shall we?" Rose halted before a passing horse.

"Promise?" Marianne's voice turned Rose around. Her friend slid her arm into Noah's and she smiled.

"Promise." As Rose watched them leave, a myriad of emotions clamored for her attention. The foremost one—fear that her friends would see Mr. Reed and arrest him—was already slipping away.

"What was all that about Mr. Reed, miss?" Amelia exclaimed as they reached the other side of the street. "I had no idea."

"Neither did I." Rose waved one last time at her friends. No sooner had they disappeared from sight than Mr. Reed popped out of the store, brushing imaginary dust from his coat as if being among so many ladies' hats had somehow soiled him.

"Thank goodness. The store owner was about to toss me from the place, accusing me of being some sort of coxcomb."

Rose would have giggled if she wasn't so busy settling her breathing.

"Thank you for not alerting them to my presence." He scanned the street.

"I had no idea you knew my friends."

His eyes met hers. "I had no idea they were your friends, miss. Nor that they hailed from Baltimore."

"Pray tell, how many more of Baltimore's citizens have you impressed on your ship?"

He smiled. "None that I'm aware of."

"Shall we go just in case?" Amelia tugged on Rose's arm, her eyes flashing with fear.

With a nod, Rose slipped her fan into her reticule and headed down the street. Though she hurried her pace, the trip back to the church seemed to drag on forever. All along the street, from every shop and every corner, curious eyes seemed to follow them. But finally, Uncle Forbes's church came into view, and Rose released a shaky breath. That was until General Smith marched from the sick house, Aunt Muira on his heels. Though the General's face was its usual unruffled mask, Aunt Muria's was quivering with distress.

Rose froze, her heart seizing in her chest.

"Thank goodness you've returned," her aunt cried out. "We must go to the Myers' farm immediately."

"Elaine?" Rose's heart clinched. The warning bells of St. Peter's rang fresh through her mind. "What happened? Is she alive?"

The general halted before Mr. Reed and eyed him with a curious gaze. The breath of relief Rose had just released crowded back in her throat.

"It was the British, dear. And yes, she's alive." But the way her aunt said the words caused Rose's hands to tremble.

"And who might you be, sir?" General Smith asked Alex.

Mr. Reed stiffened.

"Why he is our new man of work, General, Mr. Alexander Reed." Her aunt came to the rescue. "Mr. Reed, bring the phaeton around. We must leave immediately."

With a nod, he darted off.

Rose pressed a hand over the veins throbbing in her throat. "What brings you here to our church, General?"

"I heard rumors of wounded British soldiers hiding amongst our own and thought some may have wandered into your uncle's care." The general's hardened gaze followed Mr. Reed as he disappeared behind the church and remained there until he reappeared, leading the horse and phaeton. "And I wanted to inform your aunt and uncle about the attack on the Myers' farm. I know the Myers are friends of your family's."

"Yes, indeed. Rose has known Elaine for years." Aunt Muira gestured for Mr. Reed to hurry.

Rose wobbled, and Amelia slipped her arm through hers.

"Very good. Well, if you'll excuse me. I must be going." General Smith slid his bicorn atop his head. "Ladies." He bowed slightly and after they bid him adieu, he marched away.

Much to Rose's relief.

Numbly, Rose allowed Mr. Reed to assist her into the carriage. She didn't have to ask what had happened to her friend Elaine. She knew. Her thoughts drifted to Elaine's wedding last summer. How happy the couple seemed as they rode off in their open-air carriage after the ceremony, all the guests tossing rose petals at them.

"Tell me they didn't harm James." She asked her aunt after they were all settled on their seats.

"He wasn't home." Rose couldn't remember her aunt's tone holding so much pain. "I need you to be strong, Rose." Leaning forward, she squeezed her hand once again. "For Elaine."

With a shake of her head, Rose tore her hand from her aunt's grasp and lowered her gaze. "I don't know if I can." Yet hadn't she just promised herself to not allow fear to keep her from helping others?

"She's asking for you, Rose. You're the only one who can help her."

Mr. Reed leaped into the driver's seat, jostling the carriage to the right, then snapped the reins and sent them on their way. Amelia stared vacantly out the window as if she couldn't handle any more trouble for one day.

Rose agreed.

No, Lord, please send someone else. Rose stifled a sob. Every ounce of her wanted to help her friend—wanted to help all women who'd suffered as she had, but thick bars of fear kept her locked far from those in need.

"I am not strong like you, Aunt." Rose swiped a tear from her cheek. "When I help these women, it's like I'm going through it all over again."

Aunt Muira cupped Rose's face with both her hands and forced her to meet her gaze. "You are your father's daughter. There is strength in you, Rose."

"My father is gone."

"Your father lives on in you. And your heavenly Father is within you as well. Draw upon His strength."

Rose tightened her jaw. God had never helped her before. Why would he now? Yet, Elaine's sweet face drifted through Rose's mind. The way her blue eyes sparkled and dimples formed on her cheeks whenever she smiled. Rose could not turn her back on her friend—as God had done on her—not when Elaine needed Rose the most.

Within a half hour and at the direction of her aunt, Mr. Reed turned the carriage down a dirt road that wound through a valley of tall grass waving in the breeze. A small creek splashed and bubbled nearby accompanied by a chorus of meadowlarks. The happy sounds and beautiful sights were at odds with the despair threatening to sever Rose's heart. Despair for Elaine. Then as if reading her dismal thoughts, a blast of smoke-laden wind blew in through the window and stung her nose. Aunt Muira coughed and drew a silk handkerchief to her mouth. Rose leaned out the window to see a gray mist hovering over a patch of pine trees in the distance. Her stomach tightened. She faced forward again and clamped her hands together in her lap. Aunt Muira touched Rose's arm and offered her a comforting look as the carriage bumped and jostled over the uneven road.

They slowed and Rose thought she heard Mr. Reed groan. Forcing herself to peek out the window again, she saw what was left of a small cottage perched beside a pond. She drew in a gasp. Half of the small house lay in a black charred ruin, the other half, though darkened with soot, remained intact. The coach jostled over something in the road, and Rose's cheek struck the edge of the window. Ignoring both the pain in her face and the one in her heart, she jerked her head back into the carriage and searched for a breath of air. "Where is Elaine?"

"In the house, I believe," her aunt replied.

Amelia gaped out the window. "Oh my."

Mr. Reed brought the carriage to a halt before the scorched building, and Aunt Muira grabbed her satchel, opened the door, and leaped out before he had a chance to hop down and assist her.

Not that he'd intended to aid them, for as Rose took a tentative step down onto the muddy soil after Amelia had debarked, she noted that Mr. Reed remained on his seat.

Staring at what was left of the blackened house.

He glanced her way, a look of horror crossing his face, before he grabbed his crutch and jumped down.

"Come along now." Aunt Muira forged ahead, her tone that of a school matron.

But Rose couldn't seem to move her feet.

A family of ducks—a mother, father, and seven babies—glided happily over the pond to her right as if no tragedy had occurred here. But the wisps of smoke spinning off the charred wood of the cottage spoke otherwise. Movement dragged Rose's gaze to the left of the house where several yards away beneath a massive oak tree, a man halted his digging and looked up. Two fresh mounds of dirt sat amid a scattering of crosses and stones. Rose's throat clamped shut.

Abandoning his crutch against the carriage, Mr. Reed approached her. "What happened here?"

By the guilt lacing his tone, Rose knew he had already guessed. Nevertheless, she could not help but lay the charge at his feet. "Your people happened here, Mr. Reed."

Pain etched across his eyes. He swallowed and offered her his arm.

Ignoring it, Rose ventured forward.

Splinters of wood poked out from a large hole in the front door that hung limp on its hinges. Aunt Muira knocked and waited with the patience and composure of a lady making a social call. Within seconds the wooden slab swung wide with a heartrending squeak to reveal James, Elaine's husband. Wild, swollen eyes stared at them from within a red face that was streaked with soot. A torn, stained shirt did nothing to hide the cuts and abrasions across his arms and chest, and a drop of blood oozed from a wound on his head. Without saying a word, he ushered them inside.

Aunt Muira and Amelia disappeared within, but Rose remained at the threshold. The smell of singed wood, sickness, and sorrow threatened to send her back to the carriage. Perspiration dotted her neck. She whispered a portion of her father's song.

Ten thousand mile is very far away
For you to return to me,
You leave me here to lament, and well a day!
My tears you will not see, my love.

Mr. Reed remained by her side but said not a word.

Gathering her resolve, Rose ventured within. Holes in the wall to her left revealed the darkened remains of what had been the kitchen and dining room. Smoke bit her nose and throat, and Rose swallowed. Voices lured her to the back of the house where traitorous sunlight flooded a parlor that—because of what had occurred within—should have been enshrouded in gloom. Aunt Muira drew up a chair before a woman lying on a sofa and leaned over her, hiding the woman's face from Rose. But she knew it was Elaine. And she wasn't ready to face her friend just yet. Amelia knelt beside Aunt Muira and took Elaine's hand in hers, only adding to Rose's guilt at her own inadequacy.

Shards of glass littered the floor below broken windows where torn, singed curtains fluttered on the incoming breeze. The Hepplewhite side cabinet Rose had so adored lay in a pile of sticks by the cold fireplace. No doubt the rain she'd heard last night had put out the fire before it could consume this half of the house. For aside from the shattered windows, and a burn mark on the floorcloth, the parlor appeared undamaged.

Not like the lady lying on the cream-colored sofa.

James approached Rose, arms extended. "She's been asking for you, Rose."

Rose took his hands, and he drew her into an embrace. Startled by his familiarity, she hugged him in return as his body convulsed with sobs.

"I'm so sorry." Rose's voice emerged as a squeak.

He squeezed her tight, then withdrew, wiping the moisture from his face and spreading black soot over his cheek. His gaze swept to the door where a glance told Rose Mr. Reed had followed her into the house.

"And who are you, sir?" James demanded.

"I am the Drummond's servant." Mr. Reed's voice had lost its hauteur.

James's eyes narrowed, and he clenched his fists. "Your accent reeks of British nobility."

Rose stepped between them. "He is a friend." *A friend*. She surprised herself at her quick declaration.

Yet James did not seem so convinced as his lips twisted in a snarl.

Aunt Muira removed medicine and bandages from her satchel and began rubbing something over Elaine's face.

"What happened?" Rose asked James in a low voice.

Anguish darkened his face. "British raiders." His Adam's apple bobbed up and down. "I was in town when the warning sounded. I got here as fast as I could." His jaw tightened. "We caught the bloody wretches in the act before they could burn down the entire house. But not before. . ." He squeezed his eyes shut.

Rose's legs wobbled. Mr. Reed grabbed her elbow and steadied her. The air seemed to retreat from the room. She could hear her aunt whispering words of comfort to Elaine. But Rose knew full well that no kind words, no amount of medicine or herbal tinctures or thoughtful attentiveness, would ever heal the wound Elaine would carry for the rest of her life.

"Thank you, Mr. Reed." She gave him a nod, and he released her arm with a frown.

James stared benumbed at his wife. His jaw trembled. Rose lowered her chin. How could she help this man? How could she help Elaine when she couldn't even help herself? She clasped her hands together and inhaled a shuddering breath.

She must be strong.

"I saw your man digging graves," she said to draw James's mind off his wife for a moment, although even as she said the words she realized the new topic would bring no comfort.

James swiped at his moist cheeks and gazed out the window. "When we fought them off Joseph and Willie were killed."

Rose gasped. James's stableboys were but fifteen and twenty— orphans whom he had taken in to help out around the farm.

"And your wound?" Rose pointed to his bloody forehead.

"They knocked me in the head pretty good." James dabbed at it.

She grasped his hands again. "Allow my aunt to tend to you as soon as she's done with Elaine."

Nodding, he sank into a chair. "They took everything from us. Everything of value." He dropped his head into his hands.

Rose knelt before him. "Thank G—" she started, quickly amending, "but you are alive. You and Elaine." She would not give thanks to God, for there was no sign of Him anywhere.

"Rose." Elaine's weak voice tugged at Rose.

God, if You're there, please give me strength. Rose struggled to rise. Her head grew light, and she lifted a hand to steady herself. Mr. Reed's firm grip on her elbow once again saved her from embarrassment.

She wanted to thank him for his support, for his kindness, but under the circumstances it seemed highly inappropriate. His people had done this. He carried their guilt by association. She must remember that. Tugging from his grip, she made her way to the sofa. Aunt Muira stood and snapped her satchel shut. She gave Rose an encouraging nod and pressed her hand on Rose's arm.

"I've done all I can. Now she needs a friend." Then facing Amelia, Aunt Muira ordered her out of the room. "Mr. Reed," she added as she passed him at the door. "Fetch some water from the pond, if you please. Come, James. Let me tend to that wound."

Rose watched as they ambled out the door, leaving her alone with Elaine.

Lowering herself onto the chair her aunt had vacated, Rose finally glanced down at her friend. Red and purple marks swelled on her cheeks and neck, and her once crisp blue eyes melted in a sea of red, puffy skin. Fresh bandages wrapped around her right arm and forehead. She held out her hand. Rose took it and brought it to her lips.

Nausea churned in her belly.

She brushed the tangled hair from Elaine's face and closed her eyes. She could do this. She must do this.

Thunder bellowed overhead, rumbling across the sky and mimicking Alex's mood. With a snap of the reins, he urged Douglas into a trot and headed back toward the Drummond farm. A horde of emotions battled in his gut. Fury, disgust, and shame appeared to be winning. He knew this kind of thing happened in war. He had seen such atrocities from a distance the night he'd saved Miss McGuire from Lieutenant Garrick. But not until today had he ventured into the broken-down, charred home of a family who'd suffered under war's cruelty and looked into the tortured eyes of its victims. Real people who lived simple, happy lives. Innocents.

The hatred pouring from James's eyes when he'd heard Alex's accent had nearly shoved Alex to the ground. But how could he blame the man?

Worse than that was the loathsome glare Miss McGuire had given him when she'd emerged from the house. With pale face and trembling lips, she had not even taken his proffered hand when she'd climbed into the coach. From his conversation earlier with Mr. Drummond and the way Miss McGuire trembled throughout her meeting with Elaine, Alex surmised that some horrible event haunted her past. Whether it was also at the hands of his countrymen, he couldn't know.

He didn't want to know.

Her rejection stung him like a slap in the face. A slap he deserved and one that woke him up from the dream he'd been living these past ten days. His stomach soured as tiny drops of rain tapped upon his shoulders. Blast his senseless honor. He was a fool—a fool to stay with this rebel family in the hopes of protecting them while he enjoyed a brief reprieve from the rigid life of a British naval officer. He should return to his ship. It was obvious to him now that his presence caused Miss McGuire pain. And that was the last thing he wanted to do.

A gust of wind marched around him, whipping his hair and

sending a chill down his back. He wished it would blow away the smell of burnt wood that lingered in his nose, but he had a feeling that the charred scent of death would remain with him for a long while.

Like the look on Miss McGuire's face. She hated him.

The realization made his heart shrink. And if her aunt and uncle knew his true identity, they'd no doubt hate him too. Trouble was, he couldn't blame them. Everything he believed about his country—its honor, might, and superiority—seemed to splatter like the rain landing on his breeches in light of what he'd seen. He didn't know what to believe anymore. Was it right for him to pursue his goals of wealth and honor in a navy that afflicted such horrors upon the innocent? Yet how else was he to erase the stains he'd made upon his family's name and prompt his father to open the doors of their home to Alex once again? He shook his head and watched the raindrops plop onto the muddy road and the breeze thread through the dark leaves of the elm trees lining the pathway.

Lightning spiked across a darkening sky, coating the moist foliage in a sheen of eerie gray. Alex pushed his cocked hat farther down on his head. A gust of wind tainted with the scent of the sea tore over him, flapping the lapels of his coat. He snapped the reins. Thunder pounded the sky like an angry fist. As if Miss McGuire's scorn for him wasn't enough impetus to leave soon, Alex's near encounter with Mr. Brenin, Mr. Heaton, and Blackthorn in town today proved that Alex had no business being here. He didn't wish to endanger Miss McGuire or her family by his presence. Truth be told, he didn't wish to endanger his heart.

❖ CHAPTER 13 ❖

Rose crept over the sandy soil. A thick mist pressed in on her, hovering around her like a multitude of ghosts. She waved her hands through the air to swat it away, but it remained, enclosing her in a white shroud. A light appeared, its glow blossoming through the haze, forcing back the fog. Elaine emerged from the mist. She held a single candle. Her blue eyes were vacant and cold. One bruise remained on her neck. "They're coming." She swept a look over her shoulder then grabbed Rose's hand and dragged her forward. Rose followed her friend. Her heart cinched. But then the cloud swallowed Elaine up, and she disappeared. Rose's hand fell to her side.

"Elaine!" she yelled, her voice echoing through the chilled mist.

Trees formed at the edges of the haze. Rose glanced down at her torn red dress. Something cold and heavy filled her hand. A pistol. Gazing at it curiously, she lifted it. Smoke curled from the barrel. A man lay on the ground before her. Blood swelled on his waistcoat. Lifeless eyes stared up at a dark sky.

Rose dropped the gun. It fell slowly to the ground as if it sank through molasses. Then it landed with a hollow thud. Her hand burned.

She opened her mouth to scream "No!" but she could not hear her voice.

Slumping to the dirt, Rose curled in a ball and squeezed her eyes shut. "No, God, no. Please."

Light flooded all around her as if someone had opened a door. Soothing warmth swept away the chill. Something or someone lifted her chin upward. An ominous figure dressed in glowing white stood before her. The mist retreated before the light, revealing a gentle forest in its wake. Her heart took up a rapid beat. She scrambled to get away from the terrifying man when he opened his mouth and a voice emerged that sounded like the purl of a deep river. "Fear not, beloved one."

Rose halted. *Beloved one.* She gazed up at the man but the glow that emanated from him forbade her to see his face. "Fear not, for you have been chosen by God."

"Chosen? For what?" Rose mouthed, but again she could not hear her voice.

"Fear not."

Rose sprang up in bed, gasping for air. Heart crashing against her ribs, she scanned her chamber. The first rays of dawn filtered through her window, forcing the shadows of her room into the corners. Only a dream. Hadn't she wondered if they would return after she'd visited Elaine?

But what an odd dream. *Fear not, beloved one.* The words danced over her ears. Who was the glowing man? An angel? *You have been chosen.* The statement spoken with such authority and serenity tugged on something deep within Rose, something that brought tears to her eyes. She shook off the sentiment. Nothing but a nightmare—like all the others.

Swinging her legs over her bed, she plucked a handkerchief from her bed stand and dabbed the perspiration beading on her forehead and neck. Her breathing returned to normal, and she hung her head. It had been months since she'd had a nightmare. But she would gladly endure another bout of terrifying visions if she had brought Elaine a mite of comfort yesterday. They had exchanged no words. Rose had simply held her friend in her arms, and they had sobbed together. Perhaps that alone, plus the knowledge that someone understood exactly what Elaine had suffered, was enough for now.

Slipping the halter over Valor's head, Rose tightened the buckle and led the filly from the barn. Though the sun dipped low in the western sky, Rose needed to ride, needed to get away from everything and everyone. After the distressing events of yesterday and the disturbing nightmare that had woken her from her sleep that morning, she'd remained in her chamber most of the day, reading. While successfully avoiding Mr. Reed. For she couldn't be sure how she would react to him. One minute she hated him for what his people had done to her parents, her country—Elaine. The next minute, his kindness, honor, and the favorable words her friends had spoken of him, swung her emotional pendulum back to admiration. And if Rose were honest, a sentiment that went beyond admiration. But she didn't want to be honest.

She tied Valor to a post and eased a brush over the horse's back and down her sides. Despite Rose's treatment of Mr. Reed in town, her ploy to belittle him had backfired. Instead Mr. Reed had been naught but gracious as he sauntered about town—in that worn and tattered and altogether too tight livery—with the hauteur of a nobleman and the confidence of a leader of men. Any fool who looked at him twice could see he was no servant.

Even now, the mere thought of how close Mr. Reed had come to being thrown in jail—not to mention her family tried for treason—sent her chest heaving. Setting down the brush, Rose swung a blanket over Valor's back, then lifted a saddle on top of it and tightened the girth. Douglas, her uncle's steed, looked up from the field where he was grazing.

Mr. Reed had more than proven himself to be an honorable man these past days, and now with the testimony of her friends, Rose could no longer deny that he was also a good man—a kind man.

Grabbing the bridle, she ran her fingers over Valor's cheek and then kissed the filly's nose. The horse leaned against her and snorted. A humid breeze stirred the curls dangling about Rose's neck and brought the woodsy smell of horseflesh to her nose. Overhead, a billowing jumble of clouds darkened the afternoon sky even as the sun spread its golden rays over the farm from its position atop the tree line. At least two hours before sunset. Two hours to run wild through the forest and clear the confusion that kept her mind awhirl.

Clear her mind from thoughts of Mr. Reed. It was for the best. He would be gone soon. Perhaps even tonight.

She couldn't face him. Couldn't say good-bye.

Didn't want to say good-bye.

Which was all part of her confusion.

For if she bade him farewell, she knew he would see right through her facade. And she couldn't bear to let him know how deep her feelings for him ran.

"What are you doing, Miss McGuire?" Alex's voice drew Rose's startled gaze to him. Leaning against the doorframe, he crossed his arms over his chest and eyed her with suspicion. He'd been searching for her all day. After yesterday's events, he had to make sure she was all right before he left. He had to see her one last time, gaze into those turquoise eyes one last time—even if they were filled with hate.

Oddly, her face reddened. She turned away and slipped the bridle over Valor's head and adjusted the bit in the horse's mouth. "As you can plainly see, I am going for a ride."

Alex glanced at the dark clouds overhead as a blast of wind swirled the sting of rain beneath his nose. "Alone?"

Ignoring him, Miss McGuire fastened the bridle under Valor's chin then flung the reins over her neck. "You are no longer my servant or my guardian, Mr. Reed." She stepped onto a stool, put her booted foot in the stirrup, and leaped onto the back of the horse with more finesse than he expected. Straddling the beast like a man, she spread her full skirts out around her legs then grabbed the reins, and lifted her pert nose as if pleased that she shocked him with her unladylike behavior. "Besides, I often ride in the forest alone. It is far safer than town."

Alex lifted one brow. "There may be British afoot."

"Indeed, Mr. Reed, there *are* British afoot." Her pointed gaze made him wince. "Which is why I feel the need to leave." Giving Valor a nudge, she snapped the reins and sped off in a flurry of blue muslin and golden curls.

"What the deuces," Reed cursed then marched to the steed grazing in the field. He hoped he remembered how to ride. It had been several years since he'd ridden his father's horses across their estate. And never without benefit of saddle and reins. But there was no time for that. He glanced toward the web of greenery bordering the farm and caught one final glimpse of Miss McGuire's blue gown as the forest swallowed her up. Foolish woman.

Taking a running start, he leaped onto the horse's back and grabbed a handful of mane to stop himself from slipping off the other side. A shard of pain lanced his thigh. The horse snorted and stomped his foot into the dirt. Thunder grumbled in the distance. "Come on, boy, we've a lady to rescue." With a squeeze of his legs, he urged the beast forward. Nothing. "Forward!" he ordered. The steed shook his head. One large brown eye stared at him as if he were an annoying insect, and Alex fully expected the horse's tail to swat him from his back.

Infernal beast. Fury tightened Alex's jaw. "I said go!" He kicked the horse's sides. Much to his dismay, the horse lurched into a gallop. Catching his balance before he tumbled off the back end, Alex tightened his grip on the mane and leaned forward. Hot wind whipped through his hair, freeing it from its queue. The crazed pound of his heart matched the thump of the horse's hooves over the grassy, moist ground. Alex's body rose and fell against the steed's muscular back. Not until he charged into the forest did the horse slow to a trot. Up ahead, Miss McGuire made her way along a narrow winding trail.

"Miss McGuire!"

She shot a spiteful glance over her shoulder. "Go back to your ship, Mr. Reed. Leave me be."

"I cannot. Your uncle has charged me with your care."

"Well, I discharge you, sir." She urged her horse into a trot.

Ducking beneath a low-hanging branch, Alex followed her into the thick brush, his steed trotting over a soft bed of moss and pine needles. Leaves in every shade of green fluttered in the breeze around him. Tree trunks thrust into the gray sky like ship masts. Insects buzzed. Birds chirped, and Alex drew in a deep breath of earth and life tainted with the fragrance of wildflowers and fresh rain.

Lightning flashed above the canopy, transforming the greens into sparkling silver.

He urged his horse onward. "Miss McGuire, if you please."

"Go away!" she shouted before the foliage swallowed her up once again.

A clearing up ahead afforded Alex a view of her as her horse leaped over a small creek. But after casting one glance over her shoulder, she galloped out of sight.

Coaxing his horse into a sprint, Alex hoped the steed would clear the brook with the same skill. He leaned forward, feeling the beast's muscles tense and stretch beneath him. The horse thrust his hooves into the wind. They flew through the air for one brief, glorious second before they struck the dirt on the opposite bank. The horse bucked. Alex lost his grip. He slid off the steed's back and thumped to the ground. Pain speared up his spine and something sharp struck his head.

"Blast it all," he moaned as he toppled over onto a pile of leaves.

Seconds later, golden curls and glistening blue eyes appeared in his blurry vision. "Mr. Reed, are you all right?" Her fresh feminine scent filled the air between them, luring him from his daze.

Alex shook his head and attempted to rise. Gentle hands gripped his arms and pulled him up.

How mortifying. Shame heated his face, and he closed his eyes.

"Are you injured?" she asked.

"I don't believe so." He glanced over the clearing where their two horses grazed happily on a patch of moss.

"Oh my word." Her eyes sharpened. "You are bleeding." Yanking a handkerchief from her sleeve, she scrambled to the brook and dipped the cloth in the water.

Alex felt a trail of warm fluid slide down his cheek. He raised his hand to wipe it away, but she knelt and dabbed the cloth on his face before he could.

"I told you not to follow me," she scolded.

Pain etched across his forehead. He lifted his hand to his wound again, but she batted it away. "I could not in good conscience allow you to put yourself in further danger, miss."

"Mr. Reed." She sat back. "I know these woods better than you know your ship. I simply wished to be alone." She glanced down.

But not before Alex saw her red nose and puffy eyes. "You've been crying."

Tossing the cloth into his hand, she leaped to her feet and turned her back to him, adding to his confusion.

"I hope I am not the cause of your distress." Alex pressed the cloth to his forehead. Pain burned across his skin.

Dark clouds stole the remaining light of the sun and lured shadows out from hiding.

"You must leave." Her shoulders slumped. "There is no other recourse."

A breeze danced among the loose curls hanging to her waist. Alex shook his head. Was she upset about him leaving? Absurd. "I fear you mistook me. I meant, are you upset because I followed you?"

She swung around, a horrified look on her face. "Of course, I understood you perfectly." She swiped her cheeks and drew a deep breath. "It is this war, meeting my friends in town yesterday, Elaine." She took up a pace across the leaf-strewn ground as thunder growled in the distance.

Alex's eyes followed her as she stormed back and forth across the clearing. The sway of her silky hair, the gentle curve of her cheeks and chin, her delicate nose, her eyes the color of the Caribbean sea, and her moist lips in constant motion as she expounded on the day's events. He swallowed. How lovely she was—this backwoods, rustic farm girl.

He longed to pull her into his arms.

What the deuces was wrong with him?

"And I miss my mother and father more than I can say," she continued, her eyes misting again.

Alex wondered if he should inquire. Would she only hate him more for asking? She ceased her pacing and dropped beside him. Taking the cloth from his hand, she dabbed it over his wound again. "It's just a scratch. You'll live."

"Again you tend to my wounds, Miss McGuire. This could become a habit." He smiled, hoping to lighten her mood, but his words only deepened her frown.

He drew himself up onto a fallen log and pulled her up beside him, glad when she didn't resist him.

Perhaps it had only been thoughts of her mother and father that had prompted the tears he thought were for him. Yet her tenderness toward her parents created an ache in his own heart. Alex had been nothing but a disappointment to his father—to his entire family. But never had they expressed such affection for him or for one another in life as this woman had for her parents in death.

Seconds passed in silence as the warble of birds faded with the encroaching night.

"May I ask what happened to your parents?" He caressed her hand, warm and soft.

She swallowed. Slipping her hand from his, she glanced toward the creek frolicking over rocks and pebbles and sending creamy foam onto the banks. A gust of rain-spiced wind toyed with her golden curls. "My father obtained a commission aboard one of our naval ships, the USS *Chesapeake*. Perhaps you've heard of it?"

Alex flinched as if he'd been struck. The USS *Chesapeake*? He stared down at the mud at his feet. Thunder announced his doom. He felt as though a thousand needles stabbed his heart. "Yes." He didn't want to hear anymore. He knew exactly what she would say.

"Your HMS *Leopard* fired upon her when Captain Barron refused to allow a boarding party to search for British deserters." Though her voice wobbled, it retained the sting of anger.

Alex nodded and lowered her handkerchief. He stared at his own blood staining the white cloth and suddenly felt as though he deserved the wound and so much more.

"Three men were killed that day. Eighteen wounded. One of them my father."

Hope taunted him for a moment. Wounded only? Perhaps he had not been killed by the British after all.

"He died at the Marine Hospital at Washington Point," she continued, crushing his hopes. A few raindrops splattered on the nearby leaves, mimicking the tear that spilled from her lashes. "At least four thousand citizens stood along both sides of Market Square while his coffin was carried in a long procession. Artillery fired minute guns from onshore, and all the American vessels in the harbor displayed their colors at half mast." She sniffed and ran the back of her hand over her moist face.

Alex clasped his hands together if only to keep from holding her as he longed to do. "He must have been quite a gallant officer and well loved." He could think of nothing else to say.

Her jaw tightened. Another tear slid down her cheek. "He was but a simple boatswain, not an officer. But he was well loved. And we were not at war, Mr. Reed. The *Chesapeake* was unprepared to defend herself. Her guns were not primed for action. Why would they be?" She stood and stepped away, as if being close to him disgusted her.

Alex struggled to his feet and moved behind her, longing to take away her pain.

Lightning flashed, glinting everything in gray.

"My mother died a week later of a broken heart." Her voice cracked as she hugged herself. "And I became an orphan at age fifteen."

Alex's heart sank to the dirt. No wonder she hated the British. No wonder she hated him. He placed a hand on her shoulder, but she moved from beneath it.

"Your British navy stole everything from me."

Alex swallowed. "My association causes me great shame."

"You do not know all that I have been through."

Heavy rain drops tapped like war drums on the leaves overhead.

"No, I do not." Alex sighed. "But I will listen if you wish to tell me."

At the sound of sincerity in Mr. Reed's voice, Rose turned around. Hazel eyes, as deep and fathomless as the sea he sailed upon, gazed back at her with concern. And something else. . .an affection that sent her heart fluttering. She would prefer hatred, animosity, even excuses. Those she knew how to react to, what to say. But not this.

"You were fifteen." He shoved a wayward strand of his hair behind his ear. "Yet your aunt said you've only been here five years."

The care pouring from his eyes wrapped around her wounded heart and lured her to tell him her sad tale. She tore her gaze away. "Why do you wish to know?"

He rubbed his stubbled jaw and his gaze softened. "Because I care."

Rose narrowed her eyes. The *rap, rap* of rain on the canopy filled the air like steady musket fire. Water misted over her, and she collected her hair over her shoulder. *He cared, indeed.* She would not believe him— could not believe him. She took a step back and lowered her gaze. "If it helps appease your guilt, it was not your countrymen who. . ." Her throat closed. "Who caused me further pain."

His warm finger touched her chin, bringing her gaze back up to his. "My guilt is not the issue here. I only wish to ease the pain I see in your eyes."

Thunder bellowed and Rose turned her back to him and moved farther away—away from his touch that sent an odd tremble through her, not a fearful one, but one that felt like a thousand fireflies swirling in her stomach. "A dear friend of my father's took me in after my parents died. I didn't know of my aunt's and uncle's existence at the time because of their estrangement from the family."

She heard the crunch of pine needles behind her as he moved closer. She gazed at the creek, the sturdy brown tree trunks, the leaves swaying in the wind. Anything to tether her to reality and keep her from spilling her heart to this man. Yet her words poured from her mouth as unstoppable as the water dashing in the brook.

"What I thought was concern for me and love for my father was merely an interest in the fortune left to me by my parents." Out of the corner of her eye, she saw Mr. Reed slip beside her.

"He made me a servant in his home, treated me with indifference and cruelty. All the while he proceeded to spend my inheritance as if it were his own." She glanced at Mr. Reed, but his expression remained stoic as he gazed at the creek.

"Nearly two years later, I was cleaning the desk in his study and came across a letter my mother had written on her deathbed explaining the existence of my aunt and uncle in Baltimore and asking him to ensure that I was placed in their care."

Mr. Reed's jaw bunched.

"I took what was left of my inheritance and ran away. I procured passage on a merchant vessel traveling to Baltimore."

"Alone?" Even now, fear sparked in his eyes.

"I had no choice, Mr. Reed." She would not tell him what happened on that fateful voyage. She could not.

Stooping, she picked up a stick and fingered its rough bark. Her resolve threatened to break beneath the memories filling her mind, but she shoved them back behind the thick door of forbidden thoughts.

Mr. Reed approached, anguish twisting his handsome features. Rain slid down his face. His wet shirt clung to his firm torso, accentuating his muscles beneath. Rose blinked the water from her lashes, realizing for the first time that she was alone with a man in the forest. Where no one would hear her scream. Yet, she found not an ounce of fear within her. Instead, the strangest feeling came over her. She felt safe. Completely and utterly safe. As if nothing could happen to her as long as she was with him. She'd never felt that way before, at least not since she'd been a little girl. The sensation made her giddy and sad at the same time.

He halted before her, peering down at her with such sorrow and longing that Rose nearly melted into him. She wanted him to hold her, wanted him to touch her.

He reached for her and tried to pull her close.

But she couldn't allow that. He was British. He was leaving. It might be already too late for her heart, but she would not endanger herself further. Jerking from his grasp, Rose backed away. "Forgive me, Mr. Reed. I shouldn't have disclosed such personal details."

"No apologies necessary, Miss McGuire." His brow wrinkled. "I'm glad you trusted me with the tale."

"What does it matter?" Rose waved a hand through the air and forced a lighter tone into her voice. "You will be gone soon. Killing more of my countrymen."

"I'm truly sorry our countries are at war."

Lightning flashed. Rain dripped from the tips of his dark hair onto his collar. He shifted his boots in the puddles forming at their feet and cocked his head. Then lifting his hand, he stroked her cheek with his thumb.

Warmth sped through Rose. Her heart thumped against her ribs, and she leaned into his hand. Just for a second. For one glorious second. That was all she would allow herself.

Before she stepped back and forced indifference into her tone. "Leave me be, Mr. Reed. Return to the house."

Disappointment flashed in his eyes. He fisted his hands at his waist and scanned the foliage. "I cannot allow you to wander about without protection. It is too dangerous."

Anger rolled all sentiments away. "I am not a crew member aboard your ship, Mr. Reed, that you can order me about."

He crossed his arms over his chest. "Go then, ride wherever you wish. But I will follow you."

Thunder boomed above them.

"I will simply wait until you fall again." Rose smirked. "Only this time I will not return."

He leaned toward her, a sultry smile on his lips. "Why *did* you come back?"

"I see now it was a mistake." Rose started to leave.

Mr. Reed gripped her arm and turned her to face him. "Your uncle grants you too much liberty."

"We are in America, sir, where freedom is a way of life. Something I wouldn't expect you British to understand."

Mr. Reed smiled. "You have dirt on your face."

Rose grimaced and ran the back of her hand over her cheek. Reaching down, she grabbed a clump of mud and eyed him with mischief, fingering its cool grainy texture. Then before he could grab her hand, she rubbed it on his jaw. "So do you." She grinned.

A look of incredulity overtook his stiff features, as if he couldn't fathom that she would do such a thing. He wiped the dirt and gazed at it as it slid between his fingers. Then one imperious brow lifted, and he spread the mud on her other cheek. "You seem to enjoy it more than I." He grinned.

Rose's blood boiled. Stooping, she gathered a larger blob, then tossed it at him. It splattered over his white shirt. "It suits you as well."

He chuckled and caught the mud before it fell from his shirt. He held it up as if he would throw it at her.

"You wouldn't dare!" Rose backed away.

"Wouldn't I?" And for the first time, a mischievous glint took residence in his otherwise austere eyes.

Rose chuckled and Mr. Reed joined her.

As their laughter faded, the sound of a gun cocking sped through the clearing. Mr. Reed froze and shot a worried gaze her way. Before Rose could react, he dropped the mud, clutched her arm, and dove into a bush.

❖ CHAPTER 14 ❖

Rose curled up against Mr. Reed's firm chest and tried to still her rapid breathing. He reached for his hip as if searching for a sword. But when his hand came up empty, he swallowed her up in his thick arms and motioned her to silence. Leaves tickled her face and a branch jabbed her side, but she remained still. A twig snapped, and the sound of a footfall echoed their doom through the forest. A trapper? But Rose had never come across any trappers this close to town. It had to be a British raiding party. And if one of them recognized Mr. Reed, they would assume he'd deserted his ship and haul him away for trial—or whatever they did in the British navy.

She didn't want to consider what they might do to her.

Rain splattered over the leaves, the soft sound blending in with the increased sound of footfalls heading their way.

A tremble coursed through her. Mr. Reed tightened his embrace. The strength and assurance in his arms eased across her nerves. Their breath intermingled as he pressed her head gently against his chest and held it there, stroking her wet hair.

Rose had not allowed any other man to touch her in years. My word, why did she feel so safe in the arms of this British officer—even in the midst of danger? The scent of wet linen and Mr. Reed filled her nostrils and eased into her lungs like a soothing elixir. She wished more than anything that the world would disappear around them and she could stay in his embrace forever.

But that was not to be.

Another twig snapped, and a pair of brown buckled shoes halted before the bush they hid behind.

Thunder shook the sky. The horses neighed.

The dark gaping eye of a musket plunged through the leaves toward them, pushing aside branches. Rose stiffened.

"Whoever is in there, I demand you toss your weapons on the ground and come out!"

Rose jerked. She'd know that voice anywhere. "Mr. Snyder?" She tried to free herself from Mr. Reed's grasp, but his arms refused to release her.

The musket pushed in farther, spreading the foliage apart until Rose gazed up into the angular face of the councilman. The fear braiding his features fell into a confused frown.

"Egad, what mischief is this?" he barked, his eyes flashing.

Mr. Reed released her, and Rose scrambled to her feet. Swatting leaves and branches aside, she made her way out of the bush. Mr. Reed crawled out behind her and unfolded to his normal towering height.

"No mischief, I assure you, Mr. Snyder." Rose glanced down at her muddy dress and tried to brush off the dirt but only succeeded in smearing it over the blue fabric. With a huff, she lifted her gaze to his.

The muscles in his cheeks bunched and released. His slit-like eyes swept from her to Mr. Reed. He raised his musket toward Alex. "Explain yourself, sir, or I shall be forced to shoot you where you stand."

Mr. Reed's right brow lifted as a smirk played upon his mouth.

"Mr. Snyder." Rose approached him, more angry than frightened. Angry that this buffoon had given them such a scare. Angry most of all that he had interrupted her time with Mr. Reed. "It is not as it appears. What—"

"What it appears, Miss McGuire, would be too scandalous to voice." He gestured with his musket toward Mr. Reed. "Did this man accost you? If so, I'll deal with him here and now."

Rose lifted a hand to her forehead where a headache formed. She gazed up at the canopy. Between the treetops, white lightning flashed across a gray sky. A drop of rain struck her eye, and she blinked.

Mr. Reed folded his arms over his chest as if there were no musket pointed at his heart. Rose stepped toward Mr. Snyder. She must force him to lower the gun trembling in his grip. Just the sight of the vile weapon sent a chill through her. "I assure you, Mr. Snyder, Mr. Reed has done me no harm. We heard your gun cock and thought perhaps the British were afoot given the recent alarms." She raised a quivering hand to the barrel of the musket. Cold, slick steel sent an icy shard through her fingers and up her arm. She forced the weapon down, snapping back her hand as soon as it was lowered. "So, you see, the situation is completely innocent."

Mr. Snyder's lips drew into a tight line. Rain dropped from the trees above and splashed onto his cocked hat before trickling off the sides. "What were you doing out here in the first place alone with this man?"

A tight band stretched across Rose's shoulders at the man's impertinent questions. "He is my servant, sir. In truth, he followed me to ensure my safety."

Mr. Snyder laid the musket across his arms and shifted his stance. "Yet who is to protect you from him?"

Mr. Reed finally spoke, his voice deep and confident. "I would never harm Miss McGuire, and I resent the implication, sir."

"Do you?" Mr. Snyder snapped. "We shall see about that." He faced Rose, his blue eyes stark against the shadows of the forest. "By the by, your aunt and uncle may have a different opinion when they hear of this."

Rose longed to kick mud on the man's pristine trousers, but instead she merely released a sigh.

His face softened. "Are you all right, Miss McGuire? Did he harm you?" He scanned her from head to toe as if he only now noticed her condition. "Scads, you are covered in mud."

Rose clenched her jaw. "Whatever are you doing out here in the woods, Mr. Snyder?"

The rain ceased and a low rumble of thunder bade farewell from the distance.

"Your aunt invited me to dine with you this evening." Eyeing Mr. Reed, My Snyder tossed back his shoulders and stretched out his neck as if he was trying to make himself appear as tall as the British officer.

"And?" Rose planted one hand on her hip.

"When I inquired after you, your lady's maid informed me that she saw you gallop into the forest." He tipped his head toward Mr. Reed. "With this man chasing you."

Rose shook out her gown and swiped wet strands of hair from her forehead. "Well as you can see, I'm perfectly safe."

"Rubbish. You are drenched in rain and have mud from the hair on your head to the hem of your gown. Hardly proper behavior for a lady." He clucked his tongue, then scratched the auburn whiskers lining his jaw.

Mr. Reed cleared his throat. "And sneaking about the forest, pointing muskets at unsuspecting ladies, is hardly proper behavior for a gentleman, sir."

Mr. Snyder's brow darkened. "Rather insolent for a mere servant, Mr. Reed. I'd hold my tongue if I were you." He thrust the barrel end of the musket into the mud as if it were his cane. "Now, make yourself useful and fetch my horse."

Mr. Reed shook the water from his hair, then raked it with his hand. His saturated shirt revealed every knot of muscle, each one tightening by the second. Despite her own wet gown, Rose warmed from head to toe at the sight.

"If I may make a suggestion, Mr. Snyder." Mr. Reed addressed the councilman with the tone of one addressing an inferior. "The next time you take it upon yourself to thrust a musket into a bush, make sure its occupants are unarmed. Only a fool exposes himself to an enemy without knowledge of what weapons he possesses. Upon my honor, I could have shot you where you stood before you knew what hit you." He smiled. "Before I knew it was you, that is."

Mr. Snyder's lips curled in a sneer. "Retrieve my horse at once."

Mr. Reed glanced toward Rose, and she reluctantly nodded. Better to appease the man rather than increase his suspicion.

With a huff, Mr. Reed passed Mr. Snyder, bumping his shoulder. "Forgive me, sir." His voice brimmed with sarcasm.

Hatred burned in Mr. Snyder's eyes. "His insolence is not to be borne," he said to Rose. "He should be dismissed immediately."

"Yet that is not your call to make." Rose hugged herself against a sudden chill.

Leaning his musket against a tree, the councilman shrugged out of his overcoat and flung it over her shoulders. "You are nearly soaked through, Miss McGuire."

Not wishing to accept the man's garment, but not wanting to anger him further, she drew it around her. "How kind of you." Though the rain had ceased, water still fell from the leaves all around them, echoing drip-drops through the darkening shadows.

Mr. Snyder leaned toward her. "Forgive my outburst, miss, but I am only concerned for you."

She gave him a tight smile in reply as Mr. Reed tossed the reins of Mr. Snyder's chestnut gelding to him before proceeding across the muddy clearing to retrieve Valor and Douglas. Unable to resist, Rose gazed after him, studying his strong jaw, peppered with evening stubble, his deep eyes, and confident gait. A longing gripped her to be alone with him again, to feel the safety of his arms around her.

After assisting Rose onto her horse, and mounting his own, Mr. Snyder rode by her side. When they arrived at the house, Mr. Reed led all three horses to the barn while Mr. Snyder, taking Rose's arm with one hand and his cane in the other, ushered her toward the front door, babbling on about city politics, and offending her nose with his moldy bergamot scent. Her nerves tightened at his touch, creating a whirlwind of confusion in her mind. How could she feel so safe in the arms of a British navy officer and so troubled upon the arm of an American councilman? She glanced over her shoulder, hoping for one last look at Mr. Reed.

But he had already disappeared into the barn.

Something had happened between them that afternoon in the forest. A wall had been broken down—dare she even say, an affection had sprouted? But what was she thinking? She faced forward and silently chastised herself as Mr. Snyder opened the door. Mr. Reed had promised that he would leave soon, and he was too honorable a man to break that promise.

Alex circled the table and poured persimmon beer into the pewter mugs of each seated guest. First Mr. and Mrs. Drummond, then Amelia, who never failed to give him a coquettish smile, and now the lovely Miss McGuire. He moved behind her chair, hoping for a glance into those turquoise eyes. Not a speck of dirt marred her lovely complexion or the creamy white gown trimmed in pink ribbon she'd donned for supper. The lace bordering her neckline rose and fell with her heightened breath. Did his presence invoke the reaction? Or was she merely nervous that Mr. Snyder would find him out?

The sad story she had told him of her parents' deaths and the family friend who had stolen her wealth fired through his mind like grapeshot, igniting his fury. How could anyone have abused the trust of a young girl who had so recently lost her parents? And what tragedy had befallen her on her trip to Baltimore? Though Alex could guess, he hoped with everything in him that he was wrong. Regardless, his heart soared that Rose had entrusted him with such intimacies.

Alex had loved only one woman in his life—a woman who was now his brother's wife. A woman whom he'd thought returned his love. But he had been terribly mistaken—brought on by his foolish emotions. Perhaps he was equally in error now. Yet the moments he and Miss McGuire—Rose—had shared in the forest, as the rain misted down upon them, caused his heart to swell as it never had before. He could still feel her quivering body against his, the way she molded into him as if they were made for each other, and the way her trembling ceased when she leaned against his chest. Alex shook his head. What the deuces was he thinking? He could never entertain thoughts of such a connection. He and Miss McGuire were worlds apart. Enemies. He poured her drink and avoided looking at her further.

Making his way around the edge of the table to Mr. Snyder, Alex gazed out the open window where a cool breeze ruffled the calico curtains. The rain had ceased, and stars blinked against a coal black sky.

He wove around the table, silently cursing himself for allowing his feelings for Miss McGuire to rise and for staying among these rebels as long as he had. Pure foolishness. For the longer he stayed, the harder it was for him to go.

He tipped the decanter of beer over Mr. Snyder's mug—smiling at the devious idea that struck him—and filled it to the brim.

The councilman turned from something he was saying and stared at the glass. "You daft loon, how am I expected to sip this without spilling it?"

"My apologies." Alex bowed slightly and gave Miss McGuire a coy glance. Finally she met his gaze. A smile danced across her eyes.

Mr. Snyder gave a frustrated sigh as Alex made his way to the kitchen to help Cora carry in the platters of food. As soon as he entered the bright room, smells of turkey, pastry, and warm bread enveloped him, prompting a growl from his belly and making him wonder why he never remembered such comforting scents in the Cranleigh estate back home.

"Well, it be about time." Cora huffed his way. "This food's gettin' cold."

Alex grabbed the first platter that held two large meat pies, amazed that even the cantankerous cook warmed his heart. "You are ever a delight, Miss Cora." He winked.

With a shake of her head, she flattened her lips, but then she smiled and batted the air with a cloth before dropping it onto the table. "Now, you go on, Mr. Reed. Your charm don't work on this old gal." Picking up a platter of biscuits in one hand and a bowl of fried greens in the other, she followed him into the dining room where they placed the food in the center of the table. Cora left while Alex stood against the wall as he'd seen the footmen do in his father's estate during meals. He chose the wall opposite Miss McGuire, which afforded him a clear view of her.

"Shall we ask God's blessing on this glorious feast?" Mr. Drummond said.

Glorious feast? Alex shook his head. Surely his father would not think so of the meager meal.

"We thank You, Father, for the abundance You have provided and for Your continued protection over us during such tremulous times. May Your will be done on earth as it is in heaven. Amen"

"Amens" sounded around the table, and Alex was once again struck with not only the simplicity and genuineness of the prayer but with the way Mr. Drummond addressed Almighty God as Father.

Mrs. Drummond passed the plate of biscuits to Miss McGuire. "Dear, Mr. Snyder brought us a pound of sugar today. He knows how you enjoy it in your tea."

Miss McGuire nodded toward the councilman, but her smile faltered on her lips. "You are too kind, sir."

"Anything for you, Miss McGuire." His gaze remained overlong upon her before he rubbed his hands together. "As I was saying, General Smith was all up in arms this afternoon at the fort."

"Indeed. Whatever for?" Mrs. Drummond asked. "We saw him earlier and he seemed only concerned with finding British spies and, of course, with the Myers' tragedy."

A look of sorrow passed between Rose and her aunt.

Alex swallowed.

"Indeed, I hadn't heard." Mr. Snyder addressed Rose. "What happened?"

Rose shook her head. "I do not wish to discuss it."

With a shrug, Mr. Snyder resumed his tale. "It appeared the entire British fleet was heading for Baltimore!" He grabbed a biscuit from a passing plate. "That's twice now those loathsome British have turned their ships toward our harbor only to retreat when they've sufficiently terrorized the town."

"What do you make of it, Mr. Reed?" Mr. Drummond asked, his voice carrying an odd hint of amusement.

Shocked at being addressed during the meal, Mr. Reed shook his head. "Me? What would I know of it?"

A breeze swirled about the table, sending the candle flames flickering. Amelia dropped her fork onto her plate with a clank.

"Forgive my impertinence, Mr. Drummond, but why do you address a servant during supper?" Mr. Snyder glanced around the table for affirmation. "Highly irregular."

"Because, my dear fellow, out of all of us present, only Mr. Reed has actually fought in this war." Mr. Drummond's voice held more frustration than Alex expected from the kind man.

Rose coughed and grabbed her throat.

Mrs. Drummond studied Alex. "What happened to your head, Mr. Reed?"

Alex reached up and touched the small cut on his forehead. "I fell from a horse, madam. It is nothing."

Amelia giggled and Mrs. Drummond resumed her eating.

Mr. Drummond took a huge helping of meat pie. "Do regale us with your opinion, Mr. Reed."

Alex cleared his throat, then looked to Rose for permission. She nodded and he finally said, "In truth, I suspect the British fleet enjoys toying with your city, sir. They wish to test your response and keep you wondering when the next attack will be. Their hope is that you will ignore them when the real one comes."

Mr. Snyder chuckled. "Foolishness, Mr. Reed. You are a soldier, not a sailor. What would you know of the mindset of the British fleet?" He shoved a spoonful of turkey pie into his mouth.

Amelia shared a smile with Rose.

Mr. Drummond chomped on a biscuit, sending crumbs flying. "Makes perfect sense to me. I just wonder what they are waiting for. They've already burned Georgetown, Fredericktown, and Frenchtown and attacked Norfolk and several other cities along the Chesapeake."

Mrs. Drummond shook her head, her ruby earrings glimmering in the candlelight. "And now that dastardly Napoleon has been defeated, we shall have to contend with the entire British imperial sea force."

"As you know, I, for one, am against this war." Mr. Snyder thrust out his chin. "How can we expect to win against such overwhelming odds? Why, to continue fighting is nothing but a reckless and wanton hazard of life and property."

"Would you have us bow down like lame puppies and hand over our freedoms?" Mr. Drummond's ruddy face darkened.

Mr. Snyder flinched. His right hand twitched slightly as he sliced his biscuit. "I don't see that we have a choice."

"Some things are worth dying for, Mr. Snyder." Rose sipped her drink and offered him a tight smile.

He raised his shoulders. "Our Canadian campaign has been disastrous, and we have lost several ships to the Royal Navy, the USS *Chesapeake*, the frigate *Essex*, the *Wasp*, the *Vixen*." He sighed and took a bite of his biscuit.

Rose gripped the handle of her fork until her knuckles whitened. "But you neglect to mention the victories we've had at sea, sir. The USS *United States'* defeat of HMS *Macedonian*, the capture of HMS *Frolic* and *Penguin*, the sinking of HMS *Peacock* and *Reindeer*. Not to mention the many victories of our privateers."

"And the *Constitution's* defeat of *Guerriere,*" Alex chimed in as the memories of witnessing that battle from his impotent ship tumbled through him. Oddly, with no accompanying resentment.

Mr. Snyder batted a lace-covered hand over his shoulder toward Mr. Reed as if dismissing the comment as frivolous.

Mr. Drummond's gray brows rose. "Indeed, Mr. Reed." He lowered his gaze to Mr. Snyder. "Sir, I perceive you to be outnumbered in your antiwar sentiments in this house."

Mrs. Drummond laid a hand on her husband's arm. "Do not be so hard on Mr. Snyder, dearest. It is a noble quality to be so concerned for the loss of life."

Mr. Snyder smiled in her direction, but his shoulders lowered nonetheless. "Thank you, madam. That is my only concern. I am a patriot at heart. Besides, since the blockade, not many of our privateers have been successful."

"I beg to differ with you, sir." Rose lowered her spoon, ignoring her aunt's pointed gaze. "I am friends with several privateers, and they still do quite well harassing British shipping. They bring their prizes to dock in New York or Virginia, sell them there, then travel overland back to Baltimore." Suddenly her eyes widened, and she snapped her gaze to Alex as if she just realized she had divulged a grand secret that he could well take back to his British commanders.

Though the British navy was well aware of the practice of Baltimore privateers, Alex gave her a teasing smile nonetheless.

She pursed her lips and exchanged a nervous glance with Amelia before directing her gaze back to him.

Mr. Drummond took a sip of his beer, shifting his glance between them. A drop slid into his thick beard.

"Why do you keep staring at your servant, Miss McGuire?" Mr. Snyder shifted his gaze between them. Nothing but malicious suspicion exuded from the man. But Alex ignored him. The councilman was a gnat. What harm could he do? Yet when he glanced at Miss McGuire, he could see the fear in her eyes.

Rose gave a slight shake of her head toward Mr. Reed in the hopes of dissuading him from further goading Mr. Snyder. The councilman was a prig, but he also was not without power. And with the right information, the power to ruin them all. Oh why did her aunt continue to invite the man to dinner? Couldn't she see how Rose despised him?

Mr. Snyder dabbed the napkin over his mouth and proceeded to regale them with details of the city council's recent decisions regarding funding and new buildings and preparations for war.

As he babbled on, Mr. Snyder grabbed his glass and drew it in haste to his lips. Beer spilled over the sides and splattered onto his trousers.

Curses shot from his mouth as he leaped to his feet. "This is your doing, Mr. Reed!"

"Your language, sir." Mr. Drummond reprimanded the man as he wiped crumbs from his shirt.

Amelia giggled, but Aunt Muira quieted her with a stern look and excused herself to the kitchen. Covering her smile, Rose pretended to gasp in horror while Mr. Reed dabbed an extra napkin over Mr. Snyder's trousers. "No doubt you forgot your full glass, sir."

Mr. Snyder swatted Mr. Reed's hand away just as Aunt Muira returned and handed him a dry cloth. "Please accept our apologies, Mr. Snyder." She glared at Mr. Reed who gave her an apologetic look before backing up against the wall.

When Mr. Snyder had calmed himself, the group resumed their meal, but Rose found her appetite had fled into the night. She didn't know whether to laugh or cry. Amelia must have sensed Rose's discomfiture for she clutched her hand beneath the table. Rose returned her maid's comforting grasp. She could no longer deny that Mr. Reed's presence had a stimulating effect upon her or that her heart would be in danger should he tarry among them. Though she tried to keep her eyes off of him, they wandered unbidden his way nonetheless . . .over his black coat, white cravat, and slick dark hair pulled tight behind him. She remembered the way wet strands had dangled over his cheek in the forest, rain dripping from their tips. Now, he stood against the wall as regal as any nobleman. Perhaps he was a nobleman. The son of a baron or an earl. Suddenly, she longed to know more about him—everything about him. Doubt budded within her as she wondered what he could possibly find appealing about her and her common family.

Still clutching Rose's hand, Amelia lifted a spoonful of greens to her mouth. "We met Mr. Brenin and Mr. Heaton in town today."

"Indeed?" Relief filled Aunt Muira's voice, no doubt at the change in topic. "And Mr. Brenin's dear wife, I assume?"

"Yes and Miss Cassandra as well, along with Mr. Brenin's first mate and his son, an adorable young lad."

"Daniel, I believe his name is." Rose's uncle helped himself to more turkey pie. "A fitting name for him."

Amelia nodded. "You are right, Mr. Drummond, for the boy

uttered a prophecy over Rose."

Rose squeezed her hand, urging Amelia with a look to speak no more if it. The boy's words, though spoken with sincerity, were but silly notions of an adventurous mind, and Rose didn't want to arm her uncle with any further ammunition to prompt her to do something she was not yet ready to do.

Mr. Snyder dabbed honey over his biscuit. "That Mr. Heaton is quite the rogue, I hear. Untrustworthy sot."

Rose's uncle gave Mr. Snyder a quizzical look before turning to Amelia. "Pray tell, what did Daniel say?"

"He said that God had something important for Rose to do."

Rose huffed and glanced at Mr. Reed. His hazel eyes twinkled playfully in the candlelight.

"You don't say?" Rose's aunt sipped her drink.

"Very interesting. Interesting indeed." Uncle Forbes seemed deep in thought.

"The ravings of a childish mind." Mr. Snyder sipped his beer—more carefully this time.

Rose held her churning stomach.

Uncle Forbes tossed his napkin onto the table and leaned back in his chair. "I have no doubt that my niece is destined for something great."

Emotion burned in Rose's throat at her uncle's compliment. She smiled at him then turned away before anyone saw her eyes moisten.

After dinner, Rose's aunt and uncle bade her to join them in the parlor for tea with Mr. Snyder, though she tried to beg off with an excuse of a headache. Must she endure more time with the annoying man? And without Mr. Reed present, there was nothing at all to interest her. Even Amelia stole away, offering Rose a look of sympathy over her shoulder.

She sipped her tea and glanced out the parlor windows where the open shutters gave her a view of the trees in the distance standing like prickly dark sentinels guarding the farm. Yet they hadn't guarded her against Garrick's attack. Mr. Reed had done that. Risked his career to save her. After supper, Uncle Forbes had dismissed Mr. Reed from further duties. Now that he could walk without a crutch, there was nothing to keep him here. Would he leave without saying good-bye?

An emptiness gnawed at her belly. She had wanted to give him his uniform and weapons and take out his stitches before he traveled so far. But perhaps the surgeon on board his ship would do a better job. If Mr. Reed's captain believed his story. *Lord, please let him believe him.* Everything within her longed to dash outside and bid Mr. Reed goodbye, wish him Godspeed, and feel his arms around her one more time.

But it was better this way.

Mr. Snyder stood by the fireplace, one arm draped across the mantel, wondering how to bring up the sensitive topic of Mr. Reed with Miss McGuire's family. He decided on the direct approach. "Mr. Drummond," he addressed Rose's uncle who sat beside his wife on the sofa. "Now that your servant has left the room, I feel it is my obligation to inform you that I found him and your niece frolicking about in the woods, covered in mud and in a rather"—he cleared his throat—"provocative embrace."

Mrs. Drummond gasped and fingered a coil of her red hair. "Good heavens, Rose. Is this true, dear?"

Oddly, the statement brought a smile to Mr. Drummond's lips.

Rose pursed her lips, her cheeks growing red. "Not entirely, Aunt. For one thing, we were not frolicking"—she skewered Snyder with a pointed gaze—"and we were only covered in mud and huddling together in a bush because we feared Mr. Snyder was part of a British raiding party."

Her uncle chuckled and folded his hands over his portly belly.

"As I told you before, Mr. Snyder," Rose said. "My close proximity to Mr. Reed was, in short, due to your intrusion upon our afternoon ride."

Snyder stomped his shoe on the hearth and huffed. He certainly hadn't expected his accusation to sit well with the lady, but he hoped she would see the necessity of bringing the event to her family's attention in light of their future together. Couldn't she see that he was only concerned with her safety and her reputation? *Ungrateful girl.*

"There you are, Mr. Snyder." Mr. Drummond pressed down a patch of gray hair that had spiraled out of control atop his head. "Surely that explains things to your satisfaction. I assure you, our Rose is a lady of utmost propriety."

Snyder bit his lip. This was not going as planned. He had expected Rose's uncle to scold her vehemently and to forbid her to spend time alone with Mr. Reed without her maid present. But the old man remained his usual imbecilic self. "It was not my intention to indicate otherwise."

Rose stood and meandered toward the window.

Mrs. Drummond fingered the rubies hanging from her ears. "Of course not, Mr. Snyder. I thank you for looking out for our dear Rose."

Mr. Snyder gave the lady a nod of appreciation. At least someone in this house saw reason. He skirted the high-backed chair and lowered himself onto its soft cushion. Dabbing his fingers on his tongue, he pressed back the hair at his temples and leaned toward Mr. Drummond. "Surely, sir, you agree that this sort of behavior is most unseemly, regardless of the cause."

"I do." Mr. Drummond scratched his beard. "But it appears no harm came of it." A serene peace that Snyder had always taken as ignorance blossomed in the old man's brown eyes. Snyder squirmed on his seat and glanced at Rose who still stared out the window. Starlight shimmered over her, setting her hair aglow as a breeze ruffled the loose strands dangling at her neck. He swallowed down a lump of desire. Why did she shun his every advance while at the same time granting favor to a servant? He had not missed the amorous glances she lavished upon Mr. Reed during supper, nor that the infuriating man had returned them. What did the obnoxious servant possess that he did not? His heart shrank. Wasn't it enough that he lived with the shame of his family's sordid past? Did he now have to endure the rejection of a woman who preferred the company of a common servant over his?

"Forgive my impertinence, Mr. Drummond." Snyder attempted a different approach. "But perhaps if you hired another servant? Mr. Reed seems a bit. . .how shall I say"—*insidious, insolent, and far too handsome*—"unsuitable to be placed in charge of Miss McGuire."

Mr. Drummond's lips slanted. "I fear you overstep your bounds, sir." His stern tone turned Rose around and brought a smile to her lips.

Mrs. Drummond set down her tea and laid a hand on her husband's knee. "Oh Forbes, dearest, I find Mr. Snyder's concern admirable, don't you, Rose?"

But the look on Miss McGuire's face exuded anything but admiration. In fact, it bordered on disgust.

Snyder lowered his chin, his gut constricting. He would not allow this toad, this mere servant, to steal the woman he planned to marry.

Mr. Drummond glanced down at a brown stain on his waistcoat as if he had no idea how it had gotten there. "Nevertheless, Mr. Snyder, you may rest assured that our Rose is in no danger with Mr. Reed. Besides, his stay here is only temporary. You have nothing to fear from him."

"Fear, sir?" Snyder gave a hearty chuckle that sounded more spurious than he intended. "I do not fear the man. My thoughts are toward Rose's safety and reputation."

"I assure you, there is no need." Kindness returned to Mr. Drummond's tone. "It is Mr. Reed's job to protect Rose, particularly on days when we cannot be home."

"Ah yes." Mrs. Drummond took a cloth and lifted the teapot. "I fear I am not here as much as I'd like. I'm often drawn away with my charities."

"Oh do say you'll be here tomorrow, Aunt Muira," Miss McGuire said.

"I'm afraid not, dear. I must go to Washington tomorrow." She moved the teapot over Snyder's cup.

Rejecting Mrs. Drummond's offer of tea, Snyder stood. "Which brings me to my point for accepting your kind invitation tonight. There is a ball at the Fountain Inn next week, and I would like your permission to escort Rose."

"Oh, how kind of you, Mr. Snyder." Mrs. Drummond nearly leaped from her seat. Thin lines crinkled at the corners of her green eyes. "Isn't it, Rose, dear?"

Miss McGuire's gaze skittered about the room. She clasped her hands together and stared at her uncle as if seeking assistance with the answer, but his gaze was riveted to the carpet.

"Forgive me, Mr. Snyder, I am not feeling well," she finally said. "Can we discuss this at another time?" Then clutching the folds of her gown, she dashed from the room and ran up the stairs, leaving Mr. Snyder stunned in her wake.

Containing his frustration, Mr. Snyder thanked the Drummonds for a lovely evening and then saw himself out. He barreled down the steps of the front porch, hoping the fresh evening air would cool his humors. It didn't. *Ill-mannered hoyden.* How dare she treat him with such disrespect? He stormed forward, muttering to himself, and nearly ran into Mr. Reed, who stood ready with his horse.

He snatched the reins from the invidious man. "I know what is going on here, Mr. Reed, and I won't stand for it."

The servant smiled. "You do say?"

"Your behavior toward Miss McGuire is most inappropriate."

Mr. Reed chuckled and tossed the hair from his face. *He chuckled!* "And yet, since you are neither her relation nor her suitor, Miss McGuire is none of your affair."

"Neither is she yours, sir. At least not beyond your duties."

"Indeed." Finally, a frown scattered the man's insolent grin.

"Mrs. Drummond approves of me," Snyder continued, taking advantage of the small victory. "She has informed me that she intends to encourage Rose to accept not only my courtship but my future proposal of marriage."

The servant raised a brow. "And Mr. Drummond. . . ?"

"I am close to winning his blessing as well." The gelding snorted as if even the horse knew Snyder lied.

"Then, I congratulate you, sir." Mr. Reed bowed slightly. "But shouldn't it be up to the lady?"

"Silly girls do not know their own minds." Snyder tossed the reins back to Mr. Reed. Pulling his leather gloves from the saddle pack, he began to tug them on his fingers. "Rose will see the sense of our match. I can give her a good name, the prestige of my office, and a decent living."

"How could any woman resist such an offer?" Mr. Reed's annoying grin returned.

Snyder gazed into the impudent servant's face, half in shadow, half lit by a lantern hanging from a nearby post. "Indeed." He spat through a clenched jaw.

Reed tilted his head. "And you, of course, will receive her land."

Snyder stiffened. He had underestimated this bumpkin. "Why shouldn't I desire this land? It is the last available parcel that borders the Jones Falls River. And with the proper placement of a flour mill, in a few years it will be worth a fortune."

The corners of Mr. Reed's mouth tightened, and he gazed into the night. "Perhaps the lady would prefer to be desired for herself rather than for her land."

Snyder tugged on his other glove. "I assure you there is no lack of affection for her on my part. But pretty ladies are in abundance in Baltimore."

"But not pretty ladies who will inherit land such as this." Mr. Reed winked at him.

Snyder eyed him. "I see we are of the same mind, Mr. Reed."

But the servant huffed in disdain. "I am nothing like you."

Mr. Snyder frowned, his ire rising. "I advise you to forsake your pursuit of her. You know I will win."

"I have my doubts."

Snyder snatched the reins again, longing to slap them across Mr. Reed's face. "Do not cross me, sir."

"Or what?" Again, that infuriating grin.

"I suspect there is more to that despicable British accent than you admit, Mr. Reed." Shoving his shoe into the stirrup, Snyder swung onto his horse and tugged the reins. The horse neighed and stomped his front hooves. "Whatever you are hiding, I will find out your secret, Mr. Reed. Mark my words."

❖ CHAPTER 15 ❖

Alex loosened his clenched fists at his side and watched until the darkness swallowed up the last trace of Mr. Snyder. Turning, he leaned against the fence post and gazed at the Drummond home. Through the parlor window he could see Mrs. Drummond sitting on the sofa beside her husband, his arm flung over her shoulders. They leaned their heads together in deep conversation, interrupted by bouts of joyful laughter. Alex had never seen his parents enjoy each other's company. He never thought such an intimate relationship was even possible. Mr. Drummond kissed his wife on the cheek then stood and assisted her to her feet. He grabbed the lantern and then, arm in arm, the couple left the parlor and headed upstairs. Alex shifted his gaze away. It landed on light spilling from a second-story window he knew to be Miss McGuire's bedchamber. Not the sort of man who spied into ladies' boudoirs, he was glad for the thick curtains, which forbade him an unintentional peek within. His eyes moved to the final wisps of smoke curling from the chimney above the kitchen where the light from a lantern faded. No doubt Miss Cora retired for the evening.

A lump formed in Alex's throat.

Home. This quaint, rustic farmhouse exemplified the meaning of the word. Home wasn't a large estate with cathedral ceilings and marble floors, where oil paintings of the masters, exquisite tapestries, and gold-gilded mirrors decorated the walls, where drafty halls extended outward like a maze, and opulently decorated rooms stood cold and empty. No, home was a place where people loved each other and shared their lives. It was something Alex had yearned for all his life and would probably never know, aside from these few glorious days.

Blast Mr. Snyder for trying to destroy this home. Alex's hot, angry breath mingled with the humid air swirling around him. He would have loved nothing better than to flatten the man where he stood, but that would only cause more trouble for this precious family.

As soon as Rose heard her aunt and uncle's chamber door click shut, she leaped from her bed, pressed out the folds of her gown and inched toward the door. No sounds save her aunt's and uncle's quiet murmurs filtered to her ears. Opening her door and cringing at the tiny squeak, she crept down the hallway and headed downstairs. In the foyer, she grabbed a pair of scissors, some bandages, and comfrey salve from her aunt's medical satchel, which sat atop a side table, before she exited the front door. Fresh air perfumed with wildflowers swirled around her as she clomped through the mud toward the barn. After briefly greeting Liverpool, Rose climbed the loft and retrieved Mr. Reed's torn uniform and sword from a trunk. The mere sight of his pistol made her chest tighten. Unable to touch the heinous weapon, she left it there and made her way around the other side of the house to the back of the stable. Prinney, whom she'd let loose from his pen earlier, waddled after her, grunting for her attention.

"I haven't time now, Prinney."

Mr. Reed opened the door to her knock and stared at her in utter shock. He had removed his overcoat and waistcoat, leaving only a tight linen shirt across his firmly lined chest. Prinney grunted and nudged her leg.

Rose swallowed and gazed past Mr. Reed into the gloomy room.
"Miss McGuire."

"Mr. Reed." She forced her chin forward. "I have come to remove your stitches before you leave." She pushed past him, ignoring the way the light breeze frolicked among the loose strands of his dark hair.

"Why, I...Hmm." He shoved a large rock in place to prop the door open.

His act of propriety at keeping the door ajar only endeared him to her more. Prinney ambled in after her as Rose took a deep breath of the humid air that smelled of mold, hay, and Mr. Reed. A cot holding a crumpled wool blanket guarded the right corner. His waistcoat, coat, and an extra shirt and pair of breeches left by Samuel hung on hooks lining the back wall. A cold potbellied stove perched in the left corner. On a table in the center of the room, sat a single lantern and a vase holding two pink roses. *Pink roses?* She stomped over the dirt floor toward his bed. Hay crunched beneath her slippers. "I am not without a heart, Mr. Reed." She tossed his uniform and service sword onto the blanket.

He hobbled toward her. "That is one fact that has not escaped my attention."

She dared a glance into his eyes and found only sincerity—and something else. . .ardor, affection perhaps—within them. She looked away, trying to conjure up anger, hatred, anything to douse the affection burning within her. "How dare you pick my roses?" She jerked her head toward the vase. "I didn't grow them for your enjoyment."

He blinked. "Indeed? Well I have enjoyed them anyway."

Rose narrowed her eyes.

He chuckled and held up a hand of truce. "In truth, I did not pick them. One of your beasties must have trodden your bush for I found these two flowers barely hanging on and about to fall to the ground." Moving to the table, he touched one of the petals and bent over, taking a whiff. "They do brighten the place, don't you agree?"

Rose shook her head as she watched Mr. Reed's thick, rough hands stroke the delicate petals. And the way he enjoyed the flower's sweet scent. It was the last thing she expected him to do—any man to do, let alone a British officer. She threw back her shoulders. "Please take a seat, Mr. Reed."

Prinney grunted in agreement and pressed his snout against Rose's leg.

Mr. Reed sank into the chair. "Am I to assume the pig is your protector?"

At his sarcastic tone, Rose tightened her lips. "This pig is Prinney, as you are well aware. And he has been a better friend to me than most people I know." She lowered her gaze to the bandages, scissors, and salve in her hands. "And if you misbehave, I do have my scissors, sir." She cocked a brow and put on her most formidable look, but it faltered when a giggle rose to her lips at the absurdity of her statement.

Mr. Reed joined her. "In that case, I shall comport myself as a perfect gentleman."

Rose gazed out the door into the darkness. He had never behaved otherwise. She must remember what his people had done to Elaine. She must avoid gazing into those caring hazel eyes. She must avoid pondering why her heart leaped at the sight of him instead of tightened as it did with most men. She kneeled by his feet. "I need to cut through your breeches."

"Cut through?"

"It is either that or have you remove them."

A red hue crept up his face, and for some reason, it brought a smile to Rose's lips to see that a man could blush so easily. Rose took the scissors and began to cut through the black linen. "You won't be needing them anymore."

Alex's heart sank at her words. In truth, he wasn't ready to go. He longed for a few more days' reprieve from the harsh British navy—a few more days feeling as though he belonged to a family. A few more days with this precious lady. He studied the way the lantern light made her hair shimmer like fine gold. Her delicate fingers worked so gently to cut the fabric of his breeches without disturbing his wound.

She finished slicing through his breeches, then moved the lantern closer to get a good look at his thigh. "What, no complaints, Mr. Reed? No excuses why you should impose upon my family's hospitality further?"

Alex longed for a glimpse into her lustrous eyes—eyes that could not hide her true feelings—but she kept her chin lowered.

He sighed. "No. I am a man of my word. I am well enough to leave. And leave I shall."

A visible shudder ran through her. Sniffing, she gazed into the empty space of the room.

A spot of dirt marred her graceful neck, bringing a smile to Alex's lips. "You were very brave yesterday at your friend's house." He didn't exactly know why she'd been so frightened, but he'd fought in enough battles to know courage when he saw it. Her tender care in light of what she must be feeling toward him—toward all British—caused his throat to clog with emotion. He wanted to tell her how sorry he was for what his fellow countrymen had done. But he couldn't find the right words. More than likely, she would not believe him anyway.

She chuckled. "Me, brave?" Shaking her head, she snipped one edge of the stitches. The scissor blade was cold against his thigh. She tugged at the thread and a slight twinge of pain made Alex wince. "You don't know me, Mr. Reed."

Alex rubbed the stubble on his jaw. "It pains me that I will not have the chance."

She gazed up at him, her eyes misty pools of turquoise. "You speak foolishness, Mr. Reed. Are all British filled with such inane flattery?"

Alex lifted an eyebrow.

Prinney snorted, then meandered over to sift through the hay by the door.

Miss McGuire tugged on the thread again, and Alex watched it slip though his flesh. Queasiness rolled across his gut.

Her cheeks glowed like sweet cream in the lantern light, and Alex longed to brush his fingers over them. While her eyes were downcast, he leaned over and drew in a deep breath of her fresh scent if only to implant it upon his memory.

She finished pulling the remainder of the stitches, then plucked some salve from a small jar. She spread the paste over his wound—a wound that was now nothing but scarred, pink flesh. Afterward, she cut a stream of bandage from a roll, placed it over the wound and wrapped it around his thigh. Every touch of her fingers to his skin set him aflame.

"That should suffice until you see your ship's surgeon." She stood and avoided his gaze.

Alex let out a humph. The ship's surgeon was a ninny. He'd trade that man's ministrations for this lovely creature's any day.

She picked up her things and headed toward the door. But Alex wasn't ready to say good-bye. He stood and plucked a rose from the vase. "Allow me to escort you back to the house, Miss McGuire. It is dark."

She stopped but did not turn around. "Your job of protecting me is over, Mr. Reed."

Alex slipped beside her. "Well then, I thank you, Miss McGuire, for tending my wound and saving my life."

"And I thank you, Mr. Reed, for rescuing me from your comrade." A breeze wafted in through the open door, fluttering her curls. Prinney ambled outside as if bored with the conversation.

"We shall call it even then." He took her hand in his and felt her tremble. Raising it to his lips, he placed a kiss upon it.

At last she lifted her gaze to his. Eyes sparkling with tears searched his face. Tears for what?

"Forgive me. I have upset you." Alex frowned, longing to see her smile again. He held out the rose to her.

She eyed him quizzically but did not take it. Instead, she tugged her hand from his.

"A token of our time together?" He attempted a smile that did not reflect the agony in his heart. "The color reminds me of your lips."

She snatched the flower from his hand and stepped out into the darkness. "Godspeed, Mr. Reed. I pray we do not meet again." Then turning, she fled into the night.

Hoisting a burlap sack stuffed with his uniform over his back, Alex made his way to the barn—Miss McGuire's barn. Somehow being in the place she held so dear, the place where he had first seen her, made him feel close to her. And he needed one last dose of her presence before he left her forever. Mr. Snyder's threats rang fresh in Alex's mind. He must leave tonight. Should the councilman discover Alex's true identity, the entire family would be tried for treason.

And Alex could not let that happen.

He stomped forward, his boots squishing through the weeds and mud. His service sword stuffed in his belt, slapped against his thigh. But how could he leave Miss McGuire at the mercy of Mr. Snyder? With no other prospects, the Drummonds would no doubt force her to marry the nincompoop. A nightingale took up a harried call from a tree by the barn. A warning? Yes, that was what he must do. Before Alex left, he must warn Mr. Drummond of the councilman's true intentions. But how? Mr. and Mrs. Drummond had already retired to their bedchamber.

Halting, Alex gazed back at the house. A sliver of a moon peeked from above the dark treetops in the distance as if God were smiling down upon him. He sighed. When had he started thinking of God that way? If God was real and He did answer prayers, Alex could sure use some help. Pausing, he decided to give it a try. He'd never prayed before, not really. But seeing the Drummonds' faith lived out daily stirred a deep part of him, made him want to talk to God like a friend. Closing his eyes, he took a deep breath and began, "God, if You're there, I need to speak to Mr. Drummond tonight." A breeze heavy with moisture and the scent of cedar stole his whispered words away. He nearly laughed out loud at his pathetic appeal.

Shaking his head, he ventured into the shadowy barn, struck flint to steel, and lit a lantern hanging on a center post. Removing his sword, he leaned it against a post and set his sack beside it. Liverpool let out a low groan and a chicken crossed his path, scolding him as it made its way to the chicken roost against the far wall. The smell of hay and manure and leather swirled around him. He chuckled, realizing he no longer found the scents offensive. Surely the woman had bewitched him. He moved to Valor's stall and eased his fingers over the horse's face.

"What do you think, mighty Valor?" The animal nodded her head up and down, then gazed at Alex with brown, intelligent eyes that reminded him of Mr. Drummond's. Alex chuckled. "I believe you are far wiser than you allow me to believe. Much like the man of the house."

"What's that you say?" Mr. Drummond's cracked voice turned Valor's ears in the direction of the door.

Alex jerked around to see Rose's uncle approaching him, lantern in hand. Stunned, he could only stare wide-eyed at the older man. During the time Alex had been here, he'd never once seen Mr. Drummond come out to the barn. A tremble jolted him. Had God answered his prayer? Impossible.

"Talking to a horse, Mr. Reed?" Mr. Drummond's eyes twinkled.

Alex chuckled. "I seem to have more success conversing with horses than people."

Mr. Drummond set his lantern down atop a post and gave Valor a pat on the side. "Oh I doubt that, Mr. Reed, although you did stir Mr. Snyder into a dither this evening."

Alex shot a glance at his sword and pack, but thankfully, they were hidden in the shadows. "I beg your forgiveness, sir. I fear the man brings out the worst in me."

"Think nothing of it, Mr. Reed. I quite enjoyed the exchange."

Alex blinked. He'd expected a proper scolding from a man who lived his life by God's law. "Indeed? I was under the impression Mr. Snyder was a friend of yours."

Mr. Drummond swatted at a fly buzzing about his head and pressed a hand on his back. "I am quite delighted to say that I do not count him among my friends, though I do pray for his soul." Pulling up a milking stool, he sat down with a moan. "Old age, Mr. Reed. I do not recommend it." He chuckled. "No, it is my dear Muira who favors a match between the councilman and Rose, though I have been unable to ascertain her reasons."

Alex studied the elderly man. Everything he said and did slammed headfirst into Alex's long-held opinions of how clergymen should behave. But Mr. Drummond had opened a door, and Alex decided to step through it. "If I may, sir, I believe Mr. Snyder's interest lies more in Miss McGuire's land than in the lady herself."

Mr. Drummond nodded as a look of sorrow deepened his eyes. "As the good Lord has told me."

The odd words struck Alex like a wave of icy water. "God speaks to you?"

"Aye, quite often."

Valor snorted and bobbed her face up and down again.

Alex ran a hand through his hair and scratched the back of his head, hoping to ignite some insight into the man's way of thinking. "Is this an American invention? For I cannot fathom it, sir."

"American? No. I'll wager God even speaks to Englishmen from time to time." Mr. Drummond chuckled.

Alex doubted it. None of the bishops he'd met back home claimed such an intimacy with God. In truth, they seemed more interested in politics than faith. "So, your government has no say in the dictates of religion?" Alex asked.

"Indeed. We are free to worship and believe as we please."

Liverpool groaned as if uttering her approval. And Alex had to agree with the beast. At least these Americans had it right on one account for he had seen how government used the cover of religion as an excuse for all manner of hatred and ill treatment. But God speaking directly to man? "I beg your pardon, sir, but perhaps you only *think* you hear from God."

Mr. Drummond patted his waistcoat pockets. "He speaks to all his children, but many never hear Him because they are not listening or they do not believe God speaks at all."

Again, the man shocked Alex. Doubts pecked at his rising faith like vultures on a wounded beast. "Pray, tell me how He speaks to you, sir. In a burning bush, or perchance an angel appears to give you the message?" Alex snorted.

Mr. Drummond smiled and pointed toward his chest. "In here. A still, small voice, a knowing that always brings peace."

Pushing away from the stall, Alex took a step back, suddenly wondering if the man was mad. "I have never heard such a thing."

"Perhaps because you do not believe you can." Mr. Drummond's gray brows rose.

"You are a reverend, sir. If God does still speak to man—and I'm not saying He does—hearing His voice is no doubt a privilege of your profession." Alex nodded, content with his explanation.

Mr. Drummond's brown eyes flooded with wisdom and something else—a love so intense it caused Alex to avert his gaze. He shifted his boots over the dirt.

"It is a privilege of all He calls His children," Mr. Drummond said.

Children. Was Alex God's child? He didn't want to be anyone's child ever again. Children were commodities to be used or tossed aside at the whim of an uncaring parent. "You speak of God as if He were, indeed, your father."

Mr. Drummond nodded.

Alex gave the man a caustic look. "A bit disrespectful, wouldn't you say, calling the Creator of the world by so familiar a name?"

"He is the Father of all, my son." A gust of hot wind tore through the barn and Mr. Drummond coughed. "When we believe in His Son, Jesus, we are adopted into God's family and are privileged to call Him Abba, Father."

Son. Mr. Drummond had called him son again. And with more affection than Alex's own father had ever spoken his name. Family. Home. Love. All the thoughts that had recently brought such warmth to Alex now rose like a whirling tempest within him.

Mr. Drummond fingered his beard. "I believe God has brought you to us for a reason. He has told me you have an important task to complete."

"Absurd." Alex tugged on his tight waistcoat. "It only proves that no one truly hears from God, for I assure you, sir, I will never do anything of import. At least not that you would consider so." Alex frowned. No, the feats he hoped to accomplish in His Majesty's Navy were the only things important to Alex. And they would only further his own family name and wealth and hopefully gain him entrance to his home again.

Though he was beginning to wonder why he sought so hard after that goal.

Mr. Drummond folded his hands over his portly belly. "There's only one way to find out. Ask God to show you His will and then submit to His direction."

"Humph." Alex crossed his arms over his chest.

A smile—not an insolent, pretentious, or taunting smile—but a smile that bespoke a knowledge that Alex did not possess settled on Mr. Drummond's lips.

Alex rubbed a hand over the back of his neck and glanced out the barn doors. Nothing but darkness met his gaze. Thick darkness—the kind of darkness a man could get lost in and never return. Which was what Alex intended to do. He snapped his gaze back to Mr. Drummond. Golden light from two lanterns spilled over the man, surrounding him in an ethereal glow. Something in the confidence and peace in his tone, on his face, sparked hope within Alex.

But what did it matter? He must leave this place, leave this man, and leave Rose. "Mr. Drummond, I beg you to protect Miss McGuire from Mr. Snyder. I believe a match between them would cause her great unhappiness."

"Oh, you do?" The knowing smile on the man's face curved into a taunting one.

"And it is not because of any affections I may have for her."

"I made no mention of any affections." Laughter sparkled in Mr. Drummond's eyes. He cocked his head. "Is there something you wish to ask me, Mr. Reed?"

Alex studied the odd man. "No, sir," he said carefully. He couldn't afford to reveal his growing affection and then leave. It wouldn't be fair to Rose.

"Hmm. Very well."

Alex huffed. "I must leave. Go back to my sh—regiment."

Mr. Drummond lowered his chin. "As I feared."

Upon his honor, Alex could not figure the man out. "Surely you do not wish me to stay here because of my exemplary skills as a servant?"

Mr. Drummond laughed. "No, but you are good for Rose."

"I fear you are mistaken."

"Am I? I have not seen her so lively, so vibrant in years."

Alex looked away. He didn't want to hear it. It hurt too much to know that he could bring her joy only to have to break her heart. "I assure you it is not my doing."

"Hmm."

"Nevertheless, I must leave you tonight." Alex forced determination into both his tone and his resolve. "I cannot thank you enough for your kindness in offering me a position in your home."

"Tonight?" The elderly man struggled to rise. "You cannot possibly leave tonight."

❖ CHAPTER 16 ❖

Crying. A woman's crying echoed through Rose's ears, bouncing off the walls of her mind, jarring her awake. She turned on her side and drew her quilt over her head. The sobbing continued. Did it come from within her? Had the sorrow that had weighed so heavily upon her when she retired that night followed her into her dreams? Sitting up, she swiped her cheeks. No. Not her tears.

Whimpering drifted through the walls. *Amelia.* Leaping from her bed, Rose swung a robe over her shoulders and crept through the dark hallway into Amelia's chamber next door. The poor woman lay curled in a ball on her coverlet. Misty fingers of moonlight streamed in through the window, caressing her, even as her long black tresses fanned over the coverlet like silken threads. Amelia's chest convulsed. Rose inched to her side and laid a hand on her arm.

Amelia shot up, her eyes wide. "Oh miss, it's you." She gasped for air and looked down. "Forgive me, I woke you again."

Rose sat beside her and enfolded her in a tight embrace. The aged bed frame creaked. "Has something else distressed you or is it. . ." Rose hated to even mention his name lest the woman break into sobs anew.

Which Amelia did anyway at just the hint of him—Richard, her husband.

"I miss him so much, Rose." She inhaled a sob, then leaned her head on Rose's shoulder.

"I know." Rose stroked her back. "I know." Tears burned behind Rose's eyes. It had been two years since Richard disappeared at sea, yet still his young wife mourned him as if he'd left only yesterday. "Your love was one of a kind."

Amelia pushed back from her. Glassy brown eyes brimming with pain gazed at Rose. "It was, wasn't it?"

Rose nodded and wiped a moist strand of Amelia's hair from her cheek. Though she knew no man was perfect, the way Amelia described Richard as an honorable, kind, and brave man who loved Amelia deeply made Rose long to be loved by such a man. Oddly, a certain British officer filled her vision—an officer who was gone forever just like Richard. Her heart grew heavy. And for the first time, Rose felt the weight of her maid's ongoing agony. "You were blessed to have had Richard for as long as you did. Most women will never be loved so passionately."

Amelia nodded, then fell into Rose's embrace again. "Why am I not getting better? Why do I still think of him every moment of the day and dream of him during the long night?"

"Because he will always be with you, Amelia. And you, with him." Rose grabbed a handkerchief from the table and handed it to her maid. She blew her nose and gave Rose a tiny smile. "Thank you, miss." Then dropping her hands into her lap, she gazed out the window. Starlight drifted over her, transforming her skin into porcelain and her tears into silver. "Even when I play the coquette and attract all manner of attention from men, the pain does not subside."

Rose grasped her hands. They trembled.

"I am beginning to believe that no man can ever take Richard's place," Amelia said.

Rose swallowed. She wouldn't have agreed with her maid a week ago. A week ago, she would have told her to give up her romantic, fanciful notions. She would have told her that one man was as good as the next, as long as he was honorable and hard-working. But Mr. Reed had changed everything. Rose had never met anyone like him. And she doubted she ever would again. Suddenly a hint of Amelia's pain filled her own heart, and tears blurred her vision.

Amelia lowered her chin. "I need to find a husband. I've burdened your aunt and uncle long enough."

Rose gripped her shoulders and resisted the urge to shake her. "Don't be such a silly goose, Amelia. You are family now. Surely you know that." She wiped a wet strand of hair from Amelia's face.

"Well I suppose if that weren't true, they would have dismissed me long ago." Amelia's laugh came out as a sob, and Rose drew her into a tight embrace and held her until her sobs subsided and they both drifted off to sleep.

Alex hoisted the ax above his head. His muscles burned. Sweat streamed down his bare back. He thrust the blade into the wood, then repeated the process again and again until finally the log separated into two. A sound that reminded him of a ship's mast snapping shot through the air. Halting, he settled his breath as James Myers strode up to him, a bucket of water in hand, and scooped him a ladleful. Alex set down the ax and poured the cool liquid into his mouth until it dribbled down his chin. After handing the ladle back to James, he ran a hand through his sweat-moistened hair. "Thank you."

Dropping the ladle into the bucket, James scanned the scene. "It is I who should thank you, Mr. Reed." His Adam's apple bobbed up and down, and Alex followed his gaze to the house, or what was left of it.

"It would please me if you would call me Alex."

James chuckled. "It would please you? Now, aren't you the gentleman? With that accent, you could almost be mistaken for some elegant British nobleman."

Alex coughed into his hand. "God forbid."

From across the field, Mr. Drummond strolled up to them. "And just what does God forbid?" He tugged off his hat and ran his sleeve over his forehead.

James scooped some water for the elderly man. "God forbid that Mr. Reed. . .I mean Alex would be a British nobleman."

A sparkle lit Mr. Drummond's brown eyes as he snapped them to Alex. "A travesty, indeed."

Unsettled by the man's keen perusal, Alex gazed back at the house. With all the burnt rubble cleared away, the structure appeared sound.

Shards of darkened wood poked out from the remainder of what had been the kitchen, but the foundation was intact. Two young men from town, Mr. Anders and Mr. Braxton stood atop the roof joining the new frame to the existing one. A week or so of hard work should make the humble home as good as new. Not that Alex knew anything about carpentry, but he'd overheard as much from Mr. Drummond.

Alex stretched his shoulders, wincing at the ache that spread down his back. Though he'd been forced to lift heavy objects and perform various laborious tasks in the navy, he couldn't recall ever wielding so large an ax or working so hard and long in such sweltering heat—not even when he'd chopped wood for Miss McGuire. Oddly, Alex embraced his discomfort. For the first time in his life, his hard work served a noble purpose. Shading his eyes, he glanced up at the sun slinging fiery rays upon him as if the glowing orb were angry at some offense. *Which one?* Alex wondered.

Hot wind whipped around him, and he closed his eyes, allowing it to cool his chest and arms. He drew in a deep breath of air tainted with a hint of salt and sweet summer flowers.

James clapped him on the back. "Well, I thank you again, Alex." True appreciation beamed in the man's eyes. "Now I best get this water over to Harold and Jarvis and then get back to my own work." He tipped his hat and headed toward the house.

Mr. Drummond's gaze remained on Alex. "Not done much carpentry work before, eh?"

Alex chuckled and picked up his ax. "Is it that obvious?"

"Just a bit. But you're doing a great job, son. Thank you for staying. We'll have this house up in no time."

"It's the least I could do." Alex said the words before he realized their implication.

Mr. Drummond scratched his gray whiskers, and a hint of a smile flickered over his lips. "Now why would you say something like that?"

Alex gripped the ax handle so tight a splinter of wood pierced his skin. If the man only knew. "I meant after all this family has suffered." When Mr. Drummond had asked Alex to help rebuild this poor farmer's home, Alex had seen it as a way to offer penance for the crimes of his countrymen. He hated that he'd had to break his promise that he would leave last night, but how could he refuse the opportunity?

"You are a kind soul, indeed, son." Mr. Drummond's look of approval nearly forced Alex to take a step back. Then, smiling, the man turned and walked away.

Alex watched him as he left: the slight hobble in his gait as if one of his legs pained him, his gray hair poking out in all directions from beneath a wide-brimmed hat, the humble yet confident lift of his shoulders. And a longing welled within Alex, a longing to have a father like Mr. Drummond. Alex's own father had never paid him a single compliment, nor even a kind word or encouragement.

Mr. Drummond took up his spot leaning over a log, shaping and cutting the ends with a long knife while James perched atop a ladder giving water to his friends. He must have said something funny as the men atop the roof joined him in laughter. Alex shook his head. These people found joy even in the midst of tragedy, even with their country at war and the enemy surrounding them. These Americans might be a rustic breed, but they were hardy and they cared for one another. They helped one another. Alex had seen nothing like it in his life. Men willing to give up a day's or a week's worth of hard work for someone else. And receive nothing in return. Astonishing. Shame drew his gaze to the grass surrounding his boots—shame at his own reason for offering his assistance. Penance. A purely selfish reason that had nothing to do with kindness.

Hoisting the ax onto his shoulder, Alex moved to the next felled trunk and dug the blade deep into the wood, angry at himself, angry at his father, angry at his countrymen. And even angry at Miss McGuire for being so charming and wonderful.

And for stealing his heart.

Rose clucked her tongue and nudged Valor forward. After both her and Amelia's difficult night last night, Rose thought it best that they find something productive to do today. If only to keep their minds off their sorrows. So when Cora had informed her that Uncle Forbes was over at the Myers' farm helping to rebuild James and Elaine's house, Rose decided to bring him lunch, along with enough food for any other men helping out. And perhaps speak to Elaine again.

"Oh I do hope Mr. Braxton will be there. I know he's a friend of

Mr. Myers." Amelia's excited chatter drifted over Rose's shoulder even as the woman's grip on Rose's waist tightened. "Maybe he'll ask me to the ball."

Rose let out a huff, amazed that Amelia could recover so quickly from a night of such anguish. But then again, Rose knew the woman's flirtatious ways were the only thing that gave her the strength and impetus to survive another day without Richard.

She patted Amelia's hand. "Maybe he will."

Pushing up the brim of her straw hat, Rose gazed at the archway of thick elm branches overhead. Trumpet vines spun upward around their trunks and curled around branches before dangling over the dirt path like the green tresses of a forest maiden. Rose swatted one away and drew a deep breath of the fresh mossy air, trying to allay the ache in her heart.

"There they are." Amelia's arm speared out on Rose's right side.

Two men stood atop what was left of the roof, her uncle and James leaned over a massive log perched above the ground on two wooden trestles, and out in the field stood another man, ax raised over his head, dark hair blowing in the breeze.

Bare-chested.

Rose's stomach clamped tight. Her heart raced. Removing one hand from the reins, she rubbed her eyes and refocused them on the man.

"It's Mr. Reed," Amelia said with merely a hint of surprise in her voice. "What is he doing here?"

Rose 's thoughts spun in a chaotic jumble. "I have no idea."

"Oh my, look at him."

"I'd rather not."

"Why not? He's absolute perfection."

"My word, Amelia, shame on you. You shouldn't stare at him." But even as she said it, Rose's eyes shot his way again as if they had a mind of their own. He plunged the ax into a log, then yanked it free and lifted it over his head once more. Muscles as firm as the wood he chopped rippled through his chest and arms beneath skin glistening in the noon sun. She swallowed and urged Valor through the open gate and up the path to the house, where she pulled the horse to a stop. Her uncle looked up from his work and smiled. "There you are, lass."

James dug his ax deep into the wood and rushed over to assist Rose from her horse. After her feet hit the ground, she turned and took the basket of food from Amelia before James assisted her down as well.

"We brought you lunch." Rose held the basket out to James.

James leaned forward and took a whiff. "Very kind of you, Miss Rose."

The two men on the roof descended the ladder and dropped to the ground, heading their way.

Amelia pinched her cheeks then turned to face them. "Good day, Mr. Braxton." She gave the young man a coy glance.

Doffing his hat, he ran a hand through his blond hair and nodded in her direction. "Good day, Mrs. Wilkins. A pleasure to see you again."

Out of the corner of her eye, Rose saw Mr. Reed toss a shirt over his head and start toward them. "Is Elaine home, James?" she said. "I'd love to see her."

"No, I'm afraid not." James placed the basket atop a table covered with carpentry tools. "She went to stay with the Brandons in town until I can get the house repaired."

"How is she doing?"

"As well as you might expect, Miss Rose. She'll be sorry she missed you." Anguish burned in James's blue eyes before a gentle smile stole it away.

Mr. Reed's tall figure filled the corner of Rose's eyes. Part of her was furious that he had not left, the other part elated. In truth, she had no idea which part to embrace. She decided on anger. It was the safer choice. "We should be going." She could not question him now in front of these men. Turning, she tugged on Amelia's sleeve, but the woman continued talking with Mr. Braxton.

Uncle Forbes approached Rose, a smile on his face. "So soon? I'll not hear of it, lass."

"It's far too hot this time of day, Uncle." Rose batted the muggy air around her neck. "You can bring the basket home with you later."

"Come, come, my dear." He proffered his elbow. "I'll grab my lunch, and we can sit under the tree by the pond."

Mr. Reed approached James and peered into the basket. His hazel eyes latched upon Rose. Regret flickered across them along with a burning affection that caused her skin to flush.

Turning away from him, Rose took her uncle's arm. "Very well." At least she would be away from Mr. Reed. Away from his effect on her. From the way one look from him could dismantle her anger and turn her insides to mush.

The warmth and strength emanating from Uncle Forbes's arm helped ease Rose's taut nerves as they made their way to the huge oak tree. Lowering onto the soft grass, Rose spread out her skirts as her uncle excused himself to get his lunch. Untying the ribbon beneath her chin, she drew off her hat and gazed at the leaves fluttering in the breeze, the red and yellow marigolds in Elaine's garden, the ducks gliding over the pond. Yet voices drew her gaze back toward the house where her uncle stood in deep conversation with Mr. Reed. Grabbing one of the lunch bundles, Mr. Reed headed her way.

Her way?

Too late to jump to her feet and run away.

Tightening her jaw, she returned her gaze to the pond, trying to erect barriers around her heart. His shadow fell across her. He cleared his throat.

She glanced up.

"Your uncle said you wished to speak to me." A breeze twirled among the dark strands of his hair.

With a frown, Rose searched for her uncle and found him sitting with James and Mr. Anders, eating his food. Why would he say such a thing?

"Miss McGuire?" The deep timbre of Mr. Reed's voice caressed her ears.

She forced a stoic expression. "I fear he was mistaken, Mr. Reed."

"Then forgive the intrusion, miss." He nodded and turned to leave.

"Why are you still here?" she called after him.

He swung about, a puzzled look on his face. "You are angry?"

"No." Rose fingered a blade of grass. "Yes. . .I don't know. It's just that I prepared myself for you leaving."

One dark brow rose. "Prepared?" A spark of hope glimmered in his hazel eyes.

"Oh, never mind." She waved at him. "Do sit down, Mr. Reed, and eat your lunch."

He hesitated, glanced over his shoulder, then finally dropped to the ground beside her. He propped his boots on the dirt and leaned his arms across his knees. "When your uncle asked me to help today, I thought it my duty to stay and assist in cleaning up the mess my countrymen made. I hope you understand."

Understand? That he was an honorable, kind man. Yes, she did. But she wished she didn't. She wished he were a selfish, arrogant brute who would just leave.

"Rest assured, I intend to leave tonight." He raked his moist hair back from his face.

"I do not believe you." She smiled.

He chuckled and unwrapped the cloth bundle in his lap. Pulling out a chunk of yellow cheese, he offered it to her. She broke off a piece and popped it in her mouth. The sharp taste matched the angst brewing in her stomach.

Tearing off a clump of bread, he took a bite and stared at the pond glistening silver in the bright sun. Unable to stop herself, Rose gazed at him, memorizing every detail, the angular cut of his jaw, the black stubble on his chin, the way his dark hair grazed his open collar. Even sitting on the grass, he exuded strength and confidence. The wind flapped his loose shirt, giving her a peek of his chest. She turned away. Her eyes misted. She would miss him—this British naval officer.

Images of her father beckoned to her from deep within her soul. Sudden guilt followed the usual sorrow flooding her, and she lowered her gaze. Surely her feelings for this British man betrayed her father's memory. And she hated herself for it.

Amelia's giddy laughter echoed over the field, and Alex glanced in the maid's direction. The poor woman stood far too close to Mr. Braxton, clinging to his arm and waving her fan about flirtatiously.

"Your companion plays a dangerous game."

"Why do you say that?" Though Rose could imagine, she wondered at Mr. Reed's concern.

"She throws herself at every passing man." He took a bite of dried pork. "She's a sweet woman, to be sure, but one of these men will take advantage of her."

"Yes, I fear that as well." Rose handed him back the cheese, her churning stomach unable to accept another bite.

"Perhaps your uncle can curtail her behavior." Mr. Reed's tone carried no condemnation, only concern.

"No, I fear my uncle is too often gone." Rose plucked a dandelion weed. "Do not think badly of her, Mr. Reed. She is not as wanton as she may seem. Her coquettish ways cover a deep wound."

"Indeed?" Mr. Reed swallowed his meat and looked her way.

Should Rose tell him the tale? What would it matter if she did? He'd be gone soon anyway. "Her husband was lost at sea two years ago."

Mr. Reed glanced back at Amelia, but said nothing.

"She believes him dead, but it's possible that he was impressed by your navy." Rose allowed anger to seep into her voice.

Sharp eyes snapped her way. "What is his name?"

"Richard Wilkins."

Something sparked in Alex's eyes before he looked away.

Rose laid a hand on his arm, her pulse quickening. "You know him?"

He shook his head. "I don't think so. . .perhaps. The navy impresses many men."

"Indeed you do." A welcome disdain ignited in Rose's belly, and she did all she could to fan its flames. Better to be angry with this man than allow her sentiments to grow for him. "You steal them from their families, never to be seen or heard from again."

Mr. Reed's jaw bunched and he released a labored sigh. "It is an inexcusable practice, Miss McGuire, one which I have never approved of. But rest assured"—he gave her a measured look—"your American navy is not without equal blame. They hold our sailors hostage as well."

"Perhaps. But I thank you for reminding me of something."

"What is that?"

"That you are British through and through and always will be." Grabbing her skirts, Rose struggled to stand as modestly as she could. She started to leave. "Good day, Mr. Reed."

He grabbed her hand, turning her gaze back to him. "I am first and foremost a man, Miss McGuire. Neither British nor American."

She feigned a tug on his grip, not wanting him to release her. Something deep within his eyes—longing and pain—kept her in place.

He squeezed her hand. "Much to my chagrin, I have discovered that my opinion of you Americans was quite erroneous at best. Perhaps you would offer me the same courtesy?"

Warmth spread from his hand up her arm and down her back, causing her to shudder. "How can I when I know so little of you?"

With a sigh, he glanced toward the pond then back at her, still not releasing her hand. "Very well. If you'll sit back down, I'll do my best to regale you with the horrid tale of my childhood."

Snyder eased his gelding to a walk as he approached the Drummond farm. White smoke drifted from the kitchen chimney where their Negro cook no doubt prepared the evening meal. If he was correct in his assessment, she should be the only person home at the moment. Last night, Snyder had overheard that Mrs. Drummond intended to travel to Washington today and Mr. Drummond would be at the Myers' farm helping to rebuild their damaged house. Snyder had just seen Rose and Amelia ride off on horseback. And since Mr. Reed was not with them, he must be already at the Myers', assisting Mr. Drummond.

Snyder smiled at his own ability to accurately assess any situation.

Heading toward the stable, he loosened his cravat. Sweat broke out on his neck, and he dabbed it with the folds of silk. Blast this infernal heat. Rarely did he venture outside when the sun was at its zenith, but he would gladly endure all the discomfort in the world, if he accomplished his mission. Slipping off his horse, he tied the reins to the post outside the stable. With one glance toward the house, he circled the building, found the door leading to Mr. Reed's quarters and sneaked inside. The musty smell of mold and hay accosted him. Sunlight filtered through the single dirty window, twirling dust through the air as he scanned the room, looking for something, anything that would prove Mr. Reed's true identity. He took off his hat, grateful for the cooler air, as his eyes grew accustomed to the shadows. A glimmer drew his gaze to something underneath a cot in the corner. Making his way toward it, he knelt, pulled out a sack and peered behind it. Malevolent delight surged within him, for there lying in the dirt was the silver hilt of a British service sword.

❖ CHAPTER 17 ❖

Alex rubbed his stiff jaw and gazed at the ducks skimming over the glassy waters of the pond. A mother and seven ducklings. A family. Happy and carefree. He envied them. Rose sat patiently beside him. With the folds of her gown spread like creamy wings over the grass and her golden hair framing her face like a halo, she looked like an angel. She *was* an angel to him. An angel whose blue eyes gazed at him expectantly making him hesitate to divulge the shame of his youth, hesitate to watch disapproval curve those beautiful lips into a frown, for his story would do nothing to engender her good opinion of him or of his countrymen.

"Mr. Reed?" Her questioning tone snapped him from his daze.

He shook his head. "There isn't much to tell, Miss McGuire. I simply did not want to see you run off so angry."

"Well, now that I've sat down again, I would like to know more about you." She glanced toward the trees lining the other side of the pond and sorrow rolled over her face. "Even if I am never to see you again."

"Very well." Alex tied the edges of the cloth sack containing his lunch and set it aside. "My father's name is Franklin Reed, Viscount Cranleigh, or just Lord Cranleigh to his friends." He chuckled. "Among his many achievements, he is also a member of Parliament."

The corners of her lips tightened, and she lowered her chin as if the news upset her, but then she gave him a timid smile. "Then should we be addressing you as Lord Cranleigh?"

"No." Alex returned her smile, happy to see his status did not intimidate her as it often did those of common birth. "The sons of viscounts receive no title." He plucked a piece of grass and tossed it aside.

Rose's forehead wrinkled. "Was your father cruel?"

Alex leaned back against the tree trunk, amazed at her discernment. "He was not a father at all." He shrugged. "But I suppose I was not much of a son either."

"I cannot imagine that."

Her compliment settled on his shoulders like the warmth of the sun filtering through the leaves above them. "I was the prodigal son, Miss McGuire. Got into all sorts of trouble in town. Drank to excess, harassed the watch, caused great embarrassment for my family." He wouldn't tell her the rest—consorting with questionable ladies, gambling, and the two nights in prison he'd spent before his father had come to bail him out.

"Why would you do such things?" She stared at him as if she couldn't conceive of anyone defying their family in such a way.

"I was an angry young man."

"Angry at what?"

"My father, my elder brother, life. . .I don't know." Visions of his boyhood antics strolled through his mind like a nightmarish parade, showering him with remorse, yet reminding him of the inward fury and emptiness that had haunted him day and night.

"But you had everything—wealth, prestige, family."

Alex snorted. "Wealth and prestige, yes. But not family. Not the kind of family you're thinking of." Alex glanced toward Mr. Drummond who was laughing with James. "My father was a very stern man. He favored my elder brother, Frederick, and found me lacking in every way." Alex huffed as he pictured his brilliant, gifted brother sauntering into the family sitting room with the flourish and elegance of a London dandy—and how his father's eyes would brighten at the sight of him. "Where Frederick was skilled in learning and quick with books, I resisted instruction and bumbled my numbers. Where he was an accomplished horseman, well." Alex chuckled. "You saw my skill on a horse."

Rose smiled and clasped her hands in her lap, yet sorrow lingered in her eyes.

Alex stretched his back. "So, my dear father, Lord Cranleigh, sent me away to the navy. Obtained a commission for me as a midshipman aboard the HMS *Aquilon*."

"You didn't wish to go?" Rose's forehead puckered.

Alex shook his head. "I had no aspirations to fight silly sea battles across the globe."

Rose shifted her gaze to the pond where the mother duck swam into a patch of lily pads and gathered her young around her. "I'm sorry."

"It was good for me." Wind blew a strand of his hair into his face, and Alex flipped it aside. "The discipline, the hard work. I came home to visit my family for a few weeks during the summer of '06 and became quite taken with a certain lady."

"Oh." Her tone was one of dismay. Rose glanced at the hands in her lap.

"There was but one small impediment. She was my brother's fiancée." Alex studied her, gauging her reaction.

"My word." Rose gasped, but still she would not look at him.

Certainly the story was no credit to Alex's character, but the sad tale was a huge part of what had formed him into the man he was today—a huge part of what had driven him to this point. And for some reason, now that he had begun, he wanted Rose to know all of it, to understand him. If she didn't, if she turned her nose up at him in disdain, he would no doubt grieve, but it would be far easier for him to leave her forever.

"And worse, the lady encouraged my affections," he continued. "Toyed with the infatuation of a young man. I was beside myself with love." He shook his head and chuckled. "Or so I thought."

Finally Rose lifted her gaze to his. Nothing but compassion swam in her eyes. "Do not be so hard on yourself. You were but eighteen."

Alex glanced down at the grass fluttering in the breeze and swallowed the burning in his throat. "Yes, I was young, and she but a vixen in disguise. At a dinner party at our house, she lured me into the library and showered me with kisses—quite passionate kisses, I might add."

A red hue flooded Rose's cheeks, making her even more adorable.

"I proposed to her on the spot—asked her to break off her engagement with my brother and run away to Guernsey with me to get married."

Rose drew a hand to her mouth.

"Never fear, Miss McGuire." Alex gave her a sad smile. "As it turns out, the woman had some sense after all. She laughed at me. Not just a slight giggle, but a rather unladylike chortle."

Rose put her hand on his arm. Pain burned in her eyes, but she said nothing.

Alex stared at the dirt by his boots. "My brother inherited the bulk of the family fortune, you see. And marrying a seaman was beneath her."

Rose squeezed his arm. "I'm so sorry."

Alex tore from her grasp and stood. He stepped toward the pond, turning away from her, not wanting her to see the pain moistening his eyes. He no longer loved the vixen. Hardly ever thought of her. Then why did her rejection still grieve him so?

He heard Rose get up and felt her presence behind him.

"She informed my entire family of my silly proposal." Alex could hear the bitter sarcasm in his own voice. "I dare say, I was on the receiving end of everyone's jokes for days to come. And oh"—he glanced at her over his shoulder—"my dear brother called me out to a duel."

Rose eased beside him. "What did you do?"

"I nearly killed him." Alex fisted his hands across his chest. "I begged him not to fight, but his blasted honor"—Alex hung his head—"his blasted honor. . ." Sorrow choked him, forbidding him to speak.

Several seconds passed. "What happened?" Rose finally asked.

Alex dared a glance at her. "I disfigured him. Not intentionally of course, but my sword etched a thick scar upon his face and neck." He drew a line across his own face, indicating the extent of the wound while shame soured in his belly. "Last I heard, he'd become addicted to laudanum, and he suffers daily from severe melancholy."

A wisp of Rose's hair blew across her cheek. Though she uttered not a word, the air between them billowed with her disapproval.

"After the incident, my father ushered me back to the navy in the middle of the night with the admonition that I was no longer welcome at the Reed estate. He said I was worthless, not his son. I returned to my ship a different man, Miss McGuire." Alex ran a hand through his hair and gazed at the family of ducks. "I am determined to restore the honor I stole from my family, gain their forgiveness, and perhaps earn the right to return home."

Alex swallowed the burning in his throat and drew a deep breath of fresh air, hoping to clear away the memories. He reluctantly faced Rose, expecting to see disapproval in her eyes—pity. But what he saw instead made him want to take her in his arms, deny his country, his heritage, and stay with her forever. Instead, he clenched his fists and took a step back. No. He had promised himself that he would never again make a decision based on flighty emotions. He had learned the hard way that silly sentiments befuddled his mind and led him down a path to destruction. He must always rely on his mind and his good sense. And at the moment both were warning him to run as far away from this precious lady as possible.

Pain darkened Mr. Reed's features, and Rose's heart grew heavy. She wanted to embrace him, to tell him that, despite his youthful indiscretions, he was the most honorable, capable, kind man she'd ever met. Not until this moment did she realize that not everyone had fathers like the wonderful one she had experienced. "Thank you for sharing such intimacies with me, Mr. Reed." Rose knew it had not been easy to tell her of his shame. "And I no longer believe all British are evil." She waited until he met her gaze. "Knowing you has convinced me otherwise."

At first shock skittered across his eyes, then sorrow, before he lowered his chin.

A gentle breeze swirled around them, tossing Mr. Reed's loose hair and cooling the perspiration on Rose's neck. "You are not worthless, Mr. Reed. I hope you know that now."

"Perhaps, perhaps not." The lines on his brow deepened. "I'm not sure what I know anymore."

At the risk of losing her own heart, Rose stepped toward him.

Instead of a commanding naval officer, he seemed more like a lost, little boy. "I'm sorry for what happened to your brother, but he is the one who challenged you. You can hardly blame yourself."

He grimaced. "I could have run away and not met him that morning."

"Perhaps." Rose brushed a curl from her face. "We all make mistakes when we are young and impetuous." She cringed as memories of her own stupidity rose to taunt her. "My uncle says that God forgives all our sins if we are truly repentant."

Alex snorted. "Ruining someone's life is unforgivable, especially when that someone is your brother."

"Your brother was left scarred. He did not lose a leg or an arm or receive some other debilitating injury. It seems to me that his own vanity ruined his life, not you."

Alex flinched but then a smile broke upon his lips.

Rose blinked. "Why are you grinning at me?"

"Do you never fail to speak what is on your mind?"

"Why should I?"

His hazel eyes shifted between hers. "You have me quite befuddled, Miss McGuire." He lifted his hand and caressed her cheek as if her skin were made of porcelain and he feared to break her.

Rose's heart fluttered wildly. Tossing her reservations aside, she leaned into his hand and closed her eyes, imagining what it would be like to be loved by such a man. He rubbed his thumb over her cheek and released a sigh, his hot breath filling the air between them.

A soft moan escaped Rose's lips as her dreams took a turn into possibility.

But he had said he wanted to restore his family honor and make his father proud. Rose was but a common farm girl. An enemy. She would only bring him shame and worse—further rejection from his family.

Opening her eyes, she stepped away and turned her back to him.

They had no future together.

"Good-bye, Mr. Reed. I insist you leave tonight. Go back to your ship and leave me and my family alone. You don't belong here. I don't want you here." Then grabbing her skirts, she marched away before he saw the tears spilling down her cheeks.

Alex kicked a boot full of hay into the air and took up a pace across the dirt floor of his servant's quarters. More like a horse's stall for all its comforts. Then again, the workers in his father's house had far better sleeping quarters than what he'd seen of the Drummond family's chambers. He huffed. It was not the dirt floor or hay-stuffed mattress or the meager furnishings that caused Alex's stomach to fold in on itself. No, it was the look of ardor burning in Rose's crisp blue eyes earlier that day and the way she'd leaned into his caress and moaned softly.

As if she cared for him.

As if her affections for him went beyond mere friendship. Even the anger in her voice as she stormed away and told him she didn't want him to stay, bespoke of opposite feelings within.

Alex reached the log wall and spun about. He passed by the lantern flickering on the table and glanced out the window to see only darkness beyond.

He should be gone already.

As soon as he and Mr. Drummond had returned, Alex had begged off from supper and any additional duties with an excuse of utter exhaustion. The elderly man had not questioned the statement, but he had gripped Alex's shoulders in a hearty embrace and thanked him for his toil. And something else. . .he had said he would pray for Alex.

Too tired to ask why and unsure he wished to hear the answer, Alex had simply nodded and walked off—away from the rustic American preacher who used to be a thief—and the man who had been more of a father to Alex these past few weeks than his own had been in the many years he'd lived at home.

Intending to grab his sack and sword and slip out into the night, Alex, instead, found himself an hour later clearing a trail of pounded dirt across the hay-strewn ground of his quarters. His gut contorted, his heart constricted, and he struggled to release each breath. He should leave. He must leave.

Yet the thought of going back to his ship and being forced to fight against these Americans, these people whom he'd come to admire—and some even love—caused bile to rise in his throat. He shook off a sudden chill that shuddered over him and scanned the room, seeking the source. Yet he found no holes in the walls nor open window or door that would allow a breeze to enter. The hot, humid air swamped back over him, and he ran his sleeve over his forehead and swerved around to trek across the room again.

If Rose returned his affections. If she could overcome his nationality, his heritage, then maybe. . .maybe Alex could become one of these backwoods Americans. And once accepted as such, his presence would no longer endanger this precious family.

He clenched his fists until his nails bit into his flesh. He was either a fool or completely mad for even entertaining such a thought.

Perhaps both.

He stopped pacing and fell into the chair beside the table. Leaning forward, he dropped his head into his hands and squeezed his eyes shut.

"What do you want, Alex?"

The whisper rang ominous and clear, and yet it came from nowhere. Alex lifted his head. Perhaps he had gone mad, indeed. But the question remained. What did he want? Honor, position, power, fortune like his father possessed? Was his father happy? Alex searched his memories and found no moment of joy in his childhood home, no smiles upon his parents' lips, no gentle touches or embraces. Then why, when he had been so miserable as a child, did he seek after the same things? Alex shook his head.

"I love you, son."

Tears burned behind Alex's eyes as the silent words drifted over him. *Son.* Such an endearing yet powerful term, implying an affection and a bond that could never be broken. He remembered what Mr. Drummond had said about how God spoke to him—from deep within him.

Exactly where this voice seemed to originate.

Alex's breath halted in his throat. "God?" he spoke into the still air, then felt foolish and lowered his chin. Why would God bother with him? Yet hadn't God answered his prayer last night asking for the chance to speak to Mr. Drummond?

A cold chill enveloped Alex, jarring his senses. No, nothing but a coincidence. Yet hope sparked a tiny flame within him that God would actually speak to him. That he *did* care for Alex like a father cared for a son.

"Lord, if You are listening, tell me what to do. If I stay, I'll lose everything I've ever worked for and bring further disgrace to my family. If I go. . ." Alex hesitated.

"You'll lose all that I have to offer you."

Offer me? God had something for him? Alex stood and took up a pace again to settle his nerves. His mind played tricks on him. The voice surely rose from his scrambled imaginings. He threw back his shoulders, wincing at the ache that stretched across them like a tightrope. The pain of his sore muscles seemed to jar him back to reality. Back to the honor and duty of a British naval officer and the son of a viscount. He had to leave, and he had to do it now or he feared he never would.

❖ CHAPTER 18 ❖

Rose scratched Liverpool behind the ears, eliciting an affectionate moo from the cow then moved to Valor's stall. The horse lifted her head over the railing. One large brown eye assessed Rose as she approached—an eye so full of sorrow and compassion it nearly crumbled the wall of tears behind Rose's eyes.

"Oh Valor." She leaned her cheek against the horse's face, inhaling the musky, sweet scent of horseflesh. "I can always rely on you. You'll never leave me, will you?"

Valor blew out a snort in response and stomped her hoof.

Though Rose had snuffed her candle and crawled early into bed nearly an hour ago, slumber had escaped her.

Just like Mr. Reed. He was no doubt on his way back to his ship by now. *Lord, keep him safe.*

Rose kissed Valor and took up a pace across the hay-strewn ground. It was better that he left. Better for them both. Better for their countries. Then why did she feel as though her heart would dissolve beneath the pain? She swerved around and headed the other way. "Oh Lord, of all the men in the world, why did You allow me to fall in love with a British officer?" Tears escaped the corners of her eyes and spilled onto her cheeks. She didn't understand God's reasoning. But then again, she didn't understand why God had allowed any of the tragedies in her life.

The light thud of a footfall jarred her heart into a frenzied beat. Memories of Lieutenant Garrick's attack bombarded her. She swerved toward the open door.

Mr. Reed stood at the entrance to the barn—an apparition of her grieved mind. A gust of wind tousled a strand of his hair that had broken free from its tie. Still donned in the stained livery of a footman, his white shirt stretched across his thick chest like a milky band in the moonlight.

She rubbed her eyes and took a step back.

He held up a hand. "It's only me, Miss McGuire." His deep voice sent her heart into a different kind of frenzy.

Rose swallowed. Every inch of her wanted to throw herself into his arms. A seed of hope began to sprout within her that perhaps he wouldn't leave at all. Perhaps he had come to tell her he intended to switch sides, to become an American. "What do you want?"

"Forgive me. I...I...." He shifted uncomfortably. "I didn't mean to intrude. I was looking for my uniform and sword."

"I gave them to you."

He blinked as a puzzled look tightened his features. "I hid them under my bed, but when I went to retrieve them, I found them gone. I thought....I thought...."

"You thought I took them? Why would I when I want you to leave?" The lie made her cringe. His statement dried up her hope. A breeze blew through the barn, bringing a chill with it. She hugged herself.

His puzzlement turned to concern as he approached her. "You've been crying." The timbre of his British accent eased through her like warm tea on a winter's night.

Rose looked away. Sorrow constricted her chest.

Touching her chin with his finger, he moved her gaze back to his. Lantern light angled over his sharp jaw and flickered in his hazel eyes now brimming with affection. "Rose, surely you are aware of my feelings for you."

Rose's breath halted in her throat.

"The pain of never seeing you again overwhelms me." His warm hands enveloped hers and he looked down.

Rose's breath returned and gusted out of her mouth. A sob emerged behind it.

Which he must have taken as shock, or worse, disapproval. "My apologies for being so bold." He gazed down at their hands and released his grip. "But situation and time deny me the luxury of proper etiquette."

Rose finally found her voice. "Why do you tell me this when you are leaving?"

"Because I want you to know. I want you to remember me. To know that you affected me deeply—changed me."

Hope sparked in Rose's heart. "Then why not stay? Become an American."

He shook his head and stared at the ground. Dark strands of hair hung around his face, hiding his expression.

A tear slid down her cheek. He looked up.

"I've made you cry." He started to turn away, but Rose grabbed his hand. His warm fingers wrapped around hers as if he'd never let go. "You are the first man I've allowed to touch me—the first man I've felt safe with in years."

"That pleases me more than I can say." He gathered both her hands in his once again. His manly smell surrounded her like a shield. A look of complete and unfettered concern beamed from his eyes. "Rose, tell me what happened to you."

Alex watched as Rose turned and made her way to the barn door, leaning against its frame. He followed her. A breeze swirled around them, fluttering the hem of her gown and dancing among the golden curls that hung to her waist. Moonlight encased her in a protective glow as if she were too beautiful, too pure to touch.

"Remember when I told you about the so-called friend of my father's who took me in after my mother died and made me a servant?" Her voice quavered.

Alex nodded.

"I didn't tell you everything that happened to me after I ran away from him." She shifted her gaze away.

"You bartered passage aboard a merchant ship, if memory serves me."

She swallowed hard and opened and closed her mouth several times as if trying to say something.

"There is no need to tell me."

Blue eyes shot to his, cold with pain. "I want to. I want you to know."

She turned away from him and gazed out upon the farm. "At first the captain and crew were kind to me. They gave me my own quarters and fed me well."

The muscles in Alex's chest tightened. The tone of her voice, the defeated pain, said it all. Somehow he knew what was coming, and he didn't want to hear it. Didn't want to know that anyone had hurt this precious lady.

"But one night, two sailors crept into my cabin. One of them assaulted me—" Her voice cracked.

Blood pulsed hot in Alex's veins.

"During the struggle, I grabbed the pistol of the man attacking me. And I shot him." Her delicate jaw grew taut. "The captain burst into the room before the other man could react. But he was too late. The sailor was dead and I was. . ."

Alex stepped toward her.

She shuffled away. "The captain put me ashore, stating he wanted no more trouble aboard his ship."

The anguish in her tone sent a lance through Alex's heart.

"I traveled on foot, keeping to the trees that lined the coach trails, not daring to trust anyone again. Finally, two weeks later, I arrived at my aunt and uncle's house in town, starved and beaten." Drawing in a deep breath, she faced him, her features tight and a distant look in her eyes.

Alex tightened his jaw. Her sad tale had not surprised him. He had suspected as much. But now that he knew for sure, he could understand why she was frightened of everything. Why she feared even going into town. What this poor girl had endured at so young an age—just seventeen. It took all his strength to contain the rage bubbling up inside him at the sailors who had accosted Rose. But his anger would do her no good right now. Now, she needed understanding. She needed love and acceptance.

Her shoulders began to quiver beneath a sob. "I killed a man." She shook her head. "And the worst of it is I'm not sorry for it."

Alex reached out for her, but she backed away.

"I'm a murderer," she said. "The Bible says 'thou shalt not kill.' "

"I'm told by a very reliable source that God forgives." Alex grinned, hoping to lighten her mood.

"Does He forgive when I'm not sorry?"

Alex had no idea. He suddenly wished for Mr. Drummond's wise counsel, anything to help ease Rose's torment. "Is that why you abhor guns?"

"Yes." She tilted her head upward, allowing the moonlight to soften the hard lines of anguish. "What that sailor did to me was done. I am defiled. But because of that pistol, I now live with the guilt of his murder."

"You were defending yourself. No more than I or any military man does in war." Slipping in front of her, Alex took her in his arms. After a second, her stiff body relaxed, and she began to sob. He kissed her forehead and caressed the back of her head. He continued to stroke her hair and allowed her to cry even as fury tore through him. What he wouldn't give to find the remaining sailor and bring him to justice.

When her sobs were spent, Alex drew away from her and cupped her face in his hands, forcing her to look at him. Her red nose and tear-streaked cheeks glistened in the moonlight. "You are not defiled to me. You are the most precious thing I have ever encountered." He eased a lock of her hair from her face. "I truly do adore you."

"Then stay with me." The look of pleading in her moist eyes threatened to crack his resolve. No, to blast it into fragments. But what of his country, his family honor, his brother, his recompense? Would he be making another rash decision based on the passion of the moment that would only cause him further pain? Yet now as her lips parted and her eyes lovingly caressed his face, all those things seemed to drift away in the night breeze.

He lowered his mouth to hers.

Rose closed her eyes and felt Alex's lips touch hers. Moist and warm. Pressing her against him, he planted soft kisses over her mouth. His body stiffened and warmed. His kiss deepened. A surge of heat flooded her, swirling in her belly and sending pinpricks over her skin. She melted into his arms and lost herself in his scent, the feel of him, the taste of him. Her mind careened into an abyss of pleasure and love—a place she never wanted to leave.

An evening breeze wafted over them, bringing with it the scent of summer hyacinth. Silver light surrounded them. Leaves fluttered on trees as though they were laughing with delight. Rose never wanted this moment to end.

He withdrew and caressed her cheek with his fingers.

Rose was afraid to open her eyes. "I'm dreaming."

"After that kiss, I assure you, you are not." His voice was deep and sensuous.

Rose fell into him, and he swallowed her up in his arms.

"So this is the way of things?" a voice dripping in spite shouted from the darkness.

Jerking back from Alex, Rose spun to see Mr. Snyder approaching the barn, one hand on his cane, the other fisted at his waist.

"What are you doing here?" Rose's mind reeled at the interruption.

Alex groaned. Valor neighed and retreated into her stall as if the sight of the councilman sickened her.

"The question should be, what are you doing, Miss McGuire, compromising yourself with a family servant? Beyond unscrupulous." He huffed and jutted out his chin.

Alex moved in front of Rose, easing her behind him as the councilman entered the barn. "One more insult to Miss McGuire, and I shall demand satisfaction."

The spark of confidence in Mr. Snyder's eyes did not fade beneath Alex's threat, and that alone sent a sliver of dread down Rose's back.

"Fraternizing with the enemy, my dear?" Mr. Snyder twirled his cane in the air and moved toward Alex, a malicious smirk on his thin lips.

Rose's heart stopped beating, or so it seemed. The barn began to spin.

"Whatever are you babbling about, Mr. Snyder?" Alex's tone remained confident and demanding, but she could tell from the way he fisted his hands at his waist that Mr. Snyder's words had struck their mark.

The smile fell from Snyder's lips, and a hateful frown took its place. "I'm talking about your being a British naval officer, Mr. Reed."

Rose's legs nearly gave out, and she stumbled. Alex turned just in time to catch her before she fell. Wrapping an arm around her waist, he drew her to his side.

"Now isn't that sweet?" Snyder planted the tip of his cane in the dirt and leaned both hands upon it.

"You're mad, Snyder," Alex spat. "Where is your proof?"

One cultured brow lifted. "I have in my possession a certain service sword."

Rose felt a tremble jolt through Alex.

"I see from your stunned expression that you know the sword. It has an engraving, I believe." He tapped his chin. "Let me see if I can recall it. Ah, yes. Alexander M. Reed, HMS *Undefeatable*." He grinned like a cougar about to devour his prey. "An award perhaps for some courageous action?"

Rose gasped, and Alex tightened his grip around her waist. She glared at Snyder, surprised by the hatred burning in her soul for this man. "What are you going to do?" she asked.

He puckered his slimy lips and widened his eyes. "Well, nothing actually." Then he grinned. "As long as you both do what I say." Despite his assured stance, a bead of sweat forged a trail down his cheek.

"Pray tell, what is that?" Defeat and sorrow deepened Alex's tone.

"It's quite simple really. You, Mr. Reed, will scurry back to your ship or wherever you came from." He gestured with his hands as one would usher a mouse to a hole. "And you, Miss McGuire, will agree to marry me."

Nausea leaped into Rose's throat. The air thinned around her.

Rose felt Alex's body stiffen, heard the grunt of disbelief at the man's nerve.

"No doubt you know what will happen if you do not comply," Snyder pushed. "If I turn you in to authorities. . ." The rat paused for effect. "Miss McGuire and her family will be arrested for harboring the enemy." Then he waited, a malicious smirk on his face. Rose wanted to wipe it off, wanted to tell him to take a flying leap.

Finally Alex sighed. "I'll go back to my ship, Snyder, but leave Miss McGuire and her family out of this. They've done no wrong."

"Perhaps." Snyder sauntered toward Liverpool. The cow swung her head over the stall and snorted at him, halting him in his tracks. He wrinkled his nose, then turned to face them.

"Not very smart, are you, Mr. Reed?" Snyder cocked his head. "I'll still have your sword. And unless you have forgotten your unfortunate meeting with General Smith in town,"—he grinned—"ah, yes, I know about that. Well, let's just say, I'm sure he'll remember you were employed as the Drummond servant."

"We will deny that we knew his true identity." Though she tried to sound authoritative, Rose's voice cracked.

"No one will believe you, my sweet Rose." Snyder's lips slanted. "Not with the evidence I have gathered from Mr. Reed's quarters, and the fact that the British were seen on your property the night Mr. Reed suddenly appeared. Egad, the man's own regal accent betrays him."

Rose's legs trembled. He was right. General Smith was no fool.

Mr. Snyder brushed a speck of dirt from his coat, and Rose thought she saw a flicker of pain cross his face. "I am not a cruel man. I had hoped my fears of a dalliance between you and Mr. Reed were but a figment of my overimaginative mind. If so, there would be no need to resort to such measures."

The spark of hope that had ignited within her earlier, now extinguished, leaving her soul empty and dark.

Alex shifted his stance. "And if the lady refuses to marry you?"

"That would be most unwise." Snyder pointed his cane at them and chuckled. "For I can assure you that Miss McGuire and her aunt, uncle, most likely her maid and cook too will be tried for treason and executed."

❖ CHAPTER 19 ❖

Alex stormed into the servants' quarters. The wooden door slammed against the wall, raining dust upon him from the rafters. Fury blazed a hot trail down Alex's back, legs, arms, until he felt he would burst unless he struck something—or someone. He lifted a boot to the lone table and kicked it. It flew through the air and crashed against the far wall then fell, in shatters, onto the dirt floor.

Alex heard Rose's soft footsteps enter behind him. He ran a hand through his hair, tearing strands from his queue, and tried to collect his rage. But no sooner had his anger dwindled than an overwhelming sorrow threatened to crush him. He shook it off. Anger was better. It kept him focused, determined. It kept him from sinking into despair.

But a sob filtering from behind him proved to be his undoing. He turned around. Moonlight cast Rose's dark silhouette in a silver aura. He opened his arms, and she dashed toward him. The soft curves of her body melded against his chest, and he tightened his arms around her as if doing so would always keep her with him, always by his side. He stroked her hair. She trembled beneath another sob. Releasing her, he cupped her face and lifted her gaze to his. Tears streamed down her cheeks. He wiped them gently with his thumb.

"What are we to do, Alex?" Her face was etched in sorrow.

He hated to see her in such pain. Hated to feel it himself. Hated to be the cause of it. To the devil with Mr. Snyder! Alex had met scoundrels in his life. Many in fact during his time in His Majesty's Navy. One of them, Garrick, lay in a shallow grave not too far from where they stood. But the councilman surpassed them all.

He kissed Rose's forehead, then pressed her against him.

"I will die if I marry him," she cried.

Alex agreed for he felt as though he would die as well if she married that buffoon. Silently, he cursed himself for his selfishness, for staying too long, endangering this family and this precious woman.

Alex pushed away from her. Tears pooled on her lashes, and a red hue colored her nose and cheeks. Golden curls tumbled over her shoulders like spun silk. He took her hands in his. "I will not allow that to happen." Releasing her, he took up a pace across the room, not wanting her to see the moisture filling his eyes, not wanting her to see his inner conflict that surely must be evident on his face.

A sob moaned in her throat. "You could stay, switch sides, then it wouldn't matter that Snyder has your sword?"

"I can't." Alex halted and gazed at the dirt. He couldn't let his family down yet again. Couldn't make another bad decision based on foolish sentiments.

"So you would have me marry that fiend?"

"No." The thought made Alex's stomach churn and brought a sour taste to his mouth. "I will not allow that to happen."

"I don't see how you can prevent it." She turned her back to him and her shoulders lowered.

"Trust me, Rose." Alex reached up to touch her but thought better of it. Truth be told, a plan had formed in his mind even before Mr. Snyder had galloped away.

When she faced him again, her face was dry, and her eyes held the distant look of surrender. She had accepted her fate. He knew she would eventually. He knew because she was wise and strong—not a woman given to flighty, romantic notions. It was one of the things he loved about her. And a quality he wished he possessed more of, for at this moment, if she would but beg him to stay one more time, he doubted he could resist her.

"I shall pray for you, Alex. I'll pray that you can someday return to your home in England." Her voice threatened to crack.

"And I shall pray the same for you as well." He stepped toward her and fingered a strand of silky hair. "I will never forget you, Rose."

He studied her creamy face, memorizing every detail, the tiny wrinkle on her forehead that told him she was upset, her thin brown eyebrows drawn together in a frown, her high cheeks flushed with emotion, her moist lips. One last kiss. Could he steal one last kiss? He lowered his lips to hers. They tasted of tears and trembled at his touch.

Before she tore away from him and fled into the night.

Alex dashed to the door. Rose's white skirts billowed in the breeze and seemed to be floating over the ground like an angel as she receded into the darkness.

Then she was gone.

He rubbed his burning eyes. The sooner he left the better. He searched the room for his belongings and remembered Mr. Snyder had stolen them all. He had nothing but the clothes on his back. And those weren't even his. Blowing out the lantern, he stood at the door and took one last look at the room that had been his private chamber this past week. No four-poster oak bed topped with a silk embroidered coverlet, no mahogany writing desk, or rich velvet curtains, no Persian rug or marble-framed fireplace, but this small dirty room had brought him far more comfort than his elegant bedchamber at home. He closed the door, passed the house—forcing himself not to look at it—then headed toward the dirt road.

Anger simmered within him until it seared his vision and branded his thoughts with purpose. A dark cloud drifted over the moon, stealing the light and casting the dirt road into even deeper shadows. No matter. Alex knew where he was going. Well, almost.

Mr. Snyder may think he has the upper hand in this dangerous game, but Alex would be a pirate's lackey before he'd allow that snake to marry Rose. A hint of a plan had taken root in his mind even before the slimy toad had finished his threats. It was the exact carrying out of that plan that eluded Alex at the moment.

Despite his promise to himself, he cast one last glance over his shoulder at the Drummond home. Golden light cascaded from the windows, beckoning him back to the only place that had ever felt like home—to the people he'd grown to love. A shadow crossed the upstairs casement. Rose? He swallowed and fisted his hands.

"Good-bye, my love," he whispered into the wind.

The clomp of horse's hooves drew him about to see a lone rider heading his way. Before he had a chance to even consider where he could hide, the man closed in on him, Alex recognized the familiar form of Mr. Drummond. The older man pulled his horse to a stop and peered down at Alex.

"Is that you, Mr. Reed?"

"Yes sir."

"Sink me, what are you doing out here in the dark?" His horse pranced over the dirt. "Hop on and I'll give you a ride back home."

Home. "I can't go back, Mr. Drummond. Ever." He owed this man the truth and welcomed the opportunity to thank him for his kindness.

The old man gave him a curious look, then flipped his leg over the saddle and slipped from the horse with more agility than Alex would have expected. "What's that you say? Of course you can go back."

Alex shook his head, squinting to see the man's face in the darkness. A face that had always brought comfort to Alex. But the shadows forbade him a view. "Mr. Drummond, you have been very kind to me, and I thank you for taking me into your home and into your employ. And for gracing me with your friendship."

"What happened, son?" Mr. Drummond's voice grew solemn.

Alex shifted his stance, unsure of how much to disclose. "Let's just say that if I stay, I will endanger your entire family."

"I'd say you've had quite the opposite effect, particularly on Rose." The dark cloud slipped aside, allowing the moon's light to seek out Mr. Drummond and bathe him in its creamy glow.

"Believe me, sir, for your own safety and for Rose's, I must leave." Alex bowed his head and avoided looking into Mr. Drummond's brown, caring eyes. "Please extend my thanks and appreciation to your wife." He turned to leave.

Mr. Drummond grabbed his arm. "Has this anything to do with you being a British naval officer?"

A sudden breeze stole the words away before Alex's mind could grasp them. He blinked and scratched his head. "You knew?"

"Aye." Mr. Drummond chuckled.

Alex would have laughed if he weren't so filled with sorrow. This man he'd once considered to be nothing but a bumbling fool turned out wiser than them all. "How?"

"Ah, shame on me, Mr. Reed, if I don't know what's happening beneath my own roof."

"Why didn't you have me arrested? Or at least tossed out of your house?"

Mr. Drummond folded his hands over his prominent belly. "You are good for Rose. I've never seen her so happy."

The reminder opened a fresh wound on Alex's heart. "But I am her enemy—your enemy."

"Your country, yes. But not you, Mr. Reed. I count myself a good judge of character, and I could tell the first time I met you that you are an honorable man with a kind heart." He sighed and rubbed the back of his neck. "I don't much care for this war, Mr. Reed. But I also don't judge a man by color, status, money, or nationality." He tapped a finger on Alex's chest. "God judges by the heart, and I try to do that as well."

The man's words defied everything Alex had been taught his entire life. He stared at the man in wonder. "I am all astonishment, sir."

Mr. Drummond grinned. "Besides, God told me you and Rose are a good match."

"I wish that were true." Alex winced beneath another jab to his heart.

"Why not stay and find out?"

"Upon my honor, I cannot, sir. I have obligations in England to attend to. But, I fear my identity has been discovered and your family threatened."

"Mr. Snyder, eh?"

Again the man amazed Alex. "He has my service sword with my name engraved upon it."

Mr. Drummond groaned.

"He threatened to turn in your family as traitors. He forces Rose to marry him," Alex snapped, his anger rising once again.

"Well, we can't let that happen, can we?"

Alex shook his head at the man's confident tone. "She will do it to save you and your wife from the traitor's noose."

The elderly man scratched his bearded jaw. Anticipation rose as Alex waited, hoping he would offer an alternative plan. But no wise answer spilled from his lips.

Alex released a heavy sigh and gazed into the dark forest lining the path. Why torture himself? There *was* no other alternative. Yet even as his thoughts took a dive into despair, the idea planted earlier in his mind sprouted a promising leaf. "Are you acquainted with a Mr. Noah Brenin?"

"That I am."

"Would you do me the kindness of showing me where he lives?"

Mr. Drummond's eyes twinkled. "Would I be correct in perceiving, Mr. Reed, that you've got some trickery up your sleeve?"

"Aye, that I do, sir, a plan that will keep Rose from being forced to marry that callow nodcock."

"God always finds a way, Mr. Reed." Mr. Drummond grabbed his horse's reins, clipped a buckled shoe into the stirrup, and swung onto her back. "Hop on, Mr. Reed. I'll take you to Mr. Brenin myself."

Alex followed Mr. Drummond up the porch stairs of a modest two-story home, capped with a hipped roof. Golden light, along with a child's laughter and a discordant melody streamed through the open green shudders, barely glazing the tips of a multitude of flowers that must have been brilliant in the daylight.

Mr. Drummond knocked on the door. Each rap tightened the band around Alex's nerves. Was he mad? Asking help of man he had impressed and enslaved aboard his ship? If Mr. Drummond had not insisted he join Alex on his mission, Alex couldn't be sure that Noah wouldn't strike him across the jaw and have him arrested on the spot. How could he blame him?

Clearing his throat, Mr. Drummond rapped again as a light breeze laden with salt and fish blew in from the harbor only a mile away. Even at this distance, Alex could see the bare masts of a multitude of ships spear into the night like white, ghostly claws above waters churning with anxiety. A sense of unrest and dread settled over the city. Alex could feel it in the air, see it in the faces of those they passed. All due to his countrymen.

The door swung open to a tall, sallow-skinned man whose lips puckered as if he'd just drunk a mug of sour milk. Folds of skin fell over a lavender neckcloth that appeared far too tight but held the only color in an otherwise drab black suit.

"Mr. Drummond and Mr. Reed to see Mr. Brenin, if you please." Mr. Drummond brushed past the man without an invitation, and the butler's face soured even further.

"Wait here." He walked down the hall and entered a parlor on their left, where open double doors flooded the otherwise dim hallway with light and gaiety.

Moments later, the laughter and music fell silent, and the grim man returned. "Follow me."

When Alex stepped into the room, the joyous sparkle in the eyes of those present faded as each gaze latched upon him. Marianne, Noah's wife, who sat at the pianoforte, leaped to her feet and covered her mouth with her hand. A glass slipped from Noah's grip and shattered on the floor, spraying the contents over the wooden planks. A child let out a startled cry, and an elderly woman took the baby in her arms and rose from a floral-printed settee, her worried gaze shifting from Alex to Noah.

Noah stepped over the broken glass, his face tight and his skin flushed. "What are you doing here, Reed?"

Mr. Drummond's gray eyebrows arched at Alex. "I wasn't aware you were acquainted with the Brenins."

Alex cleared his throat. He hadn't wanted to tell Mr. Drummond for fear he wouldn't bring him to their home. "Yes, they had the misfortune of being impressed on my ship."

"Then you know who this man is?" Noah proceeded toward a cabinet against the far wall, flung it open and grabbed a pistol.

"Indeed I do." Mr. Drummond said. "But before you go shooting him, he is here as a friend to Rose, not an enemy."

"A friend to. . ." Noah spun around, pistol in hand.

Marianne stepped out from the pianoforte. "Then we did see you in town the other day?"

Alex nodded in her direction. "Good evening, Miss Denton. I mean Mrs. Brenin, the last time I saw you you were hanging off the stern of my ship."

"Indeed." Marianne said with a slight smile.

Noah methodically poured gun powder into the barrel, then

rammed the bullet inside with a ramrod. "Mr. Drummond, surely you know that bringing him here endangers my entire family."

The elderly woman gasped, stumbled and lowered herself and the child back onto the settee.

Mr. Drummond scratched his beard. "That will not happen, I assure you. We only need a moment of your time. Please I beg of you to trust me. Rose's future is at stake."

Noah cocked the gun with an ominous click then pointed it at Alex.

Though his insides began to clench, Alex forced a stoic look upon his face. Surely the man wouldn't shoot him here in front of his family?

Marianne wove around the shattered glass and slid beside her husband. "Mr. Reed was always kind to us, Noah. Hear him out, for Rose's sake."

The young boy, who could be no more than one grabbed a wooden doll from the elderly woman's hand and stuffed the arm in his mouth.

Mr. Drummond faced the woman on the settee. "Mrs. Denton, always a pleasure. You appear in fine health these days," he said as if there weren't a gun pointed at Alex.

"Indeed, Reverend Drummond." The woman, whom Alex assumed to be Marianne's mother, clutched the child tighter. Veins lined her thin, frail hands, yet her eyes were clear and her voice strong. "There is nothing like a grandchild to keep an old lady around past her time."

Lowering his pistol, Noah flattened his lips. "What is it you want?"

"May we speak to you alone, Noah?" Mr. Drummond asked. "It is a matter of grave importance."

Noah's eyes narrowed. He glanced at his wife who nodded her approval. "Very well." Still gripping the pistol, he led the men across the hall to another room, closing the doors behind them. Tobacco and wood smoke combined to form the masculine scent of a man's library. Bookshelves lined the right wall from floor to ceiling. A cold fireplace stood on Alex's left. Candle sconces hanging intermittently on the fore and aft walls sent flickering light across the sturdy wood furniture. A walnut desk guarded the far wall while various cushioned Windsor chairs were scattered throughout. Whitewashed walls decorated with oil paintings of ships and the sea sat above a wooden chair rail that circled the room like a ship's bulwark.

Placing his pistol atop his desk, Noah crossed his arms over his chest. "Now, what is this about?"

Mr. Drummond took a seat and deferred the question to Alex, who after taking a deep breath, spent the next few minutes explaining how he had come to be on the Drummond farm and the ultimatum Mr. Snyder had issued to him and Rose earlier in the evening.

Gripping the edge of his desk, Noah stared at the cross-stitched rug by his boots. "Egad man, what were you thinking staying with the Drummonds so long?"

Alex walked to the fireplace, placed his boot atop the marble hearth and gazed at dark coals. "I should have left as soon as I could walk. I intended to leave last night, but—"

"I enlisted his help to rebuild the Myers' house." Mr. Drummond coughed.

Noah glanced up. "You don't say? Unheard of. A British officer cleaning up the mess he made." Sarcasm stung in his voice.

Alex grimaced. "I felt obliged." Then he snapped his eyes to Mr. Drummond as the realization struck him. "As you knew I would."

Mr. Drummond shrugged. "I had to think of some way to keep you here."

"To keep him here?" Noah's face scrunched. "Are you daft, Reverend?"

"Perhaps." Mr. Drummond smiled and patted the pockets of his waistcoat as if searching for something. "He's good for Rose."

Alex turned his back to the mantel and crossed his arms over his chest. "In truth, I was having difficulty leaving anyway." Would he sound foolish if he shared his feelings for Rose with Noah?

Noah's blue eyes turned to ice. "I would think you'd be anxious to return to your ship and continue terrorizing innocent farmers."

Alex flinched beneath the blow. "If you must know, I have no desire to do either."

"Why not stay, become an American?" Noah asked. "Then Snyder's threats would be empty."

Alex hung his head. Oh how he wanted to. With everything in him. But he couldn't. Hadn't he already made enough mistakes by following the leading of his heart? "I can't."

Noah snorted.

Mr. Drummond quit his unsuccessful search and stood. His gaze shifted between Alex and Noah, finally landing on Noah. "Mr. Reed only wishes to help Rose."

Moving to the fireplace, Noah eyed Alex. A wood-encased clock perched upon the mantel marked Alex's future with an eerie *tick-tock, tick-tock.* "You love her?"

Alex said nothing.

"Yet you'll leave her." Noah's voice spiked with disdain. "For what? Title, fortune? Ah, don't want to step down off your British pedestal, become a common American, eh?"

Alex met his gaze. "That's not the reason."

Mr. Drummond stepped toward Noah. "Will you help us, Mr. Brenin?"

"What else can you do now but leave?" Noah said. "Haven't you done enough damage?"

Alex shook his head. "I can't. Not until I make things right. Not until I fix it so Rose will not be forced to marry that insolent ninny on my account."

"I don't see how you can prevent it." Noah huffed.

Alex lengthened his stance, feeling his resolve strengthen." He leaned toward Noah. "I have a plan, but I need your help."

Noah lifted one brow. "A plan?"

"Yes. To break into Snyder's home and steal back my sword."

❖ CHAPTER 20 ❖

Rose pried open her swollen eyelids to see nothing but the scratchy underside of her quilt. Sunlight filtering through the fabric twisted the threads into chaotic patterns. She traced them with her eyes until dizziness overtook her. From the top, the quilt's multicolored strands formed a beautiful pattern. But underneath they appeared disorderly and without purpose—just like her life. Birds outside her window chirped a traitorous, joyful melody. How could any creature be happy when Rose was steeped in such overwhelming sorrow?

Alex was gone.

Forever.

Why hadn't the world stopped spinning? Why did the sun keep rising? Something besides her broken heart should mark the passage of such an honorable man.

Her chamber door squeaked open. "Rose, dear." Aunt Muira's tone sounded heavy, muffled. Smells of fresh biscuits and coffee from downstairs penetrated Rose's quilt and caused her stomach to rumble. She pressed a hand to her belly—as traitorous as the birds and the sun.

"Rose, dear." Her aunt repeated as she sat on one side of the mattress. "I know you're under there."

213

"I don't feel well." Rose squeaked out, her nose curling at her own sour breath.

The quilt slipped from her face, and Rose squeezed her eyes against the bright light.

She felt her aunt's hand on her face, her neck. "You've been in bed for two days now, dear." She sighed. "You have no fever, and I can find nothing at all wrong with you."

Rose opened her eyes and blinked at the fuzzy image until her aunt's comely visage came into focus. *Nothing wrong with her?* If only her aunt knew. Rose had the worst kind of sickness. One that would never heal.

Aunt Muira brushed tangled curls from Rose's face. "Tell me what is bothering you, dear." A ray of sunlight caught one of her pearl earrings and set it aglow.

Rose swallowed. Her mouth felt as though it were stuffed with hay. "May I sleep a bit more, Aunt Muira? I'm so tired."

Her aunt's lips tightened into a thin line, and she sprang from the bed. "Absolutely not. I insist you join us for breakfast. You didn't eat all day yesterday." She swung around and the folds of her lilac gown swirled in the air making a swooshing sound. Gathering undergarments from Rose's dresser and a gown of lavender muslin from her armoire, she laid them across the foot of the bed. "Some food and fresh air will do you good." She planted her hands on her hips. "Perhaps then you will tell me what ails you." She gave Rose a sweet but determined smile before she swept from the room and closed the door behind her.

With a groan, Rose sat and punched her mattress, sending a spray of dust sparkling in the sunlight. Dizziness threatened to send her back onto her pillow. She drew a deep breath and swung her legs over the side of the bed. She had no choice. Sooner or later she had to get up and face life, no matter how empty her future seemed. Today was as good as any.

Minutes later, she entered the kitchen to find Amelia, her aunt, and Cora sitting around a table laden with platters of biscuits, fresh jam, eggs, and blocks of yellow cheese. A plethora of fragrant smells— butter, sweet cream, spice, and coffee—sent Rose's stomach lurching. Sounding like one of Rose's chickens, Amelia babbled excitedly about the ball in three days at the Fountain Inn. Apparently, Mr. Braxton had finally asked Uncle Forbes if he could escort Amelia.

"There you are, dear." Aunt Muira said.

Amelia's eyebrows slanted together. "You look horrible, Rose."

Rose slid into the wooden seat beside her aunt as Cora poured her a cup of coffee.

"You shouldn't be sayin' such things, Miss Amelia. Your mistress's been ill." Cora set the tin pot down in the center of the table and moved to the open fireplace.

"She's not ill, Cora. Rose's just upset about. . ."

Rose's glare halted her maid in midsentence. Not only did she not want Cora and her aunt to know what had happened, she didn't want to hear *his* name out loud. Not yet.

"Thank you, Amelia, for caring for my animals while I was indisposed." Rose attempted to change the topic of conversation.

It didn't work.

"Upset about what?" Aunt Muira took a delicate bite of toast smothered in strawberry jam.

Taking the silver tongs, Rose plopped a cube of sugar into her coffee. Then another.

Aunt Muira's hand stopped her from plucking yet another one from the china bowl. "Careful, dear. Those are all we have until the war ends."

Setting down the tongs, Rose stirred her coffee and took a sip, hoping the savory liquid wouldn't rebel in her stomach. The rich flavor that reminded Rose of cocoa eased down her throat and helped settle her nerves. But it needed more sugar.

Cora returned from the fireplace and placed two pieces of toast before Rose.

"Thank you, Cora, but I fear I'm unable to eat anything."

"Of course you are, dear." Aunt Muira leaned over and spread butter and jam over Rose's toast before shoving the plate closer to her. "Now, do tell us what has you so distraught. I've never seen you keep to your bed for two days. Not since. . ."

Her voice trailed off, but Rose knew what she intended to say. Not since Rose had turned up on their doorstep starving and beaten five years ago.

MaryLu Tyndall

Cora circled the table and laid one hand on her hip. "If you ask me, I'd say it has somethin' to do with Mr. Reed leavin'."

His name shot like an arrow through the room and pierced straight into Rose's heart.

"Wherever did he run off to, Rose?" Aunt Muira dabbed her napkin over her lips. "Forbes won't say a word except that Mr. Reed has gone back to join the war."

Amelia shared a quizzical glance with Rose.

Rose took another sip of coffee and warmed her hands around the cup. But her vision blurred with tears.

Cora tugged at her red scarf. Amelia set down the piece of cheese she'd been nibbling on. Aunt Muira's gaze flitted from Cora, to Amelia, to Rose. She placed a hand on Rose's back. "Oh dear, tell me your affections did not lean toward Mr. Reed."

The china cup cradled in Rose's trembling hands clattered on the saucer.

"Oh my." Aunt Muira laid a hand on her heart. "How could I have missed it? You poor dear. And now he's gone."

"I knows just how you feel, child." Cora sank into a chair and shook her head. "I felt like my heart would never recover after my Samuel left."

Amelia gave the cook a tender look. "Why did you allow him to leave?"

"I didn't *let* 'im go. He took off hisself."

"He left because you scolded him to death." Amelia offered.

"Now, now, Amelia, that isn't kind." Aunt Muira said.

"No, she's right." Cora sighed. "I didn't mean to. Just mad at the world, I guess." She fingered a folded white napkin. "If I had to do it all over again, I'd never let him go. I sees now it was my unforgiveness that drove him away."

Aunt Muira stretched her hand across the table to the cook. Cora gripped it briefly then released it as if she was uncomfortable with the display of affection from her mistress.

Amelia frowned. "But you weren't unforgiving of anything Samuel had done. How can that drive anyone away?"

Cora tossed down the napkin and stood. "Bitterness made me too afraid to love—to risk losin' that love." She gazed out the window.

"An' now he's gone."

Unforgiveness and fear, yet again. Two topics that kept flashing across Rose's path like garish actors across a stage. Pushing out her chair, she stood, skirted the table and kissed Cora on her cheek. Cora's big brown eyes met Rose's, and she saw the brokenness in their depths.

"Must every woman in this house fall in love with our servants?" Aunt Muira's exasperated voice scattered the gloomy spirit that had descended upon the kitchen.

"Not me!" Amelia waved her hand through the air, sending her raven curls bouncing. "I intend to marry a man of fortune."

"Speaking of eligible men, Rose." Aunt Muira sipped her tea and set the cup down with a clank. She gave Rose one of those motherly smiles that said she knew what was best for Rose even if Rose did not. "I've invited Mr. Snyder to supper tonight. Perhaps he can pull you out of your dour mood and make you forget all about Mr. Reed."

A nauseous brew of disgust and agony churned in Rose's stomach, threatening to erupt with fury on the odious snake of a man sitting across from her. Maybe then he would leave and stop smiling at her with that salacious grin of victory. Dinner had been unbearable, but now sitting in the stuffy parlor with him might prove to be her undoing. At least she was not alone. Amelia sat next to her on the settee, sipping her tea, while Rose's aunt and uncle sat side by side on the sofa. Mr. Snyder occupied the high-backed chair and pretended to listen to her uncle's discourse on the war.

"I hear word of British ship movements along the coast of the upper Chesapeake," her uncle was saying.

Mr. Snyder set his cup on the table and adjusted his silk cravat. "No doubt more idle threats intending to frighten us into submission." Candlelight reflected devilish flames in Mr. Snyder's eyes.

"I beg to differ with you, Mr. Snyder," her uncle said in a tone that lacked its normal solicitude. In fact, her uncle had seemed unusually ill at ease during their evening meal, making curt remarks toward their guest and offering up a chorus of groans and sighs, mimicking the silent ones grinding through Rose.

Aunt Muira had attempted to make up for his behavior by engaging

Mr. Snyder in a discussion of the city militia's readiness to fight and the council's recent decision to keep pigs from running rampant through the city streets.

Which gave Mr. Snyder the center stage he so often sought and relished in. But which had further squelched Rose's appetite for the broiled cod, potatoes, and fresh greens that stared up at her from her plate, uneaten.

"Our lookouts have spotted a new British fleet, commanded, some say, by Sir Alexander Cochrane," Uncle Forbes continued. "A formidable force of four ships of the line, twenty frigates and sloops, and twenty troop transports." He stretched his shoulders and leaned back on the sofa. "Since the British have already successfully blockaded the Chesapeake, it worries me."

"Yes." Rose's aunt folded her hands in her lap and swept green eyes filled with concern over them all. "It would seem the defeat of Napoleon in France has emboldened the British to pursue victory here as soon as possible."

For the first time since she'd met her, Rose detected a slight glimmer of fear cross her aunt's eyes. Which only set Rose's own nerves further on edge.

Uncle Forbes laid a hand atop his wife's. "Never fear, dearest. God is in control. We must continue to pray for our victory."

"Pray, humph." Mr. Snyder dabbed his fingers over his tongue then slicked back the red hair on either side of his temples. A vision of the slithering tongue of a snake formed in Rose's mind.

"We must act. We must take up arms and force these devilish British off our shores." He speared Rose with a devious, determined gaze. She knew he spoke of Alex. She averted her eyes to the open window where thick darkness seemed to pour into the room from outside like black molasses. Not even a wisp of a breeze entered behind it to relieve the dank, oppressive air that always seemed to hover around Mr. Snyder.

"All this talk of war." Amelia pouted. "Can we talk of brighter things, perhaps?" She scooted to the edge of her seat. "Like the ball at the Fountain Inn?"

"Is that all you think about, Amelia?" Rose instantly regretted her tone as her maid swallowed and stared down at the hands in her lap.

"Forgive me." Rose set down her cup and grasped Amelia's hand.

"I fear I am not myself lately."

"As much as I love a good soiree"—Uncle Forbes fingered a stain on his cravat—"shouldn't we be preparing for a possible invasion instead of dancing the night away?"

"It is good for morale, dearest." Candlelight shimmered over Aunt Muira's burgundy-colored hair, streaking it crimson. "The citizens of Baltimore need to escape the constant threat of attack, if only for one night."

If only Rose could escape the constant threat of the man sitting across from her. She flattened her lips and found Uncle Forbes's tender gaze still on her. Did her uncle know of the councilman's insidious plan? But how could he? Rose had thought it best to keep the man's threats from her family. There was no need to cause alarm over something that could not be changed.

As if Mr. Snyder's presence wasn't disconcerting enough, her uncle's odd behavior only increased the turmoil clawing at her insides. Plucking out her fan, she waved it over her heated skin.

"By the by, speaking of the Fountain Inn." Mr. Snyder's nasally voice shot through the room like a quiver of arrows. Rose resisted the urge to duck to avoid being pierced by one.

"If I may, Miss McGuire, it would be my honor to escort you to the ball."

She should have ducked.

Her stomach gurgled and a sour taste rose to her mouth. Why was he putting on such airs? He knew she could not refuse him. She could refuse him nothing as long as he threatened her family. Yet. . .she bit her lip. Perhaps he would release her from the obligation of attending this silly ball. She pasted on a smile. "You are too kind, Mr. Snyder, but I have not been well lately and wish to remain home."

"Indeed? But it is three days away. Surely you will regain your strength by then." One cultured brow rose above eyes that hardened at her denial.

"Rose, dear." Aunt Muira patted her hair in place. "A night of fun and dancing will do you good. And I can think of no better escort than Mr. Snyder."

Uncle Forbes coughed and slammed down his teacup.

"Do say yes, Rose." Amelia jumped in her seat, bouncing Rose on the settee. "Think of the fun we could have together."

Rose smiled at her maid, urging her with her eyes to remain silent and wishing she had confided in Amelia about what Mr. Snyder had done. But Rose had hardly been able to think about his threats, let alone speak them out loud.

"Yes, I insist." Mr. Snyder's tone held no room for argument.

She directed a chilled gaze his way. Was there no end to the man's petitions? Wasn't it bad enough that he had threatened her family? That he now forced her to marry him? Despondency tugged her shoulders down as she envisioned a future consisting of Mr. Snyder's iron rods of demands erected one by one around her until she was a prisoner to his every whim.

Her foot twitched. She wanted to kick him. She wanted to toss her hot tea in his face. Instead she smiled sweetly. "A gentleman never insists, sir."

"More tea?" Aunt Muira took the china pot and poured more of the amber liquid into Mr. Snyder's cup in an effort, Rose assumed, to alleviate the tension rising in the room.

He thanked her aunt with a tight smile.

"With Mr. Reed gone, who else will ask you?" Amelia gripped Rose's hands.

Rose glared at her maid.

"Aye, perhaps you should go, Rose." Uncle Forbes folded his hands over his rounded belly. "I am of the opinion that you'll be glad you did."

Rose swept a confused gaze toward him as perspiration formed on her neck. Her uncle had always seemed unimpressed by Mr. Snyder and had never encouraged a courtship between them. Was he now against Rose as well? Was everyone against her?

"It's settled then." The snake set down his cup. The clank echoed Rose's doom through the parlor. He stood and brushed invisible dust from the sleeves of his coat. "The hour is late. I shall relieve you of my company."

Relieve, indeed. Rose smiled.

An uncharacteristic alarm rolled across her uncle's face. "So soon, Mr. Snyder? Why you've barely been here a few hours."

Rose clenched her jaw. *Please let him go, Uncle.*

"Indeed, but I have some urgent business which requires my

attention." Mr. Snyder bowed. "I thank you for the lovely supper, Mrs. Drummond, Mr. Drummond. Mrs. Wilkins, always a pleasure." He turned to Rose. "Would you do me the honor of seeing me out, Miss McGuire? I wish to speak to you."

Uncle Forbes struggled to his feet with a groan. "Are you sure I cannot interest you in some pudding?" He glanced toward the kitchen. "Cora!"

"Dearest, what is wrong with you?" Aunt Muira rose and took her husband's arm. "We have no pudding prepared, and Cora has retired."

Mr. Snyder's nose wrinkled. "I am quite all right, I assure you. Perhaps some other time."

Yes, like when the oceans turn to mud. Rose followed him into the foyer.

"Perhaps a sip of brandy then?" Uncle Forbes asked.

"No, thank you, sir." Mr. Snyder turned toward Rose and gestured toward the door. "Shall we?"

"I really shouldn't go outside in the night air." She feigned a cough.

"Nonsense, dear, it's only a few steps," Aunt Muira scolded. "We'll keep the door open for propriety." She nudged Rose forward.

Retrieving his hat and cane from the coatrack, Mr. Snyder turned toward her uncle. "You really should hire another footman, sir."

"I have every intention of doing so." There was no mistaking the aversion in her uncle's voice. Then why did he suggest she accompany Mr. Snyder to the ball?

Aunt Muira opened the door, and Mr. Snyder proffered his arm toward Rose. Ignoring him, she stepped onto the porch and swatted at a bug hovering around the lantern atop a post.

She wished she could swat Mr. Snyder away as easily. Instead she followed him down the path, feeling as though it was her heart crunching beneath his shoes instead of the gravel.

Halting at his horse, he leaned toward her. "You shouldn't treat your future husband with such contempt. It may cause suspicion, my dear."

"What do you expect, Mr. Snyder?"

"I expect you to comport yourself as a lady."

The smell of the bergamot he splashed on his hair threatened to choke her. Withdrawing a handkerchief from her sleeve she pressed it over her moist neck and gazed above. A dark cloud drifted over the sliver of a moon, stealing away its light. Just as Mr. Snyder had drifted into her life, stealing away her future. *Why God?* Rose lifted up her first prayer since Alex had left. Even now her anger forbade her to pray more.

Mr. Snyder untied the reins and faced her, sorrow clouding his features. "I hate to be so disagreeable, but you force my hand. You must attend the ball with me—to show our friends and family our devoted attachment before our engagement is announced."

"And if I don't?"

His eyes hardened, but the sorrow remained. "I think we both know what will happen."

Rose sighed. "But if you expose my association with Mr. Reed and send me and my family to prison, then you will never marry me or get your hands on my property. Why risk it for a silly ball?"

He gazed at her as if for the first time he realized she actually possessed a mind underneath her golden tresses. "Indeed. Why risk it for a silly ball, Miss McGuire?" He tugged on his riding gloves then slid his cane though a loop on his saddle.

She narrowed her eyes. "So I am to attend the ball and play the part of your devoted admirer, is that it?"

"Precisely." He brushed his fingers over her cheek, and she stepped back, her stomach tightening.

"And what do I get in return?" Rose asked.

Agony pierced the hard sheen covering his eyes. "I know you are angry with me, Rose. But in time I hope you will forgive me. I can make you happy if you'll but give me a chance." He lifted his hand toward her again, but she stepped out of his reach. Frowning, he donned his hat and swung onto his horse. "And maybe someday you will come to love me."

Instead of answering, Rose gazed, benumbed, into the darkness that extended into an unforeseen oblivion.

"Until the ball, my dear." Mr. Snyder kicked the horse and sped off down the trail.

Dust showered over Rose, but she couldn't move. She hugged herself, willing her tears back behind her eyes. Young Daniel had said she had a destiny.

What he hadn't said was that her destiny was a fate worse than death.

❖ CHAPTER 21 ❖

Alex followed Noah down the streets of Baltimore. The last rays of sun slipped over the western horizon, luring shadows from the alleyways and darkened corners. A bawdy tune wafted on the breeze from the docks as lanterns atop posts lining the avenue remained as dark as the encroaching night. No need to give the British fleet a glowing target. A wise decision on the part of General Smith.

Behind Alex, Mr. Heaton's boots thudded over the sandy lane. The men said not a word to one another. A bell rang in the distance, accompanied by the lap of waves coming from the harbor a mile away. They passed a row of shops all closed for the day: cobbler, chandler, millinery, ironworks, and a bakery. Their engraved wooden signs swung in the breeze from iron hooks above their doors. A carriage rumbled by, its occupants chattering happily. Down the street, a man shouted for his son to come inside. A night watchman, armed with musket and sword, strode by them and tipped his hat. "Good evening, Mr. Brenin. Mr. Heaton." His eyes grazed over Alex in passing as Noah returned the greeting.

They turned the corner onto Howard Street. The smell of horse manure, salt, and tar from a distant shipyard stung Alex's nose. Tension pricked the air and clawed down his back.

"Just another block," Noah shot over his shoulder.

Alex thanked God for this man's help—and for Luke's. He'd been surprised they both had agreed to accompany him on his nefarious deed. Surprised and also ashamed to accept their kindness in light of Alex's complicity in the suffering they'd endured aboard the HMS *Undefeatable*. So many conflicting emotions roiled in his gut, he didn't know what to feel.

Except at the moment fear seemed to dominate the others. Alex had spent the past two days holed up in Noah's home, pacing the floor, agonizing over the mess he had caused. Now, ever since Mr. Drummond had informed Alex he had managed to lure Mr. Snyder from his house for the evening, Alex had begun to wonder if he hadn't lost what was left of his reason.

He was a British officer in the middle of a rebel city on a mission to steal back his sword from a member of the city council. Absurd!

Considering the way his countrymen had terrorized these citizens of late, if he were caught he'd be no doubt strung up on the nearest tree. And what of Mr. Heaton and Mr. Brenin? They risked the same by helping him.

No, not for him, to help their friend Rose. Which spoke volumes as to her character. Something he could well attest to, for he would do anything to ensure her happiness.

Even if her future wasn't with him.

Alex clenched his fists. He hoped Mr. Drummond had not invited Snyder to the farm. The thought of the depraved councilman being anywhere near Rose caused Alex's stomach to fold in on itself. But there was nothing to be done about it.

At least not yet.

Rows of houses stood at attention on either side of the street. Slivers of light peeked from behind closed shutters and curtains, but otherwise the homes remained shrouded in darkness. Noah stopped before a modest, single-story cottage at the end of the street. The simple home gave no indication that a councilman lived within. A garden that boasted of more weeds than flowers filled the small front yard, while an iron gate that hung loose on its hinges did a pathetic job of barring entrance. No wonder the man sought after Rose's property.

"I would have expected Mr. Snyder to live in a more stately home."

Alex stopped beside Noah.

Luke laughed. "Indeed, the man has an uncanny ability to play the part of royalty when, in truth, he lives like a pauper."

A group of gentlemen emerged from a house across the street, and Noah nudged Alex and Luke into the shadow of a tree beside the fence. "Truth be told, Mr. Reed," Noah whispered, "Mr. Snyder cannot claim a very noble pedigree. In fact"—he scratched his jaw and watched as the group of men sauntered down the street and out of sight—"his father was hung for horse thievery and his grandfather for piracy."

Alex flinched and gazed back at the house. "Upon my honor."

"Honor has nothing to do with it." Luke snorted and flipped the hair from his face.

"This was his father's house." Noah studied a passing horse. "The only thing left him after he paid his family's debts."

"How did he become a councilman?" Alex asked. No man so dishonored could ever hold such a prestigious office in England.

Noah shrugged. "He's intelligent and has a way with words. And Americans don't tend to hold a person's parentage against them." He gazed toward the harbor. "I suppose because so many of our ancestors came here to escape their pasts."

Alex ran a hand through his hair. So unlike his homeland where bloodline and title were everything. Yet one more quality to admire about these Americans.

After scanning the street one last time, Noah pushed open the broken gate. The loud squeak of rusty hinges frayed Alex's already pinched nerves as Noah led them down the dirt path to the front porch.

"How are we to get past the servants?" Alex whispered.

"There's only one—a middle-aged spinster who runs the house." Noah stepped over a fallen branch.

"And?" Mr. Reed raised his brows.

"Why do you think I brought Mr. Heaton?" Noah halted at the porch steps then dipped his head to the left. "This way, Mr. Reed."

Luke winked at Alex as he proceeded up the steps. A *rap, rap, rap* echoed through the air even before Alex rounded the corner of the house.

"Mr. Heaton," a female voice exclaimed. "I'm sorry, but Mr. Snyder is not home."

Alex followed Noah through a sea of tall grass and weeds to a darkened window at the back. Balancing on a pile of firewood stacked along the wall, Noah pressed on the wooden frame of the window. The bottom half slipped upward.

"Ah, God is good to us, Mr. Reed. We don't have to break the glass." Hoisting himself up on the window frame, Noah squeezed headfirst through the opening. A thump sounded from the room, and Noah's hand appeared in the window. "Hurry, the two of us can search much faster together."

The opening proved a more difficult obstacle for Alex's larger frame, but with Noah's assistance, he soon landed on the wooden floor of what he assumed to be Mr. Snyder's bedchamber.

"You are looking more lovely than ever, Miss Addington." Luke's deep flirtatious tone filtered beneath the door.

A woman's giggle was the only reply.

Noah fumbled among the objects sitting atop a desk in the corner then struck flint to steel and lit two candles. He handed one to Alex "Hurry. We don't have much time before Mrs. Addington sees the light beneath the door."

Alex scanned the room, which was filled with a shabby bed and an assortment of chipped furniture. Unexpected pity welled inside him for the humble way in which the man, who put on such haughty pretensions, actually lived. How difficult it must be to keep up such airs.

"Oh, you shouldn't say such things, Mr. Heaton." The giddy female voice echoed down the hall. "You make an old woman blush."

Alex scanned the room as Noah flung open the drawers of a pine dresser and sifted through the contents.

"What makes you think he's hidden my sword in here?" Alex searched behind the volumes of books lining shelves on the far wall.

"I know this man," Noah said. "It's far too important for him to keep anywhere else."

Easing open the drawers of the small oak desk perched in the corner, Alex examined the contents: foolscap, quill pens, a pocket watch, ink, a pistol, and a key.

Noah swung open the doors of a cabinet, sending an eerie creak through the room. They both halted. The tap of steps padded across the floor outside the chamber.

"Don't you run away from me, Miss Addington." Luke's deep voice halted the footfalls. "If you would honor me with your charming company, I would be happy to await Mr. Snyder's return."

Noah rubbed the back of his neck and lifted the candle over the contents of the cabinet. Only breeches, shirts, hats, stockings, and cravats stared back at him. He swung about. The candle flickered the frustration in his eyes. "Confound it all, where could he have put it?"

Alex ran a sleeve over his moist forehead, not willing to give up. His sword had to be here or all was lost.

Dropping to his knees, Noah peered beneath the bed.

"Oh no, Mrs. Addington. Please give me another moment of your time." Luke's sultry voice slithered through the door cracks.

"Mr. Heaton, you do make an old woman feel young again."

The scraping sound of wood on wood jarred the silence, and Alex turned to see Noah pulling a small trunk from beneath Mr. Snyder's bed. He yanked on the lid. "It's locked."

The key. Pulling open the desk drawer, Alex retrieved the key, knelt beside Noah, and inserted it into the lock. A click sounded and the latch loosened.

Luke laughed and Mrs. Addington joined him.

"God is good." Noah smiled.

Alex lifted the lid, wondering at the way the man always gave credit to the Almighty.

A glint of gold reflected the candlelight. Alex's sword. Beneath it laid his tattered uniform. He grabbed the hilt in a firm grip as if it were an old friend and stood, swinging it through the air.

"Oh, here you are Mr. Snyder. Mr. Heaton has come to call on you, sir." Mrs. Addington's voice lost its coquettish tone.

Alex's heart slammed into his chest. Noah's eyes widened. He plucked up Alex's uniform, closed the lid, locked it, then shoved it back under the bed. Alex took the key from him, slipped it into his pocket, and blew out his candle.

"What is it, Mr. Heaton? I have neither the time nor the inclination to talk with you at the moment." Mr. Snyder's squeaky voice ground against Alex's nerves.

"I daresay, Mr. Snyder, if you could spare a minute, I'd like to discuss the city's plans for a water aqueduct from the spring," Luke said.

"At this hour?" Snyder's tone stung with annoyance. "Go away, Mr. Heaton."

Tucking the uniform under his arm, Noah squeezed out the window and dropped to the ground with a thud.

Alex tossed the sword to him then flung one leg over the window ledge. Bending his body, he attempted to shove it through the small opening.

But the creak of a door sounded behind him.

Entering her uncle's makeshift hospital, Rose lifted a hand to her nose at the putrid stench. Amelia drew out her handkerchief and flapped it in the air as if she could bat away the smell. Looking up from one of his patients, Uncle Forbes squeezed the man's arm, then stood and approached them. His brow furrowed at Amelia's discomfiture. Handing her a bucket, he sent her out for fresh water.

He faced Rose. "Thank you for coming today, lass."

Rose removed her hat and gloves and hung them on a peg. "My pleasure, Uncle. I'll do what I can." Anything to keep her mind off a certain British officer. Grabbing a stained apron from a hook, she wrapped it around her waist and tied it in the back. Her uncle's brown eyes shifted over her as if he could read her mind.

She wished he could. She wished she had someone to talk to about Alex, someone to confide in about Mr. Snyder's nefarious plans. But her uncle didn't know Alex was a British naval officer. And, for his own safety, it was better that way.

"Just encourage those that are awake, lass. And see if they need anything. Dr. Wilson already tended to their wounds yesterday." He patted his pockets and plucked out his spectacles. "Ah, there they are." He grinned.

An hour later, Rose drew up a stool at the last man's cot. He was asleep, though his eyelids fluttered. A nightmare perhaps. She knew all about nightmares. Across the aisle from her, Amelia read the Bible to an aged man, whom Rose's uncle had found begging on the street, his feet eaten up with gout. Though the comforting words from the Psalms should have eased Rose's nerves, they seemed to have the opposite effect.

Uncle Forbes pulled up a stool on the other side of Rose's patient. "Good. He's asleep for now. Doc said he had an infected bullet wound, but looks like his fever finally broke. Brave man, this one. He got shot protecting a settler he didn't even know."

Brave. It seemed an unattainable trait to Rose.

"Lass, before I forget, your aunt and I will be traveling to Washington after the ball at the Fountain Inn."

Fear coiled around Rose's heart, confirming her prior assessment. "Why must you go as well?"

"Your aunt has a wagon full of supplies to deliver and can't manage them herself. Besides, it's been awhile since I've had a chance to visit with Reverend Hargrave." He cocked his head. "Never fear, Mr. Markham has offered to stay at the house."

Rose shook her head. "Why am I always afraid, uncle?"

From behind his spectacles, his brown eyes warmed. "Fear is not God's plan for us, lass. In fact, His Word says 'There is no fear in love; but perfect love casteth out fear: because fear hath torment.'"

Torment. That was exactly how Rose would describe her constant fear—tormenting. But how could she rid herself of it? After all she had endured, what normal woman wouldn't be overcome with fear? And what did love have to do with fear? Her love for Alex had only caused more fear. "But I cannot seem to help it. Bad things keep happening to me."

He reached across the cotton coverlet and gripped her hand. "You have been through many frightening things for one so young."

His hand felt hard and scratchy like the bark of a tree.

"Others have as well," Rose said. "You and Aunt Muira have suffered much. Yet you both have such courage and strength."

He chuckled, and the lines at the corners of his mouth scrunched together, lifting his beard. "Courage? I wouldn't call it that. I prefer to call it faith."

Faith and courage. Love and fear. Confusion once again scrambled Rose's thoughts. "It seems the more I love, the more afraid I become." Rose withdrew her hand and twisted her finger around a loose curl at her neck. "When you love someone, doesn't it make you terrified to lose them?"

"That's not the love God is speaking of, lass." He smiled.

"What other kind of love is there?"

"God's love. Only His love is perfect."

Rose rubbed her temples where a sudden ache began to form. "What does that have to do with fear?"

Uncle Forbes's spectacles slid down his nose. "You don't believe God loves you, do you?" His tone held a drop of sorrow.

Rose gazed at the sleeping man. His lips twitched. His eyelids flitted. So agitated even in slumber. Just like her. "The Bible says He loves me."

Her uncle tapped his chest. "But you don't know His love in here."

Rose huffed. "I don't understand."

"When you truly believe God loves you and have experienced it in your heart, there's nothing to fear. Don't you see?" He removed his spectacles and placed them on the side table, then leaned over the man to take her hand once again. "The Bible says that if God is for us, who can be against us? 'He that spared not his own Son, but delivered him up for us all, how shall he not with him also freely give us all things?' " He squeezed her hand. "You see, when you're God's child, there's nothing to fear."

Rose frowned. "But that's where you're wrong, uncle. There is much to fear in this life. Bad things happen to God's children. What of me? What of Elaine and James Myers?"

"Aye, but you mistake me, lass. I didn't say bad things would never happen. I said regardless of what happens, there's nothing to fear. Because God loves you, everything has a purpose. Everything will work out for good in the end. That's a promise."

Rose wished she could believe that, desperately wanted the peace that believing those words would bring. If she could, then she needn't worry about her future. She needn't worry about being forced to marry Mr. Snyder and never seeing Alex again. Somehow things would work out for the best, and God would see her through.

"You must first let go of your bitterness and unforgiveness, child." Her uncle's brown eyes held such wisdom, such peace. "Perhaps that is what is keeping you from truly receiving God's love in your heart."

Withdrawing her hands, Rose clasped them in her lap and lowered her gaze. "I don't know how to let go."

"Then those who have done you harm will always have a hold on you. They will always dictate your happiness. Do you want to give them that power?"

Rose shook her head. She hadn't thought of it that way. "But if I forgive them, doesn't that mean they have escaped without punishment?"

"Escaped?" Her uncle snorted and pressed down a strand of his unruly gray hair. "No, lass. If they don't repent, they will have to answer to God on judgment day. And if you don't forgive them, you will as well."

❖ CHAPTER 22 ❖

Rose gazed out the window of Mr. Snyder's hired coach and tried to drown out his incessant babbling. Beside her, Amelia, dressed in a beautiful gown of creamy satin embroidered in glistening emerald, pinched her cheeks with excitement. Next to Amelia, light from the lantern perched outside the carriage transformed Aunt Muira's satin burgundy gown into shimmering red. Across from the ladies sat three gentlemen, Uncle Forbes, Mr. Braxton, and Mr. Snyder, who had insisted he provide their group with a plush hackney to convey them to the ball. And who now regaled them with the tale of how he had convinced the council to adopt a provision for another theater to be built in town that would "greatly enhance the city's reputation as a bastion of civilization."

Or so he declared.

Rose pressed down the folds of her own gown of royal blue silk trimmed in white satin netting—a gown drawn from the collection her aunt had kept from her youth and altered to fit Rose's smaller frame. She tugged at the white sash around her waist. A matching ribbon adorned her hair, which had been pinned up in a cascade of curls and decorated further with jeweled pins and a spray of tiny wildflowers. A gold necklace, embedded with rubies and pearls—also her aunt's—hung over a neckline that was a bit low for Rose's taste. Nevertheless, the elegant attire made her feel like a princess. At least until Mr. Snyder had appeared at the house, with black top hat in one hand and his ever-present cane in the other, wearing a grin that reminded Rose of Prinney's pink snout after a fine meal of kitchen slops. And suddenly, instead of a princess, Rose felt like the icing on a cake about to be eaten by the devil himself.

Wind gusted through the coach's window, and she closed her eyes, imagining she was on board a ship with Alex, sailing to an exotic port where it didn't matter from whence they hailed: America or Britain, France, or even the moon. She wondered where he was at that moment. What he was doing. Was he safe? Had his captain accepted him back on board without repercussions?

Was he thinking of her?

Rose shook her head, trying to scatter the thoughts away. They served no purpose other than to feed an ever-growing depression that hovered over her like a dark, icy fog.

Amelia slipped her hand into Rose's, and she felt the woman's tremble of excitement even through her gloves. Rose smiled her way and then dared a glance at Mr. Braxton, whose gaze had not left Amelia since he had entered the carriage. Perhaps her maid would find true love again after all.

As Rose had found. If only for a few days.

But now that she had experienced it, nothing else would do—especially not the man sitting across from her. She felt his eyes upon her, but she refused to honor his sordid stare with a glance of her own.

Instead, she studied her uncle sitting across from his wife. She'd never seen him looking so dapper in his black overcoat, embroidered satin silver waistcoat, and breeches. He tipped his hat toward her, drawing a smile from Rose, yet something in the curve of his lips, the depth of his gaze, gave her pause. It was as if he knew some grand secret. Returning her gaze to the window, she released a sigh. Fairy tales and dreams were for little girls. Not for women like Rose, who had seen too much of the cruel world to no longer believe in happy endings.

Mr. Snyder tapped his cane on the floor. "I daresay, it promises to be a glorious evening. I am quite looking forward to it."

Uncle Forbes lifted his hand to his mouth to cover what sounded like a chuckle but ended as a cough.

Aunt Muira frowned at her husband before responding, "Indeed, I do agree, Mr. Snyder. This ball is just what this city needs to take our mind off the war."

"And what is your opinion, Miss McGuire?" Mr. Snyder addressed Rose in a tone that dared her to speak her true heart.

She flashed a caustic smile his way and tugged upon her long white gloves. "I fear I do not share your enthusiasm, Mr. Snyder."

Amelia looped her arm through Rose's. "Oh I do pray you will cheer up. We shall have so much fun." The woman's lavender perfume swirled around Rose, mingling with the rose oil she had dabbed on her own neck.

"I agree." Aunt Muira's tone was scolding. "Count your blessings, dear, or they shall be taken away from you and given to someone more appreciative."

Uncle Forbes coughed again, and Rose swept a gaze his way again. Was he ill? But no. A smile creased the corners of his mouth.

Blessings, indeed. Rose tapped a gloved finger over the window frame in an attempt to count out those blessings. But the few she recollected were instantly shadowed by the disastrous future looming before her.

Soon the hackney turned down Light Street, which was aptly named this evening for the many streetlights setting the block aglow—the ban on city lights apparently lifted for this gala event. A parade of ladies in flowing gowns, escorted by gentlemen in top hats and coats, drifted down the avenue toward the Fountain Inn. Coaches, curricles, and chaises, along with gentlemen atop horses swarmed the cobblestone street. The *clip-clop* of horses' hooves, the rattle of carriage wheels, and the laughter and chatter of the crowd rose in a chorus of gaiety that thumbed its nose at the British troops blockading the port.

The driver pulled the coach to a halt before the Fountain Inn, an elaborate structure that rose several stories into the night sky. Light shone from the upper windows onto iron-grated balconies before spilling down upon the crush of people swarming to enter the front doors. The gentlemen leaped from the carriage, the footman lowered the step, and Mr. Snyder's bony hand appeared in the doorway. The audacious jewel on his middle finger winked at Rose in the lantern light. She drew a deep breath. She could do this. She could endure one night with this hideous man. Just one night at a time—although he insisted on many more. But she could not think of that now, or she feared she would lose all desire to live.

Avoiding Mr. Snyder's outstretched hand, she clutched her gown and descended the steps, searching the crowd for any sign of Marianne or Cassandra. She could use a friend tonight. The ladies' coiffures adorned with ribbons, flowers, and plumes bobbed alongside waves of black hats that swept through the front door like seawater pouring through a crack into the hold of a ship. With her hand all but hovering over Mr. Snyder's arm, she allowed him to lead her through that crack, wondering all along if she would drown in the agony of her heart.

Once inside, Mr. Snyder ushered her through the main courtyard of the inn, where a large trickling fountain was the centerpiece in a flower garden set aglow by flickering lantern light. Rose gazed up at the inn's chambers perched upon levels of terraces that circled the gardens. Several couples stood near the fountain or sat on the iron benches in deep conversation. She glanced over her shoulder to see Amelia hanging on Mr. Braxton's arm, her eyes sparkling with excitement as they scanned the surroundings. From behind Amelia, Aunt Muira offered Rose a gentle smile. Rose knew her aunt meant well. And by all accounts, Mr. Snyder was a perfect match for any young lady. Until he revealed the devil buried beneath his polished facade.

Following the swarm of chattering guests, Mr. Snyder, with his head held high, led Rose through another set of doors to their left. A few heads turned their way as they moved into the brightly lit ballroom. The elegant tones of a minuet began at the far end of the hall where musicians sat on a raised stage. Two massive crystalline chandeliers hung from an arched stucco ceiling that was etched with flowers and gilded in gold. Mirrors on either side of the room reflected the light from dozens of candles. The smell of sweet punch, beeswax, and a myriad of perfumes tickled Rose's nose and made her long for fresh air.

After their names were announced, Rose scanned the ladies who stood at the edge of the dancing couples, gossiping behind fluttering fans like a gaggle of geese flapping their wings. No sign of her friends anywhere. Rose's heart sank even lower. She turned to ask Amelia if she had seen Marianne, but Mr. Braxton had already swept her out onto the dance floor.

Aunt Muira and Uncle Forbes soon followed, gazing into each other's eyes as if they were the only ones in the room.

Rose swallowed a lump of sorrow. Her aunt and uncle shared an intimate, eternal love Rose had but tasted, but would never know in full.

"Would you care to join them?" Mr. Snyder's blue eyes studied her, and Rose searched her mind for an excuse.

It came in the form of her dear friend, Marianne, who hurried to join her from across the room in a flurry of pink satin. She grabbed Rose's arm. "I was so glad when I heard you were attending."

"How did you hear?" Rose turned from Mr. Snyder and gave her friend a questioning look, glad for the excuse to avoid his question. She had only just agreed to attend three days prior and had not spoken to anyone since.

"Oh, never mind." Marianne smiled and nodded toward Mr. Snyder. "Good evening, Councilman."

He scrunched his lips together as if tasting something sour. The music stopped and those who remained on the floor lined up in two rows as others joined them, men along one side and women on the other. "Mrs. Brenin." Mr. Snyder said. "If you'll excuse us, Miss McGuire and I were about to partake of the country dance."

He grabbed Rose's arm to drag her onto the floor when Noah wove his way through the crowd to stand before him. "Mr. Snyder, I have a matter of great importance to discuss with you, sir. Would you join me in the other room for a glass of port?" He flashed a smile toward his wife. "I'm sure the ladies can entertain themselves in our absence."

"Importance, you say?" The councilman's chest seemed to expand beneath his velvet waistcoat. "Can't it wait?"

"Not unless you wish to keep the mayor waiting."

Snyder peered around Noah toward the side doors. "Mayor Johnson wishes to speak to me?"

"Indeed. He asked for you directly." Noah's tone was serious, but his blue eyes held a twinkle of mischief.

"Of course. No doubt he seeks my wise council on a matter of urgency." Mr. Snyder jutted out his chin. Releasing Rose's arm, he faced her. "I shall return shortly to claim that dance, my dear."

Rose shot a pointed gaze at his back as he left. She breathed a sigh of relief as music filled the room once again.

Cassandra, decked in a shimmering gown of emerald, appeared out of nowhere and sidled up beside Rose. She made a face at Mr. Snyder as he exited the room with Noah.

"You shouldn't behave so, Cassandra." Rose covered her mouth to hide her unavoidable smile.

"Why not? He deserves it." Cassandra fingered the lace on her glove and gave Rose a coy glance.

Marianne's eyes sparkled. She clutched Rose's arm again and seemed ready to jump out of her shoes. If Rose didn't know her friend better, she'd think it was the ball that thrilled her so. But she *did* know her friend. And Marianne had never been overfond of such social functions. Rose's gaze shifted to Cassandra, who wore an unusually sly look, even for her.

Rose lifted a brow. "What's going on with you two? Did Noah purposely steal Mr. Snyder away for some delightfully foul purpose?" Not that she would object. But what confused her was how her friends would know to aid her in such a manner. She'd never spoken to them of her aversion to Mr. Snyder or of his recent threats.

Cassandra batted the air with her white glove. "What does it matter? He's gone." Her green eyes scanned the crowd as if looking for someone. They locked on something in the distance, and Rose followed her gaze to see Mr. Heaton standing by himself across the room, drink in hand. His normally unruly black hair was slicked and tied at the back of his neck as he stood tall and handsome in a well-tailored suit of black lute string with velvet trim. His dark eyes focused on Cassandra as if there were no one else in the room worth looking at. He raised his glass toward her with a nod.

"My word." Rose leaned toward Cassandra. "Mr. Heaton presents quite the handsome figure tonight."

Marianne smiled. "And it would appear he only has eyes for you, Cassandra."

Cassandra tore her gaze from him. "Don't be absurd. Mr. Heaton has eyes for anything in a skirt." Her giggle faltered on her lips.

Rose glanced back at Mr. Heaton and found his gaze still directed their way before he turned and slipped through a side door.

"Doesn't he captain your ship, *Destiny*?" Rose asked Cassandra.

"Yes. And he's already made quite a fortune in prizes." Marianne's delicate brows lifted.

"He's a rogue and not to be trusted." Cassandra spat. "I have begun to regret investing in his privateer." She pressed down the folds of her emerald gown.

Several gentlemen approached the three ladies, requesting dances with both Rose and Cassandra. Rose politely refused each one, forbidding them to even sign her dance card. Cassandra, however, at least allowed them that small encouragement, although, in truth, she appeared more than aloof.

Rose hadn't danced since her father had twirled her around their parlor when she was a little girl. The thought of a man touching her, even briefly, in such a seductive dalliance made her heart cinch. That was, any man but Alex. And with him gone, she'd never have the opportunity. Even the cheerful music rasped in her ears like a contentious chime. Truth be told, she'd rather go home and bury her head beneath her pillow.

Rose fingered the heavy jewels around her neck, as out of place on her skin as she was at this ball. Her glance took in the dancers floating over the marble floor like swans on a crystalline pond. She spotted Amelia as she executed the steps of the quadrille with perfection—steps the young maid had practiced with Rose and her aunt in the parlor all week. Amelia's face glowed with delight, and Rose smiled, happy for her companion, despite the agony weighing down her own heart.

Two more gentlemen approached. Rose politely declined the taller man's offer to dance while Cassandra batted the other one away.

"Why not dance with the gentleman, Rose?" Marianne gripped her arm and swept her gaze over the room as if looking for someone. "It may help to lift your humors."

"I agree." Cassandra waved her silk printed fan about her face. "You shouldn't be so glum at so gay an event. Who knows when we'll have another evening such as this one with this war going on?"

"Then why aren't you dancing?" Rose asked Cassandra.

"Because I have become, shall we say, more selective regarding whom I choose to pair up with on the dance floor."

Marianne leaned close with a smile. "Which means she's waiting for a particular gentleman to ask her."

Cassandra huffed, but a grin played with the corners of her lips.

Rose would have giggled if her insides didn't feel like they'd been run over by a carriage. "Please go enjoy yourselves. I'm afraid I'm not good company tonight."

"Rubbish." Marianne said. "Why don't we go get some punch before the two of you break every gentleman's heart in the room?" She tugged on Rose's arm and led the way toward one of the side doors.

A billowing crowd of chattering people packed the refreshment parlor, helping themselves to the libations on a buffet lining the far wall. Men circled gaming tables perched about the room, playing whist or faro. The smoke of a dozen cigars hovered over them like storm clouds. Rose drew a hand to her nose.

"Oh no, there is Mr. Snyder." Marianne dragged Rose to the side. "Perhaps we can get a drink without him seeing us."

"He knows I'm here, Marianne." Rose gave a cynical snort. "Besides, he appears to be quite in his element."

Standing beside Noah, Mayor Johnson, General Smith, and two other councilmen, Mr. Snyder held a drink in one hand and his cane in the other. His voice—which sounded much like the squeaking of a rusty hinge—rose above the crowd and ground against Rose's ears. By the bored expressions on the faces of his audience, he no doubt regaled them with his grand vision for the city. Noah stood at his side. Mr. Heaton suddenly appeared and handed Noah a glass of red liquid, which, after relieving Mr. Snyder of his empty one, Noah placed in the councilman's hand.

Craning to see between the undulating crowd, Rose eyed them with curiosity. Neither Noah nor Mr. Heaton were the type to flatter someone in power, nor had they ever expressed an interest in Mr. Snyder's affairs or politics in general.

She leaned toward Marianne. "I must thank Noah later for keeping Mr. Snyder occupied. But I don't wish to keep your husband from you all evening."

"Oh think nothing of it." Marianne eased her toward an oblong table laden with cold tea, punch, and spiced wine. Rose selected a glass of punch and had barely taken a sip when Mr. Snyder, Noah, and Mr. Heaton descended upon them.

Mr. Snyder's eyes carried a distant glaze that seemed at odds with the man's normal intense focus. He extended his arm. "A dance, my dear?"

"I do not feel—" she began to protest.

"Nonsense." He dragged her through the clamorous mob and out onto the dance floor where they joined a row of couples lining up for a reel. One glance to her side told her that Marianne, Noah, Luke, and Cassandra had followed. Oddly, their presence brought her some comfort.

The music began, and Rose bowed toward Mr. Snyder, whose gaze skittered about the room like a bird who'd lost his flock. They stepped toward each other. "Are you all right, Mr. Snyder?"

"Yes, of course." Yet his voice wobbled slightly. He coughed and stepped back. They circled around and met again. When he moved toward the lady beside Rose, his face grew flushed, and he stumbled.

They stepped together. Rose placed her hand upon his upraised one and they floated down the middle of the rows, with the ladies on one side, the men on the other. "Did the mayor say something to upset you?" Rose asked.

"No, of course not. Naturally, he wanted my opinion on the defenses of the city."

Naturally. Rose strung her lips tight as they made their way down the line of dancers. Marianne and Noah grinned at her in passing.

"You are marrying an important man, Miss McGuire," he added, though his tone lacked its usual rigid pomposity.

He stepped away, then back again. "Perhaps now you won't find the idea so disagreeable?" His grin broke into an odd giggle.

Heads turned their way.

Beads of sweat sprang upon his forehead.

Rose took his arm and swung beside him. "Mr. Snyder. I fear you are unwell. Would you care to sit down?"

He shook his head as if to rid himself of whatever ailed him. His breath became labored, and he nodded. "Perhaps I should."

Rose led him to one of the velvet stuffed chairs that lined the walls, but he refused to sit. Instead he began to pace, placing a hand over his heart. The dance ended, the music stopped, and the room instantly filled with chatter.

Noah led Marianne from the floor, and Mr. Heaton did the same with Cassandra. They headed toward Rose who was helping a pale Snyder walk without stumbling. People began to stare.

"It would appear your Mr. Snyder has partaken of too much spirits." Cassandra cocked her head, a devilish smile on her lips.

Rose stared at the councilman. So unlike him.

"Pure madness! I had but two glasses of wine." Mr. Snyder hissed and tugged upon his cravat.

A few ladies at the outskirts of the crowd moved away.

Luke crossed his arms over his chest and grinned.

Rose resisted the urge to chuckle. At least she wouldn't have to dance with him again. Perhaps if the man drank himself unconscious, she could convince her aunt and uncle to leave early.

Mr. Snyder halted his pace, drew a deep breath as if he were choking, and then sank into a chair.

The chattering subsided as if a predator had entered the forest.

Heads swerved toward the door. Fans began to flutter. Gentlemen and ladies leaned toward one another in whispers.

The announcer's voice rang through the room. "Mr. Alexander Reed."

❖ CHAPTER 23 ❖

M r. Alexander Reed."

The name drifted through the air like sweet music, a glorious tune from Rose's past. Until it sharpened and shot straight through her heart.

Was this some cruel joke? Rose shifted her gaze between the grins on Marianne's and Cassandra's lips.

Mr. Snyder muttered something then dropped his head into his hands.

Rose stood on her tiptoes and peered over the crowd.

Then she saw him. Standing at the entranceway, a head above most of the other men. A gold satin waistcoat, trimmed in black velvet, peeked out from beneath his dark coat. A pair of black pantaloons were tucked into Hessian boots. His hair was tied behind him, revealing the strong set of his jaw. Hazel eyes as rich as the velvet of his coat locked upon hers.

Rose's breath shot into her throat. Her head spun. She stumbled. Marianne and Cassandra gripped her arms, steadying her.

"Alex is here? How. . . Why. . .?" Alarm tightened the skin on her hands, her arms, her neck until they tingled. "He shouldn't be. . ."

"Go to him." Marianne gave her a gentle nudge.

Rose gaped at her friend. "You knew?" She swept her gaze to Cassandra on her other side. "You too?"

They both smiled.

A thud sounded behind her, and she swerved to see Mr. Snyder slumped onto the floor. "My word." She headed toward him, but Noah and Luke hoisted him up between them.

"He'll be all right, Miss Rose." Luke winked. "He just needs to sleep it off now."

Sleep *what* off? The crowd parted amid a flurry of gasps and condemning glances as Noah and Luke dragged the councilman away.

Rose faced forward, her mind reeling with confusion. The throng split again. This time for Alex, who glided toward her with the authority and ease of a ship parting the sea. Her heart raced.

He gave her a sultry smile, then bowed and took her hand. "Miss McGuire, you look lovely tonight."

Rose wanted to laugh, to cry, to fall into his arms. "Why, thank you, Mr. Reed."

Music began and laughter and conversation joined in a chorus around them as the party resumed. Rose opened her mouth to ask the thousand questions rolling on her tongue, but nothing coherent emerged.

"Would you care to dance?" His deep eyes drank her in as he gestured toward the dance floor.

The haze in her mind refused to form a logical thought. Rose nodded as she kept her eyes fastened upon him, expecting him to disappear at any moment. Alex couldn't be here. He'd be caught— locked up as a prisoner of war. Strong fingers curled around hers, and a jolt of heat coursed up her arm and into her head, adding to her dizziness.

Either she was dreaming or she had gone completely mad. She'd gladly accept either option as long as she never woke up or regained her sanity.

Alex led her onto the floor and entered the parade of couples moving in a country dance. The music, the candlelight, the jewels, plumes, and colorful sashes all swirled around Rose in a blur as she gazed at the man she loved.

They stepped toward each other.

"I don't understand," she whispered.

He arched a questioning brow.

"Why? How?" Rose asked.

"Does my presence displease you?" He swung her around, leading her across the floor with the skill and grace evident of his nobility.

"Quite the contrary." Rose dipped and swung around the gentleman to her left.

Alex took her hand once again. "Then let us enjoy the moment." A speck of sorrow stained his otherwise jovial tone.

Rose did her best to silence the questions, the fears, and embrace the seconds of pure bliss as Alex moved her around the floor. Dare she hope he had decided to stay? She gazed up at the firm cut of his jaw, his regal nose, and dark brows above eyes that scanned the throng for possible enemies. Always ready. Always alert. His masculine scent filled the air between them. The brief moments of contact with him heated her skin, leaving it cold when he moved away, only to be warmed once again by his presence, his touch, the adoring look in his eyes. If this was a dream, it was a dream that brought all her senses to life.

He spun her around another couple and then allowed his gaze to travel over her face as if he was memorizing every inch of her. As they passed the edge of the crowd, dozens of curious eyes followed them. Jeweled heads leaned together behind fans in heated whispers, no doubt trying to guess the identity of this dark, handsome stranger, all the while wondering what he was doing with an unsophisticated girl like her.

The music stopped. Alex released her, and the room suddenly chilled. He proffered his elbow. "Would the lady care for a stroll in the gardens?"

Rose laid her hand on his arm. "The lady would."

Ignoring the stares of the crowd, they sauntered from the floor as if they were king and queen. Rose searched for her friends, but they had conveniently disappeared. Instead, at the far end of the hall, her uncle smiled her way before ushering Aunt Muira into the next room. Was he part of this scheme as well? So many questions. But they would have to wait. All that mattered now was Alex.

He wove his way through the crowd with ease toward the door.

General Smith and two officers stood to the side of the entrance. Rose stiffened, but then remembered Alex had been introduced to the general as their footman. Though Alex's presence with her would be considered unusual, it would not raise undue suspicion.

Fresh evening air swept over her, cooling her skin and fluttering the lace at her neckline. A crush of people filled the garden. Laying his hand over hers, Alex led her through the back opening into additional gardens behind the inn where only a few couples lingered in secret assignations.

He stopped beneath an arbor of climbing roses and slowly turned to face her. The light from a nearby lantern reflected a mixture of agony and admiration in his eyes. He brushed his fingers over her cheek, and Rose closed her eyes, hoping, wishing to keep him with her forever.

The sweet scent of roses, honeysuckle, and Alex wafted about her. "I hope I never wake up."

Alex said nothing, though a tiny smile graced his lips.

Alarm snapped Rose from her dream. She glanced over her shoulder. "If Mr. Snyder sees you. . ."

"He won't. Your friends have seen to that."

Tears filled her eyes. "I had no idea they even knew about Snyder or my feelings toward you."

Threading his fingers through hers, he kissed her glove, all the while keeping his eyes on her. "I thought I would never see you again." His voice deepened in sorrow.

"I fear for you, Alex. I do not know who Mr. Snyder may have told." She gripped his hand. "Why have you come back?"

Whispers from a couple sitting on a bench across the way drew his gaze. He scanned the surroundings, then turned to her and smiled. "I have something to show you."

"What could be so important that you risk your life?" She fell against him. Strong arms engulfed her. His strength washed over Rose like an elixir that soothed away all her fears. If only she could bottle it and save it forever. "I could not bear to see you imprisoned. . .or worse."

He kissed her forehead and took a step back, then lifted the flap of his coat. A flicker of gold glimmered in the lantern light. The hilt of a sword. Why had she not seen it before? He drew it from its scabbard.

His service sword. A giggle bubbled in her throat but never released. "How did you get this?"

He slid the blade back into place. "I stole it." His eyes sparkled mischievously.

"From Mr. Snyder?"

"I had some help."

Rose threw a hand to her throat as realization struck her. "Noah and Luke?"

"Indeed." Alex nodded.

"And they didn't turn you over to General Smith?"

"Your uncle convinced them to help me in order to save you from Snyder."

Rose drew in a breath. "They risked being arrested for me."

Alex nodded and brushed a thumb over her cheek. "And they allowed me this one last chance to see you, to tell you in person that you don't have to marry that beast."

Pain stabbed her heart. "Before you leave."

"Yes. They are allowing me to go back to my ship, and for that I am grateful." Alex rubbed the back of his neck. "I know they could all be arrested for treason should anyone find out."

"And my uncle too. What a dear man." The air around Rose grew warm as she began to understand what her friends had risked for her. Tugging off her gloves, she gazed up at Alex and stroked his firm jaw, memorizing the scratchy feel of it.

He placed his hand atop hers. "I could not leave knowing you would be forced to marry that vile man because of me."

A tear slid down Rose's cheek. He gazed at her for a moment then leaned toward her. His warm breath tickled her throat and sent a quiver through her. Then his lips found hers. Lost in his taste, Rose melted into him, fighting back the tears that threatened to spill once again from her eyes.

"He's here. I know I saw him!" Mr. Snyder's slurred voice shot into the garden. Rose jumped from Alex. Her wide eyes met his. A chill enveloped her.

"I assure you, sir, the Drummond servant left their employ last week." Noah's urgent tone sped past them. One glance over her shoulder told Rose, the councilman headed toward them, Noah and

Luke on his heels.

Alex pulled Rose into the shadows.

"Go!" she whispered, her tears flowing freely now. She pushed him away. "Go." Agony rent her heart in two.

Gently clutching her face in his hands, he kissed her once more. Then releasing her, he turned and ran into the night.

Alex plodded down the weed-infested trail, his heart so low in his chest it felt as trodden as the pebbles beneath his feet. The rhythmic stomp of boots and beat of war drums reminded him that he was back among his people. Brushing aside a vine, he gazed through the thick forest toward the west where the setting sun wove bands of auburn and gold through the trees and across the path. He stepped through one of the glittering rays but felt none of its light and beauty. In fact, he'd begun to wonder whether he would ever feel joy again.

Two days had passed since he had left Rose at the Fountain Inn. After he'd slipped into the shadows, he'd turned for one last look at her as she stood, tears spilling down her cheeks, staring into the darkness. He'd nearly shed his own tears at the anguish on her pretty face—at the pain in his own heart. But naval officers did not cry. Especially not British naval officers.

Which was what he was once again.

At least that's what he kept telling himself. For as he marched through the Maryland countryside alongside British soldiers, he felt none of the patriotism, pride, or loyalty toward his country that had been inbred in him since his youth.

Truth be told, he felt more like a traitor now than he ever did when he lived with the Drummonds.

Sweat dripped down his back beneath the dark coat of his uniform. Save for the shade of a few trees, the sun had pummeled the men mercilessly as they marched all day with barely a respite. Forbidden to shed the outer coats of their uniforms, many had fallen by the wayside, too exhausted from the heat to continue. Alex pressed onward, embracing the scorching heat, the blisters on his feet, the ache throbbing in his thigh, hoping the discomfort would dull the pain in his heart. He shifted his musket into his other hand and shook out the cramp that had formed in his arm. The smell of unwashed bodies along with the occasional groans filled the air around him.

He tried to shake off his ill feelings. He must forge ahead. He must do his duty. He must not allow foolish sentiments to lead him astray. Yet something deep within him had changed. Something at the core of his being. His very beliefs and values had been turned upside down, and he doubted he'd ever be able to set them aright again.

Nor did he want to.

No, he was no longer the same man. It was as if he had been blind his entire life only now to be given sight. Doffing his hat, he dabbed at the sweat on his forehead as orders ricocheted through the trees, sending the band of men turning to the right.

He must keep his focus. He had his family's honor to think of.

Yet the word *family* in connection to his childhood home seemed blasphemous when compared to what he'd come to know of the true meaning of the word with Rose and the Drummonds.

At least after Alex had left Baltimore and traveled all night, he had no trouble finding a boat to row him back to the HMS *Undefeatable*. He supposed he should thank God that Captain Milford accepted his woeful tale of being shot and cared for by a Loyalist farmer for nearly three weeks until Alex had been able to walk on his own. The captain posed no question as to the whereabouts of Lieutenant Garrick. No doubt most of the men on board, including the captain, were not sorry to see the first lieutenant gone. Alex felt a pang of sorrow for the man who had inspired not an ounce of mourning for his loss.

Yet, no sooner had Alex settled into his berth than he'd been ordered to join a group of marines and seamen who were to rendezvous with a band of troops under the command of General Ross at Marlboro. Their orders were to drag one six-pounder and two three-pounder cannons over the asperous terrain to an undisclosed battlefield. Unable to convince the captain he had not regained his full strength, Alex now found himself, once again, trudging across American soil. Something he had promised Noah and Luke he would do all in his power to avoid.

Last night when they'd camped at Marlboro, the British soldiers had helped themselves to the American settlers' homes and food. They'd stolen sheep and horses and stripped crops and fruit trees like a swarm of locusts. At least they had not murdered or ravished any of the farmers' wives in the process. For that, Alex was grateful. And surprised. Since Admiral Cockburn had joined General Ross, Alex had expected far worse, for the admiral's insatiable lust for American blood had claimed many lives along the Chesapeake.

Alex's agony increased with each step he took. Perhaps if he prayed, God would hear him. Yes, he would pray to Mr. Drummond's God. Not the God Alex had grown up with in the Church of England. No, Alex had come to see that the true God was a God who loved unconditionally and who heard and answered prayers. Bowing his head, Alex could think of no appropriate words to start the dialogue. Yet, oddly a powerful presence encompassed him as if a good friend had stepped into the ranks beside him. A voice spoke, an internal, soothing voice that Alex realized must be the voice of God, repeating the same words over and over again.

"Trust me, trust me."

No matter what happened, Alex determined to do just that. Yet he also prayed that part of his destiny did not entail firing upon the American people he'd come to admire as if they were his own countrymen.

His own countrymen. The words rang so loud and clear within him that he nearly shouted them out loud. Not only did the revelation burst in his heart, but it settled in his reason as if it were pure wisdom.

God, are you telling me to become an American? Excitement heightened his steps.

What of his family? What of gaining their favor once again? A flurry of letters filled his vision—letters he had sent back home begging his brother and his father for forgiveness.

All of them unanswered.

"There is One more whom you must ask."

Alex swallowed and stared down at his muddied boots as he marched onward. He had never asked God to forgive him. In fact, Alex had never forgiven himself. "I'm sorry, God. I'm sorry for what I did to my brother," he whispered.

A weight seemed to roll across his shoulders and fall to the dirt beside him. He stretched his back and gazed upward into the blue sky. Unexpected joy filled him. His skin buzzed with excitement. God had forgiven him. God had forgiven him! How could Alex not forgive himself?

He bowed his head. *Thank You for Your forgiveness, God. I forgive myself. Please help me never to do something so foolish again.*

He cringed and raised his gaze. Yet wasn't staying with Rose just another foolhardy, irrational move?

No. It wasn't just a frivolous sentiment. Though Alex's heart was elated, becoming an American also rang true in his mind and in his spirit—the spirit that now was connected to God Almighty.

Alex chuckled out loud, drawing the gaze of a few of the soldiers. Perhaps he was the half-wit his father had so often called him. Here was the proof. What son of a wealthy viscount would turn his back on his family, his inheritance—egad, even his country—for a farm girl who spoke to pigs and cuddled chickens? A woman who feared everything and yet saved the life of an enemy whose people had killed her father.

A woman who loved without measure.

The lure of home, family, love, and a pair of luminous turquoise eyes made all the things he had sought for his entire life seem suddenly unimportant—trite. He would give up all the fortune and titles in the world, even the throne of England itself, to make Rose his wife.

Later that night Alex squeezed between two seamen and lowered himself to a rock before the blazing fire—one of many that dotted the landscape. The boldness of his countrymen! Setting up camp so brazenly in the middle of their enemy's land. As if the Americans hadn't the wit or the bravado to attack them. Quite astonishing. Yet hadn't Alex been a willing participant in that enormous British ego most of his life?

The seamen and marines under Alex's command greeted him as they dipped bread into the stew filling their tin plates. The scent of beef and unwashed men swirled about his nose, and he grabbed his own plate, hoping his appetite had returned. But the sounds of the men slopping their grub reminded him of Prinney, and sorrow clamped over his heart once again. He set the plate down.

He wanted to leave. Find his way back to Rose's farm. Tell her he loved her. Become an American. But he must be careful. The countryside was flooded with British soldiers on high alert. If he were caught, he'd be put in irons and sent back to his ship. If the Americans caught him before he could explain, they'd shoot him on the spot. He couldn't risk it. The best strategy would be to wait until they spotted the American army. Then he could slip away in the night, white flag in hand, and report to their commanding officer. But so far, they'd not spotted a single American troop.

He gazed across the dark night to a field dotted with white canvas tents that reminded him of a fleet of ships at sea. But where was General Ross leading this fleet? Alex had sent one of his own men, Mr. Glasson, to loiter about Ross's quarters and glean what information he could about the general's objective.

And there Mr. Glasson came now, emerging from the crowd of soldiers milling about the camp as he rushed to their small group. He knelt beside them, his eyes twinkling in the firelight. "I found out what you asked, Mr. Reed. I ran into Lieutenant Scott, one of Admiral Cochrane's men."

"So, where are we heading?" One of the men asked before he took a swig of water.

"Tomorrow we march into Washington." Mr. Glasson smiled and rubbed his hands together. "To burn her to the ground."

❖ CHAPTER 24 ❖

Rose knelt beside the pigsty and eased her hand through the wooden posts. Prinney waddled toward her, snorting and grunting in glee. Memories drifted across her mind, of Alex's face twisting in indignation when he'd discovered whom she'd named her favorite pig after. A traitorous smile lifted her lips. The first in days. Three days, in fact, since she'd last seen Alex in the gardens of the Fountain Inn. That entire evening seemed like a dream to her now. Like one of those mystical childhood fairy tales where the prince arrives at the ball and sweeps the princess off her feet. Only to be separated later by some evil wizard.

Which was a perfect description of Mr. Snyder.

Thank goodness the laudanum Noah had slipped into his drink had befogged his faculties enough to give her and Alex time to say good-bye one last time. That Alex had risked so much to see her softened the blow of his leaving. He loved her. Then why did he have to leave at all? Perhaps, he just didn't love her enough.

She ran her fingers over Prinney's rough hide. The pig nuzzled against her hand. "At least I still have you, Prinney."

He grunted in return, encouraging his fellow pigs to join in the chorus.

Rose stood, pressed a hand on her back and glanced over the

farm. The noon sun capped the field in a bright bowl of glistening light, transforming ordinary green into emerald, browns into copper, and yellows into saffron. Even her ripe tomatoes sparkled like rubies. A light breeze, plump with the scent of cedar, hay, and horseflesh, stirred the tall grass into swirling eddies of green and gold. Chickens crowded around the hem of her gown. Grabbing a handful of dried corn from the bucket, she scattered it across the dirt. The birds clucked and flapped and strutted back and forth, snatching up the tiny seeds.

Picking up the bucket, Rose headed toward the barn. Even the beauty of this place could not penetrate the fortress of gloom around her heart. She already missed Alex so much, she had no idea how she would endure the rest of her life without him.

Wind whipped through the barn doors, tossing loose strands of her hair into her eyes and blinding her for a moment. Groping her way to Liverpool's stall, she brushed the curls from her face.

And ran straight into a man.

Rose screamed and leaped back. Mr. Snyder stood before her, cane planted in the dirt, and a look of deviant fury warping his face.

Terror gripped her. Her aunt and uncle had left for Washington DC the day before. Cora and Amelia had gone to town on errands, and Mr. Markham was no doubt asleep in the parlor. "What are you doing here?"

A caustic smile twisted his lips. "To inform you, my dear, that I know what you and your friends did. Malicious and traitorous gnats. I should have you all arrested."

Annoyance swept her fear aside. "Why don't you then?"

He shook his head and stepped toward her. "You think you have won, Miss McGuire, but you have not." He grinned. "You will still marry me"—he clipped her chin between his thumb and forefinger—"or I will inform General Smith that you harbored a British naval officer in your home for weeks." His bergamot cologne stung her nose.

"I beg you to do so, sir." Rose snatched her chin from his fingers and thrust her nose into the air. "You have no proof and Alex. . .Mr. Reed is gone."

"Ah yes, gone back to join the troops who attack us daily. Why, in fact, your beloved naval officer may be at this very moment marching into a trap."

Rose stiffened. "What do you mean?"

Victory flashed across Mr. Snyder's contemptuous gaze. "I heard from General Smith that a band of British troops are headed toward Washington." He brushed dust from his coat. "As if they could occupy our capital. Bah!" He chuckled then studied her. "Oh, I see fear on your pretty face. Now, don't fret about the lives of your fellow Americans, my love, I'm sure the regular army and Maryland militia will give the British quite a welcome. Hopefully one which obliterates every last one of them."

A dozen thoughts spun in Rose's head until it grew light. Her aunt and uncle were in Washington. Did they know about the attack? Were there enough American soldiers to protect them? And what of Alex?

She took a deep breath and gripped the edge of Valor's stall. "Mr. Reed is no doubt back on his ship."

Mr. Snyder cocked his head and smiled. "Ah yes. One would think so, but I also heard there are several naval officers among the British horde. *Tsk tsk.* It would be a shame to see him killed. And by one of our own."

Rose's legs wobbled.

"Which brings me back to why you will still marry me," he continued, twirling his cane in the air. "Who do you suppose General Smith will believe, a prominent councilman or a British doxy?"

Rose longed to wipe the supercilious smirk from his lips. "A rather inebriated councilman, from all appearances at the ball. Perhaps he'll believe me, over you, sir."

"Humph." Mr. Snyder tugged on his cravat, then pressed his fingers through the red hair at his temples. "You are nothing but a British strumpet, a sullied orphan girl."

Rose tried to ignore the insult, but it slipped into her heart anyway. "I insist you leave at once, Mr. Snyder. You are no longer welcome here."

A spark of fury seared in his gaze. It grew larger and larger until it seemed to consume his eyes like a wildfire. Rose swallowed and took a step back.

"I will take down your entire family." Lifting his cane, he slammed it over the post. The ominous snap of wood shot through the barn like musket fire.

Liverpool let out a long mournful groan as the chickens scattered in a frenzy.

A wave of acid flooded Rose's belly. She hadn't thought Mr. Snyder capable of violence, but suddenly she was not so sure.

Mr. Snyder tossed the broken stick to the ground, then clutched Rose by the throat.

Clawing at his hands, she gasped for air.

He thrust his face into hers until she could smell the sausage he'd had for breakfast. "I will have this land and you as my wife if it's the last thing I do."

Valor let out a thunderous bray and kicked her stall.

Rose scratched at his hands, her lungs screaming. Visions of another man's harsh grip upon her throat blasted through her mind. *Oh God, no!* Panic set in, first clenching her heart then weaving its way through every muscle and tissue. Just when she thought she might lose consciousness from lack of air, Mr. Snyder released her, shoving her back against Valor's stall.

Lifting a hand to her throat, Rose coughed and gulped in air, shifting her gaze between the open barn door and Mr. Snyder, lest he come at her again. Instead he stood there, his chest heaving, his expression one of shock and self-loathing. "Forgive me." Then suddenly, spinning on his heel, he marched from the barn.

A minute later, Rose heard his horse gallop away. She wanted to succumb to her trembling legs and crumple to the ground. She wanted to cry. She wanted to run and lock herself in her chamber.

But she couldn't. Her aunt and uncle were in the center of a city about to be attacked by the British. She couldn't count on the military evacuating them. Despite what Mr. Snyder declared, Rose's aunt had informed her that Washington was often left largely unprotected because most of the army stationed there was called out to battle in other locations. No one in their wildest dreams considered an attack on Washington DC possible.

And perhaps it still wasn't.

But how could she be sure?

Daniel's words of destiny rang in her ears. *God has something important for you to do.* She hadn't believed him. Not until this moment. Now she feared the destiny he had spoken of was fast approaching.

She must go to Washington to warn her family.

Climbing to the barn loft, she retrieved Alex's pistol from a trunk. She hated bringing the heinous thing but it might come in handy. Thoughts of Alex caused her heart to shrink. Was he indeed marching on Washington? If so, he'd be forced to shoot Americans. Which made him her enemy once again. Not to mention put him in grave danger. And the worst of it was, if he died, she would never know. She didn't know whether to pray for him or her countrymen. Perhaps both. After climbing down the ladder, she prepared Valor to ride, stuffed the pistol in the saddle pack, and led the horse out of the barn.

No sooner had she reached the open field than her legs went as limp as blades of grass, her chest felt as though Liverpool were sitting on it, and her head spun around a pounding ache.

She could not go to Washington!

Alone.

What was she thinking?

She gazed over the grassy field beyond. Her home. Her sanctuary. Would it remain that way? Over the treetops the afternoon sun sped toward the horizon as if frightened of the coming night. Distant thunder rumbled from slate gray clouds looming in the east.

Oh Lord, please protect my aunt and uncle.

Even at a gallop, the trip would take her at least four hours. She might already be too late.

She sank to the ground and dropped her head into her hands. "I cannot go. Lord, what if I'm attacked again?"

"I love you."

God? Rose glanced around her but heard only the rustle of the wind dancing through the tall grass. "What if I don't make it in time?"

"I love you."

Did God love her? Memories of the dream she had a few weeks ago filled her thoughts. The man in white had said she had something important to do for God, just like Daniel had proclaimed. Rose wiped her sweaty palms over her gown.

"Go." The inner voice again. Gentle, yet not demanding.

"Me? Lord. I'm nothing but a frightened little mouse." A heavy wind swept over her, twirling the dirt beside her into a whirlwind. She hugged herself. "I don't know if I can do this."

"*Trust me.*"

Trust. Indignation forced her to her feet. She fisted her hands at her sides. "Trust!" She shouted into the sky. "Where were You when I was attacked? Where were You when I was ravished?" Her voice cracked.

"*Right beside you.*"

"Lord." she sobbed.

"*Precious daughter, forgive them.*"

Rose closed her eyes. Light and shadow battled across her eyelids. The warmth of the sun embraced her as the wind caressed her hair and cooled her moist cheeks. Forgive. She didn't feel like forgiving the sailors who had assaulted her, the family friend who had used her. But maybe it wasn't about feelings. Mr. Snyder had asked for her forgiveness before he'd stomped out of the barn. Could she forgive him as well?

Rose clenched her fists. "I forgive them, Lord. I forgive them all."

Love such as she'd never known before instantly fell upon her, cloaking her, filling her. More than the love of her earthly father, this love was like a fire, consuming all fear in its path.

She opened her eyes. And suddenly she knew. It didn't matter what happened to her. She belonged to God. The Almighty Creator of the universe was her father. He would always be with her—even through the bad times. There was a plan.

A purpose behind the agony.

Half-giggling half-sobbing, she lifted her arms out to her sides, thirsting for more of this love, wanting to soak it in, to bask in it. She twirled around like a child frolicking among a field of wildflowers until she nearly stumbled with dizziness. So this was what Uncle Forbes meant when he said, "*Perfect love casts out all fear.*"

"Thank You, Father."

Thunder groaned in the distance again, reminding her she hadn't much time.

Wiping her face, she drew a deep breath and swung onto Valor's back. She clutched the reins and faced southwest. Fear still lingered within her. She felt its tormenting claws grinding over the fortress of love that held it at bay, clamoring to be released, but with God's help, she would not allow it. Not ever again.

Snyder urged his gelding down the trail leading back to the Drummond home. No sooner had he reached Madison Street than he regretted his harsh treatment of Rose. He hadn't intended to be so vile. In fact, quite the opposite. But the smug look of victory on her face had unleashed the devil within him. How dare she toss him from her farm like so much refuse? The audacity! Never in Snyder's life had he been treated with such brazen impudence. Especially not from an orphaned farm girl.

Snyder's own inferior birth and dubious heritage rose to sneer at him, but he shoved the unsavory thoughts aside. He had risen above the legacy left him by his father and grandfather. And he would rise further still.

For he had every intention of marrying Miss McGuire, despite this temporary setback.

With Mr. Reed gone, the lady had no other worthwhile prospects. Certainly none as advantageous as himself. His housekeeper, Miss Addington, had reminded him of that fact last evening as he stormed about his parlor, shoving vases and trays to the floor in his fury. "Easier to catch bees with sweet nectar than with tar," she had said. He wished he'd taken her advice instead of behaving the ignoble beast. But who could blame him after all she and Mr. Reed had done? Nevertheless, he determined to make amends immediately, before her anger festered. He would swallow his pride and apologize for his behavior. Sooner or later, she was bound to see him in a favorable light and forgive his past indiscretions.

Adjusting the bouquet of wildflowers he'd picked along the side of the road, he snapped the reins and smiled at the assurance of his success. He was handsome, accomplished, and had much to offer the lady. Now all he needed was a bit of charm and a barrel of patience, and soon this prime land would be his.

A band of sooty clouds lined the eastern horizon, but the afternoon sun still beat down on him. Withdrawing a handkerchief, he mopped the sweat from his brow as he led his horse through the farm's open gate and glanced toward the barn where he expected to find Miss McGuire. His eyes were rewarded with the sight of her standing beside her horse.

Urging his gelding into a trot, he headed her way when, much to his surprise, she leaped upon her filly, kicked the beast's sides, and galloped across the field, disappearing into the forest.

By herself! Did she know there were British afoot?

Snyder stared after her as a gust of wind swept away the cloud of dust kicked up by her horse. Of course she knew there were British afoot. Perhaps that was why she'd left in such a hurry—to rendezvous with a particular British naval officer.

Snyder ground his teeth together. *The tramp.* Tossing the flowers into the dirt, he flicked the reins and sped across the field after her.

❖ CHAPTER 25 ❖

Alex had barely slept ten minutes before a bugle blared and drums pounded through the camp, waking the troops to a new day.

A day his countrymen intended to march into the American capital and crush the heart of this fledgling nation.

Struggling to rise from the hard ground outside the tent, he stretched the ache in his back and rubbed his eyes, trying to shake the fog from his brain.

Soon men in red coats emerged from tents like fiery wasps from their nests as officers stormed by on horseback shouting orders. After a cold breakfast of dried pork and water, the men tore down the tents, packed the supplies, and lined up in formation. Cool morning air, whispering the promise of a reprieve from the summer heat, drifted over the tired soldiers as they marched double-file into an immense forest where thick branches and a plethora of leaves in all shapes and sizes formed an archway of green overhead that shielded them from the sun. Behind Alex, the seamen in his charge heaved on thick ropes attached to the ship's guns. It would have been much easier to pull the iron cannons in a wagon but due to a shortage of horses, none had been provided. They were good men, brave and loyal, some barely sprouting whiskers on their chins. The guilt of Alex's treason ground hard against his soul. He bowed his head. *Lord, please allow no deaths this day. Please save this wonderful nation and her capital.*

He felt a stirring in his soul. A mission. The American capital must not fall.

He didn't know why. But he felt God telling him, assuring him that these rebel Americans would remain a free nation.

That they must remain a free nation.

His eyes locked on the service sword swinging at his side and the brass buttons lining his blue naval uniform. They seemed out of place on his body—as if they belonged to someone else. He raised his gaze and shifted his shoulders beneath an oddly pleasing sensation. He no longer felt like an Englishman. Instead he felt like an American. Longed to be part of this nation that stood for freedom and liberty and a man's right to pursue his own path to happiness—a nation that did not honor a man simply because of his pedigree.

Soon the cool air of morning dissipated, ushering in a blanket of muggy heat. A groan rose in Alex's throat, and he tipped up his bicorn and wiped the sweat off his brow. The task before him seemed insurmountable. Not only did he have to do his best to avoid battling the Americans, but he had to slip away from the British undetected, and make his way to the American troops without being shot by either side. The more he pondered it, the more impossible the task seemed. And the more dangerous.

After another hour the British troops emerged from the forest into an open field. Though the sun stood only halfway to its zenith, heat struck Alex with such ferocity, he felt as though he'd walked straight into an oven. Dust from the hundreds of boots that had preceded him rose to clog the air. Alex coughed and gasped for breath. His eyes stung. Not a wisp of wind stirred to clear the air or cool his skin.

On their right, they passed bundles of straw and the smoking ashes of campfires strewn across a field, evidence that a large body of men had camped there the night before. Farther ahead, the fresh imprints of hooves and boots sent a tremble down Alex.

The American troops were close. Alex's heart leaped. Perhaps he could escape before the fighting began.

Yet the unrelenting heat punished them without mercy. Seasoned soldiers fell by the wayside, too exhausted and dehydrated to continue.

Alex took a position beside his men and aided them in pulling one of the cannons. Sweat soaked his coat, shirt, and breeches and dripped from the tips of his hair. His breath heaved and every muscle ached as he followed the ranks onto a huge field dotted with thick groves. An eerie silence fell. Everyone seemed to hold their breath, waiting for the signal to form a square for battle.

Alex loosened his cravat and wiped the back of his neck. In the distance, a heavy dust cloud appeared. Drums beat the forward advance, and the troops continued down another road, passing a small plantation on their right before climbing a grassy knoll.

Ignoring the blisters on his hands and the burning in his thighs, Alex tugged on the thick rope. The soldiers who marched before him slowed. Their bodies stiffened like masts. The air twanged with tension. The clomp of horses' hooves joined the shouts of commanding officers. Releasing the rope to another seaman, Alex darted up the hill and pressed through the throng of sweaty men.

Across a field of tall grass, not half a mile away, stood line after line of American soldiers, some in uniform, others not. All well armed. And beyond them in the distance, Alex could barely make out what must be the buildings of Washington DC rising into the afternoon sun.

Alex's muscles tightened. He gripped the musket on his shoulder. The battle would begin in seconds.

Rose galloped into Washington DC and headed down Maryland Street toward the Capitol. Reining Valor to a trot, she scanned the city. Unlike Baltimore, which boasted cobblestone streets through the main part of town, this road and all the ones that spanned from it were nothing but patches of mud and dust. Brick buildings rose on each side and a ditch filled with sewage and stagnant water lined the avenue. The stench curled Rose's nose even as the sight shocked her.

This was the capital of their grand country?

Clucking drew Rose's gaze to a group of chickens prancing off the side of the road. A massive pig snuffled through a pile of garbage to her left. The only signs of life in the otherwise vacant city. After the long ride, the familiar sight of animals loosened her tight nerves if only a bit before she turned right toward Delaware Street where she knew her aunt's orphanage was located. Up ahead a black man ducked in between two buildings. Rose called to him, but he did not reappear.

Despite the heat of the day, a cold chill slithered down her spine. Where was everyone? Then it occurred to her. She'd ridden unhindered into the capital. No one had stopped or questioned her. Not only that, but she'd not spotted a single soldier, American or British. Had Mr. Snyder been misinformed?

Rose scanned the buildings framing Delaware Street. Up ahead, a two-story, whitewashed home drew her gaze, and she slowed before it. The words SUFFER THE LITTLE CHILDREN TO COME UNTO ME stood out in black letters on a sign that hung on a post just inside a tattered fence. Taking a deep breath to calm her thundering heart, Rose dismounted, tied the reins to a hitching post, and grabbed the pistol from the sack. The front door stood ajar. No light or sound emerged from within. Creeping forward, she gripped the handle of the gun and nearly laughed at her own hypocrisy. She could never use the vile weapon even if her life depended on it. Never again.

She stopped before the door and listened. Only the mad rush of blood through her head pounded in her ears. She pushed the door open wider, sending an eerie creak chiming through the house.

"Aunt Muira! Uncle Forbes!" She stepped inside the shadowy foyer. Open books, toys, and children's clothes littered the wooden floor as if the inhabitants had fled in a hurry. The sweet scent of children and innocence and aged wood drifted past her nose.

Footfalls sounded from the back of a long hall. Rose's heart pinched. "Aunt Muira?"

"She's not here." The gentle voice of a man preceded his appearance around a corner. Smiling, he approached Rose. Short-cropped gray hair matched a cultured beard that ran the length of his jaw. Caring brown eyes assessed her. "You must be Rose."

Rose lowered the weapon. "Reverend Hargrave?"

"Yes." He examined the gun and his brows scrunched together. "Why have you come here? It's not safe."

"I heard the British intended to attack Washington, and I feared for my aunt's and uncle's safety." Rose stuffed the pistol into her sash and clasped her hands together to keep them from trembling.

"Oh dear girl, how kind of you." He released a sigh. "Indeed. We heard the same horrendous news. But they've all left. Your aunt and uncle and Miss Edna. They took the children in our wagon and fled the city not two hours ago."

Rose glanced out the door, then back at the reverend, her mind and heart spinning. "Where did they go?"

"I have no idea, my dear. I'm so sorry." He laid a hand on her arm. "But never fear, they are safe."

Relief eased through Rose, and she sighed. Moving to the door, she gazed over the deserted street. "Where is the army, the militia? Why aren't they defending the city?"

"They marched out hours ago." The reverend's footsteps rang hollow over the floor. "Although I do believe there are still some troops down at the naval yard."

Rose swerved around. Though she'd rather hop on Valor and head straight home, certainly God had sent her here for a reason. Perhaps that reason lay at the naval yard. "Where is the yard?"

"Down Virginia Avenue beside the east branch of the Potomac, miss." Concern tightened his features. "But you needn't worry about them." His tone turned urgent. "I beg you to return to Baltimore where you'll be safe."

Rose stepped toward him. "What if the British make it past our troops? What about you?"

He stooped to pick a book off the floor, then smiled. "One of the children is sick and couldn't travel. Besides, they won't trouble a man of the cloth."

Rose did not share his confidence. Yet the peace that surrounded this man put her fears to shame. "God be with you, Reverend."

"And with you." He gave her a reassuring nod.

Turning, Rose fled out the door, dashed toward Valor, and swung onto the saddle. Shielding her eyes from the setting sun, she urged the horse into a trot and headed east.

Past the Capitol building that centered the town. Though not yet completed, its tall white columns stretched to the sky like unrelenting monuments of freedom. The Hall of Representatives stood on the right side—a massive oval surrounded by Corinthian pillars. A wide wooden boardwalk connected its two wings, where they no doubt planned to build an enclosed walkway. Rose galloped past. No time to admire the majestic buildings.

"Oh Lord, please help me," she whispered, but the wind slamming over her face tore her words away along with the pins from her hair.

Flinging strands from her face, Rose raced onward. She tightened her grip on the reins. Her fingers ached. Her heart crashed against her ribs. Fear beckoned to her, begging for release. But something had changed. Rose now knew that God loved her and would never leave her. She may feel fear, but it no longer enslaved her.

She galloped down the street toward the white brick wall that enclosed the navy yard and was surprised once again to find the outside gate abandoned. In fact, no one manned the guard house at all as she led Valor onto the sun-bleached yard. Tall brick buildings framed the inner courtyard. Beyond them loomed the massive arched buildings where the ships were made. Cannons, their muzzles pointed through the battlements of a long stone wall, guarded the yard from seafaring invaders. In the distance, bare ship masts stretched like spires into the sky, stark white against the black clouds lining the horizon.

Rose slid off Valor and headed toward what appeared to be the main headquarters when a thin, bald-headed man with tufts of hair sprouting like brown thickets above his ears emerged and nearly ran her down.

"Miss! What are you doing here?" He placed his cocked hat atop his head, his blue eyes flashing.

Rose threw a hand to her chest. "Sir, are the British marching on Washington?"

He gave her a skeptical look and chuckled. "Where have you been? Why haven't you left town?" He glanced over his shoulder. "You need to leave immediately, miss."

A dozen men emerged from the same building and flooded the yard, some giving her a cursory glance as they passed. Their arms were laden with weapons and cans of some kind of powder.

Rose frowned and gave the man a venomous look. "Who are you, sir, and what are you doing to defend this city?"

He snorted and narrowed his eyes. "I am Commodore Thomas Tingey, miss. And who, pray tell, are you?"

"Rose McGuire from Baltimore." The smell of tar and gunpowder stung her nose. "Where is the militia? Where are the troops defending Washington?"

He gave a sardonic chuckle. "Troops defending Washington?" His bitter tone sent a chill through Rose. "What troops we had marched off to cut off the British advance yesterday." He swallowed and gazed into the distance, sorrow claiming his dusty features. "I have just received word that they have been defeated at Bladensburg."

"Defeated?" Rose's knees wobbled.

"I'm afraid so, miss." He touched her elbow to steady her. "The British could be here any minute."

Valor neighed, and Rose sent a harried gaze over the barren yard where evening shadows began to creep out from hiding. "Aren't you going to do something?"

"Miss, I have but a handful of sailors. I've been ordered to fire the yard at the first sign of the enemy."

"Fire the yard?" Rose glanced to the grassy fields that extended to the Potomac River.

"Aye, we've already set up explosives. Our last task is to lay trails of gunpowder, so we can ignite the blast when the time comes."

Rose glanced at the bare masts of several ships at dock and a few being built on land. "What of the ships?"

Tingey scratched the stubble on his chin. "A shame indeed, miss." His gaze shifted to the docks. "I won't mourn the old frigates, *Boston* and *General Greene,* but the sloop *Argus* and the new frigate *Columbia.* Now, those will be hard losses." He eyed her. "But would you prefer they end up in British hands, along with our naval stores and ammunition?" He brushed past her, shouting orders to the men, then flung a glance back her way. "Now, miss, I urge you to leave the city immediately." His stern tone and the commanding look in his eyes brooked no argument.

Rose nodded, defeat settling like an anchor in her gut. "I will, sir. Is there anyone else in town I can assist in evacuating?"

Commodore Tingey pursed his lips. "I understand the first lady stubbornly resists leaving. I have orders to gather her up on our way out of town."

"Mrs. Madison?" Rose heard the excitement in her own voice. "Can you direct me toward her house?"

Commodore Tingey gestured with his hand. "Past the Capitol, on Pennsylvania Avenue. You can't miss it. Good luck. She's a stubborn one." He tipped his hat at her and marched off shouting "Godspeed to you, Miss McGuire" over his shoulder.

"God help us all." Rose swallowed, then mounted Valor and rode out of the yard, feeling suddenly small and useless. "Why have You sent me here, Lord?" The wind whipped over her, swirling taunting voices in her ears. *You have no destiny. Foolish girl. There is nothing important for you to do here.*

Fear, her old familiar friend, surged through her like a prisoner suddenly released, giddy with delight. Pulling Valor to a halt, she stared at the deserted streets of her nation's capital. The setting sun cast a rainbow of orange and gold over the homes and government buildings. She blinked and rubbed her eyes as if she'd just awoken from a dream. What was she doing here? So far from home. With no one to protect her.

"Oh Lord," she sobbed. "What can I do against an entire British army?" She nudged Valor into a slow walk. Hope spilled from her with each tear that slid down her cheek. The British would take Washington.

And there was nothing she could do about it.

Boom. A distant cannon sounded. Rose clutched the reins. The leather bit through her gloves into her skin.

Their glorious country would fall, and its people would once more be subject to the tyranny of a king who lived across the sea. How could that happen?

"Trust me."

That voice again. So sure and strong, resounding from within her. Created out of her own desperate need to be valued, loved, and cared for? Or truly the voice of God?

She turned down Pennsylvania Avenue, fear threatening to rise and choke the breath from her lungs, her throat. The sun dipped below the horizon, stealing more of the daylight. She should go home. Now, before the troops arrived. Before the soldiers found her—a woman all alone, vulnerable.

And she suffered the same hideous fate all over again.

She would rather die.

A beautiful white mansion rose among the smaller homes along the street, its front door wide open. No doubt the president's home. A carriage with two horses and a footman waited out by the street. It appeared Mrs. Madison was in no need of assistance. Rose kicked Valor to pass the house and head out of town when a woman's scream blared from one of the windows.

❖ CHAPTER 26 ❖

Alex knelt beside the lifeless body of Mr. Kennedy, a seaman under his charge. Blood oozing from several bullet holes in his chest marched like a maroon death squad over his brown shirt. Though not a bruise or cut marred his young face, his vacant eyes stared at the blue sky above—serene, yet empty. Alex brushed his fingers over them, closing them forever. Somewhere back in England, a mother had lost a son. And she was not even aware of the tragedy. Nor would she be aware of it for months.

Ignoring his throbbing thigh and the ache spanning his back, Alex rose and scanned the scene. Exhausted from the stifling heat and the harrowing battle, soldiers had dropped to the ground wherever their weary legs had deposited them. A group of men cleared the British dead from the field while another band picked greedily through the pockets of the dead Americans. From what Alex could tell, more British than Americans had been killed, although neither total reached one hundred.

Plucking his keg from his haversack, Alex uncorked it and poured tepid water down his throat. Despite the temperature, the liquid cooled his parched mouth and filled his empty belly. He lifted his arm to wipe his lips and jolted at the sight of blood splattered over his sleeve. Not his blood, thank God. But someone's blood. Perhaps Mr. Kennedy's or another unfortunate soldier who had slipped from earth into eternity. He prayed they'd gone in the right direction.

To his left, a pair of hollow blue eyes stared at him from within a face blackened by soot. Seaman Miller sat among a group of sailors and offered Alex a sad smile. Despite the horrific chaos raging around him, he had remained at his post by the six-pounder Alex had ordered him to command. Not once had he hesitated in his duty. Alex nodded his approval toward the man of a job well done.

A shout of orders drew Alex's gaze to a large group of captured Americans being led by a colonel who pranced before them in the pomp of victory. He hoped they would be treated humanely but knew they'd probably be either impressed into the Royal Navy or transferred to prison hulks for the remainder of the war.

Tugging off his stained cravat, Alex mopped the sweat from his neck and brow and glanced at the sun halfway on its descent in the sky. He guessed it to be about four in the afternoon, which meant the battle had lasted three hours. Three hours that had seemed like mere seconds—terrifying, agonizing seconds. Though Alex had been in many battles at sea, there was something different, something far more gruesome about fighting on land. Everything moved slowly and methodically upon the sea; on land, everything occurred with such intolerable rapidity and chaos. At sea, as the ships maneuvered for the next broadside, the men had time to clear off the wounded and catch their breath, even say a prayer. But on land, the bullets had never stopped whizzing past Alex's ears, the cannons never stopped firing, the explosions never stopped blasting.

And the men never stopped screaming.

Two soldiers lifted a wounded man off the dirt and placed him on a stretcher. He groaned in agony. Nausea bubbled in Alex's belly, nearly forcing it to spew the water he'd just consumed. He corked his keg and placed it back into his haversack. Bowing his head, he thanked God that he'd not been forced to fight face-to-face with any of the Americans, for he doubted he could have looked straight into the fire of freedom burning in their eyes and willingly extinguished it.

In the end, it must have been the British Congreve rockets that had sent the enemy fleeing. The rocket's shrill screech still rang in

Alex's ears. Despite their ominous sound, they were grossly inaccurate, and Alex doubted any of the rockets had met their mark. But the bone-chilling howl—a roar that Alex imagined sounded like a legion of demons escaping from hell—was sufficient to invoke terror in the staunchest soldier.

Certainly terrifying enough to send the untrained, undisciplined American militia into a panic. Even so, their rapid, chaotic retreat surprised Alex. And disappointed him. He had hoped for more bravado from these Americans he had come to know as both courageous and determined. Of course slipping away and joining them in the heat of battle had not been an option. He'd have been shot on the spot. And now the Americans were gone again. Alex was beginning to think that he wouldn't be able to desert the British until the entire war was over. At least it seemed that way until a minute ago when Admiral Cockburn had stormed up to Alex and selected him to join the march into Washington.

Rose dashed through the open door of the White House and halted, listening. Another scream blared from the right. Clutching her skirts in one hand and plucking her pistol from her sash with the other, she sped up the stairs, slowing when she reached the top.

"I order you to leave my house at once, sir!" A lofty female voice, tainted with a slight quaver, drew Rose down the hall to the right.

"Not a step farther, sir. Do you know who I am?" the woman shouted.

"Yes, madam, the mistress of this rebellious squalor of a country." The man's strong British lilt coupled with his invidious tone sent a wave of dread over Rose.

Ducking beneath lit sconces and framed paintings, she inched over the ornately woven rug toward an open door at the end of the hallway. Her legs shook like branches in a storm.

"How dare you?" the woman's superior tone resounded through the hall.

Lord, help me. Rose stopped at the side of the open door and dared a peek inside. A soldier in a red coat and white breeches stood with his back to her, leveling a sword at an elegantly attired lady wearing a feathered turban. From what Rose had heard about the president's wife, the lady had to be Mrs. Madison.

Mrs. Madison took a step backward and nearly bumped into one of the high-backed chairs surrounding a long dining table at the center of the room. A flick of her eyes told Rose the woman had seen her. Ducking back beside the doorframe, Rose leaned against the wall to quell her sudden dizziness. She had the advantage of surprise.

And a gun. She should shoot him.

But she couldn't.

Not again. But she could hit him with it. Knock him out. Her hands shook. The pistol slipped in her sweaty palms. She tightened her grip, gulping for air that seemed to have retreated with the rest of Washington's inhabitants. If she failed to rescue Mrs. Madison, the soldier would no doubt turn on Rose and then kill the president's wife anyway. Closing her eyes, she silently hummed her father's song, hoping to find solace in the words.

> *O can't you see yon little turtledove*
> *Sitting under the mulberry tree?*
> *See how that she doth mourn for her true love*

Rose shook her head. It wasn't working. Terror kept her frozen in place. Yet hadn't she just declared herself to be free of fear's bondage?

"I hate to inform you, madam, that we have taken your capital and that you are now a prisoner of war." The man chuckled. "Or should I say, prize of war."

"I am no one's prize, sir."

"We shall see, madam."

Rose closed her eyes. *Why has my fear returned, Lord? Where are You?*

"Trust me."

I can't.

"I love you. I will never leave you."

Rose drew a deep breath. She wasn't alone against this British soldier. The Creator of the universe was with her. Pretty good odds, she'd say.

If she believed it.

Rose lifted her chin. *I do believe it. I do believe You, Lord.*

Clutching the barrel of the pistol with both hands, she held it above her head and charged through the door. Before the soldier could turn around, she slammed the handle of the weapon on his head. He dropped to the floor in a heap. A red puddle blossomed like a rose on his blond hair.

The gun slipped from Rose's hands. It fell onto the wooden floor beside him with a *clank*. She raised her gaze to Mrs. Madison.

The lady's wide eyes softened, and a smile grazed her painted lips. "Why, thank you, my dear. The buffoon was becoming quite annoying." Opening her arms, she gestured for Rose to enter as if welcoming her to an evening dinner party.

As if there weren't an unconscious British corporal lying on the floor.

Rose stepped over him. Her legs shook and she stumbled. Mrs. Madison clutched her arm to steady her. "There, there, dear. It is all over now."

Rose glanced at the soldier, then back at Mrs. Madison. "It appears the British have already arrived in the city. You should leave at once."

Releasing Rose's arm, Mrs. Madison flapped a gloved hand over the man as if to brush him away. "Just a scout of some sort." She sighed. "Now, pray tell, who are you, and how did you come to be in my home?" The woman smiled, lifting the circles of red rouge painted on her cheeks. Candlelight sparkled in her eyes and glimmered off the gold jewelry around her neck.

Rose glanced at the long, elegant dining table behind Mrs. Madison. Exquisitely painted china plates framed a white linen cloth that held candlesticks, pitchers, crystal glasses, and platters upon platters of food. Candlelight reflecting off the silverware and brass brightened the entire room. Only then did the scent of beef pudding, wild goose, cornmeal, and sweet pickles reach her nose. Rose shook her head at the odd sight.

"I am Rose McGuire from Baltimore, Mrs. Madison. I was riding past your house when I heard your scream." Rose's heart refused to settle, and she pressed a hand over it. "I beg your pardon for entering uninvited, but the door was open."

"You beg my pardon?" Mrs. Madison's laughter bounced over the room with a friendship and gaiety at odds with the situation. "My dear

Miss McGuire, your boldness saved my life." She studied Rose from head to toe. "And such a slip of a girl too. But so full of bravery."

Brave? Rose found the compliment difficult to swallow.

Mrs. Madison glanced at the open door. "I do wonder where Jean ran off to, as well as Mr. Jennings. If they had been here, this wouldn't have happened."

Plucking a telescope from the table, she glided toward an open window. The swish of what Rose assumed to be a silk Parisian gown—for she'd never seen anything so exquisite—drifted through the dining hall.

"I haven't seen my husband all day." Mrs. Madison lifted the glass to her eye and peered out the window into the darkness beyond. A night breeze ruffled the red plume atop her embroidered turban and fluttered the rich damask curtains. "He left early this morning to meet with his Cabinet at the navy yard. Pray don't think poorly of him." She glanced at Rose over her shoulder before lifting the scope to her eye again. "Mr. Madison did leave a troop of men to guard me, but they ran off to Bladensburg. Who knows what happened to them? God, be with them." She lowered the telescope and released a sigh. "All day long, I've been watching with unwearied anxiety, hoping to discover the approach of my dear husband and his friends, but alas, I can descry only groups of military wandering in all directions, as if there is a lack of arms or of spirit to fight for their own firesides."

"Mrs. Madison." Rose moved to stand beside her. "I hesitate to relay such bad news, but I've heard our troops were defeated at Bladensburg."

She waved a gloved hand through the air. "Yes, so I heard, though I can hardly believe it. Major Blake has come twice to warn me of the danger, but how can I leave my own house?" She faced Rose and shrugged. But then her jaw tightened and fury rolled across her face. "Ah, would that I had a cannon to thrust through every window and blast those redcoats back to England."

Rose couldn't help but smile. What a charming, courageous woman. She lowered her chin. "Mrs. Madison, how can you be so brave when you are all alone, defenseless against the British troops that are surely heading your way?"

Mrs. Madison smiled and grasped one of Rose's hands. "Please call me Dolly. And I am not alone, Miss McGuire. God is always with me."

Her statement jarred Rose while at the same time bolstering her own convictions. Hadn't God said the same thing to her only minutes before?

A shuffle at the door sounded, and Mrs. Madison released Rose's hand. "Jean, there you are."

A tall, wiry man with short-cropped brown hair stared down an aquiline nose at the British soldier on the floor.

"Yes, remove him, if you please, Jean. Tie him up and set him on a sofa somewhere."

"What happened, madame?" The man's French accent was unmistakable.

Mrs. Madison turned toward Rose. "Miss McGuire, may I introduce Jean Sioussa, my doorman. Jean, this is Miss Rose McGuire out of Baltimore. She saved my life when this"—she pinched her lips together—"man tried to accost me in my own dining room."

"Mon Dieu." Jean's curious gaze drifted from the soldier to Rose, and finally landed on Mrs. Madison. "I am sorry I was not here."

"It is nothing, Jean."

"Madame, I have loaded everything onto the carriage: the trunk of cabinet papers, documents from the president's desk, the large chest of silver, velvet curtains, clocks, and the books we packed earlier."

"Thank you, Jean."

Shaking his head, he knelt, grabbed the soldier beneath the arms and hoisted him up. The injured man emitted a low groan, and a wave of relief spread over Rose. In the melee, she hadn't thought to check if she'd killed him.

"I'll attend to this man and be back for you, madame," he said before dragging the soldier off down the hall.

Mrs. Madison set the telescope on the table and glanced over the elaborate meal. "I serve dinner promptly at three o'clock, you know." Sorrow stung in her eyes. "Though Mr. Madison often complains, I always invite as many distinguished guests as I can." She ran her finger over the carved mahogany of one of the chairs. "But no one came today."

Rose laid a hand on Mrs. Madison's silk sleeve. "I'm sorry."

"But I did manage to save the portrait of dear George Washington.

It used to be displayed there." She pointed to the wall where a magnificent gilded frame hung empty like a vacant eye. "Jean managed to extricate it intact on its inner frame." Mrs. Madison's eyes regained their sparkle. "We gave it to some reliable friends who promised to take it away to safety. God knows what the British would do to it."

The pounding of horses' hooves drummed outside, and Mrs. Madison darted to the window. Rose followed and peered below to see a Negro man waving his black hat through the air.

"Clear out! Clear out! General Armstrong has ordered a retreat," he shouted, his voice heightened in fear.

"Why, that's James Smith." Mrs. Madison gripped the window frame. "He accompanied my husband to Bladensburg."

The man dismounted and rushed toward the house. Mrs. Madison swung around just as he barreled into the room and handed her a note. Breaking the seal, she unfolded it and began reading. Her face paled. Even the heavy rouge on her cheeks seemed to fade. "Mr. Madison orders me to flee." She swallowed and glanced over the room. "So that's the end of it. I must leave my home in the hands of those implacable British oafs."

She turned to Rose. "Please come with us, Miss McGuire. I promise you'll be safe."

Rose grasped her gloved hands. "Thank you, Mrs. Madison, but I have a horse outside. I promise I'll leave for Baltimore posthaste."

"Very well. Godspeed to you, dear." She squeezed Rose's hands. Her eyes glazed with tears. "Pray for our country. This is a dark day indeed. But our God is bigger than any force on earth, even the British." She lifted one cultured eyebrow and drew a deep breath.

Releasing Rose's hands, she swept past the dining table, snatching as much silverware as she could hold along the way and stuffing it into her reticule. Jean followed her out the door, leaving Rose all alone.

Hugging herself, Rose moved to the window. Mrs. Madison leaped into the waiting carriage with a servant girl in tow. The driver snapped the reins, and Rose watched as the vehicle dashed down the street until darkness stole it from her view. Thunder roared from the east. A chill struck her.

She had saved the president's wife!

That must have been the important thing Daniel had said she

would do—her destiny. Despite the fear, the terror, she had pressed through and done what God had asked of her. *Thank You, Lord.*

And yet it appeared her country was about to fall under tyranny once again.

Turning, she gazed at the fine fare set on the table. A shame it would all go to waste. Releasing a ragged sigh, Rose headed toward the door. She must leave the city and head back to Baltimore before the British arrived in full force. Head down, pondering her best escape route, she rounded the doorframe.

And ran straight into a British soldier.

The same soldier she had knocked unconscious. He tossed the remnants of ropes from his wrists to the floor and lifted a hand to touch the wound on his head. Dark eyebrows bent above eyes that smoldered with hatred.

Shifting his weight, Alex winced at the pain from the blisters on his feet. His glance took in the band of two thousand troops, mostly redcoats, milling about among lit torches on the east lawn of the Capitol building. *In the heart of Washington DC.* Doffing his hat, he ran a bloody sleeve over the sweat on his brow and gazed up at the nearly full moon that drifted in between masses of dark clouds. Thunder bellowed. Or was it cannon fire? He couldn't be sure. His ears rang constantly with blasts of guns from earlier that day. Would the pounding ever cease? Or would it always drum in his ears as a reminder of the day he'd helped to defeat freedom?

As quickly as he wiped it away, sweat beaded once again on his brow. Though the sun had long since set, its oppressive heat remained. Only a slight evening breeze offered any relief. He supposed he should at least be thankful for that. Unavoidable anger swelled inside him. Anger that the British had won. Anger that they now intended to strip this great nation of its freedoms. And anger that he was being forced to partake in such a travesty.

Tugging off his cravat, he ran it over the back of his neck as he listened to the excited chatter of the men around him. Voices, once stinging with fear, now buzzed with the excitement of victory.

They'd entered the capital city of America without opposition, save for a volley of fire from a house when they'd first marched down Second Street. A house Admiral Cockburn had immediately torched, much to the dismay of anyone who had remained within. Now, as they waited before the seat of American power for someone—anyone—in authority to come out and discuss the terms of surrender, Alex began to wonder if a single soul remained in the city at all.

Boom! An enormous blast lit the eastern sky. The soldiers snapped to attention, gripped their muskets, and stared aghast at the yellow and red flames flinging into the darkness at the end of Virginia Avenue. Fear silenced every tongue as they waited to be attacked. But no bullets whizzed past them, no cannon blasts thundered. Finally, a scout galloped off on horseback to investigate. No doubt, the Americans had destroyed something they didn't want the British to confiscate. Which meant the city, indeed, belonged to the British.

Several minutes after the scout returned, Admiral Cockburn leaped on his horse and ordered the men to storm the Capitol building. As Alex filed in behind the troops, sharpshooters at the front of the line fired a volley through the windows of Congress. Admiral Cockburn thrust his sword into the air. "Storm the rebel bastion!" And the troops dashed forward in a chaotic wave of hatred and greed, breaking windows and bursting through the front door of the House of Representatives. With a heavy heart, Alex followed them inside. His defiance of the order would be too obvious.

The Senate chamber was a stark contrast to the rustic appearance of the city streets. Velvet-curtained balconies circled the room above a marble trim on which some words had been etched. Rows of rich wooden desks and chairs lined a red and gold embroidered carpet. Ornate white columns guarded the main floor that opened to a painted oval ceiling above.

While the troops scoured the building for objects of value, Alex took a spot just inside the chamber doors and watched as Admiral Cockburn sauntered through the impressive room, his face a mask of shock. "Indeed," he turned to the officers following him. "I am all astonishment. This American senate chamber is a much more imposing spectacle than our own House of Lords." He gave a sordid chuckle, straightened his coat, and mounted a platform. He sank into an elaborate wooden chair from which, Alex assumed, either the president or some other important government official conducted business.

The admiral banged the gavel for attention. "Shall this harbor of Yankee democracy be burned? All for it, say aye."

"Ayes!" rang through the room like gongs of doom.

General Ross marched into the chamber and halted. Frowning, he folded his arms across his chest, and Alex got the impression he was not at all pleased at the way Cockburn conducted himself. Yet after a few minutes, the general slipped out, doing nothing to stop the insolent mayhem.

As the men began gathering furniture to burn, Alex's gaze landed on a large black book atop a curved mahogany desk at the front of the room. It seemed to beckon to him, and before he knew it, he had eased from his spot by the door and inched closer, trying to avoid attracting the attention of Admiral Cockburn still sitting in the elevated chair. The closer Alex got to the book, the faster his heart beat. A Bible. And beside it on a placard, were painted the words, "In God we trust." He raised his eyes once again to the unfinished engraving on the marble trim lining the room. "In God. . ." it began.

Alex retreated to his spot by the door and scratched his head. Mr. Drummond had told him that the government in America prided itself on staying out of religion. Alex had assumed that meant that the government had nothing to do with religion and faith. But from the presence of the Bible in their Senate chamber and the words engraved on the placard and started on the trim above the room, the truth of the matter appeared to be quite the opposite. Americans deemed that government should stay out of religion, but they in no way wanted religion to stay out of government. In fact, this government appeared to embrace faith in God.

Vile laughter shook him from his thoughts as the men flung burning lanterns on top of a massive pile of desks, tables, and chairs in the center of the room. Alex's throat went dry. He fingered the hilt of his sword. He must stop this madness. But how? He was one against thousands.

Cockburn marched from the room, laughing.

Alex resisted the urge to plunge his sword into the admiral's heart and instead, ground his teeth together as the flames began to lick the wooden legs and arms of the furniture. A swarm of troops fled the room behind the admiral, flinging obscenities in their wake. Soon, the whole chamber blazed with a heat so intense the glass of the lights began to melt. Alex darted out the door and stepped outside for some air only to see more flames leaping from the Senate chamber's windows. The temporary wooden bridge that separated the two wings also burned, as well as a few nearby homes and the Library of Congress across the way. In truth, the whole city seemed ablaze as red and orange flames reached their flickering fingers up to God pleading for mercy.

Blood rushed to Alex's head as a wave of nausea struck him. He stumbled to his knees beneath a tree and tried to collect himself. Tears burned in his eyes. This honorable, God-fearing, free nation had seen its last days. It didn't seem right.

Cockburn and Ross mounted their horses, and Alex gleaned from the excited chatter around him that their next target was the American president's home. Was nothing sacred? Alex gazed toward the distant forest, longing to return to the Drummond farm—to beg their forgiveness and forget that he once knew a nation of proud, free people.

But he couldn't. Tensions were too high. He'd never make it alive.

Instead, he struggled to his feet, rubbed his eyes, and fell in behind the raucous crowd. The city that only moments ago had been shrouded in darkness now lit up as bright as day. Waves of heat from the flames swamped Alex as he dragged his feet over the sandy street. He hung his head, wanting to pray but not finding the words.

Clearly God had deserted them all.

❖ CHAPTER 27 ❖

Clutching her throat, Rose backed away from the British soldier. Though he was not much taller than she, the broad expanse of his shoulders beneath his red coat spoke of great strength. A white baldric crossed his chest and disappeared beneath the red sash tied about his waist. The bloodstains on his red coat and gray trousers were the only marks on his otherwise pristine uniform.

She opened her mouth to ask him what he wanted, but her words emerged in a pathetic squeak. It didn't matter. She could tell from the hatred and fury storming in his blue eyes that he wanted to kill her. Once again, he dabbed the blood-encrusted patch of hair atop his head. "You churlish American chit!" He reached for a sword that no longer hung at his side then glanced down at his belt for what she assumed were his pistols.

Also gone. *Thanks be to God.*

Rose drew a breath. "I'm sorry I had to hit you so hard, sir, but I could hardly have allowed you to murder my first lady."

He grunted and surveyed the room.

"If you're looking for Mrs. Madison, she has left." Rose lifted her chin and met his gaze with defiance, though she felt none of the bravery that Mrs. Madison had attributed to her. Instead, her legs quivered like wet noodles.

"Dashed off like a coward, no doubt." He sneered. "Like all the cowards in this city."

Rose gripped the back of a chair to keep from crumbling to the ground. "What do you expect, corporal? We are but innocent women and children."

His gaze wandered over the food-laden table, and he licked his lips. "None of you rebels are innocent."

He took a step toward her, staggered, then shook his head. A spark lit his eyes, and he bent over and plucked up a knife tucked within his boot. Twisting it in his hand, he grinned with delight. Rose cast a harried gaze over the floor for her pistol. There it was, by the door where she'd dropped it. Out of her reach.

She would die soon. An odd peace settled upon her at the realization. She had fulfilled her destiny, and now God would take her home. It was for the best. Without Alex, and with the prospects of forever living under Mr. Snyder's threats, she had no reason to go on. She prayed only that her passing would not be too painful.

The corporal advanced. This time there was no wobble in his step.

Rose squeezed the back of the chair until her fingers hurt. "I could have killed you, sir."

He tugged at his white collar and grinned. "You should have."

Reaching behind her, Rose groped across the table, seeking anything with which to defend herself. Her fingers latched onto a fork.

The corporal took another step toward her. The candlelight glinted off his knife.

Lord, help me. Rose clutched the fork and started to swing it forward when the sharp cock of a gun behind the corporal cracked the air. The soldier halted.

"Ah, just as I suspected." The male voice bore no British lilt. But its familiar cadence caused Rose's heart to collapse nonetheless. She peered around the soldier.

Mr. Snyder's stylish figure filled the doorframe. His pistol swerved between Rose and the British soldier.

The corporal's eyes narrowed, more with disdain than fear. Tucking the knife beneath his coat, he turned to face this new threat, slowly raising his hands in the air.

Rose stared aghast at the councilman. She blinked, thinking her eyes must surely be playing tricks on her. "What are you doing here, Mr. Snyder?"

His brows rose above icy blue eyes. "Why, I followed you, Miss McGuire."

"Followed. . .my word." Rose's head spun. She dropped the fork onto the table. "Thank God you arrived in time. As you can see, this soldier—"

"What I see, Miss McGuire"—Mr. Snyder seethed between clenched teeth—"is that you are consorting with the enemy."

The British man moved, and Snyder snapped the pistol toward his chest. "Ah, ah, no you don't, you odious redcoat. I'd have no qualms about shooting you where you stand."

Rose's thoughts whirled in shock and confusion. "Consorting with. . .are you daft?" Anger tossed her fear aside, and she fisted her hands on her waist.

The corporal lowered his gaze to the floor.

"Quite the opposite, I assure you. Wasn't it bad enough you fraternized with one of them on your own farm? Now, I find you here in Washington"—he gave an incredulous snort—"in the White House of all places, delivering vital information to this officer."

"Deliver. . ." Rose slammed her mouth shut to cool her temper and collect her chaotic thoughts. "I came here to warn the president of an impending attack, you buffoon. And this man was about to kill me."

"Yet, I see no weapons in his hand. Or on his person, for that matter." Mr. Snyder smirked. "No, my dear, this time, I have caught you in the act. And if justice is served, you will be tried as a traitor to your country. Even I cannot overlook such bold treason."

The soldier lifted his gaze. A bold, malicious look flashed in his eyes.

Ignoring the shiver that ran down her back, Rose stepped toward Mr. Snyder. "Don't be absurd. Now, if you please, let's bind up this man and be on our way. I fear the British are marching into the city as we speak."

"No thanks to you, I'm sure." Mr. Snyder eyed her with disgust. "I daresay, I am quite disappointed to discover that you are, indeed, a traitor, my dear. I was willing to lower my standards in order to gain your land, but I could never endanger my career as councilman by marrying a British spy." He sighed. "More's the pity. Now I shall have to find someone else to marry."

Frustration bubbled in Rose's gut.

An explosion thundered in the distance. The floor quivered. Mr. Snyder's wide eyes flew toward the window, and the corporal darted toward the door and stooped to the ground. Rose's gaze followed the reach of his hand, but before she could react, he grabbed the pistol Rose had dropped earlier. In one fluid motion, he leveled it at Mr. Snyder and fired.

Rose screamed.

Shock rolled over Mr. Snyder's face. The pistol shook in his hand. He fell backward through the open door and the corporal leaped toward him. Mr. Snyder's weapon discharged. The soldier halted in midstride, let out a shriek, and clutched his chest. Crumpling, he toppled to the ground. Mr. Snyder stumbled backward. Red blossomed on his silk waistcoat.

Dashing past the soldier, Rose grasped Mr. Snyder's arm to steady him. He glanced down at the blood bubbling from his chest. His breath rasped in his throat. His legs gave out, and Rose eased him to sit on the floor.

"My word." She scanned the room for anything to stop the bleeding. Dashing to the dining table, she grabbed a bundle of napkins and ran back to Mr. Snyder. He slumped to the wooden floor. Placing the cloths over his wound, she pressed as hard as she could. "We have to stop the bleeding."

Mr. Snyder moaned.

"Never fear, Mr. Snyder. It's just a bullet wound. I've dealt with them before." Her mind drifted to Alex and the wound in his thigh. Beneath her fingers, the maroon circle advanced on the cloth like an unrelenting army. Her stomach knotted. This was a much more serious wound. *Dear Lord, please help him.*

Shouts blared in through the window from outside. British voices. Jubilant voices accompanied by the bray of horses and the ominous thud of many boots.

Mr. Snyder's wide eyes locked on Rose's as he whispered, "The British are here."

Amassed in a crush of exultant soldiers, Alex entered the American president's house. Each step of invasion into the private home of the great leader forced his shoulders lower in shame. His comrades were not of the same mind. In fact, Admiral Cockburn, who had sauntered in ahead of Alex, seemed quite giddy as he declared to the poor young American bookdealer he'd corralled for a guide, "Ah, Jemmy's palace at last!" He tipped up the front of his cocked hat. "Do give me a tour, lad. I wish to collect souvenirs that I may presently give to the flames." He faced the troops standing in the foyer and waved a hand through the air. "Men, at your pleasure." His release sent the soldiers scattering like ants from an anthill in search of treasure.

Alex wanted no part of it. Instead, he ambled behind the twelve officers who followed the admiral upstairs. Best to keep his eye on Cockburn and salvage anything of import during the mayhem, for Alex could think of no other reason God had allowed him to partake in this madness. If simply to witness the cruelty of his nation, he'd already seen enough. What other purpose could there be for his presence here besides to save some important document or national artifact from the angry flames?

The band of imperious men sauntered down a long hall to an open door from which spilled bright, flickering candlelight. The scent of beef and goose along with the metallic smell of blood and stench of sweat formed a malodorous blend that made Alex cringe. Thunder bellowed outside, mimicking the fury storming within him. As they approached the door, a dark shadow halted the admiral. A dead British soldier lay crumpled in the corner. Alex made his way through the crowd. No, not dead. A faint lift of the man's chest and flutter of his eyes gave evidence of a lingering, yet dwindling life. A large crimson stain darkened his red coat. Kneeling, the admiral gazed at the man. "Crenshaw, go fetch the surgeon." One of the men dispatched from the group and darted down the hallway.

"You." Cockburn stood and pointed at Alex. "What is your name, lieutenant?"

"Reed, Alexander Reed, sir."

"Stay with this man until the doctor arrives."

"Aye, aye, sir."

As the men filtered through the open door, Alex knelt beside the poor fellow. His ashen face, blue lips, and the gurgling sound in his throat, did not bode well for his surviving the night. Leaning back on his haunches, Alex peered into the large room, which from all appearances must have been the president's formal dining room.

Cockburn surveyed the table with a hearty laugh. "Egad, how thoughtful of Jemmy! Up until now, I had considered him to be nothing but a fatwitted ruffian." He took a seat at the head of the table and gestured for his officers to join him. As each man sat around the elegant spread, Admiral Cockburn snapped his fingers for the bookseller. "Pour me a drink, good fellow." The thin, timid man filled the admiral's cup from a pitcher of ale on the table.

He raised it in the air. "To Jemmy's health."

"To Jemmy's health," the men repeated before they all burst into a bout of devilish laughter.

Alex tore his gaze from the scene and closed his eyes. Such insolent lack of respect. The sounds of glass breaking, wood splitting, and raucous laughter drifted down the hall as the soldiers ransacked the mansion from cellar to garret. The clank of silverware and the moist slap of lips from the dining room told Alex the men now brazenly partook of the president's meal.

The soldier mumbled, and Alex opened his eyes to find the wounded man staring at him. The intense look on the man's face nearly sent Alex backward. He opened his mouth and seemed to be trying to speak. Leaning forward, Alex brought his ear near the soldier's mouth. "Rebels in the house. I shot one. The other's a lady," he managed to squeak out between strangled breaths.

Alex nodded and squeezed the man's hands. "Hold fast. The doctor is on the way."

The corporal shook his head. "They couldn't have gotten out."

"Another toast to Jemmy, gentlemen." Admiral Cockburn's insidious voice slithered over Alex from the dining room. "For being such a good fellow as to leave us such a capital supper."

"Here, here," the men chanted as another bout of pretentious laugher ensued.

Alex's stomach churned.

The wounded corporal's hand went slack in Alex's and fell to the floor by his side. He released one final ragged breath, and Alex brushed his fingers over the man's vacant eyes. Then bowing his head, he prayed for the violence to end. For this night to end.

Alex had seen enough death for one day.

Rising to his feet, he peered at the admiral and his officers shoving food into their mouths and drinks down their throats as they regaled each other with bombastic anecdotes.

Rebels in the house? Alex headed down the hall. Perhaps that was why God had sent him here. If there were injured rebels in the house, Alex had better find them before the British soldiers did.

With one hand, Rose dabbed her handkerchief over Mr. Snyder's slick brow and cheeks while she kept the other pressed over his wound. He moaned, and Rose adjusted the pillow she'd made from his overcoat. The hollow thud of boots and the bone-chilling screech of laughter echoed through the thin walls of the small unfinished chamber Rose had discovered at the other end of the house. Intended to be servants' quarters or perhaps a storage area, the room was barren of furniture— save for the velvet-upholstered sofa she and Mr. Snyder hid behind. No rugs covered the wooden floors, no desks or chairs stood about, nothing hung on the walls, and no curtains framed the two large windows. The dark, empty chamber seemed to accentuate the noises around her: ominous footfalls, glass shattering, drunken laughter, crashes and thumps that kept her heart tangled in fear.

It had taken every ounce of her strength to haul Mr. Snyder to his feet and then—with him draped over her shoulder—assist him down the long hall in search of a hiding place. She had lugged him toward the back of the house and then up another flight of stairs before she could go no farther.

"Rose," he whispered, his voice as ragged as his breathing.

"Shhh, Mr. Snyder. I'm right here." She dabbed his forehead and looked at his blue eyes in the shadows—eyes that had lost the sting of arrogance and determination. Though she pressed as hard as she could on the wound, Mr. Snyder's once gold waistcoat had transformed into a brown pond. Too much blood.

He was losing far too much blood.

Boots thumped nearby, and a door slammed in the distance. Rose swallowed a lump of terror. If any of the soldiers entered the room, she prayed the obvious lack of valuables would force them to leave. Unless, of course, they took the time to walk over and peek behind the sofa. If they did, perhaps the Lord would make her and Mr. Snyder invisible. Why not? Surely the Creator of the universe could perform such a simple task.

Despite the mad thumping of her heart and the sweat trickling down her back, Rose felt an inner peace. Whether God saw her through this harrowing night or took her home, she was content that His will would be done. And that it would be for the best. What a wonderful change God had worked in her heart from just a few days ago! Yes, some of her fear remained, but God's peace had removed the sting from it, rendering it impotent.

"I'm sorry, Rose." Mr. Snyder coughed. A trickle of blood spilled from the corner of his mouth.

Rose flattened her lips and stared at the man who had threatened her family, who had sent her beloved Alex away, forever destroying Rose's chance at true love and happiness. She searched her heart for any animosity and strangely found none, as if his life-threatening injury or perhaps God Himself had swept it all away.

A flash of lightning lit his face, and Rose nearly gasped at the gray pallor of his skin. Beneath her hand, his heart still beat, though its pulse had weakened. A tear slid down her cheek. She bit her lip. *No, Lord. No. Please do not let him die.*

Yet. . .a shameful thought skipped across Rose's mind. If Mr. Snyder died, Rose and her family would be safe from his threats. She sighed and wiped the blood from Mr. Snyder's lips. Even still, she did not wish him dead.

Withdrawing her right hand from his wound, Rose placed her other one upon it, then shook out the cramp in her palm. Not that holding the wound was doing any good. This amount of blood indicated a major organ or artery had been penetrated. If only her aunt or Dr. Wilson were here. Then again, what could any of them do in the middle of an enemy-occupied city?

"I have been a beast, Rose." Mr. Snyder's voice cracked. "I wanted your land. And I wanted you." He attempted to smile.

"It doesn't matter now."

"But it does. I want you to understand." His voice rasped like the scraping of wood on wood. "I longed to be a man of importance, of prominence. I wanted recognition, status, I wanted to be admired." He coughed and another stream of blood spilled from his lips. "And someday, maybe even loved." His sorrowful eyes met hers.

Thunder pounded on the walls of the house. Rose's heart collapsed in anguish for Mr. Synder's pain. "A man's true value is not measured in his wealth or status, but in his honor and charity," she said.

Understanding flashed in Mr. Snyder's dull eyes. "Yes, I see that now."

Somewhere a window shattered. Hideous laughter ensued.

"You must leave, Rose." Mr. Snyder's tone grew urgent. "Before they find you. I am done for."

Rose gripped his hand. "I won't leave you."

His forehead wrinkled. "After all I've done?"

The patter of rain sounded on the roof like the march of a thousand soldiers.

She squeezed his hand.

His eyes misted. "Forgive me, Rose?"

Rose dabbed at the sweat beading in the red whiskers that lined his jaw—the ones he always kept so expertly trimmed. "Yes, of course." A sudden fear gripped her as she watched his life ebb away—fear for his eternal destination. "But it's God's forgiveness you need to seek."

He nodded, coughing. Sprinkles of blood flew from his mouth.

Rose smiled and wiped the tears spilling down her cheeks.

He coughed again, then expelled a deep breath.

And went completely still.

A flash of lightning revealed eyes devoid of life.

Releasing the pressure on his chest, Rose curled up into a ball on the floor beside him and began to sob.

Thunder cracked the sky with a loud boom.

The door squeaked open. Swallowing a sob, Rose peered beneath the sofa. A breeze wafted around her with the scent of rain and sweat and smoke. Boots, immersed in a circle of light, thudded over the wooden floor. Black Hessian boots. Rose held her breath.

Oh Lord, make him go away.

Inching to the edge of the sofa, Rose dared a peek around the corner. She gasped.

Alexander Reed stood in the center of the room.

❖ CHAPTER 28 ❖

Too shocked to move, Alex stared at the woman he loved. He shook his head. He'd gone mad. There was no other explanation, for Rose would not have traveled this far from home. Holding up the lantern, he took a step toward her. Rain tapped an eerie cadence on the roof. Lightning flashed outside the window, coating her in silver. Alex blinked and rubbed his eyes, trying to settle his heart. Only a vision. Just a vision conjured up by his despair.

Thunder rumbled through the walls. He snapped his eyes open.

The vision moved. It gripped the sofa and slowly stood. Wide, lustrous blue eyes gaped at him.

He inched toward her. "Rose?"

She flew into his arms. He wrapped one arm around her and dropped his face into her hair. The smell of hay and honeysuckle confirmed what the warmth flooding his body told him.

She was real.

She began to sob. "I thought I'd never see you again."

Withdrawing, he set the lantern on the floor, then gripped her shoulders and glanced over her, looking for any injuries, as sudden fear dashed away his joy. "What the deuces are you doing here?"

Sadistic laughter barreled down the hallway.

Rose wiped the tears from her face and fell into him again. "My aunt and uncle were at the orphanage. I came to warn them."

Alex bundled her in his arms and kissed the top of her head. "You foolish, wonderful lady."

Lantern light flickered over her face as her eyes, bounding with love, sought his. He stroked her cheeks and lowered his lips to hers. They tasted of salty tears and Rose. She moaned, and he pressed her against him and ran his fingers through her hair. "I love you, Rose."

"You love me?"

"Yes." He brushed the hair from her face. "And I want to stay with you. Become an American."

She blinked and took a step back. "Then what are you doing here?"

"Trying to find your military so I can desert mine, trying to stop the destruction." Alex ran a hand through his hair. "I'm not sure anymore."

"I can't believe you want to become an American." Rose approached and cradled his face in her hands. "Is it true?"

"Truer than anything I've ever known." Alex smiled and leaned his forehead against hers.

A loud blast from inside the house jolted him back to reality. Releasing Rose, he gripped the hilt of his sword, stepped to the door and peered out. Fear tightened his gut. "Your aunt and uncle?"

"They were already gone when I got here."

"Then what are you doing in this house?"

"I came in to warn the president's wife." Tears streamed down her cheeks, and she raised a hand to cover her mouth. "Mr. . .Mr. . ." Her voice quaked. "Mr. Snyder."

Alex turned to give her a questioning look. "What of Mr. Snyder?"

"He followed me." Her eyes snapped to the only piece of furniture in the room. Thunder growled outside. "He's dead." Rose shuddered and stared at the sofa.

Picking up the lantern, Alex skirted the velvet couch. Blank eyes stared up at him above a blood-soaked cravat and waistcoat. He tore his gaze away and looked at Rose. "How?"

"A British soldier shot him."

Alex swallowed as realization settled. Yes. The soldier who had died by Alex's side. More footsteps pounded outside the room, joining the tap of raindrops atop the roof. Alex grasped Rose's hand once again.

This time he noticed how cold and moist her skin was. Terror like he'd never felt before consumed him. He must keep Rose safe.

"We have to get you out of here. Soldiers are searching the entire mansion. They will find you."

The ominous clap of a footfall sounded behind him. Alex spun around.

The dark figure of a British soldier stepped inside the room. "Ah, I see you've found a sweet American tart, my friend. Care to share?"

The soldier sauntered into the room, pistol in one hand, a bottle of liquor in the other. All hope fled Rose before an advancing onslaught of fear. Her pulse roared in her ears. No matter what happened, she would never forget these final minutes God had allowed her with the man she loved.

Alex moved in front of her as if he could shield her from this man. From the world. She wished he could. *Oh Lord, please protect him. Please don't let him do anything foolish.* She glanced over the room, searching for anything she could use as a weapon, but found none. Mr. Snyder's pistol was in the dining room where he'd dropped it beside his ever-present cane.

Alex's hand flew to the hilt of his service sword. "The woman is my prisoner."

"Egad, man. She's a rebel wench." The soldier, a sergeant, evidenced by the three strips on his red coat, peered around Alex. "And a comely one at that." Desire burned in his dark eyes. Rose's stomach soured.

"Besides." The man wobbled past Alex. "Admiral Cockburn has given us his leave to take whatever we find in the house." The smell of alcohol emanating from the brute burned Rose's nose.

Alex moved in front of her again. His muscles seemed to ripple beneath his dark navy coat. But then his shoulders relaxed, and he let out a sigh of compliance. "Very well. I suppose I'll oblige you, sergeant." He gave a chuckle that would have convinced Rose of his sincerity if she didn't know him better. He pointed toward the soldier's pistol. "No need for that, is there? We are on the same side, after all."

The sergeant glanced at the weapon in his hand as if he'd not realized he held it. Stuffing it in its holster, he hefted the bottle to his lips and took a big draught. He wiped his mouth and handed it to Alex.

Alex took a sip then gestured toward the hallway. "Do get the door, sergeant, while I get the wench ready. We don't want to be disturbed, do we?"

Lightning flickered outside, flashing an eerie gray over the sergeant's angular face. His wide grin reminded Rose of a row of dead bones standing at attention. "Aye, I like the way you think, sir." Removing the tall black shako from his head, he set it on the sofa, scouring Rose with a salacious gaze before he turned and started toward the door.

Alex didn't hesitate. Drawing his sword, he struck the man's head with the hilt. With a moan, the sergeant folded to the ground like a used piece of foolscap.

Rose gasped and stared at Alex.

Thunder roared, rattling the windows.

Alex flashed a smile her way, then knelt by the man and began unbuttoning the brass buttons on his coat. "Quick. Take off your clothes."

"What?" Rose shook her head as if Alex's words had somehow become jumbled.

"Your clothes, Rose." His voice was urgent. "I'll turn my head."

Slipping into the shadows, Rose hesitated for a moment until she realized what he intended to do. She wanted to protest the mad idea, but her voice once again would not cooperate. Instead, she clutched her gown and lifted it over her head.

Alex made quick work of the man's brass buttons and tore off his coat, then began fidgeting with his fatigue jacket beneath. "Your petticoat, Rose. I need your petticoat." His voice was gentle, but commanding, brooking no argument—just as Rose assumed he sounded when he shouted orders aboard his ship.

Lifting off her petticoat, she tossed it to him. It landed by his side as he removed the man's linen shirt. Shouts and laughter echoed through the house. Rose's fingers shook as she attempted to unhook her stays. Without success.

Rain pattered on the roof, matching the frenzied beat of her heart. Smoke filtered into the room. An off-key ballad chimed from somewhere in the house. She cleared her throat. "I need. . . I need help with my stays." Too embarrassed to face him, she turned around and stared at the cracks in the dark wall.

She heard his boots clap over the floor, felt his warmth at her back, his breath on her neck, and his fingers groping at the laces. "Upon my honor, how do you wear these infernal things?"

Rose suppressed a giggle, felt her stays loosen, her breath release, and heard him depart. She swerved about to see him with his back to her again. Such a gentleman. He removed the man's shoes then began tugging down his trousers as Rose shrugged out of her stays. They fell to the floor, leaving only a thin chemise between her and the world. Between her and this man. A chill struck her and she hugged herself and receded farther into the shadows. Two months ago, she would have been horrified to be so scantily clad in a man's presence. But she trusted Alex more than she'd ever trusted anyone. And despite their terrifying circumstances, she found an odd comfort in that realization.

Alex gathered the man's clothing in a pile and pushed them toward her. "Put these on."

Rose stooped to pick them up. "Surely they won't fit."

"We'll make them fit. It's the only way."

The shrill tear of fabric echoed through the room from Alex's direction. Rose donned the trousers, then slipped on the linen shirt, fatigue jacket, coat and shoes. Her feet swam in the buckled black boots, and the coat hung nearly to her knees. She had to hold the trousers up to keep them from falling. How would she ever pass for a British soldier?

Using the strips of torn petticoat, Alex bound the man's feet and hands, then stuffed a gag in his mouth. He stood. "That should hold him until we get away."

"I'm dressed." Rose said, her voice emerging as a squeak.

Alex spun around, grabbed the man's tall shako from the sofa and handed it to her. "Do your best to stuff your hair into this."

Rose placed it atop her head and began forcing her thick tresses inside it while Alex tightened her belt around her waist and buttoned the coat buttons. Even with her hair stuffed beneath it, the silly hat kept slipping down her forehead.

Alex stepped back, shook his head and chuckled. "We must keep to the shadows and pray most of the men are well into their cups."

Lantern light twinkled in his eyes and gleamed off the brass buttons lining his coat. "For I doubt any man with half his wits about him would think you are anything but an alluring female."

Amazed at his nonchalant attitude, Rose searched her heart for even a speck of courage to match his. Instead, fear knotted in her throat. "Are you sure this will work?"

Alex grabbed her hand and pulled her to the door. "No."

Not the answer she wanted to hear.

Stopping, he faced her. "Stay behind me. Say nothing and keep your head low."

Rose nodded. Air seized in her throat. "Lord, help us."

"Yes, indeed." He gave her a half smile, cupped her chin, and kissed her. "It will be all right." Then he lengthened his stance, threw back his shoulders, and marched from the room as if he owned the night.

Rose followed him down a long hallway to a flight of stairs. He led her down them as the sounds of mayhem and madness assailed her from all directions: crashes, thumps, and the crackle of fire. Smoke stung her nose. Thunder bellowed and drunken laughter grated on her nerves. A mob of soldiers passed on their left, torches in their hands. The smell of alcohol wafted over her. Rose's knees quaked. But the men seemed more intent on setting fire to the house than on paying her and Alex any mind.

Rose's teeth began to chatter. Perspiration slid down her back beneath the heavy coat. She tried to keep her eyes on Alex's back, to gain courage from the commanding cut of his uniform, from his confident gait. He led her down another hall to the main set of stairs. Down below, the front entrance of the house beckoned to her. *Freedom. Escape.* But it might as well be as far away as Baltimore, for a crush of sailors and soldiers mobbed the foyer.

Yet Alex didn't miss a step. No hesitation. No fear.

Heat swamped Rose, and she turned to see flames bursting from the dining room. A lump formed in her throat. She fought back tears. There would be time to mourn for her country later. They started down the stairs. Two sailors brushed past them, laughing. A band of marines huddled near the front door.

They reached the foot of the stairs. They were almost there. Almost free.

Alex nodded at the marines by the door and exited the house. Rose lowered her chin, raised her shoulders, and stepped out behind him. Not until they reached the outer gate did she feel the rain pelting down on her or the breath returning to her lungs. One glance around her told her that Valor was no longer tied to the post. Sweet Valor. She hoped some British redcoat had not confiscated the poor horse. *Please take care of Valor, Lord.* A gust of wind whipped over her, and she pressed a hand upon her hat and followed Alex down Pennsylvania Avenue.

Hurrying her steps, she eased beside him. The clomp of her oversized shoes echoed her betrayal. Rain misted on her, cooling her skin. Bright lights plucked at her curiosity, yet she kept her face down, hidden. When they had walked at least two blocks and the cacophony of destruction had lessened, she dared to lift her chin and scan the surroundings. Fires raged across the city. Unaffected by the rain, flames leaped out of windows and shot from roofs toward heaven. Smoke rose like prayers into the night sky, obscuring the stars and moon.

Rose's heart collapsed. Her throat burned, and a shiver overtook her despite the heat of the night and the fires. "Dear God, how could this happen?"

Alex started to take her hand, then pulled it away. "I'm sorry, Rose." Light from the flames flickered determination in his eyes. His jaw tightened. "I'm ashamed of what my countrymen have done."

Musket shots peppered the sky. An explosion shook the ground.

Alex cast a worried gaze across the scene. "Follow me." Turning down Thirteenth Street, he plodded forward, head down.

The drum of boots and the clomp of horses tightened Rose's nerves. She dared a peek at a band of troops heading their way, led by two officers on horseback.

A pig crossed the path in front of them. It stopped, stared at them for a moment before grunting and ambling away.

"Friend of yours?" Alex teased.

Rose flattened her lips. "How can you joke at a time like this?"

"It relieves stress."

"It's not working." Rose glanced down at the oversized attire and her massive footwear that clomped over the sand so loudly—they'd no doubt betray them to the passing troops. She wanted to laugh, wanted to cry. Instead she softened her step, lowered her chin, and kept her mouth shut. The soldiers passed.

A gust of wind blasted over them. Before she could stop it, Rose's shako flew from her head. It clunked to the ground, releasing her long golden tresses down her back. She shrieked.

"You there, halt!" A voice blared over them from behind.

Without so much as a glance over his shoulder, Alex grabbed her arm with one hand, withdrew his sword with the other and dashed down the street. Rose ran as fast as her legs and enormous boots would allow. Horse hooves followed them like war drums. Shouts and hollers of jocularity filled the night as if the men were engaged in a fox chase on the English countryside.

Alex ducked in between two brick buildings, batting shrubbery aside with his sword. His breath came hard and heavy. The mad crunch of pebbles beneath their feet sounded like gunshot. His tight grip on her hand was the only thing that kept her going—that gave her hope. One glance over her shoulder revealed flaming torches bobbing atop an incoming wave of soldiers.

"There they are!" one of the men shouted.

Rose's feet burned. Her heart crashed against her ribs. One of her boots slipped off. Then the other. Sharp rocks tore the skin on her feet. She cried out in pain.

Halting, Alex glanced at her feet then swept her into his arms and continued to barrel down the alleyway out onto a narrow dirt street. His steps were heavy and thick and their pace slowed even as his breath increased. The shouts of their pursuers grew louder.

He set her down and cupped her face gently, lifting her gaze to his. His heavy breath filled the air between them. "Go, hide in that house." He gestured over her shoulder to a small one-story brick structure. "I'll draw them away from you."

"No, I want to stay with you!" Rose tugged on his arm, unable to fathom losing him again.

A sea of torches turned the corner at the end of the street and rumbled toward them like a tidal wave. "They will find us, Rose. There's no time. Do as I say!" he barked.

Tears filled her eyes and Alex's figure blurred before her. "Please Alex, don't leave me."

Leaning over, Alex kissed the tears flowing down her cheeks then brushed his lips over hers. "I'll find you. I promise. Now go!"

Turning, Rose forced her feet to run to the house. Opening the door, she slid inside and ran to peer out one of the broken windows. Glass cut her foot and she squelched a cry of pain—pain that she felt both outside and inside as Alex's dark shape disappeared down the street. A second later, a horde of angry men who appeared more like fire-breathing dragons flew after him.

Leaning back against the inner wall, Rose threw a hand to her chest to slow the frantic beating of her heart. The cold brick of the walls seeped through her gown. "Oh Lord. Please protect him."

Alex waited long enough to see that Rose had followed his orders, but perhaps he delayed too long. One glance over his shoulder told him the mob of soldiers was only yards behind. Sprinting with all his strength, he forged into the darkness, thankful that this part of town had not yet been set to fire. He heard the stomp of a dozen boots behind him, the diabolical laughter and devilish chuckles of his own countrymen. Men he had supped with, trained with, and marched beside. How quickly things had changed.

One more glance told him that none had separated from the group. They had not seen Rose slip away. Thank God.

Alex dashed between what appeared to be two shops. His thigh cried out in pain. His lungs slammed against this chest.

"There they go!" a belligerent voice trumpeted behind him.

He glanced once more over his shoulder to see a myriad of bobbing torches like lit cannons on the wobbling deck of a ship. Lit to fire at him. Too close. Far too close.

Lord, please don't let them catch me. For Rose's sake.

Alex swung his gaze back forward, tripped over a rock, stumbled past a bush whose sharp branches tore at his coat. He righted himself. A pop of a pistol rang through the air and the shot zipped past his ear.

He burst from the alleyway onto the street and turned right, not hesitating to choose which way. He chose the wrong way. The dark gaping hole of the barrel of a musket nearly impaled him. He stopped just in time before it did.

"One more move and I'll shoot," the soldier ordered.

Alex raised his hands in the air as he struggled to regain his breath. In moments he was surrounded by the torch-wielding mob. Sweat streamed down his forehead into his eyes, stinging them. He scanned the faces, twisting and undulating in the flickering torchlight, like sinister demons released from hell.

One man approached him and spit at his feet. "Where is the woman?"

"What woman?"

The man struck Alex across the jaw, sending him reeling to the side. The pain spiked into his mouth and down into his neck.

"Never mind. We shall find her." The lieutenant snapped his fingers. "Bind him. We'll see what Cockburn has to say about this traitor."

❖ CHAPTER 29 ❖

The distant pop of a gun startled Rose as she stood inside the small house. Turning, she glanced out the window once again. A different band of soldiers sauntered by. Others separated into smaller groups and wandered among the buildings across the street. Was the shot directed at Alex? *Oh Lord, please protect him.* As her eyes became accustomed to the darkness, shapes began to form: a settee, oak tables, a pianoforte, and a rocking chair.

Groping her way among them, Rose made her way toward the back of the house. With all the British running around, she had best find a place to hide. Even though everything within her wanted to run out and find Alex, rescue him as he had rescued her. A tear slid down her cheek, but she brushed it away. No time to be frightened. No time to be weak. She was not alone. And neither was Alex.

"Yes, I will never leave my children."

The voice within her confirmed her convictions, bringing forth another tear from her eye. But this time, a tear of joy.

Laughter and more shots tore in through the window from outside. She ran her fingers over the wallpaper lining the hallway and bumped into various sconces and pictures hanging there. Finally, she entered a room in the back that appeared to be a storage room filled with bulky

301

sacks, crates, and shelves lined with jars. A table in the center had been pushed aside. Rose squinted into the shadows, searching for somewhere to hide, when her eyes landed on a dark square beneath the table. Kneeling, she discovered it was a hole that led to a cellar beneath the house. The trapdoor lay pushed aside, along with a crumpled rug that no doubt was used to conceal the opening.

Footsteps thundered outside. Closer. Closer. Shouts. The neigh of a horse.

Rose's muscles tensed. Then the sounds faded.

"Is anyone there?" Rose whispered into the dark cavity. "I am a friend." But no answer came. Grabbing the rug, she hugged it to her chest, imagining that the family who lived here must have hidden down below from the British. She wondered what had happened to them.

She didn't have time to consider it. The front door blasted open and heinous laughter filled the front parlor.

Alex tugged from the pinching grips of the men on either side of him and met the imperious gaze of Admiral Cockburn. The man before him, though powerful on earth, had proven himself to be a cruel and heartless man who used his God-given power to abuse and subjugate those beneath him. Alex did not fear him. God was with Alex. Truth was with Alex. And no matter what this man did to him, truth and love would win in the end.

At last, Alex understood how Mr. Drummond's eyes could be so filled with peace in the midst of the storms.

Cockburn eyed him up and down as if he were but another bug to squash. "What have we here, Lieutenant?"

The man to Alex's right threw back his shoulders. "A traitor, Admiral. At least that's what he seems to be. We found him running through the streets of Washington with a woman dressed in a sergeant's uniform."

The admiral chuckled and the smell of alcohol spilled over Alex. Which did not bode well for his sentencing. Often during the long day, Alex had witnessed the fiendish effect drink had on the admiral's sensibilities.

"Indeed, and where is the rebel wench?" The admiral slapped the telescope he was holding against his other palm.

The lieutenant looked down. "Got away sir. But we'll find her."

"That you will, Lieutenant, or I fear you'll meet the same fate as this poor man."

Alex could hear the lieutenant gulp.

Admiral Cockburn raised his chin and looked down his nose at Alex. "Mr. Reed, did you say? What have you to say for yourself?"

Lengthening his stance, Alex gazed behind the admiral where flames still devoured the Capitol building. Though they stood yards away, he could feel the heat, and it only sufficed to fuel his anger. How dare they destroy these symbols of freedom? He met the admiral's gaze. "I was only protecting an innocent woman from being ravaged, Admiral. There's no crime in that."

"No crime you say? Ha." The admiral glanced over his men. "No crime save leaving her untouched, I'd say."

Some of the men chuckled.

From the left of the group, a soldier aided another man to the center—a sergeant dressed in nothing but his underclothes. He rubbed his head and his eyes nearly fired from their sockets when they landed on Alex. "Aye, that's the man. He struck me over the head."

Alex shrugged. "He was going to ravish the woman."

Cockburn leaned toward Alex. "It's what the rebel wench deserved. So you let her go?"

"I did."

Cockburn's jaw twitched. He nodded toward the lieutenant on Alex's right, who hauled his arm back and slugged Alex across the jaw once again. At least it was on the other side this time. Renewed pain tore across his cheek.

"She could have possessed valuable information, Mr. Reed." Cockburn continued while Alex rubbed his jaw. "Why else was she still in Washington? Egad. The incompetence! Such insubordination for a second lieutenant in the Royal Navy." Cockburn shifted his stance, the fringe on his epaulets quivered. "Wait until the Admiralty Board hears of this. You'll not only be cashiered my friend, but hung as well."

Alex allowed the words to enter his mind and then slither down into his gut. Not a pleasant way to die. But as he thought back on the events of these past weeks, he wouldn't have changed a thing.

Alex's silence evoked rage from the admiral, who immediately growled. "Tie him up and stand watch over him while we finish destroying the city. Tomorrow, we'll escort him back to the flagship. I'll wager we can gather up enough captains to host a court-martial right here in the Chesapeake. Then before we even set sail, we can hang you from the yardarms."

Rose dove into the cellar, nearly stumbling down the ladder. Reaching up, she placed the rug atop the trapdoor, and then from below, she eased it over the hole, cringing when it snapped into place. Lowering her shaky legs rung by rung, her feet finally found the cool hard dirt of the cellar floor. Pain etched across her soles. She winced. Chilled air tingled over her neck. The smell of sweet herbs and mold whirled about her.

The hollow thump of at least a dozen boots thundered overhead and shook the trapdoor. Dust rained over her. Covering her mouth and nose, she suppressed a cough as a plethora of male voices trumpeted through the rooms above. Thunder growled in agreement of her dire predicament even as footfalls continued to pound above her. The squeal of a rat somewhere in the cellar sent a shiver down her back.

Furniture legs scraped over the wood. The sound of cloth flapped like sails in the wind. A pair of shoes tromped over the trapdoor again and halted. The boards creaked and wobbled. With her hand still pressed over her mouth, she closed her eyes.

"What a night, eh?" one man said.

"Cowardly rebels!" Another man chortled. "Leavin' their capital for us t' plunder."

"Aye, wait till my lady sees the silverware I'm bringin' home—" his voice heightened with scornful insolence—"compliments of the citizens of Washington DC."

The man moved off the trapdoor and sauntered about the room. He must have shifted the rug aside for a sliver of lantern light spilled through a tiny crack in the boards.

"I ne'er seen such an easy conquest. Why, we should be able t' take the rest of these despicable colonies within a fortnight and be home before Christmastide."

Insidious chuckles pummeled Rose like hail.

"An' tomorrow," another soldier piped in. "Admiral Cockburn says we can finish burnin' the rest o' the city."

Footfalls rumbled over the floor again, but this time, their hollow thuds receded.

"This looks like a fair place to hole up for the night," one man declared, his voice fading as he walked into another room.

"Milford, did ye bring the bottles of brandy we found?"

"Aye, I said I did."

Insolent rogues. Rose didn't know whether to be terrified or furious. As long as the soldiers stayed, she was trapped and couldn't go in search of Alex.

Alex. He had come for her! Saved her once again! Rose pictured him as he marched into the empty room in the president's mansion in his dark naval uniform with long coattails, brass buttons, and service sword glittering at his side. He wanted to stay with her! Her heart should indeed be soaring. If it weren't so twisted with fear. And fury. She must find Alex. But how, with all those soldiers sleeping above her?

Blinking she strained her eyes and gazed over the dank cellar. Soon objects began to form out of the darkness: barrels, crates of what appeared to be potatoes or apples, sacks of grain. Above her, bundles of herbs hung from the rafters like sleeping bats.

Kneeling, Rose felt her way over the dirt floor and sat, leaning her back against the support wall. She drew her knees to her chest and laid her weary head upon them. "Lord, help me."

Hours later, above her in the front parlor, the men's drunken revelry quieted.

Even the thunder and lightning fell silent, and the rain ceased its march across the roof. A deceptive peace descended on the house as if the abominations of the night had not only drained the city but the earth and sky of all their energy.

Including Rose. All the stress of the evening, the fear, the horrors, spilled from her. Her eyes grew heavy. Cool, dank air crept over her. She shuddered. Then a sudden warmth enveloped her—a strange supernatural warmth—and she closed her eyes and fell into its embrace.

Alex shifted his back against the rough bark of the huge tree he sat beneath. He gazed upward. A hickory tree, he thought, though it was hard to tell in the darkness. He twisted the thick ropes binding his hands together. Pain spiraled up his arms. Though he'd been tugging against the bindings for hours, the only thing he'd accomplished were patches of raw bleeding skin around his wrists. From his spot, sitting atop a grassy knoll just outside the city limits, he had an excellent view of Washington. To his right a group of soldiers hovered around a campfire. They played cards, laughed, drank, and told off-color jokes, all the while over their shoulders the bastion of freedom burned to the ground. The flames that rose over Washington would have been a beautiful sight with all their brilliant oranges, reds, and yellows dancing in the night like some garish ballet.

If it wasn't such a horrendous scar on the history of mankind.

Alex's thigh throbbed, his hands were a bloody mess, and his back ached, but the largest pain of all came from his heart. He had promised Rose he'd come back for her. And now, he doubted he could keep that promise. Thoughts of her hiding somewhere in that burning city, frightened and alone, waiting for him, gnawed at his gut like some satiated predator intent on giving him a slow death.

No, Alex couldn't help Rose. But God could. Bowing his head, Alex spent the next several hours in prayer. For Rose, for her family, and for America to survive this devastating night. Somewhere amid the crackle of fire and the fading shouts of men, Alex succumbed to his exhaustion and fell asleep.

A slap across the face jarred him awake, and he peered up into the smirk of one of the soldiers who had been guarding him. "Wake up, traitor. You should witness us finishin' off your precious rebel city." The sting on Alex's face was nothing compared to the pain etching across his soul at the man's words. He shifted his gaze to the city, now bathed in dawn's glow and to the smoke rising from the buildings like incense to heaven. He prayed the scent made it all the way to the throne of God.

The soldier spit to the side of Alex, gathered his things, and along with several of the other men, left Alex tied to the tree with only a single soldier to guard him. It might as well have been a thousand for as tight as the ropes were about Alex's waist and hands. Even if he made it through the ones binding his wrists, his entire body was tied to the trunk of the tree.

He watched the solders descend the hill laughing and slapping each other on the back in anticipation of another day of plundering and destruction.

Scanning the city, Alex tried to find the house where he had left Rose, but the smoke and remaining flames obscured his view. "Lord, watch over her. Please get her home safely."

"Pray for a storm."

The silent words couldn't have been clearer within Alex. He shook his head. Was he destined to go mad along with everything else?

"Pray for a storm."

Alex glanced over the city. Sunlight shot bright arrows down between puffy gray clouds. They'd had a small storm last night, but today the sky appeared to be clearing. "A storm, Lord?"

"Yes."

Emitting a sigh of submission, Alex bowed his head. "Very well. Father." He nearly choked with emotion at the title with which he now addressed God. He finally had a Father who loved him—who would never close His home to Alex. And if Alex should indeed hang from Admiral Cockburn's yardarm, God would welcome him home forever. "Please bring a storm upon this land, this city," he continued, feeling his zeal rising. "One that will send these British back to their ships and back to their country!" He laughed at his own foolishness then leaned back against the bark.

If God didn't intervene soon, Alex didn't want to contemplate what would happen to Rose. "Thy will be done."

The thud of shoes and the crackle of morning voices permeated Rose's slumber. The men's voices grew louder, and she stirred, rubbing her face. When reality forced itself into her dreams, she bolted upright and opened her eyes. Shouts and curses flew through the air above them. Footfalls pounded. A door slammed and then all grew silent. Above her, a sliver of sunlight speared down into the cellar, indicating that a new day had dawned. Struggling to her feet, she shook off the last vestiges of slumber, chastening herself for falling asleep under such dire circumstances. Yet she remembered nestling into the peace of a warm hug. A dream? Or her Father in heaven? She smiled and tilted her ear to the ceiling. No sounds. The soldiers had gone. Why hadn't Alex come to get her? Renewed fears leaped up to grab her heart.

There was only one explanation. Alex must have gotten caught. She clenched her fists and gazed upward. She had to rescue him. But how? Terror gripped her at the thought, but she forced it back. "I am not alone. I am not alone."

Slowly creeping up the ladder, Rose lifted the trapdoor, holding it slightly ajar. No movement. No sounds. Placing both hands against the wood, she moved it from the hole, sliding it to the side. The bitter smell of brandy and sweat bit her nose as she emerged from the cellar into the storage room then inched to the door and peered down the hall. No movement, no voices. Nothing to alert her. Making her way down the hall she entered the front parlor. What had appeared last night to be a neat and nicely furnished room now resembled more of a tavern after a violent brawl. Broken furniture, crumpled rugs, and empty bottles of brandy and rum that lay on their sides, mouths open, as if they too were intoxicated.

Shoving down her disgust, Rose dared a peek out the front window. Redcoats filled the streets, some marching in formation, others crowding in groups laughing and no doubt regaling each other of their conquests the night before. Some still carried torches.

Rose ducked back to the side of the window and felt like crying. She wasn't going anywhere. At least not for a while. "Haven't they done enough, Lord? Oh please make them stop." She dropped her face into her hands and sobbed.

"Pray." A strange sensation overcame Rose—a presence so strong it seemed the room could not contain it.

"Pray for a storm." The voice resounded within her, sweet, yet strong, like a harmonious chord from a violin.

A storm? Rose didn't understand. What could a storm do against the entire British army?

"All right, Lord." Lowering herself to her knees, Rose clasped her hands together and prayed. First she thanked God for His love, His mercy, and for allowing her to see Alex one last time. Then she prayed for rescue for them both, for America to survive, and lastly, for a storm to strike the city.

Rising to her feet, she took up a pace across the parlor floor, keeping an eye on the soldiers outside, and wishing she had more faith to believe God would perform the things she had just prayed for.

BOOM! An enormous explosion thundered in the distance. The ground shook. The hickory tree shook, jarring Alex from his prayers. The soldier, who guarded him, dashed to the edge of the hill, musket ready. Beyond him, a massive plume of smoke rose in the air from the area of town Alex remembered as Greenleaf Point where the city's arsenals had been kept. Tortured screams etched across the sky and sent a chill down Alex's back. Pieces of rocks, shells, and bricks shot through the air like grapeshot leveling some of the men as they dashed away from the blast. When the smoke cleared, even from this distance, Alex could see bodies—and what used to be bodies—scattered over the ground.

The Americans had no doubt left the British a surprise. War made devils out of men. Alex shifted his gaze away and closed his eyes. "Lord, please help them." He didn't know what else to pray for, save that this hideous war would end. His prayers for a storm all morning had gone unanswered. Perhaps he hadn't heard from God at all. Yet, despite the unanswered petition, a peace surrounded Alex as if God was somehow pleased that Alex had been obedient. The approval of a Father who loved him. Alex savored the foreign sensation. Yes, indeed, he could get used to having God as his Father.

No sooner had the wounded been carried off to the hospital that General Ross had set up near the Capitol building, than the *tap tap* of a light rain drummed on the leaves above Alex. Distant thunder accompanied the continued shouts and stomp of troops through the city streets.

The tapping increased in both tempo and speed. Water dripped on Alex's face. Shaking it off, he gazed into a sky that had darkened to near black in a matter of minutes. Angry clouds boiled in fury above him, marching across the city. Soon thick blades of rain fell upon them as if a giant armory had been opened in heaven. The solder guarding

Alex ducked beneath the tree alongside him. He drew the edges of his coat together and held down his hat, sharing a wary gaze with Alex, as the torrent of wind and water increased.

The fierce gusts grew and grew until Alex could no longer keep his eyes open. Tucking his head between his upraised knees, the realization struck him that his prayer had been answered. Awe swept through him while at the same time the wind threatened to carry him away. Lightning crackled the air around him, painting his eyelids silver and buzzing over his skin. He smelled the electricity and something else—burnt flesh. Not his. At least he hoped not. Thunder pounded. The ground shook as if God Himself walked through the capital of America.

Screams and shouts assailed Alex, but still he could not open his eyes. In fact, he could barely move. The wind tore at his coat, at his breeches. The ropes on his hands loosened. He felt rather than saw large objects flinging through the air around him. Something struck his tree. The trunk trembled against Alex's back.

Still the wind howled. Rain pelted him like the sharp tips of a cat-o-nine tails. The massive truck of the tree groaned and began to sway. The wind lifted Alex off the ground. The ropes around his waist tightened until he felt they would cut him in two. If they broke or if the tree fell, Alex knew he would surely die.

❖ CHAPTER 30 ❖

The tiny house shook beneath a blast of wind. Rose peered once again out the window to see pieces of wood, buckets, and sand flying through the air. Soldiers, bent at the waist, struggled to walk, bracing their shoulders to the wind. Some crawled over the ground like spiders.

A storm! Just like she had prayed for. Above her, an eerie crack sounded. A plank loosened from the roof and flapped up and down, banging out a warning. It flew away and wind tore through the parlor.

Rose should get below. Making her way to the back room, she lowered herself into the cellar and replaced the trapdoor.

Thunder cracked and roared and fumed. What little light that drifted down into the cellar instantly blackened. Torrents of rain fell from the sky as if the very gates of heaven had been flung open to release God's wrath. Backing into the shadows, Rose gazed upward, waiting for the floor to cave in. Thunder growled again. Louder and louder it grew, as if a million-man army galloped toward her.

Turning, Rose groped her way through the darkness and dove behind a stack of crates. Hugging herself, she trembled and prayed. Something massive struck the house. Rose screamed. The walls shook.

Raindrops that surely were as thick as hail struck the house from every direction. Eerie sounds like a thousand voices screaming and the crash of mighty waves whipped the small building. Rose couldn't think. Couldn't breathe. All she could do was huddle in the darkness and pray.

WHAM! An ominous crash blasted over Rose's ears. The trapdoor flew open. It slammed shut. Then it opened again. Over and over, it opened and shut like a giant mouth that dared to scold the storm for disturbing its rest. Air whipped into the cellar, spinning in a chaotic whirlwind. The crates in front of Rose performed a deranged dance. Potatoes and apples flew through the air. One struck the back of her neck. Pain shot into her head.

The door slammed shut, and something heavy landed on it, silencing it.

Rose's ears grew numb to the deafening sounds around her.

Minutes that seemed like hours went by.

Finally the winds abated. The rain lessened and the thunder retreated.

Light peered through the cracks in the trapdoor as if seeking survivors. Water dripped around its edges.

Still trying to calm her thrashing heart, Rose stood on shaky legs, and made her way up the ladder. The trapdoor wouldn't budge. She had to get out of here. She had to find Alex. Groaning, she hefted her back against it and pushed with all her might. Finally the wooden slab moved, and she shoved it aside. Closing hers eyes against the light, she ascended one more rung of the ladder. A gust of wind and rain slapped her face.

Which meant the house was no longer standing. Preparing herself for the inevitable scene, she opened her eyes. Nothing but shards of wood and broken glass remained of the structure that had sheltered her. Or of the buildings beside it or the ones across the street. A cannon sat where the foyer had once been—a testament to the power of the wind. The red coats of slain soldiers dotted the gray landscape. In the distance, the setting sun cast an orange glow over the round dome of the Capitol and the sidewalls of the president's mansion. Both still standing. Other than that, nothing but complete devastation met Rose's eyes, as if the city had been blasted with enemy cannons for days. But this was no enemy.

This was the hand of Almighty God.

Alex opened his eyes to a sight that he had never expected to see and one that would be forever imprinted in his mind. Scattered across what was left of Washington were the red and blue coats of slain soldiers, dead horses, pigs, and the towering remnants of government buildings that had not fully succumbed to the fiery flames.

He raised his hand to find ropes no longer binding them, then tugged at those around his waist. After a few short pulls, they too fell to the ground. He stood, wobbled beneath a wave of dizziness, then leaned a hand on the tree for support. The hickory tree. He studied the trunk, nearly stripped of its bark. "Thank you, my friend." He patted it. For if he had not been tied to it, he would have surely been swept away with the other men. What he had thought had been a prison, God had used to save his life. *Thank You, Father*.

A bird flew overhead, and somewhere a horse neighed. Drums beat a march of retreat in the distance. The British were leaving. Alex scanned the devastation again. Most of the homes and buildings were flattened or gone. *Rose*. His heart shriveled. *Oh my sweet Rose*. Alex barreled down the hill, weaving his way through debris and death with one purpose in mind. He must find her.

Amid praises to God for her deliverance and gasps in horror at the death and desolation around her, Rose made her way toward the Capitol. Her feet ached and bled, but it didn't matter now. She must find Alex. "Oh God," she cried, forcing back thoughts that he was a prisoner of the British—or worse, dead. "Please help me find him."

Yes, Rose finally believed God loved her. She could still feel His presence all around her. And bad circumstances didn't mean she would lose His love. She drew in a deep breath. If Alex had not survived, she would still not give up on God. She now believed that God had a plan, and she must trust Him no matter what. She only prayed His plan involved Alex being alive and well.

Halting, she wiped her moist face then held up her arm to shield the sun while she glanced over the broken city. Her eyes locked on a figure moving toward her in the distance. It blurred beneath the steam rising from the puddles. Friend or foe? She swallowed and continued, but made her way toward a broken wall to her right—a place she could hide behind should the person turn out to be her enemy.

Yet there was something about the man, the lift of his shoulders, his confident stride that kept Rose's eyes on him. A dark blue navy coat formed out of the dull gray around him. *British navy.* Alex? Rose shook her head. What were the chances? She'd better hide. Yet when she tried to move her feet they wouldn't budge. An invisible band seemed to have been strung between her and the mysterious man, keeping her in place.

Still he continued marching toward her. Dark hair the color of cocoa blew against his collar.

Her heart jumped.

He stopped. "Rose!" That marvelous deep British lilt released her feet from bondage, and clutching her oversized pants by the belt, she dashed toward him, ignoring the pain spiking up her legs. "Alex!"

He ran to greet her. Rose flew into his arms, laughing and sobbing all at the same time. He flung her around, showering her with kisses, then lowered her to her feet and held her face in his warm hands. "Thank God."

Rose took his hands and kissed them, smiling up at him. "I love you, Alex."

His arms swallowed her up again, and he lowered his lips to hers. "I love you so much, Rose." He kissed her, at first gently caressing her lips, before claiming her mouth as his own.

Rose forgot about the war, forgot about the destruction, the death, just for one glorious moment. All that mattered was Alex. And that he was alive. And that he loved her.

Releasing her, Alex planted a kiss on her nose and drew back, rubbing his thumb over her cheek. "Are you unharmed?"

Rose nodded. "You?"

He kissed her forehead then swung an arm over her shoulder and turned to survey the city.

"What now, Alex?" Rose asked.

"Let's go home."

Five hours later, Alex halted the horse at the edge of the Drummond farm. Rose leaned back against his chest and drew in a deep breath. She'd never remembered such a beautiful sight. Coated in moonlight, the fields, the barn, and the house glinted in sparkled silver as if the place had been dropped on earth from a better world somewhere far away.

"Home at last." Alex's warm breath eased down her neck.

It had been a long journey. And the longest two days of her life. If not for the incessant ringing in her ears, Rose would have thought she'd only imagined the storm that had set them free.

Had set her nation's capital free.

But visions of death and destruction kept popping unbidden in her mind.

After finding a pair of mismatched shoes along the side of the road for Rose, Alex had led her through the vacated streets of Washington in search of some means by which to travel home. Averting her eyes from the death around her, Rose had kept her gaze on Alex's back and her thoughts on God. Finally, they found three fully saddled and harnessed horses grazing in an open field across from the Capitol. No doubt spooked by the storm, the animals must have returned to the city only to find their masters gone. Alex managed to catch one, while the other two galloped away.

They passed the first few hours of their journey in silence, too numb, too in awe, to speak. But eventually Alex began singing an old church hymn, and Rose joined him. They spent the next hours thanking God for sparing them and for bringing them together. A few somber moments passed when they spoke of Mr. Snyder's tragic death. Neither of them had wished the councilman any harm. The man had simply chosen the wrong path.

Just like all choices in life. One path led to greater light while the other led deeper into darkness.

During the last hour of the journey, Rose had leaned back against Alex's chest and thought about the paths God had laid before them. Daniel had been right. She and Alex each had something important to do. God had used them mightily—had used her mightily. Rose found the feeling both overwhelming and humbling.

"I wonder if God would have sent the storm without our prayers," Alex said as if reading her thoughts. "It baffles me that the Almighty needs the petitions of mere man to do anything."

Rose gazed at the light spilling from the parlor window of her home. No doubt her aunt and uncle were awake worrying about her. "Uncle Forbes says that our prayers are powerful and effective and rise like incense before the throne of God." She stretched her legs and winced at the ache that spread through them from riding so long. "The prayers of God's people have stopped rain from falling, closed the mouths of lions, and raised the dead. Though I don't suppose God needs our prayers, I do believe He uses them to do His will."

The horse snorted and pawed the dirt, and Alex gripped the reins. "I am in awe that He used someone like me to help save this great nation."

"And me as well, little terrified me." She laughed. "Yet now without my fear, I feel God's gentle nudge to help women who had suffered as I have—to help them past the shame and let them know God loves them."

Alex wrapped her arms around her. "I'm so proud of you."

Rose stared at the farm she'd grown to love. "I wonder what else God has for us to do?"

Alex nudged the horse forward. "Let's go find out."

Sliding from the horse, Alex tied the reins to the post and turned to reach up for Rose, but she had already dismounted. Dragging her oversized trousers in the mud, she limped past him. With her mismatched shoes clomping a discordant tune over the ground, her red coat hanging nearly to her knees and her golden tresses brushing against her waist like silken threads, she was, by far, the most adorable foot soldier he'd ever seen.

They mounted the steps to the front porch, and Alex swept open the door.

"Rose!" Mrs. Drummond flew toward her and swallowed her up in her arms. Amelia emerged from the parlor, her face pale, and dashed toward Rose's other side.

"Dear, where have you been? Your uncle and I have been so worried." Mrs. Drummond glanced over Rose's attire and her brow furrowed. "My goodness, what, pray tell, are you wearing?"

Mr. Drummond appeared behind them, hands folded over his portly belly and a knowing smile on his lips. "Perhaps she joined the British army, dearest." He winked at Alex.

Amelia giggled, and Mrs. Drummond swung a stern gaze his way. "Oh you do enjoy teasing me, Forbes." She faced Alex. "And you, sir. A British naval uniform? Has the world gone mad?"

Alex opened his mouth to respond, but Mrs. Drummond continued her frantic speech. "We only just arrived home last evening, but the storm kept us from searching for you."

"Where are the children?" Rose asked.

"They are well." Mrs. Drummond exchanged a glance with her husband. "We left them in Lewisville with friends of Reverend Hargrave. But we were worried you would panic when you heard the British were marching on Washington, so we came home immediately."

"Then when we found you gone, lass," Mr. Drummond added, "I'm afraid we were quite distressed. We intended to head out at first light."

"We were in Washington." Rose said.

Amelia gripped her arm. "We heard the British set fire to the city!" Rose exchanged a sorrowful look with Alex. "Indeed they did."

"Oh my." Amelia covered her mouth.

Mrs. Drummond withdrew a handkerchief. "Oh the shame of it." She dabbed her eyes. "Mr. Markham informed us he could see the flames from Federal Hill. But, dear, you overcame your fear and went to find us?"

Rose clasped her aunt's hand. "What else could I do?"

Mrs. Drummond's eyes glistened. "Oh you poor dear. You must have been terrified."

The kitchen door flew open, and Cora sped into the room, halting as her eyes settled on Rose. "There you are, child." She ambled forward and stood by Mr. Drummond.

Rose smiled. "Good to see you, Cora."

Alex winked at the cook and the woman rolled her eyes.

"But do tell us what happened?" Mrs. Drummond waved her handkerchief through the air. "How did you come to wear this hideous uniform?"

"It's a long story, Mrs. Drummond." Alex took Rose's hand and glanced at Uncle Forbes. "God rescued us and the entire city."

"Indeed?" Mr. Drummond cocked his head, then moved beside his wife. "Come, let us sit down in the parlor. I cannot wait to hear it. Cora, bring some tea and biscuits."

Alex squeezed Rose's hand. "First, there is a matter that cannot wait."

One gray eyebrow rose on Mr. Drummond's face.

Casting a glance at Rose, Alex cleared his throat, suddenly feeling more nervous than he had during all the terrifying events of the past week. What if the man said no? For the first time in his life, Alex had nothing to recommend himself—no land, no money, no prospects. In fact, why on earth would Mr. Drummond accept his proposal? Sweat blossomed on Alex's forehead and neck. "Sir, if I may." He glanced at Rose who prodded him on with her eyes. "If I may."

"If you may what, Mr. Reed?" Mr. Drummond smiled.

"With your permission." Alex blew out a sigh. Better to get it over with. "May I have your niece's hand in marriage?"

Mr. Drummond grinned and slapped Alex on the back. "Yes, indeed, you may! I thought you'd never ask."

"Marriage? Oh my." Aunt Muira shook her head and gripped Amelia for support.

Cora chuckled. "Heaven be praised."

Amelia squealed in delight and hugged Rose.

Alex faced Rose and found her looking at him with so much love and admiration, he nearly fell backward. Mr. Drummond, Mrs. Drummond, Amelia, and even Cora crowded around the couple, offering words of love and congratulations as they welcomed them home.

Home. Alex smiled as warmth spread through him.

He was home at last.

❖ SURRENDER THE NIGHT— AUTHOR'S HISTORICAL NOTE ❖

In the early evening hours on August 24, 1814, after defeating the Americans in battle at Bladensburg, British Major General Robert Ross and Rear Admiral Cockburn led some fifteen hundred British soldiers and sailors, unhindered, down the streets of Washington DC. The troops halted in an open field east of the Capitol building and waited for someone in authority to emerge and discuss surrender terms and prize money. But no one came. After the Americans blew up the naval yard, Admiral Cockburn led a party of men into the Capitol building. Thus began a night of revenge, drunken mayhem, and devilish destruction as British troops went on a rampage through the capital city, stealing valuables left behind by its citizens, and setting fire to every government building they could find. Among the buildings destroyed were the Capitol, the Library of Congress (housing 3,000 volumes along with many maps and charts), a home owned by George Washington, the president's house, the War and Treasury building, and the office of the *National Intelligencer* newspaper (which had slandered Admiral Cockburn).

Dolly Madison, the president's wife, barely escaped her home before the troops arrived, carrying as many paintings, documents, and artifacts she could hold. (Although, there is no record of a British soldier or lady from Baltimore in her house on that day, the possibility exists!) Admiral Cockburn, in a raucous display of vengeful arrogance, did indeed partake of the dinner Mrs. Madison had laid out for her husband's men, as well as offer a multitude of insulting toasts to the president whom he referred to as "Old Jemmy."

Early in the morning of August 25, the British aroused themselves with the intent to set fire to any remaining buildings and wreak as much additional havoc as possible. But this new day would not afford them success. At two in the afternoon, a detachment of two hundred redcoats marched to Greenleaf Point to finish off the arsenal and destroy any remaining buildings left by the Americans. However, before leaving, the Americans had concealed a large quantity of kegged powder in a dry well near the barracks. One of the British artillerymen accidentally dropped a lighted portfire into the well. The resulting explosion rocked the city, unroofed houses, and shot pieces of brick, stone, and earth into the air. Twelve British died and thirty were wounded.

Soon after the explosion, a terrifying storm struck the city. One eyewitness commented, "Of the prodigious force of the wind, it is impossible for you to form any conception. Roofs of houses were torn off by it, and whisked into the air like sheets of paper. . . . The darkness was as great as if the sun had long set. . .occasionally relieved by flashes of vivid lightning streaming through it, which together with the noise of the wind and the thunder, the crash of falling buildings and the tearing of roofs as they were stript from the walls, produced the most appalling affect I ever have or shall witness. . . . Our column was completely dispersed as if it had received a total defeat."

The two-hour storm not only doused the remaining flames, but killed thirty British soldiers, scattering the rest over the landscape. The British gathered their survivors and quietly withdrew from Washington.